Still Human

Kerry Heavens

Published by Kerry Heavens.
© 2013. Kerry Heavens.
Still Human
All Rights Reserved.

No part of this book may be reproduced or transmitted in any form or by any means, electronic or mechanical, including photocopying, recording, or by any information storage and retrieval system without the written permission of the author, except where permitted by law.

ISBN-13: 978-1493793587
ISBN-10: 1493793586

Editor: Kelly at Ultimate Proof Ltd.
Cover image used under license from istockphoto.com
Cover Design: Kerry Heavens

For Steve

You be the anchor that keeps my feet on the ground,
I'll be the wings that keep your heart in the clouds.

&

My Angels,
I love you to the moon and back.

Prologue

Liv.

"Please Liv, you have to eat something," begs Max.

I tighten the covers around me. I'm not hungry, but I keep quiet. If I speak, even about food, he'll think I'm ready to talk. There's nothing else to say. I poured it all out when I got home and there's nothing left. He stayed with me all night, held me tight while I cried and now he is fussing around. He wanted to call everyone to tell them I was safe. But I warned him not to call Danny. I said he could let Mum know I was okay but that was it. No details and under no circumstances were any of them to make any contact with Danny either. I can just imagine Mum and Grace as vigilantes and, while I want him to hurt, he isn't worth it.

"I'm going down to check on things, I'll bring you something up anyway." He says quietly. I don't respond.

In the silence of my flat, my ears ring. I hate silence, I always have and without thinking I get out of bed, wrapping myself in a blanket, and sit in front of the TV. I find a film on a movie channel I've seen before and sit and ignore it. It's better than the deafening silence. Now that I'm upright, I ponder what to do next. I know I have to pull myself together today, Connie is flying home. Ugh! She won't let me just wallow, she'll make me talk. I need to get up, shower and go to work. Keeping busy is my only option, it'll keep people off my back.

As I adjust the temperature of the shower, I examine my options. I don't really have any. It's not like life was going well before I allowed Danny to walk in and screw me over. I have to just try my hardest to get back to normal as quickly as possible. I should have trusted my instincts. Danny was just human after all, hurting me was almost inevitable. Sadly, I knew that but the naive teenager in me just got sucked in for old time's sake. I knew this would happen, I was safer with Mark, at least I could take that on the chin.

Max is waiting when I come out of the bedroom dressed for work.

"I brought you some coffee and…" He starts as he turns to me. His face falls as he sees me. "Liv, you're not going to work?"

I walk across to where he is sitting and pick up my coffee. Taking a sip, I smile a tiny smile and sit beside him.

"What should I do then?" I ask softly.

"We have it all covered downstairs. You need to sort your head out."

"I'm not going to do that here, trust me. I need the distraction." I put my hand on his knee. "Thank you for looking after me, but I have to get back down there before I drive myself insane."

He sighs. "Well, you aren't going anywhere until you eat something." He holds up a muffin on a plate.

I smile sweetly and dutifully take the muffin. Then, with some physical effort, I force some down. I may as well start now, Connie will be much harder to deal with.

Satisfied, Max sits back and seems to relax slightly. I can hear his cogs turning though and I know he wants to talk. So when he parts his lips to say whatever it is I know I don't want to hear, I say "I don't want to talk about it." Then, getting to my feet, I take the coffee and the muffin and go to the door.

"Coming?" I ask innocently as I head down to the diner.

*****

Danny.

Jen places a coffee on my nightstand and sits on the edge of the bed. "If they know any more, they're not saying," she says softly.

She was just on the phone to Liv's sister, trying to get more information. But I know all I need to know. They found the note last night when they got back; it said she was going home.

It didn't say why, but I know.

She doesn't love me.

She found out I was going to propose and she ran.

Again.

Last night after the dust settled, Jen found the ring bag screwed up in the trash. I'd left it out on the counter when I went to go meet Liv at the party and it doesn't take a genius to see what happened. Liv came back just after I left, saw the bag, figured it out, freaked and then packed her things and left.

Scott and Jen left me alone last night, but only after I insisted. Jen came back first thing this morning though, to make sure I was okay. She wants me to get up and go over to Grace's to find out what they know, but I don't want to hear it. I can't face their pity and I'm too angry to see Connie. This is all her fault. Liv and I were getting on with our lives quite happily until she interfered. Now I'm left with that old open wound and I have to start getting over her again. Except this time, I don't think I can.

"Danny, come on, drink your coffee." Jen urges. Reluctantly, I sit up and take a sip.

"Thanks," I say distantly.

"So what are you going to do now?"

"Nothing," I tell her.

She watches me as I drink, until I can't take it any longer. I throw the covers off and get up.

"Are you going over there?" she asks hopefully.

I turn and see her optimistic face. "No," I say firmly. "I have unpacking to do."

"Danny! You can't just give up."

"Why not?" I scoff. "She has."

One.

The nights are the worst.

Danny.

I shower and throw on some shorts and a t-shirt. I've successfully managed to work through the hellish night. The nights are the worst, but this one was particularly bad as it's precisely a week on from the night Liv walked out on me. Jen had some ridiculous idea of me having dinner with them, but that sounded like my worst nightmare. Why would I want to mark the occasion with a sombre dinner when I could be working away in my pit, unaware of the world and all the pain within it? I'm so glad I have this job to do right now, or I would have driven myself nuts. But, it's Saturday morning and if I don't show my face for the obligatory pancakes I'm going to be in for a world of shit. Besides, there is something I need to discuss with them both.

Scott is up, dressed and looking particularly chipper when I arrive laden down with groceries.

"Wow! You realise it's A.M. right?" I rib as I put the groceries down.

"Yeah, yeah," he dismisses.

"So how are you?" asks Jen with her well-rehearsed tone.

"I'm doing okay," I say, trying not to brush her off. I know she is worried about me, but I can't do what she wants me to do. I'm not chasing Liv. Jen has tried cajoling, nagging, yelling and crying. There is only bribery left, but she seems to have risen above that. She wants me to be happy, but she is wrong about how I can achieve that. I should have left the whole thing alone. But I went against my gut and this is the result. I won't make that mistake again. I'm staying put. Screw Liv.

"Working hard?" Jen asks, this is more of an accusation.

"Yes," I say like a sulky teen. "But it's what I need right now. Anyway, I need the money…I've a huge credit card bill to pay." I joke, referring to the ring. But there is little humor to be found, even when the joke is my own. I sigh. How did I become the guy with two unwanted engagement rings to his name?

Jen doesn't push further.

"So whose turn is it to cook?" I ask, knowing full well it's mine, I'm just trying to change the subject. Jen rolls her eyes and sets about making coffee. Scott takes the morning papers over to the table, his usual position. I've no idea when he became exempt from cooking, but Jen and I take turns.

I get on with mixing the batter, it's second nature now, and Jen and I move about the kitchen in perfect sync with one another. I wonder distantly, how I thought it would be easy to give this up and move. I love these guys.

We make Scott do all the donkey work after breakfast; it's only fair that he cleans up. Jen and I poke fun at him for our own amusement, from where we sit in the garden.

"I'm just not used to seeing him this alert on a Saturday morning," I tease.

"We went for a walk on the beach this morning," Jen says with a knowing look. "We had stuff to talk about."

"And?" I ask, knowing full well the subject they needed to discuss. They have been back and forth all week on this sperm donor thing. I know Jen is terrified, but Scott sees it as no big deal and just wants to get on with it. I really admire the guy; hell, it's quite a dent in the old masculinity. But as far as he is concerned, it's just a blip. Any child that is conceived as a result would be his and his alone. Jen has just read one bad example and it has her all in knots. She's worried that Scott won't feel connected to the baby and she'll be left all alone. That just wouldn't happen.

Scott joins us just then and they smile at each other. "I talked her around," Scott says, never taking his eyes off Jen as he sits beside her. God, he loves her.

"That's great!' I exclaim and put my arms around Jen lifting her slightly out of her chair. "So what happens now?"

"Well…we start looking," she says with a nervous smile. "It's a long process and we need a few months to figure out my ovulation issues."

Okay, here goes. I can't handle any more rejection this week. "I don't know the best way to approach this," I say, looking them in the eye in turn. "But, when you're ready, I was hoping you would consider me."

Silence descends on the garden.

I fidget in my seat. "Okay, I can see you guys are having a hard time processing what I've just said, but I've done a lot of research." I waffle through the awkward silence, while jogging into the kitchen. From the bag on the counter I produce a wad of papers. "I've looked into ways to do this sort of thing and it seems like people do it all the time." I pause for breath and lay the pages on the table. Waiting nervously to see who speaks first, I feel like I've crossed a line and it could go either way. Have I just wrecked my closest friendship? It wouldn't surprise me, I seem to be on a roll.

Scott looks at Jen and after a moment smiles. They both smile.

"What?" I ask.

"The thing is, when we talked this morning, we said it was a shame we can't ask you." Jen giggles.

I watch them for a moment, "So you would consider it?" I ask.

"Yeah," replies Scott. "I think we would." He looks to Jen for some indication of where she stands on the issue.

"Really?" I say. I thought they would reject the idea outright.

"Um, yeah." Jen nods slowly. "I mean, we would have a lot to discuss, but if we could all agree, you would be my first choice."

I grin. This is amazing. From the very first day that they thought they might be having problems, I've thought about offering to help them. But when we found out that the problem was mainly with Scott and I could indeed do something productive, I had to re-think. I was with Liv, moving to England and was planning to start a family of my own. I would do anything to secure Jen's happiness, but when I thought Liv and I had a future, I thought it would be too much to expect her to accept my idea.

But that is all off the table now and even if I'm able to dust myself off and find a new future, it will be a long way off. I want to do this. I want to invest in something really worthwhile. They will be great parents and I could be a part of it.

"That's so cool," I murmur, almost to myself. My spirits lifted by this show of faith from my dearest friends. Then something occurs to me… "But why couldn't you ask me?"

Scott frowns. "It's a lot to ask. You can't just go crashing in, asking your best buddy to father your child." He laughs.

"And you're not in the best place right now," Jen adds.

"I've thought about this for months, guys." I'm keen to assure them that this is not a knee-jerk reaction to the break-up. "And we could do it on whatever terms suit you. There are several ways."

"I know, I've been reading up too," says Scott.

"We can do it through all the legal channels. I don't want it to come between us in any way. I just want you two to be parents." I look to Scott. "I know this is hard on you and I don't want to make you feel worse by offering…"

Scott shrugs. "Hey, if we need a donor, we need a donor. I can't think of anyone I'd rather ask."

"Me too," agrees Jen.

"Well, I think you two should talk it all through, I'll leave it with you and when you decide, I'm here…and if you decide to go another way, I'll still be here." I'm relieved that went well, but I think they should talk about it together now, so I change the subject.

After I left them to discuss everything on Saturday, I took the Shelby out for a drive. If things had gone how I planned, I may never have driven her again, so I thought it would be nice to give her a run out. Santa Barbra and back took up a nice portion of the day, but I had to play music loud because I didn't want Liv in my head. When I got home, I slept for a couple of hours then threw myself straight into an all-nighter. Hardly sleeping, bar a few naps for a couple of days paid off, because when I finally stopped working early Sunday morning, I was so tired, I slept all day. I either need to be really busy, or so dog tired I can actually sleep; it's the only way I can survive right now. After another full-on night last night, I was just finishing up when I got a message from Jen.

'Breakfast before you go to bed? Jx'

I had to laugh, she knows me too well. So, after picking up coffee and bagels from the deli, I pull in behind the store.

"Hey!" she says looking up from her laptop.

"Hey yourself," I say, flopping down on the sofa beside her and kissing her cheek while she finishes typing.

"Did you bring me a bagel?" she asks excitedly, recognising the bag I'm holding.

"Yeah, but they ran out of Lox." I tease. I got her usual, Lox, cream cheese, tomatoes and onions. But I always make out that they only had peanut butter left in the whole place. It isn't a funny joke, but I can't not do it.

"Shame," she says, grabbing the bag and whipping out her favorite breakfast. She has bitten a chunk out of if before I can protest and I have to snatch the bag back, before she devours mine too. "So…" she says through a mouthful of bagel. "How've you been?"

"I'm fine." I bite into my bagel so that I don't have to elaborate. "What about you?" I ask as I finish chewing, to turn the tables.

"Great thanks, you left us with a lot to think about Saturday and I wanted to see you, to talk it through."

I wait, but she says nothing. "So?" I ask after a long enough pause. She's doing it on purpose.

She takes a deep breath. "Well it's a huge decision," she says. "We're both blown away by your offer and we really want to take you up on it, but there are a few things to discuss first."

"I'll sign anything you want me to sign. I don't want either of you worrying that I'll decide I want a say, or access or something. I just want to be Uncle Danny." I babble, this has all been whizzing around my head and sounds too rehearsed now.

"Oh, I know, that's not my concern," she says, putting her hand on my knee.

"Is it Scott?" I ask. "This was what I was most afraid of."

She looks puzzled. "What about Scott?"

"Well he can't…you know… and I can. Or at least I assume I can." I mumble. "I just don't want him feeling inadequate, especially against me."

She laughs. "Oh, you don't need to worry about that, he's surprisingly okay with that side of things. He wants to do it and we would both rather know who we are picking." She grins. "He actually feels more comfortable about it if it's you…and I've always wanted you for your genes anyway!" She winks at me.

I smile, I know she would be more relaxed about her abandonment fears if I'm involved, but I haven't exactly been able to voice it to her. I didn't want to put Scott's nose out. "Listen, I couldn't say this to you in front of Scott. We both know he would never freak out on you, but you also know if he did, I would never let you raise a baby on your own…especially if it's mine." I say quietly. This already kinda goes against my previous 'not wanting any sort of stake in the kid' statement, but I need her to know it anyway. It would never happen, it's just an irrational fear.

For a second my own irrational fears creep into my head, the ones that just turned out to be a reality, never say never, hey?

She smiles affectionately. "I know, thanks. I think we can make it work." She pauses. "But one thing really worries me."

"What?"

"Liv," she says quietly.

I look at her in disbelief. "Why the hell would she be a factor in all this?"

Steeling herself, she explains. "You should be together, Danny, having your own family." She pauses, leaving it hanging in the air. I feel like I'm going to suffocate. Jen just watches me.

"Fuck Jen, why are you doing this to me?" I snap. "I don't want to hear her name again."

"But you still love her and you can't tell me there isn't a chance she still loves you."

I shake my head and stare out of the window.

"Danny, a week ago, you were going to give up your whole life here to make a new one with her. That doesn't just go away." She tries to take my hand but I pull it away. "Scott and I have talked and we both agree, you need to talk to her, find out why she left."

"I'm not calling her, Jen. She's made it clear that she doesn't want me. It's over."

"Danny, you don't know why she left. She may have seen something between you and Brooke and thought you cheated."

"Nothing happened with Brooke!"

"I know that, but would she?" She reasons. "You said Brooke was already undressed when you came out of the shower. Liv could have seen that."

"Or she just didn't love me." I stand up and walk to the window.

"Danny, be realistic. You know she loves you and it's too much of a coincidence that she left the night Brooke pulled her little stunt. Now I've let you do this your way for over a week, but if neither one of you is going to give in and call the other, then I'm afraid I'll have to fight dirty."

I spin around to face her, "What the hell does that mean?"

She stands and puts her hands on her hips. "If you want us to consider your offer, then you have to call her."

And there it is…the bribery, now she's pulled every trick from her hat and she looks so pleased with herself.

"Careful," I warn. "I'm not playing."

"Neither am I." She holds firm.

We have a standoff for a moment and then she lays it on the table. "We don't want to take your first child Danny, it's not fair. Call her. Sort this thing out. Live happily ever after…Then and only then will we accept your very generous offer, *if* Liv agrees too. We can wait."

I shake my head, the gloves are really off. I'm too stunned to speak.

"If she did leave for the reasons you think, then I won't mention it again. But you have to find out for sure."

Feeling the anger rising up in me, I grab my keys. "I can't handle this." I say as I storm past her and out the door.

I'm fuming as I back my truck out of the parking lot. Who the hell does she think she is? This is emotional blackmail. I expected better of her.

When I get in I slam my keys on the counter and pace back and forth. I really needed to sleep, now Jen has got me so worked up, there is just no way that's going to happen. It's not like I didn't call her, when she was missing I was frantic. She has dozens of messages from me and she didn't have the decency to put my mind at ease. I had to hear from her family that she had flown home, at least she left them a note! As if I would call her now. She left me. Even as I'm thinking this while pacing around like a caged animal, the idea that she may have left for another reason starts to incubate. I haven't given it a thought before, I've been too angry. I'm still too angry I think, shaking it out of my head.

I sit at my desk and fire up the computer. My fingers drum while they wait for something to do. As soon as I'm in, I start furiously hammering the keys. Work will block this ridiculous chain of thoughts out.

Twenty minutes in, I've made so many mistakes and had to retrace my steps too many times. I put my head in my hands. This can't be happening. Work was the only distraction I had and now, thanks to Jen, Liv has crept into that too.

I drop onto my bed and close my eyes. Not to sleep but just for lack of other inspiration. What if Jen's crazy notion is right? What if Liv thinks I did something wrong? Surely I would have had a call from someone if they thought I had wronged her? If I thought Scott had cheated on Jen I would have been all over it. Max would have done the same wouldn't he? Maybe I should call him. Then I don't have to chase Liv, I can just find out what I need to know from him and put this mess to rest once and for all.

Before I know it I'm dialling his number, I've always been slightly impulsive. My stomach is in knots. It rings and I hold my breath.

"Hi," he answers with a tone of uncertainty.

"Hi," I respond, not sure how to proceed.

"What the hell happened?" He cuts straight to the chase.

I sigh. "I don't know where to start."

"Well you don't have to go back to the beginning, you can just fill me in from the bit where your ex-girlfriend is doing the striptease in your bedroom." He sneers, anger and disgust oozing from his voice.

Strangely, I heave a sigh of relief. I pause to take this all in.

"Wait. Is that why she left?" I stupidly ask.

"Yes, that's why she left. Wasn't that obvious?" He spits, mystified that I could question him. "And she made me promise not to call you, but trust me, if I see you again, I'm going to break your neck."

"So it wasn't because she found out about the proposal?" I mutter in a daze, not taking in what he is saying to me.

"WHAT PROPOSAL?"

"The night she left, I was going to propose," I say quietly.

"What, after you fucked your ex?"

Silence...his words just hang in the air. My mind goes into overdrive. Max has just confirmed that all my worst fears were unfounded. She didn't leave because she found out I was going to propose. This *is* about Brooke. Thank fuck for that! Even as I'm thinking it, I know how ridiculous the whole thing sounds. I would rather Liv thinks I cheated on her, than find out she didn't love me. But, I realise, that is the truth. I hate myself for being relieved, as it dawns on me the pain she must be going through. But this can be fixed, I know it.

Fleetingly, I wonder if I should be upset that she would think so little of me. But I know I made her question my honesty and I remind myself, it was only a couple of months ago that she found that sleaze Mark with her friend, in her own bedroom. No, this isn't about me and if I'm ever going to get her back, I must focus on making her trust me again. I need Max to understand the facts.

"Max, I don't know what she saw. But she didn't see enough." I assure him. "I came out of the shower and Brooke was in her underwear lying on my bed. She stole a key a couple of weeks ago and let herself in.

As soon as I saw her, I threw her out, straight away. Then I called Liv to tell her what happened, because she asked me to be completely honest with her. But she didn't pick up and I haven't heard from her since." I pause, he says nothing. "I'm not asking you to believe me, but it's the truth. I love Liv and I would never do anything to hurt her." The words come from deep inside, they bypass the thought process. My brain is still in the hurt, angry state it was in five minutes ago, it hasn't caught up with this turn of events. Yet I'm saying how much I love her and I know instantly that I will fight for her. Whatever it takes. Fucking Jen was right. Shit.

"She saw you, Danny," he says, more unsure of his argument now.

"No, she didn't, ask her. She didn't see me put a finger on her, because I didn't. The only time I touched her was when I was shoving her out the door." I shudder at the memory. "Ask her, please."

"Why don't you just leave her alone? She's been hurt enough."

"Because I love her and I'm going to get her back."

"Oh really, you love her so much, you left it over a week to bother finding out why she left?"

"I was convinced she left because she didn't want to marry me. I've been a real mess."

"Why would she do that? She loved you."

I sigh. I've been so stupid and selfish. "Because…" I hesitate. Outside of Jen and Scott, I've never discussed this with anyone and all of a sudden, my lifelong insecurities because of it seem so irrational. "Because, when we were kids and I was going away, I bought her a ring, I worked up the guts to propose to her, but before I could get the words out, she told me to go, she said I should make the most of the opportunity. She said it would be best for both of us. She must have known what I was going to do and was pushing me away so that I didn't do it…I just thought she was doing it again."

"You wanted to marry her?"

"Uh-huh. Then and now." I sigh.

"She didn't know, mate. Trust me, I picked up the pieces after you left. She thought you didn't fight hard enough, she wanted to go with you."

"You're kidding me?" I can't handle this. "I'm such an idiot," I whisper.

"You're telling me!" he sneers.

I think about what to do next. I have to talk to her.

"I have to get her back." I think aloud.

"Please just leave her alone, she can't handle any more heartache." The thought of her so hurt is like a knife to the chest.

"Max, please, I've done nothing wrong. Please just ask her, I'm begging you."

"I have to go." He hangs up. Fuck! I slam my cell onto the bed. This can't be happening. I have to get her to listen to me. I grab the cell again and select her name.

'This is Liv, leave a message.' Her cell is off, it didn't even ring. I don't leave a message, I wouldn't know what to say.

I don't know what to do now. On auto-pilot, I slowly gather myself up and drift to my truck. I find myself back at Jen's store less than an hour after storming out.

"Danny?" Jen calls as I walk in from the back door. I sit down on the sofa with a bump and put my face in my hands. Jen has a customer, so I try to remain inconspicuous while she finishes up. Lost in my thoughts, I don't notice her standing right in front of me. I jump at her proximity when I finally lift my face up to look around. I look up at her and hold her stare. She waits to hear what I have to say.

"She thinks I cheated on her with Brooke," I say in barely more than a whisper.

Jen sits beside me and touches my arm. "I knew it." She rolls her head back. "So did you explain?" she asks gently.

"I didn't talk to her, I called Max."

"You should talk to her."

"Her cell is off, I tried."

"Will Max talk to her for you?"

"I don't think he believed me, he hung up."

"Shit."

"What do I do?".

"We should look at flights," she says, opening her laptop. While we wait for it to load up, she strokes my back. My face is in my hands again. How did I let it get this far? I'm so fucking stupid.

While I mope on the sofa, Jen has a look at flights for me, but we both agree I should try to make contact again before charging in. If Max doesn't believe me, I could be opening myself up to some pretty serious wrath. Given the week I've had so far, I could really do without getting my neck broken. I've tried her cell again, but it's still off. The phone at the flat just rings out, she must have switched off the machine and I wouldn't want to leave a message when there is so much to say. I could call the diner, but I don't think it's fair to do this to her at work. So I try Max again.

Prepared to leave a message, I'm shocked when he answers.

"Did you talk to her?" I ask, hopeful that he might have had enough faith in me to at least ask the question.

"Yeah, I did," he says in a hushed tone. "So what are you going to do?" he asks, reluctant to admit that he believes me for fear of betraying his friend, but certainly with a slight change of tune.

"I have to talk to her and I can't get through, so I'm looking at flights."

"I have her phone, she threw it away. I doubt she'll see you."

"What do you suggest then?"

"Give me a few days with her. I'll keep in touch."

"Stay here you mean?"

"I think it's best. If you push her now, you might blow it for good." Then there is a loud crash on his end of the line "Fuck, Liv!" he yells and then the line goes dead.

"Max?" What the hell just happened? "MAX?" I yell.

"What?" says Jen when she sees my expression.

"I don't know," I say quietly. "But I think something just happened to Liv."

Two.

You're the clumsy one.

Liv.

I've survived the Connie onslaught. She was easier to deal with than I expected mainly due to the fact that she feels responsible. She revealed to me that she contacted Danny in the first place. I was furious. For a few days, I was so angry I could hardly talk to her, but then I realised that I was just disappointed. It was just more proof that Danny didn't really love me, he didn't contact me without a push. Connie and I are okay now, I can't stay angry with her.

I've spoken to Mum and persuaded her to stay in LA because Grace needs her far more than I do. She's promised me that she won't get involved and go and see Danny. I've even left the phone plugged in upstairs so that she can call me, she was pretty pissed off that I cut myself off completely. The problem is, I dread going back up there now. I've no idea if, when, or how many times Danny has called me since I left, but now he could leave a message if he wanted to. He hasn't reached me on my mobile because I threw it away, it's full of messages and photos I can't face. Who needs a mobile anyway?

But still, it has been eerily quiet since I got back. I was expecting more of a fight, he didn't know I saw them together, so he can't have known why I left so suddenly. He must have been worried, frantic even. The fact that he didn't follow me is both a relief and a crushing disappointment. I don't want to see him or listen to anything he has to say, but he hasn't even tried to fight for us…again. This just proves it was all me again, like it was before.

Work has been thankfully busy and the new furniture for the garden arrives tomorrow, so I'm getting everything ready. I decided to close the outside area this week and we have cleared all the furniture out. I'm spending the day jet washing, which is very therapeutic and everyone is leaving me alone to get on with it. It's just what I need. But there is so much to do and now there is one less pair of hands to help me do it. He was going to put up the canopy of fairy lights for me. But it looks like Max and I will be up the ladders.

Soaking wet from jet washing, I pop upstairs to change. The light on my phone is blinking. I bloody knew it, I should have left it unplugged. It could be Mum and if it is and I don't reply, I'll get another bollocking. Shaking my head, I go and turn the shower on. I need to get out of these wet clothes. But I can't leave it and I have to go and listen to the message. I can't help myself, this is why I left it unplugged, what if I'd been here, answered it and it was him? I can't trust myself to be strong, but I press the button anyway.

Time stands still as I wait for the beep, then I hear Mum's chirpy voice. Relief and devastation briefly do battle for control over me. I can't handle the emotional ups and downs at the moment. Mum is bleating on in the background, hoping I'm eating and looking after myself, but I barely hear her. All I can think is, why hasn't he called? But if he did, I'd be angry. It's impossible. Mum finishes waffling and I switch off the machine. I don't have a choice about having the phone on, but if I heard his voice it would kill me, I can't take the risk. Reluctantly, I trudge to the shower.

Max has a coffee waiting for me when I get downstairs. He's sitting in the booth at the back sipping his and I slide in opposite him. We haven't really done this since I got back. I suppose I've been swerving any probing discussions. I take charge of the conversation straight away to stop him from talking about…him.

"So, shall we start the lights before it gets dark?" I suggest. "I'd like to get at least half of it done tonight."

"Only if you sit with me first," he says seriously.

Here we go... "Max, I really don't want to..."

"Liv, stop." He interrupts. "I've given you some space and I haven't pushed you, but this is getting ridiculous, it's been a week." He looks at me with concern in his eyes. "I thought one of you would have made the first move by now."

A wave of nausea washes over me. Why hasn't he tried to call? I swallow hard. It's not as if I want to talk to him anyway, I remind myself. "There's no first move. It's over." I tell him firmly.

"Liv, what you have with Danny can't be over without a discussion, or a huge fight, or something. It's not something that you would both just let go of like that."

"Max, he cheated. I've let go, that's it."

"Okay, that's why you let go, what about him?"

I stare at him. This is the question I've been trying not to ask myself all week. Tears sting my eyes and I want to run away. Max stares me out, he isn't going to give in. "I don't know." I sniff.

"What exactly did you see?" he finally asks.

I sigh. "I told you what happened; I really don't want to talk about this again, Max."

"You told me he cheated with that girl, but what exactly did you see?"

"I saw her taking her clothes off in his bedroom."

"Where were you?"

"I was outside. I saw her through the window before I got to the door, I saw her and I left." I play down the drama of my departure.

"And where was Danny?"

I sigh, why is he making me go over this? "I don't know...there somewhere, obviously."

"But you didn't see him?"

"No, there was only a small gap in the curtains and I didn't hang around."

"So you don't know if he actually touched her?"

Where is he going with this?

"Oh of course he touched her, he's a man!" I immediately regret my outburst, as I once again count Max out of his gender group, not because of his sexuality, but because he would never, ever hurt me. The rest, however, are bastards. Danny included.

"But..."

"What?"

"I don't know. I was just thinking, if you didn't see him, how do you know he did what you think he did?"

"Well she was taking her clothes off in his house, which I very much doubt she was doing without his permission." God, this is exhausting. "Now I really just want to forget about this whole thing, so can we please go and do some way-out-of-our-league DIY?"

"Sure." He smiles.

It's big job, but I haven't budgeted to get someone else to do it. The outdoor lights, plus having the outdoor sockets installed, cost more than I wanted to spend. The electrician that did the sockets has also suspended two beautiful, budget-busting outdoor chandeliers, so we have no choice, DIY it is. In truth, the budget was long since blown on the retractable guttered rain shelters that have been installed above the lighting, making it an all-weather outdoor paradise.

We have marked out the line of bricks on both sides of the alley, so that the light canopy hovers just above the huge chandeliers. Now we just have to staple the lights to the bricks either side all the way down until we have the desired look. We have everything we need including a brilliant power stapler Max hired for the job.

Max starts up on his ladder, pinning the string to the wall at the first bulb. Then as he descends, he tacks the spare wire down the wall until he reaches the socket. Then it's my turn. Max passes me the lights then the stapler and I head to the top of the ladder. It's not so difficult although it's over 10ft up and the stapler has a slight recoil. But we can do it.

A few feet down the alley, we reach the end of the string of lights and Max hands me the next set. We are in the swing of it now. I love jobs like this, very satisfying and a bit exciting using big tools. I pop the stapler into the wall and my ladder wobbles. "Whoa!" I exclaim and laugh as I climb down to shuffle along to the next point.

"Jesus Liv, be careful!" says Max as he takes the stapler from me and climbs up the other ladder.

"I'm fine," I say. "You're the clumsy one." He gives me a withering look.

As he comes down from his turn, his phone rings and he moves down to the end of the garden to take it. I carry on with the next fixing on my side then, seeing that he is deeply engrossed in conversation, I do his next one as well. As I take the first step down the ladder, the hem of my jeans catches on the top step and I fall, seemingly in slow motion.

I land right foot first and as my leg buckles beneath me I come down with a bang on my side. The industrial stapler, still in my hand, slams to the ground on top of my fingers and, with the momentum of the fall, I'm unable to stop the side of my head from hitting the ground with a thud. I hear Max yelling my name, as he comes running.

"Fuck, Liv!" he shouts, then as he lands on his knees beside me he asks, "Are you okay?"

I think about this for a second, my ankle really hurts, but more in that way that your elbow hurts when you hit your funny bone. My head hurts, but not badly. My fingers hurt but I can flex them so they're okay. All in all, I'd say I'm okay.

Josh comes out to see what's going on and he recoils when he sees me lying on the ground.

"Call an ambulance," Max barks at him, as he sits behind me and strokes the hair off my face.

"No, no," I say as I try to sit up. "That's a bit dramatic..." I wince as the pain shoots through my ankle. I immediately stop trying to move.

"Liv, just lay still and do as you're told for once in your life." Max turns back to Josh. "Call them."

"Where does it hurt?" he asks in a panicked voice.

"Here." I point towards my foot.

"Okay, just lie still. It'll be okay." Somewhere his phone is ringing but he ignores it.

When Josh returns, he has the first aid kit. He quickly opens it and hands a packet to Max. I watch with interest as Max unwraps the large pad, which he then places on the side of my head. I hadn't realised I was bleeding.

"Gloves?" Josh offers Max.

Max looks at him with a 'what do you think?' glare. Josh gets the point and puts them away. I watch all of this distantly while I focus on the hurting bits of me, none of which are my head, so I don't know why they are fussing.

It feels like an eternity until the ambulance arrives, but the paramedics are so lovely. They give me gas and air to help with the worsening pain, while they ask me questions and give me other drugs. They are concerned about my ankle and put it in a splint, but I don't see the point of the big fuss. I've got the giggles a bit and I think they're making a mountain out of a molehill. It certainly didn't seem worth cutting straight up the leg of my perfectly good jeans. Max explains what he saw and once they ascertain the height I've fallen from and the fact that I bumped my head, they start shining lights in my eyes and all sorts.

They put a neck brace on me as a precaution and I'm carefully rolled onto a back board. They put that orange box thing around my head. It seems all way over the top and it's like an out of body experience. Max is holding my hand and looks really pale. Then, quickly, I'm put onto a rolling stretcher and into the ambulance. Max is allowed to come with me, as he doesn't have his car at work to follow and we set off.

The pain is much more severe now that I'm lying flat on a hard surface and I start shaking from the shock. Max is sitting across from me strapped in and one of the paramedics is fiddling about, but I can't see anyone because I have my head in a box. I feel so alone and for the first time in a week I really want Danny. I just wish he was with me. I wish he hadn't wrecked everything and then he would be. I know Max will look after me, but without Danny I feel empty.

We arrive at the hospital in a few minutes and I'm whizzed straight through to a curtained-off area. Several people jump into action when I come to a stop and I quickly lose track of who is doing what. I'm asked a very similar set of questions to those the paramedics asked me. How did I land? Did I black out? Where is the pain?

I find this rhythm comforting as it takes me out of the anxiety I'm feeling. Max holds my hand, I'm so glad he's with me. They tell me that I'm going to be sent for x-rays shortly and suggest that Max wait outside.

The doctor performs a thorough examination and is fairly happy that my spine is unaffected so he carefully removes the orange box and neck brace. Then he and two nurses roll me gently so that they can remove the back board. Despite the agony of rolling, it feels so much more comfortable to be lying on a cushioned surface and have the full use of my neck. They sit the bed up and at last I can see what is going on around me.

After several x-rays, I'm wheeled back to where I was and Max is allowed to join me again. He smiles a warm and comforting smile and sits beside me.

"That's better," he says. "I was freaking out when they put that collar on you!"

"It was just a precaution." I reassure him.

He looks at me and winces. "I saw you fall. I shouldn't have been on the fucking phone."

"Oh stop it. It was an accident." He nods and eyes me up and down.

"So what's going on?" he asks.

"I don't know. They're looking at the x-rays I suppose."

"How do you feel?"

"Like an idiot." I laugh and fidget, sending a twinge of pain through my foot.

"Shit, what is it?" Max jumps to his feet.

"Laughing made my ankle hurt!" I whimper. Max gives me a stern look as if now is not the time to be laughing anyway, which only makes it worse. Maybe it's the drugs.

As I'm calming down, a doctor appears around the curtain and introduces himself as Dr. Andrews from orthopaedics or something.

"I understand you took a tumble." He jokes, trying to put me at ease.

"It was a ten-foot ladder," Max says, not rising to the humour. "She fell from the top." Max is very dry and serious. This familiarity of my friend's anxiety puts me at ease more than the corny line from the doctor could have ever hoped to.

"Well, then I'd say you have been very lucky." He smiles. "You'll probably be quite bruised tomorrow and we'll have to stitch that cut on your head." He pauses. "But I'm afraid you have a significant fracture to your ankle which will require surgery."

I look at him while I take it in. "My ankle doesn't even feel that bad," I muse aloud.

"Well you have a trimalleolar fracture, which is complex. But we have it nicely immobilised and we are managing your pain, so you should have a comfortable night."

"You can't do it until tomorrow?" Max asks, incredulously. It's about 6pm, what does he expect?

"That's correct," the doctor replies.

We discuss what I'll be having done tomorrow, which involves screws and possibly a plate, but won't be decided until I'm in surgery. Then he briefs me on the recovery I'm facing. Six weeks in plaster and a possible second surgery. It sounds pretty rough, but he has advised me to take it one day at a time, rather than as a whole, scary picture. I get emotional when I realise that I'm going to be dependent on Max and I don't have Danny for support. The doctor mistakes this for nerves about the operation and assures me that this is just another day at the office for him; he sees this type of injury all the time. Then he leaves us and we wait for a nurse to come and stitch my head.

Twelve stitches later, I'm moved to a ward. Max leaves to go and get me some things from home and I'm left alone with my thoughts. I'm trying not to panic about how out of action I'm going to be and how we will manage at work. I'm in quite a lot of pain and I just wish I had Danny here. God, this has really been the worst week of my life.

It suddenly occurs to me that someone might tell Danny! I must tell Max that I don't want Danny to know this has happened. He might come rushing over and I'm not strong enough to push him away right now. Or worse, he won't come and I can't handle that kind of disappointment. Why did I get so caught up in all of his? It was never going to work out. I fight back tears, I can't cry now, not here. I feel so sorry for myself. Being alone is not good for me. I'm thankful that Max has got me a card for the TV and phone and pulled it over next to my bed, I put some nonsense on and drift off to a medicated sleep.

Pain and whispering wake me sometime later and I open my eyes to find Connie and Max bickering at the end of my bed.

"What's up?" I ask, sleepily, instinctively stretching as my body wakes up and then recoiling in pain as I'm reminded that today has not been the best of days.

"Liv, darling, what have you done to yourself?" Connie gushes as she hurries around to my side. She takes my hand and finds a small unbandaged part of my forehead and strokes it. "Look at the state you're in."

"I'm okay, what's with all the whispering?" I ask.

"Oh, nothing," she says, innocently. "Max forgot to bring your dressing gown." I don't have the energy to probe any deeper.

"How are you doing?" Max asks, coming to the other side of me.

"Alright," I say half-heartedly. "What did you bring me?"

"I got you some clothes, some magazines and your old iPod, because I'm guessing you still don't want your phone."

"No." I sulk.

I realised Max fished my phone out of the bin after I chucked it away, because I went back to rescue it myself a little later and it was gone. I know it was rash throwing it in the bin, but I'm still not ready to look at it yet.

"Okay, well good job I found this for you then." Max places the iPod and headphones on the bed next to me.

"Now, what time are they doing your surgery tomorrow?" Connie asks.

"Early, I think." I reply, a bit hazy from the drugs. "Nine-something."

"I'll need to let your mum know," she says.

"Shit, Mum...Don't tell her, she'll worry and leave Grace, this is their time." That would be all I need right now, Mum staying with me while I'm housebound.

"She already knows," says Max guiltily. "I rang her...but it's okay. We convinced her to stay put for now."

I give him a look. "For now?" That's not reassuring. "I'll talk to her in the morning, tell her you made the whole thing up." I giggle. Then my smile fades, "Oh and Max. I know none of you would talk to him, but under no circumstances is Danny to know about this."

As I finish the sentence, I catch a look flit between them. What does that mean? They wouldn't...I dismiss the thought, they just wouldn't.

"Everything is fine at work by the way." Max jumps in, changing the subject. "Josh called everyone to tell them what happened and, between them, they've rearranged everything so that you and I are not needed at all. They all send their love." He squeezes my hand.

"Well you tell them I love them too." I say, feeling overwhelmed.

"Oh and they've finished the lights."

"Finished them?"

"Yep." Max nods, amused. "The day shift stayed behind for an hour and did it between them. There was plenty of ladder-holding!" He laughs, then his smile vanishes. "I'm so sorry I was on the phone." He whispers, glancing again at Connie. What is going on between these two?

I'm just about to ask, when the nurse comes round with my medication. Seizing their moment to escape, Max and Connie arrange that Max will come back in the morning and wait while I'm in surgery and Connie will get everything ready for me at home...Then they are gone. Once again I'm alone and feeling sorry for myself. Fucking Danny, selfish bastard. I hate the silence, I'm in a two-bed room, but the other bed is empty. I unravel the headphones and put on some music, then I close my eyes and drift into a restless, painful sleep.

Three.

Can I have a hug?

Liv.

My face is lightly brushed by a soft hand and it snaps me out of the deep darkness. A warmth surrounds me and I feel a peace that I haven't felt for at least a week. Fleetingly, I want to know who the hand belongs to, but I'm deep in a foggy state and I instinctively know I'm not even close to the surface yet.

The hand skims over my skin again. It's bringing me forward from the depths of sleep, but only enough to be aware if the comfort it brings. Comfort I want so badly it aches. The fingers traces the line of my jaw, but then withdraws and I'm left with the darkness again.

My eyes don't want to open as I tune into the sounds in the room. I can hear Max talking to someone, but it isn't clear who. They are speaking too quietly. My mouth is dry and my throat is sore, but I'm just not awake enough yet to tell them. Vaguely, I recall a spell in the recovery room, but I can't place when that was. As I fight through, I manage to prise open an eye and then lift my hand. What a horrible feeling, like trying to run through treacle. But, quickly, I start to win.

"Liv," says Max. "She's coming round." He says to the someone else. The someone else mutters a response.

Max pulls a chair next to me and sits down, holding my hand. "Hey, Liv," he says gently.

I peel both eyes open and blink at the blurriness. "I need a drink." I manage in a hoarse whisper, my throat so dry it feels stuck together.

"The nurse is just bringing you some water." he soothes.

It feels like evening, but it must still be morning, unless the operation took way longer than expected. The room is dimly lit and cosy. I blink and look around. The curtains are closed and the slightest trace of daylight is trying to peep around them. A nurse appears and greets us warmly.

"How are we?" she asks.

"My throat is sore," I tell her.

"Yes, that's from the breathing tube they use during the op. Let's get you a sip of water."

I try to sit up, but the nurse puts her hand on my shoulder. "Just relax, these beds do all the work for you, you know." She unhooks the control from the side of the bed and begins raising me into a sitting position. From here I can see better and I glance around for another person, feeling like not everyone is accounted for. But it's just Max and the nurse going about her business. My heart sinks with disappointment, I don't know what I was expecting, but I felt whole again for a moment when I was awoken by a loving touch. I know I hate Danny, but I know in my heart I thought it was him in the room and in that split second everything seemed right with the world. It was obviously a drug-induced dream and the reality is far more of a nightmare.

"Are you in any pain?" she asks.

Not physically, I want to say. It's just this aching hole in my chest where my heart should be…But I keep it in. "No, not really." I reply, forcing myself back to the present. I can't wallow in this right now, tempting as it is. I have to get better.

"Well, if you feel like it is getting too much just press this button and one of us will see about a top-up." She busies herself with checking my pulse and blood pressure. Once she is satisfied, she says, "Dr Andrews will be along a little later to chat to you, but I understand the surgery was a complete success. Now you just rest."

After she leaves us, I turn to Max. "Who were you talking to?"

He frowns. "When?"

"Just before, I could hear your voice, but I couldn't work out who you were talking to." Max's face blanches and he looks guilty, but maybe I'm looking for something that isn't there. He thinks for a moment and then shrugs. "Just the nurse probably." I sigh in disappointment. In my hazy dream-state, I hoped Danny had come. I hate myself for it, but for that moment I felt like it would make everything okay again. How desperate am I? I'm not going to admit that to Max though. It's far too humiliating.

"How are you feeling?" he asks.

Pathetic, I think ..."Tired." I reply. I had as good a night's sleep as it is possible to have in hospital. At about 3am there was some sort of emergency down the corridor. The alarm went off at the nurses' station just outside my door and every pair of feet in the place seemed to go thundering down the corridor. With all the excitement happening around me, the constant observations carried out by the nurses and the pain, it wasn't a restful night.

"Sorry I wasn't here when you went into surgery this morning," he says.

"That's okay, they took me earlier than they said."

"Can I get you anything?"

"You can find out if I'm allowed to eat something, I haven't eaten since yesterday lunchtime and I'm starving. What time is it?" I ask.

Max looks at his watch. "Four thirty."

"What? How long did the surgery take?"

"About an hour and a half, you came back here at eleven and you've been in and out ever since."

"Oh."

"The nurse has been backwards and forwards, she says it's normal. Some people just go under fairly deep."

"Have you been here the whole time?" I ask.

"Yep." He smiles. "I'll go and find out if you can eat. What do you want?"

"Something good." I grin and sip my water.

For the first time I think about my ankle and as Max goes out to the nurse, I have a look under the covers at what is keeping me here. At first I'm surprised that it's not in a cast. Instead it's wrapped in bandages. It looks like a comedy broken leg, it's huge. Fear stops me testing it and as I look at it I feel strangely detached. Luckily the cut on my head is nothing, because I didn't black out. I suppose I might have a scar, but I scar myself willingly in every colour of the rainbow, so a natural one isn't exactly something I will worry about. It's right in my hairline anyway.

Max comes back with a thumb's up. "She says you can have whatever you like, so Josh is on his way over with a goody bag from Jake."

"You're a star." I smile. I don't know what I would do without him. But things should have been so different.

"No problem." He grins. "Anything else?"

"Yeah, can I have a hug?" I feel suddenly needy and emotional. He rushes over and squeezes me a bit too tight, but I don't care. I need him.

"Hey, it's okay," he soothes. "I'm here."

"Sorry," I say, my voice strained with emotion as I wipe big tears from my eyes.

Max sits back and assesses me while keeping hold of my hand. He says nothing, just stares. Maybe he doesn't know what to say. It's almost unheard of for him to not know how to help me. We are so in tune that we normally alienate people, so this is a strange experience. I know he completely disagrees with my decision to cut Danny off. But he is usually more vocal when we have a difference of opinion. He probably feels like he can't say anything because I'm fragile now. Who knew injuring myself would actually protect me?

I'm just finishing my club sandwich with a side of chips, when the surgeon appears at the door. I guiltily put the rubbish in the bag and Max scurries away to dispose of it.

"Don't stop on my account he insists, we like a healthy appetite around here." He jokes.

"It's fine, I was finished anyway," I say and wipe my mouth.

"So, everything went perfectly this morning," he says, all business. He goes over to the light panel on the wall beside me and switches it on. Then he slots my x-ray onto the front. It looks grizzly.

"You can see here, you have shattered everything in this area. We call it a trimalleolar fracture." He sounds way too jolly. "To repair it, we have made two incisions here and here." He points to each side of my ankle. "And we have used a plate and screws to secure the pieces of bone where we want them and hold them there while they heal back together."

He swaps the x-ray for a new one that looks a million times grizzlier. Max walks back in at that moment and baulks at the sight of the x-ray, which looks like something from a hospital drama. The surgeon points to a large screw that goes horizontally across the ankle. "This screw is temporary, we will need to remove it in a few weeks. The rest are permanent." He smiles.

"Now, you won't be able to bear any weight whatsoever on this foot for about six weeks until the bones have sufficiently knitted together, particularly while this screw is still in. Once we have taken out your stitches, we will put you in a proper cast. Until then, you are sporting this." He laughs. "It's a metal back slab, it will be quite weighty."

"Wow. That's a lot to take in." I exhale.

"We will give you pain relief and anti-inflammatories to take home. You will need to keep it elevated as much as possible, I'd say the majority of the time. You'll obviously use crutches to get around, making sure that this foot stays off the ground at all times." He thinks for a moment. "I might even see if I can get you a wheelchair for a couple of weeks."

"Brilliant," I mutter. Max stifles a laugh.

"Are you able to organise things at home to accommodate you while you recover?"

Max isn't able to stifle the laugh this time. "Well I live alone, in the flat above my busy restaurant and bar and the only access is via a long staircase." I reply, while shooting Max a 'thanks-so-much-for-your-love-and-support' look.

"Oh," he replies.

"She can stay with us." Max kindly offers.

"No, I want to be at home," I insist. "Once I'm up, or down, the stairs, I'll be fine. You will have to help me."

"We have to make sure you can safely negotiate stairs before you go home. The first couple of weeks will be the hardest, while you have this heavy bandage, but I want you to try and rest with your leg elevated as much as possible, so you'll be fine."

He leaves us, promising that I would be discharged tomorrow morning after meeting the physio and being checked over once more.

"Can I push you around?" Max asks excitedly, falling about laughing. "And can we get some of those flashing wheels?"

"Oh fuck off!" I snap.

"Sorry," he says, hanging his head slightly.

The physiotherapist arrives at my doorway bearing crutches and a wheelchair. Max is once again incorrigible. She shows me how to get myself into and out of the chair and how to put the leg rest up to keep it elevated. I'm astonished at the weight of this massive bandage, it weighs a ton. I'm glad I'm supposed to rest it as I don't fancy carting it around much.

Once she's happy that I'm not a complete danger to myself, she gets me up on the crutches.

"This thing is so heavy, how am I supposed to keep it off the ground?" I ask in frustration.

"Well you will be resting it most of the time. I just need to show you how to do the basics."

Stairs on crutches are a nightmare! I give it my best effort and she seems satisfied, then she shows me two exercises she wants me to do every day, to keep everything moving, and then finally leaves me alone to rest.

"Please go home, Max. You've been here all day and I haven't been much company." I've been very lucky that no one has been put in the other bed, so visiting hours have been overlooked by the staff.

"It's okay, I don't want you to be on your own," he replies.

I stroke his cheek. "I'm fine, honestly. Go on, have some dinner and see your man. He'll have forgotten what you look like."

"If you're sure. What will you do?"

"Sleep probably."

"Okay."

Max spends ten minutes, fussing around, putting everything within reach, insisting on helping me to the loo and buying me a couple of drinks and a bar of chocolate.

"See you in the morning." He kisses me on the forehead before he goes.

"See you," I reply cheerfully as he walks out of the door.

I don't want him to know how I really feel. I was dreading being on my own, to the extent that I forced him to go, just to get it over with. I'm at a really low ebb. The stuff that has happened to me over the past couple of weeks is too much to digest in one chunk. I can't take any more. Fighting tears, I plug my headphones into the TV and put some home improvement show on. I wish I had a film to watch. Music is too meaningful and I don't want to think right now, so I try really hard to watch the program without drifting into thought.

Danny's hand slides over my stomach as his tongue twists around my hard nipple. I've never wanted him more. It feels so urgent, like it could be taken away at any second. "oh!' I moan, startled by the sound. Why does it feel odd to make that sound?

His fingers slide into my underwear and I groan again, another strangled sound which takes me by surprise. My whole body aches for him, but he misses out the place I want him most. I try to move to guide his fingers, but this just makes him move further away.

He pulls his lips away from my nipple and I gasp. I beg him to take me, but he laughs. His gaze falls over something behind me and I turn to see what has taken his attention from me. But my body lets me down, I can't turn. I can only lie flat and the ache I thought I felt for Danny now feels like a physical pain, restricting my body. A woman appears beside me, it's her…Brooke.

"Look at me," I beg him. "I need you." Tears sting my eyes.

They both laugh at this. With his hand still circling inside my underwear he begins to kiss her. I watch helplessly, sobbing and pleading with him to love me. I cry out as he finally pulls his hand away from me and turns it to her. My pained cry jars me and my tears have made my head hurt. I'm shaking from the violent sobs wracking my body.

Danny reclines beside me and watches her as she slowly pulls her hair out of its pins and shakes it loose. I beg him not to watch but he ignores me. She unzips her tight black dress and lets it fall to her feet. I try to turn away, I can't watch. But my strange immobility keeps me flat on my back. Danny encourages her to come to him and I plead with him to stop this, but it's too late as she climbs over him. I sob and sob until I wake with a start.

It was a dream, but the tears were real. My head is heavy from crying so hard and my body aches. I want to curl up in a ball, but I can't turn over. Real or not, what I've just witnessed is so cruel that the emotional pain physically hurts as I succumb to it. I weep for a long time; short, stuttered breaths plague me even once the tears have dried. I lie awake on my damp pillow, staring at nothing, fearful of closing my eyes again.

Four.

You gave us all a fright!

Liv.

"I can do it." I snap at Max as he fusses around behind me. I've managed to get myself to standing on the curb and I'm just organising my crutches. Max is trying to erect the wheelchair, but I'm not being wheeled across the threshold in that thing.

"I'm sure I can manage the ten feet to the door if you could just make yourself useful and open it for me," I say with an irritable tone. If there's one thing I don't tolerate well it's the loss of my independence and I just know I'm going to be taking it out on those I love, namely Max. The thing that irritates me the most is that I know how unreasonable I'm being. I didn't really sleep last night after that heartbreaking dream. I know it wasn't real, but it was so devastating, I still feel tears prick my eyes if I think about it.

Before it happens again, I start off towards the door and Max scoots ahead to open it for me. I'm greeted warmly by the staff and a couple of customers who are surprised to see the state of me. I sit on the nearest chair slowly, so that I can just rest for a minute. Using crutches doesn't exactly come naturally and my hand isn't helping either. My middle two 'gripping' fingers are quite sore from being slammed into the ground by a power tool. As it turns out, the forefinger and thumb alone, have very limited gripping power, especially when burdened with the weight of a whole person. The little finger is obviously of no use whatsoever...so I can hardly grip the crutches, well the right one at least. It looks like I will need that fucking wheelchair if I hope to see daylight anytime soon.

Well at least I showed everyone that I can stand on one of my own two feet, for a minute. I just couldn't face them feeling sorry for me being pushed around by Max. Me, with no boyfriend, back from America all sad and now I can't even walk, so pathetic. I can feel myself getting angry today. I refuse to feel sorry for myself so I have to direct it somewhere. Fucking Danny. This is all his fault. If he wasn't so selfish, none of this would be happening. Thankfully my thoughts are broken by some of the kitchen staff coming out to see me.

"You gave us all a fright!" says Jake. "Let me make you some lunch," he adds, as always trying to fix it with food.

"Thanks Jake, I'll get settled upstairs first, then send Max down for something. Where is Max?" I ask, realising he has disappeared.

"Taking your stuff upstairs," says Ali.

"Here he is," says Jake.

"Here I am," says Max, looking all pleased with himself. "Come on then, let's get you upstairs."

I roll my eyes at Ali, who giggles sympathetically. "Text me if you need anything," she says.

"Thanks," I mouth at her as I'm helped to my feet.

Slowly, I make my way to the back of the diner and Max holds open the door for me. I stare up the staircase, it's longer than I remember, but I suppose the diner has high ceilings and all sorts of ducting. It's like a floor and a half at least. Taking a deep breath, I try the first step and wobble. My weight tips back and I feel like I'm losing my balance. Luckily, Max is just behind me and I'm prevented from needing to put my foot down to steady myself.

"Just let me carry you," he says.

"No!" I insist. "Here," I say, handing him my crutches. Then I carefully turn and sit on the first step. My plan is to climb up backwards on my bottom. But as I put my hands on the step behind me and try to take my weight, pain radiates through my chest. I feel like I've been run over by a bus today, everything aches. Even lifting the bed covers off me in the hospital hurt. I suppose I did fall from quite a height. I burst into tears and drop my head in my hands.

"You are so fucking stubborn!" Max tuts. I feel his arms around me and I'm gently lifted. With ease, he carries me up the stairs to my flat and puts me down carefully on the sofa, kissing the top of my head as he lets go.

"Thanks." I sniff. What would I do if I didn't have Max?

"Hey." He sits beside me and lifts my leg onto a footstool I don't recognise. "Don't get upset. It will just take some time."

"I know." I sob. "But work was keeping me sane. Now I'm stuck here." I gesture at my surroundings. Then I notice all of the changes. Firstly three huge bunches of flowers are dotted around the room. The largest display is on the table beside me along with several envelopes. The whole place smells clean and fresh. The furniture in the living area has all shifted slightly and as well as this footstool, there is a table on wheels that I can pull over my lap, with Danny's Mac set up on it. I wipe my eyes and notice that on the arm of the sofa are the remotes for everything including a small silver one I don't recognise.

"Why is it all different?" I ask.

"We got some stuff ready for you, so that you can keep busy while you get better." He smiles. "Computer, remotes, footrest, your laptop is in your room, we got you a TV in there too and linked it to your Sky. That way, wherever you want to be, you don't have to carry anything. If you want to watch TV but lie in bed at the same time, you can."

"Wow. But this isn't mine," I say pointing at the computer.

"I know, but it's in your flat, so I say, use it." He winks. "I've had a look at it, it's hardly been used. I've set up your emails and Facebook and copied your iTunes onto it, so there is no trace of it being anyone else's." He means he has cleared all evidence of Danny off it. Well, I'm not going on it anyway. I don't want to check my emails or Facebook, for the same reason I binned my phone.

"What's this?" I ask holding up the tiny silver remote.

"The best bit!" Max says like a kid at Christmas. He switches on the TV and then presses a button on the remote. The Apple logo appears on the screen and in a few seconds he shows me that I can access my iTunes library. "You can watch all the films you have on iTunes."

"I don't have any," I say incredulously.

He selects films on the screen and there are a dozen or so of my favourites. He grins at me. "You do now." He laughs, "And it's in your room too!"

"How have you managed this? I've only been gone a day and you've been with me most of the time."

"I had some help." He says and disappears into the kitchen. He comes out with a jug of water and a glass, goes to my bag and fetches the pharmacy bag from the hospital. "Now, you need to take these and then I'll get you some coffee and lunch from downstairs."

I huff as Max puts pills into my hand and hands me the glass of water.

"What do you fancy for lunch?" he asks.

"Surprise me," I say as I flip through my new films on Apple TV. I must go on about these films more than I realised because it's like my all-time favourites list, some I haven't seen since my teens. How did he know? I put 'The Secret of my Success' on because I haven't seen it in years. Then I take my jumper off carefully, still feeling like I've been run over, and settle down. I still feel so tired, maybe it's all the painkillers.

Max comes back with coffee and sits on the sofa with me.

"Is your foot warm enough?" he asks. I frown. "I know it's an odd question, but I always look at people with their toes sticking out of a cast and think they must get really cold."

"It's fine thank you." I laugh. "What are we having for lunch?"

"Burgers. Is that okay?"

"Lovely." He settles down with me to watch the film.

"Connie is coming later. I told her not to miss her painting class," he says absently after a few minutes.

"Who are the flowers from?"

Pointing to them in turn he says, "Connie, your mum and..." There is a light tap on the door and he jumps up to open it. Our burgers are here. I might be stuck at home, but I sure do live in the right place.

We tuck in and watch my film. Then Max clears the plates away and comes back, looking more fidgety.

"What's up?" I ask.

"I want to give you this and I know you're not going to want to take it." He pulls my phone out of his pocket.

I pull back from the phone slightly, not wanting to be too near it. "Not yet," I say quietly.

"Here's the problem. You need to be in communication with everyone, you might need one of us urgently and we need to check you are okay. You're just going to have to suck it up. It's for your own good." He drops it into my lap. "It's on too."

"Max. I don't want to hear anything he has to say, can you at least delete the messages?"

"There weren't any. Apart from, you know, a couple that night."

I draw in a deep breath and desperately hope that I don't look as gutted as I feel. I walked out on him almost two weeks ago, with no explanation whatsoever, and he hasn't even texted me. He is such a selfish, fucking bastard. If I hadn't seen what he did, I could be living with him now, setting myself up for an even bigger fall.

"None?" I can't help myself.

"No, but…"

"What?"

"…You should call him, you know." He

sounds afraid of the repercussions.

"No fucking way! He doesn't even know why I left and he still doesn't give a shit." I rant. "He only cares about himself."

"Liv, that makes no sense. He flew five thousand miles just to see you and then when he fell in love…" I start to interrupt, but Max silences me. "When you both fell in love, he happily and without hesitation let go of his friends, family and home to be with you." He sighs. "You certainly can't say he only thinks about himself."

"But he cheated!" How can Max think like that?

"Did he?" Max responds. "Did you actually see that happen?"

I recoil. Where is this all coming from? I thought he supported me. Why would he be saying these things? Then it dawns on me. He must have spoken to Danny.

"I think you should talk to him," he says.

"Have *you* spoken to him?"

Max stands up and walks towards the door, turning before he opens it. "Just hear him out, Liv," he says and is gone.

I'm left, mouth open, staring at the back of the door. I can't believe this. I actually feel betrayed by Max, something I thought was impossible. I drop my head back on the sofa and stare at the ceiling. A tear rolls down my cheek.

I wake with a start. I'd drifted off to sleep, bloody drugs. The phone is ringing and for a second I can't get my head together. I start to get up, sending a jolt through my ankle in the process. It's the first time I've accidentally tried to move it in such a way that it really hurts, and for a second I think I'm going to throw up. I breathe deeply to clear the queasiness and ouch! My ribs protest. I'm such a mess. The phone continues to ring. I'm more awake now and my knee-jerk attempt to answer it seems ridiculous in the light of day. I don't need/want to speak to whoever it is and I'm trying to kill myself to get it.

It rings off. We have a code in my family for times like these, let it ring once and hang up, then ring again. So if it was Mum, or Grace or Connie, I would know. It could have been anyone, it could have been…Oh God, my heart bangs hard in my chest. It could have been him! Although, if he was too selfish to call me when I left him, why would he bother now? Even so, I'm thankful I turned off the answer machine a few days ago. I sit up and get myself together. I need the loo, this should be interesting. Having shuffled around until the footstool isn't in my way and I have my crutches, I wiggle to the edge of my seat and stand up. It's harder than you would think not being able to put my foot on the floor at all, especially as it's so heavy. I'm just in the bathroom when I hear Connie calling me.

"Liv? Where are you? What's happened?" She sounds worried.

For God's sake! "I'm on the loo!" I yell back, it's not an international emergency.

"Do you need some help?" she says from the other side of the door, which I'm thankful now that I closed.

"Er, no. I think I've got it," I say.

When I emerge, she is still hovering. "Come and sit down," she fusses.

"Alright, I can manage."

Although, having said that, as I sit down, I pass the point of no return and the sofa is low, so I'm left with the choice between either banging my foot down or banging the rest of me down. It hurts.

"Careful!" admonishes Connie as I suck in air between my teeth.

"Thanks," I say sarcastically. "I forgot."

"Oh, we are in a sour mood today, aren't we?" Connie takes none of my nonsense.

I sigh. "Sorry, I'm just so frustrated."

"And you've had a disagreement with Max."

"Actually, we are yet to have the disagreement, he ran away." I sneer. "But it's coming."

"Come on, he's looking after you."

"I think he's talked to Danny and now I can't trust him."

"What's the big problem if he has?"

"Well, now I feel like he isn't completely on my side. He hasn't tried to defend him, or pass on any messages, but he has heard him out, so now I feel like he has fallen for some kind of lie." I huff.

"So you think Max would believe Danny and then turn on you?"

I shrug, knowing I'm being trapped.

"That's all you think of Max?"

"No, I just…"

"You're just wallowing in self-pity."

I stare at her, daring her to continue, but she isn't intimidated.

"Max loves you dearly and has looked out for you since the day you became friends. You should trust his judgement and advice. He would never put you in the path of harm."

"But he thinks I should hear Danny out." I scoff. "Not, mind you, that he's beating down my door with an explanation. But even if he was, why would I listen to lies?"

"What if they're not lies?" she says and holds my stare.

"He's got to you too hasn't he?" I say slowly. I'm staggered that I've lost everyone to whatever lie he is spinning.

"No one 'gets' to me," she argues. "But you're not seeing reason right now and I'm just asking you to remember who is and will always be on your side." Pausing, she strokes my hair. "If Max thinks you should talk to him then maybe you should."

I shake my head. "I'm going to go and lie down," I say absently. I start to shuffle my way up to my feet and Connie stands to help me. "I can manage," I snap.

"Okay." She holds her hands up and steps back so that I can pass. "I'll check on you later then," she says as I go into the bedroom. I feel really guilty as I sink into my freshly made bed and turn on my new TV, all courtesy of Max. There's another small silver remote on the bedside table and a satellite remote like the one in the living room, which controls the same box, via a little sensor thing sitting beneath the TV. He has really thought of everything to make me comfortable...I'm being a real bitch. I just don't know which way to turn right now and I wish I had one person I could talk to about it, that wasn't a Danny sympathiser.

Hopefully, they'll drop it eventually, when they see I'm not budging. I try to find a comfortable position and close my eyes. Drifting, I start to wonder what Danny could have said to Max that would make him switch like that. I suppose I can't really blame Max, I couldn't believe that Danny could treat me like this either. Maybe believing the lie was easier than accepting the disappointing truth.

"Liv." I stir and feel Max standing beside me. "Liv, you need to take your tablets," he says gently.

I ignore him and keep my eyes closed.

"Liv, come on. You can hate me, but you need to take these. Remember what the doctor said about not letting the pain get ahead of you."

Reluctantly, I open my eyes and sigh. I then have to suffer the indignity of Max watching me trying to sit up, although giving him his due, he just lets me get on with it. He silently holds out the tablets, which I sulkily take and swig back with the glass of water he hands me.

It's not Max's fault and deep down I can't stand pushing him away, but I can't stop myself. I know he's talked to Danny and while I need him desperately right now, I'm hurt too.

"I bought you a coffee.' he says bluntly. "And you left these on the coffee table." He puts my mobile and the home phone on my bedside table. I know I left them there, it was deliberate. The home phone has rung about six times while I've been in here and I've gladly ignored it. God knows who keeps phoning, but there is no one ring code, so I'm not picking up. I doubt he would suddenly start ringing now, but I'm not taking the chance. I'll continue to ignore it, except it will annoy me more now that it's right next to me.

"Thanks," I say with as much sarcasm as I can muster.

"You're welcome." He mirrors. Then he abruptly leaves. I heave a sigh of relief. I need to sort this out, I can't fall out with Max over anyone, least of all a weasel like Danny.

I prop myself up on some pillows and try to get comfy. The phone rings again, so I diligently ignore it while flicking through channels, then, to my horror, the answer phone kicks in…the fucker has put it on! I'm frozen to the spot as the beep sounds. To make matters worse, my stupid, fucking phone plays the audio from the handset as well as the base unit, when they are not connected, so I can't even get away from it. It's right beside me and in the living room on loud speaker.

"Liv?" Danny's voice rings through the flat. "Oh thank God, I thought I was going to get a brick wall forever!" There is a long pause. "Please call me, or at least check your emails…Please Liv. I love you." He sighs and then it cuts off.

I'm still frozen as I digest the sound of his voice, the pain and urgency in his tone. I snap myself out of almost feeling sorry for him. I don't care if he says he loves me, he's blown it, it's finished.

I snatch my mobile unthinking, to call Max and give him a piece of my mind and before I realise what I'm doing, I'm looking at the screen.

Shit! I didn't want my phone back. Twelve missed calls from Danny, all today. Thank goodness for silent mode. I toss it on the bed beside me in disgust. What now? I feel like the phones are both my enemies now too. Trapped and frustrated, I start to cry. I wallow in it for as long as I can stand and then feel really angry with myself. Look at the state I'm in.

The phone rings again. "Liv, please check your emails there is too much to say on a machine and if you won't talk to me…Please, read them. I love you." He pleads once again. He hangs on the line for a moment more before hanging up.

I shudder. This is such a head fuck. I battle with the surge of emotion that comes from hearing his voice and the sickening feeling when I think about what he has done. I can't check my messages, not just because nothing he says could ever make it alright. But also because I can't stand the fact that he thinks he has said something in those messages that would make me change my mind. He knows how I react to cheating. Who does he think he is? Oh this is too much, why right now? I just can't cope. I pull the covers over my head. It's right that I'm angry, but I can't get over being angry with him. It's another sad step on the road to putting him out of my life for good. I'll stick it out a bit longer and if he won't stop calling, I'll get my number changed.

Five.

You're such a control freak.

Liv.

I gave serious consideration to actually picking up the phone when he called this morning, just to tell him to fuck off. It's been five days since the first message and I'm getting sick of hearing his voice now, pleading and begging. Check my emails, blah, blah. He loves me, yeah sure. He loves me so much he shags some other girl while I'm out for the day. The problem is the rollercoaster of emotions it has put me on. Sometimes, when I hear his voice, instead of anger and irritation, I feel anguish or worse, comfort. His voice has always been my weakness and on my machine it fills every corner of the flat, there's nowhere to hide. I need to get out of here.

I sit on the edge of my bed and contemplate my wardrobe. Connie took my washing away yesterday and now I'm running out of clothes. Only loose bottoms fit over this damned leg and I don't feel up to wearing a skirt. I rummage around in the places I can reach and find a pair of jogging bottoms that at first I don't recognise. Then I realise, they're Danny's. I instinctively hold them up to my face and smell them. Why would I do such a stupid thing? They smell of him and this sends my emotions brimming over again, I burst into tears. How can I move on, when I'm so helpless and trapped in my flat, while he bombards me with calls?

I wash at the sink then, feeling sorry for myself, I pull on yesterday's bottoms, the only thing that Connie isn't washing, a clean t-shirt and a hoodie. I text Max.

'Can you help me get down the stairs please x.'

We haven't exactly been speaking for the last few days. I'm still angry with him for going behind my back. But he's still been fantastic, which only makes it worse. I'm treating him like shit and I need my friend back, so I hope I've worded the text in such a way that suggests that I need his help. I want to start again, but I really don't want to discuss it.

I find a small across-the-body handbag on the hooks by the front door and I put my purse and keys in it. I find my sunglasses next to the phone and put them on top of my head. Then I put my bag over my shoulder and head for the door. As I open the door at the top of the stairs, the one at the bottom flies open.

"What are you doing? You should be resting," Max says incredulously.

"I need to get out of here," I insist and, taking off my crutches, I start to lower myself to the floor.

"For fuck's sake, Liv, let me help you." He bounds up the stairs.

"No, I can do it. I just need a bit of help getting down to the floor I think." I giggle, paused hovering above the ground, holding the banister, unable to commit to the final few inches.

Max laughs too as he approaches me. He holds me under my arms and gently lowers me the rest of the way.

"Thanks." I smile.

He shakes his head. "You're such a control freak."

"I know." I grin, making no apologies for it.

"So how are we doing this?"

"Slowly," I say, easing myself down the first stair, keeping my leg off the ground, straight out in front of me.

"I'll just go ahead of you…you know, in case." He picks up my crutches and stops several stairs in front of me.

It takes a couple of minutes for me to negotiate the twenty-two steps and then I need to rest for a minute before I can stand.

"This is exhausting!"

"Here," says Max, lifting me up to standing and arranging my crutches for me. I smile gratefully, as he holds open the door into the diner.

"I'll just sit in here," I say, sliding myself into the back booth and lifting my foot onto the seat.

"Coffee?" Max asks rhetorically. Of course I'll have a coffee.

"Please, and can I have the phone too."

It takes a minute to adjust to the hum of the diner after being upstairs for days. I didn't intend to become a hermit, but I've been in a lot of pain. Anytime my leg isn't elevated it's agony, so I've been pretty bed/sofa bound.

Max comes back with the phone and two coffees and sits with me.

"So why aren't you resting?" he asks, concerned.

"I'm hardly running a marathon down here, I'm sitting," I say, sounding like a sulky teenager.

"You know what I mean. You are supposed to have your foot up."

I point at my foot on the bench seat and give a little 'see' look. "I'm wearing the only trousers I have left that I can get over this monstrosity. I need to go shopping. I'm going to ring Connie and ask her nicely to wheel me to the centre, so I can buy some more."

"I'll take you," he says.

"No, I need you here," I say firmly.

"I told you, they have things all organised here, so that I can look after you. The only reason I'm down here now is because I didn't think you were talking to me. But I was lurking in case you needed anything."

I take his hand in mine and smile. "Of course I'm talking to you," I say softly. "I just don't want to talk about 'that'."

Max sighs. "Right, so where are we going?" he says with slight reluctance. I know he won't just give up, but I'm grateful for the reprieve.

"Ultra-glam…The sports shop. I need more of these." I point to my trackies and take a sip of my coffee. "Can we have some breakfast first though? I'm hungry."

"Certainly Madame, what can I get for you?"

—

I can feel Max grinning as he pushes me through the door of the lift in the shopping centre. He's loving this. Luckily the crowd is very sparse on a Monday morning, so I doubt we will run into anyone we know. In addition to delighting in my embarrassment, he has somewhere to hang his shopping, so he can go on forever. We got some tracksuit bottoms for me and some expensive trainers for him. I spent a ridiculous amount of money on skin care products, which really isn't me, but as I've nothing much else to do, I thought I should at least start moisturising. We stop at the book shop and Max insists I buy the Fifty Shades trilogy to keep me occupied. Normally I would have no time to read, but I'm fairly free these days. Then we stop for a coffee in the new coffee shop at the bottom of the hill. Nice, but they're beginners, nothing I will lose any sleep over.

When we get back to the diner, Connie is sitting at the counter, waiting.

"You should have called me, I could have taken you," she says.

"No, it's fine, Max fancied a spot of shopping anyway." Max pushes me back to where I was sitting earlier and I ease in, while he collapses the wheelchair and stows it in the back.

"I'll just put all this upstairs, then I'll come back for you," he says.

I nod and turn to Connie as she sits opposite.

"So you two have made up?" she asks.

"We didn't really fall out, but yes, we're okay, so long as we steer away from certain subjects."

"He only wants what is best for you."

"I don't want to talk about it with you either." I warn.

"Darling, there is only one person you should talk to about it and you know that," she says, reaching for my hand. I don't offer it. "I was up there earlier, looking for you, he called and left a message. He sounds desperate. Maybe you should hear him out."

"He calls about three times an hour," I say. "I don't think I can take much more."

"Then tell him to stop."

"I can't answer," I admit quietly. "I don't trust myself."

"You don't trust yourself?"

"I'm too vulnerable, I can't give him an inch, he'll be able to walk all over me."

"Maybe he won't. Have you looked at your emails yet? He was asking you to look at them. Maybe he has explained himself," she says gently.

I shake my head.

"But you want to?"

I slowly nod. "God, I'm so weak." I sigh, dropping my face into my hands.

"Right, I'm coming up with you, we are going to do this right now, no more hiding. I'll hold your hand." She says with purpose, getting to her feet.

"Where are we going?" Max asks, back down to help me.

"Liv and I are going upstairs for a little girl time." She winks at me.

I subtly brush a single tear from my cheek as I slide to the edge of the seat. I allow Max to help me stand, but then insist on getting myself up the stairs.

Once on the sofa, I settle myself in and Max brings us coffees. Then he makes his excuses and leaves us to it.

"I don't think I can do this," I admit to Connie.

"You have to, or he will never leave you alone. At least you can hear what he has to say without actually talking to him."

I lean forward and pull his computer over so that it's hovering over my lap. I've seen him switch it on before, so I reach behind and feel for the button. The screen comes on and, while I wait, I feel sick. The desktop appears and I wait for everything to load up. The email icon shows 348 messages. Hopefully not all from Danny. I click it. Scrolling through the messages, the first few are irrelevant. So I search for his name in the bar at the top. A new list appears and there are several. I scroll down to the first unread one and, with a deep breath, I open it. Connie holds my hand.

28th May 2012

Liv,
Please call me. I need to talk to you.

28th May 2012
Nothing happened I swear, please talk to me, we can straighten this out.
D x

28th May 2012
Dear Liv,
I really didn't want to do this by email, but you're leaving me no choice. I have to explain.

It has been over a week since you left. I'm sorry that I'm only just trying to contact you. I'm sorry I didn't chase you…I'm just sorry. I thought you left because you didn't love me. I was devastated. I realise now why you left and, although I wish you thought more of me, I know that you not trusting me is totally my fault. I want to tell you what really happened that night. I know you don't want to hear me out and that you have already decided for yourself what happened, but I have to try.

After I took you to your sister's place, I finished packing and ran a few errands. I felt like you were still punishing me for not being honest with you about Brooke. But I knew once we got home to the UK we could put it behind us. I hated the idea of meeting you at the party, but I agreed because I wanted you to spend some time with your family before we left. After I finished up, I took a shower. When I came out of the bathroom, Brooke was lying on my bed in nothing but her underwear and some slutty heels. It turns out, she stole a spare key that day she came by and cried on my doorstep. She had every intention of using it to try and seduce me or break us up, or something. Fuck knows what goes on in that girl's head.

I freaked. I told her to get out. We yelled at each other back and forth, and I threatened to call the cops and report her for breaking and entering. I even dialled the number. In the end, though, I managed to get her out the door and I told her if she didn't leave us alone I would report her to the cops and the school board and she would lose her job.

After she left, the first thing I did was call you. I promised to be completely honest, so I didn't hesitate in calling you to tell you what had just happened. You didn't pick up though and I haven't heard your voice since.

When I couldn't reach you, I went to the party as planned, but you didn't show up. I was frantic with worry at first. But then Grace called to say they found your note. I was devastated, I thought, well it's not important what I thought. It was all self-pity. But I was wrong. You didn't leave because of how you felt about me. You left because you thought I cheated on you. I completely understand.

But I'm going to make you trust me again. Nothing happened with Brooke. I don't know what you saw, but I do know you didn't see me do anything wrong because I didn't. I would never do anything to jeopardise what I have with you. I want to grow old with you.

I love you with all of my heart and I hope you still love me.

Please call me so that we can talk about this.

Danny x

Silent tears are running down my face when I look up at Connie. She pulls a tissue from the box on the side table and hands it to me. I wipe my eyes and sit staring into nothingness. How can I believe him?

"What do you think, darling?" Connie utters beside me.

I shrug and shake my head, there are no words, I'm utterly empty.

I glance back at the screen. He sent it the day of the accident.

"He seems sincere." She offers. "There are more, are you going to open them?"

I click on the next one.

28th May 2012

Liv,

Please, talk to me. You're not answering my calls. I know you're hurt but we have to talk about this.

I miss you.

Danny. x

Then I click on the next one.

30th May 2012
I can't stand not hearing your voice. Please pick up. I love you x

30th May 2012
I think about you every minute of every day. I should be with you, this is killing me. Please talk to me. X

30th May 2012
Liv,
I wish you had confronted me that day, you would have seen that I had nothing to hide and we would be together right now. Instead, we are apart and I can't get through to you. You're hurting and there is nothing I can do to make it better. Please, give me the chance to try. I know I can make you happy.
Danny x

"I need to lie down," I say, making a start on standing up. There are more, at least one for each day since, but probably more. I expect they all say the same thing, but I've heard enough.

Connie bolts up and pulls the computer out of the way, while I get my crutches organised. Slowly I hop to the bedroom.

Connie follows me in and sets my coffee down on the bedside table. She hands me the phones. I sigh, they are like a millstone around my neck. She sits on the edge of my bed and strokes my forehead.

"Do you want me to stay with you?" she asks. I shake my head. "Well call one of us if you need anything and don't forget your tablets."

"Okay," I mutter. She leaves me alone and I just stare at the ceiling.

Danny's words spin around my head. I just can't deal with any of this right now. If he knew what had happened to me he might give me a break. But the chances are he would use my vulnerability against me. Why is he pursuing me this hard now, after I meant so little to him that he would cheat on me? The image of them together in my dream comes into my mind and I sob. I'm so glad I didn't see it for real, the knowledge is painful enough.

When Max came up to see how I was later, he found me in the dark and in pain because I'd forgotten my medication. Once that pain takes hold, or gets ahead of you as the doctor termed it, it's really hard to get back on top of it. Max forced me out of bed and sorted me out then, while I was waiting for the medication to kick in, he distracted me from the pain by making me talk. At first I didn't want to talk about it, I was still angry that he seemed to have spoken to Danny and was convinced he had fallen for the lies. But since reading Danny's emails, all of them... I succumbed and finished reading them...I haven't felt so, so...Oh, let's face it, I've softened. This is the reason I was so determined not to hear him out.

Six.

Let's get a few things straight shall we?

Liv.

Mum came home from LA on Sunday night and after spending Monday at home doing her washing, she came to see me on Tuesday. After sitting with her and Connie for a morning, I felt so claustrophobic. Not because I don't love them both, I really do, but I had severe cabin fever. So when Mum suggested that I come back to Brighton with her for a few days, I jumped at the chance. I switched off my answer machine and left my laptop behind. I did take my phone at Max's insistence, but kept it on silent. I guess Max must have told Danny I went away, because he didn't bother me. There were no emails and only two missed calls.

I went through it all again with Mum. She confessed that she went round to see Danny to have it out with him, but he wasn't home. She tried a couple of times but had no luck. She was sympathetic to my point of view, but I could just tell that she thought exactly the same as Max and Connie. In the end, I refused to talk about it anymore. I had a quiet, relaxing couple of days, sat in Mum's garden mostly. She pushed me along the seafront and we drank coffee and window shopped. If I wasn't a desperately sad singleton, recovering from the loss of the love of my life and my independence, I would have thoroughly enjoyed myself.

Mum dropped me home this morning and, as if he were telepathic, Danny emailed me first thing. I ignored it for as long as I could. I had coffee with Connie, brunch with Max and then I sat downstairs for as long as possible, but the Friday lunch rush was a bit busier than normal and I had to vacate my booth. Max stowed me upstairs again in my prison, but then he had to go as they needed him downstairs. I put on a film to distract me, I tapped and I pondered, but in the end I had to read the email. He is getting under my skin and it's infuriating.

8th June
Dear Liv,
I forced myself not to email you for a couple of days. I felt like you needed a break, but it was hard. I miss you. Life isn't the same without you. I miss your smile, your voice, your beautiful face, your touch, the fun we have, the way you make me feel. I miss everything about you. I have so many plans for the future and they all involve us being together. I was packed and ready to be with you, do you really think I would risk all that for some final fling? Never. As long as I live I will never want anyone else. It has always been that way. Why do you think I've never settled down? Losing you before was the worst experience of my life and now I'm living it all over again. Except this time I'm not quitting. I love you too much.
I don't expect you to reply, but when you are ready I will be here.

I love you xxx

Okay, there is nothing new there, but each time he finds a new and believable way to say it. He hasn't over explained it either, he told me what happened once and hasn't kept going over it. Every other email is just about his feelings. You might say that if he was guilty, he would keep explaining himself. I can't deny that I'm starting to think that there is more to this than I wanted to believe.

Max still hasn't told me what was said, or who instigated their contact. But it's clear that he's willing to give Danny the benefit of the doubt and, despite my determination, I can see why. Max has made some compelling points in Danny's favour and I would have to agree with each of them. However, I refuse to overlook some of my own points and this maintains my state of anger and devastation. First and foremost, Danny bought that bitch jewellery, so no matter what he says about the events of that night, something was still going on between them. When I mentioned this to Max, he seemed to want to argue, but didn't have anything. How can you argue with the facts? He quickly stopped trying. Then, the fact that Connie asked him to look me up in the first place is a huge issue, because it means that he never would have done so of his own accord.

Those things plus the image of her undressing for him will never go from my head, so I don't see how, or indeed why, I should get past it. His explanations don't make any difference to whether I trust him or not. I check my watch. 15:45, it should be quieter now, I text Max, hoping he can break this perpetual thought cycle.

'Save me from myself! X

I drum my fingers waiting for a response, but strangely I hear nothing. Since I fell, he has been hiding in the shadows the whole time, so it's strange that he is unavailable. I suppose as it's Friday afternoon, one of the first really nice ones, he's busy downstairs. I should be down there too, maybe I could get myself down the stairs and find out how things are. My phone lights up beside me, at last! I look at the screen, but it's not Max, it's Danny.

1 Facebook Notification From Danny Morgan.

Hi,

How are you? I'm trying Facebook, in the hope that you might be online too. It might be easier to talk, if we don't actually talk, what do you think? I know this is really hard and I wish I was with you.

Since I figured out why you left I've had to fight myself at every turn, my gut instinct was to come straight to you. But I was persuaded to make contact first. I know that having me around isn't currently what you want, but you know it's what I want and I feel so helpless away from you. It's hard to make you see that I'm telling the truth, when we're not face to face.

I wish you would give me a chance. There is so much to discuss.

We should be together, we should have always been together. I never should have left you twelve years ago.

I wanted to stay with you, but you pushed me to go. You said it was best for both of us, but I didn't think it was best for me. The day you told me I should go, I was going to ask you if we could find a way that I could stay. I thought we could get a flat or something. I was going to tell my parents I wasn't leaving you and that they would just need to accept it. But you wouldn't let me speak, you had all these reasons why me leaving was going to do us good in the end. I thought you wanted a fresh start and that it meant that you didn't love me as much as I loved you. I hurt so badly after that, that I just went quietly.

Maybe you thought it was what I wanted, because I said nothing to make you think otherwise. In the end, I didn't have the confidence to fight for what I wanted and neither did you. But now that I've had you in my life again, I will never stop fighting. We are meant to be together and I know this is hurting you, but it's just a glitch.

I know you trust me, you think you don't, but that's just a reaction. You know it too, it's not me you don't trust, it's yourself. Please let me back in. We have wasted too much of our lives apart.

I love you.

Talk to you soon x

This message leaves me with a flood of emotions, but I quickly push most of them down and settle on boiling mad. How dare he? Who does he think he is? Telling me I trust him, but not myself. Quite the opposite. I will never trust him again, or possibly anyone else. Oh and this is just a glitch is it? I would hate to think what would have to happen for him to think things had really gone wrong. Deep down, I know I'm only focusing on the easy-to-target bits of his argument, but it's better this way. I can't over analyse the fact that he's directly addressed all of my insecurities about why he didn't try harder to be with me before.

Fucking Max! Obviously he's been running his mouth off and now

Danny is playing on all my weaknesses. Well I may be vulnerable at the moment, but only emotionally as far as he knows. He doesn't know that I'm incapacitated, Max has promised me faithfully he won't tell him. If he did, I wouldn't stand a chance. But I'm not going to let him take advantage of me in any way. He has blown it and he can't use insider knowledge to get round me, I'm not buying it. Holding onto my rage, I wait for the laptop to start and when it does, I launch straight in to my rant.

'Let's get a few things straight shall we? Firstly, it's all very well telling me what you think I want to hear about the past, but it's just that, the past. In my opinion, you did give up too easily. I looked into going to college in LA so that I could be with you, I would have followed you to the end of the earth, but when you put up no fight whatsoever, I knew that you didn't want that and I let it go. You say that I pushed you away, but I was just supporting you in what you seemed to want to do. I was prepared to do something totally life changing for you, something real. So you can't just paint a picture of how neither one of us was prepared to fight for what we wanted, I applied to UCLA Arts for fuck's sake. Behind my parent's back. I got an interview. What did you do? NOTHING!

Then you come waltzing back into my life, being all wonderful. But it wasn't planned though was it? You wouldn't have thought of it yourself, would you? No. Connie asked you to do it. Yeah, Danny, I know about that. I feel so fucking special now, let me tell you. The fact is, you never would have thought of me again if you hadn't had the idea handed to you and I fell for it, hook, line and sinker. But I see through you now.

You claim that what we had meant too much to you to risk on a final fling. Well that's bollocks. Whatever you say happened that night, I know one thing for sure, you bought jewellery for that woman, so don't pretend nothing was going on.

Who the fuck do you think you are? Telling me who I trust. I don't trust you, or anything you say.

Please leave me alone.'

I'm shaking with anger by the time I finish writing and I hit send before I decide to edit it. I feel sick. I take a few deep breaths, I can't throw up, I couldn't get to the bathroom fast enough. I just have to hold it together. I rub my forehead and cover my eyes with my trembling hand. My mobile signals a text, but I can't look. I just sit and survive for a minute. Then the text signal sounds again, a reminder this time.

"Okay!" I bark at my innocent phone. Then I'm relieved to see it's just Max.

'Sorry, really busy down here, be up soon x'

Shit, I have to be by myself for a while longer. This is torture. I want to be behind my bar, where I belong. Busy, occupied, surrounded by noise and friends and, most importantly, feeling powerful. Not prisoner to my flat, stuck with nothing but a stalking ex for company. The laptop signals another Facebook message. Of course…I read it.

'I'll leave you alone if that's really what you want, but there are a couple of things you have to know.

Connie may have put the suggestion out there that day, but I'm so glad she did. I wouldn't have contacted you, but not because I didn't want to, because I thought I was respecting your wishes. She made me think that maybe you would want to hear from me and that was all I needed.

As for what I was or wasn't prepared to do to fight for us in the past…you'll never know the lengths I went to.'

For fuck's sake, what does that mean? I feel panicked, like I've hurt him, or pushed him too far. Why should I care? I squash my concerns into the background and focus on the anger.

If you did something, went to some significant 'lengths' that would change my opinion of you, now is the time to speak up, sunshine. Otherwise, it's just words. I start to write this as my reply, when Max appears at the door. Quickly, I delete it. What is the point? If I respond, it leaves the conversation open. He said he will leave me alone, maybe I should just let it go.

"You alright?" asks Max. It's as if he knows words have been exchanged.

"Not really." I sigh.

"What's happened now?"

"Oh, I don't want to bore you with the details."

"No, come on, it's what I'm here for," he says sweetly.

"I just had a bit of a run-in with Danny on Facebook. Apparently, I trust him, it's myself I don't trust. Can you believe the nerve?" Max swallows hard and looks terrified. After an awkward silence, I know he agrees with him. This is going to end in an argument.

"Don't hate me," he says cautiously, "but maybe he's right."

I stay calm. Max just stares. He's brave, I'll give him that, I'm not in the most reasonable frame of mind at the moment. I watch him for a while, shakily holding his ground and it occurs to me that although he's not taking sides as such, he has all the information. He's heard both sides in full and, try as he might to be completely behind me, he can't help but sympathise with Danny.

"You think I should trust him?" I ask slowly, in a measured tone.

Max nods.

"Do you?" I ask.

He pauses then nods again. "I think you want to as well," he adds quietly.

I draw in a deep breath to disagree, but a surge of emotion chokes me.

"Hey," he soothes, moving closer. "It's okay." I break down in his arms.

Max holds me while I gather my thoughts. I allow myself to test the waters of believing Danny. If I did, then it would mean that all of this would go away. He could come back and we could be together. But would it all go away? Wouldn't I have a nagging doubt, always? Then he would be here and I wouldn't be happy. He will have given up everything and I would end up having to send him away. Oh God, why is this so complicated? I could choose to forgive him. That would be different, because that would be acknowledging what happened but moving past it.

But then what kind of over-trusting idiot would that make me?

"I honestly don't think he did anything wrong," says Max, trying to help me.

I sniff and look up at him, wiping my face. Maybe Connie is right. Even if I don't think I can trust Danny, I should at least be able to trust Max's judgement, right?

"I think you should talk to him," he says firmly.

I nod absently. Not realising it looks like I'm agreeing.

"You will?" he asks, hopefully.

I shrug, I don't have the energy to clarify. "He's just told me he will leave me alone. I can't go back on it now."

"It's never too late," says Max. "You should call him."

"No," I answer, feeling railroaded all of a sudden. "Too much has happened. It's better just to leave it."

Max sighs and releases me. He sits back. "You really are infuriating sometimes," he snaps. His phone beeps in his pocket and he pulls it out, still shaking his head at me in exasperation. He glances at the screen. "Shit, they need me downstairs. Sorry, big delivery, I've got to go." He stands up and fixes me with his stern look. "Don't throw this away, Liv. You'll always regret it," he adds as he leaves.

I'm so sick of this emotional torment, I can't take anymore. I wish I could go away again, but Max is flat out, Connie has her own stuff and I've been to Mum's already, she needs some time at home with Dave after a month away. I can't go anywhere by myself. Feeling self-pity brimming out of me I weep again. I let myself sink into a cushion and sob. It's a conscious decision to wallow, because I could do something. I could call Connie. I could get myself downstairs, I could get a cab somewhere, but it's all too hard right now so I wallow. The phone rings and I ignore it. He just said he would leave me alone, some willpower he has. If I do decide to speak to him, it won't be when I'm like this.

I pull a crumpled tissue from my pocket as the answer phone begins its familiar message. But the caller hangs up. Maybe he really has given up, it briefly occurs to me. My stomach turns over at the thought, but I shouldn't care, I just asked him to leave me alone. Yet the thought of never hearing from him again is worse than anything else.

The phone rings again and I let out a frustrated growl, half choked with tears.

"Leave me alone!" I sob. I hear the beep, expecting it to cut off again, but I hear him breathe. The sound makes me freeze.

"Liv, please…" He begs, sounding emotional. "I'm begging you, talk to me…" There is a pause, I realise I'm holding my breath.

"I'm not giving up, Liv. I will fight for us…" he says. "I let you go too easily once before, I should have fought harder, but I was a stupid kid." I struggle to sit up. I look at the phone, wanting desperately to pick it up. "But I won't make that mistake again…"

I sob silently, so torn. I hate him for what he has done but I feel so weak. I wished he had fought harder when he left, so hearing this obviously weakens me further, but he didn't fight. It's too late now.

"Liv, I love you…deep down, you know…I wouldn't do what you think I did…" He sighs. "Please…pick up the phone…" His voice fills the air, I can't hide from it. I don't think he will ever go away. After another long pause, he almost whispers, "…please, just pick it up…"

With shaking hands I reach for the phone, an unthinking response to his heartfelt request and press the button as I put it to my ear.

"Liv?' he asks quietly.

"Yes," I whisper, crying as silently as I can manage. But then I hear him break down and I can't hold it back any longer. For a moment, we each battle with our own emotions.

"Sorry." He chokes, trying to gather himself.

I remain quiet.

"Are you okay?" he asks.

"No," I say. What am I supposed to say?

"I miss you," he says softly.

Again I stay silent. I can't say anything that might seem like reciprocation, even though I do miss him, desperately. My heart is breaking all over again, talking to him, knowing I have to let him go.

"I love you so much," he continues.

Summoning what little strength I have, I try to speak. "Danny…I…"

"No, don't," he interrupts. "You don't have to say anything. I know you are angry and I know you are hurt. Picking up the phone is enough…Please don't say anything to end things between us. We can work it out, you just need to let me back in."

I swallow hard. "I can't handle this at the moment." I manage to say with a steady voice.

"I know, I'm sorry." He sighs. "I'm sorry for everything…I didn't mean to upset you before and I know I said I'll leave you alone, but I can't."

A small sob escapes my lips and I fight to rein the emotion in. I can't speak when he keeps saying things like that. I wait for him to say something else…

Seven.

Go back to your life Danny and I'll go back to mine.

Danny.

She says nothing, so I continue. "I didn't do it, Liv." I whisper, again fighting tears. "I know you don't want to say you believe me, but…"

"Danny, it's just too hard. Maybe we were better off before."

"No." I insist. "How can you say that?" I push back from the table in frustration and pace the room.

"Because…" She pauses, finding the words. I dread what she's going to say. She sighs, she can't find a good enough reason to quit. I still have a chance. I touch the door with my fingertips and think about how much she needs me right now. It's killing me, not being able to help her, hold her. I can't even tell her I know about the accident, because how could I justify not rushing to be by her side? I have to wait until she's ready. Max warned me about pushing her, but he thinks she might be coming round, I can't risk ruining it now. I turn and lean against the door.

"Because it was easier." She sighs. Is that the best she can do?

"Than this, sure. But not easier than us being together."

"But we're not together now," she says. I'm just thinking of the best response when she starts to make her escape.

"Look, I've got to go. I'm snowed under here." She lies.

I half smile, "Okay. Can I call you later?" I ask, ever hopeful, I don't want to but I have to let her go, now that she has picked up, I hope I will have other chances.

"I don't know, we're really busy." Another lie.

I try not to let the smile reflect in my voice. "Well, I'll call anyway, pick up if you're available."

She hesitates. "Okay."

There is silence between us. I can tell she doesn't really want to go.

"Goodbye then," I say as gently as I can. "Thanks for picking up."

"Goodbye," she replies.

"Oh and Liv."

"Yes."

"I love you." Then summoning all of the strength I have, I hang up before she has chance to reply. I let out a long breath and stand up straight. I turn towards the door again and lightly touch the wood.

"Hang in there man," Max says as he squeezes my shoulder. I pat his hand, grateful for his support.

"Come on," I say, trying to snap myself out of my funk. "Let's get this delivery in before it gets busy again."

I work the bar like a man possessed. I can see why Liv loves it. I can see myself here, working side by side with her. I've got quite good at it too, these past ten days. When I first arrived I just wanted to help in any way I could. I was picking up glasses and all that stuff. But I've got really into it. I've done it before and it's not that different. I'm not mixing cocktails yet, but I can make myself useful and at the very least take some of the slack off the other guys. This place really misses Liv. She's the life and soul of it and you can tell the difference when she's not here. I have my own work to do as well, but after she left me I did nothing else for days, so I'm really ahead. Then whenever Liv comes down I have to disappear, so I go home, to Max's where I'm staying for now and do as much as I can.

I'm really surprised that I've not been sprung by anyone. All of the staff know the situation, they're cool. But I'm surprised no friends have called her and accidentally mentioned my presence. Max is running interference and it helps that Liv has been incommunicado. The past couple of days, she has been away, so I've been able to move freely around without fear of being discovered. Max and I finished the garden and it's full of happy customers right now. I feel awful that Liv had her accident doing something that I should have done for her. But knowing Liv, even I would not have been able to stop her and her control freakiness from taking stupid risks.

I've tried twice to find the time to call her tonight, but I can't get far enough away from the crowd noise. Eventually, I tell Max I'm taking off for ten minutes and I walk around the block. I find a quiet street and sit on a low wall and dial her number. I'm ready for it to go to the machine, so I'm floored when she answers.

"Hello?"

"Hey." I begin nervously, knocked off my feet by this unexpected turn of events. "How are you?"

"I'm okay," she says. "You?" It's not exactly what you would call concern, but the fact that she asked has blown me away.

I think for a moment about how to answer this. I don't want to make this about me, but if I don't show that I'm suffering, she will think I don't care. 'I'm lost without you." I hope that was the right way to go. "I'm surprised you're there." I admit.

"So am I." She sighs. "I had a break." She lies again. "You just caught me."

"Oh, okay, good timing then." I humor her.

"I suppose."

I have to think on my feet, I'm so used to having this conversation one sided that I can't think of anything to actually say to her. The silence stretches out before me.

"I don't know what to say," I admit.

"You called me," she points out.

"I know, but I wasn't expecting you to answer."

She sighs. "Danny, this is pointless, you have to stop calling me."

"I can't," I whisper.

"It's over," she says with no conviction at all.

"But, I love you," I tell her, "And you love me. So how can it be over?" I feel stronger now, she's coming around.

She doesn't reply.

"I wouldn't do anything to jeopardise our future."

"I saw her, Danny."

"Nothing happened," I say calmly.

She lets out a long breath. "It doesn't matter. It's too late."

"Liv, it's…"

"Don't, please. We never should have started this. It was always going to end this way. Go back to your life Danny and I'll go back to mine."

"It doesn't have to end at all," I say softly. "I know you love me. Tell me you don't."

"It's too hard, you're too far away." Her voice is choked with emotion. Then, after a short pause, the line goes dead.

My heart is pounding and I have to fight the emotion. I stand in the street, not knowing what to do. Think…THINK! She didn't say she doesn't love me and I'm not too far away…I'm right here…I start running.

Rounding the corner, I run all the way back. I yank open the door to the diner, ignoring the surprised look on Ali's face and run to Liv's door. I hammer the code into the keypad and take the stairs two at a time, freezing in front of the door, I knock gently.

"It's open," she says, her voice strained with tears.

Holding my breath, I turn the handle and push open the door.

Liv looks up from the sofa, tears running down her face and gasps. For a moment I just stand in the doorway. She is a beautiful mess. Her leg is resting on a stool, and she has been crying a lot, I can tell because her face is all blotchy. She isn't dressed to go out and she self-consciously pulls her cosy sweater tightly around her. I swallow hard. Look at what I've done to her. I don't care how she looks, she is always beautiful, but she is normally so strong and in control. I hate seeing her this way.

I'm still breathing hard from running, so I try to steady myself.

"Can I come in?" I manage, my own emotion affecting the reliability of my voice.

She is still speechless, so I step inside and shut the door.

"What are you doing here?' she asks breathlessly.

I shrug. Where do I start? "You said I was too far away. I wanted to show you I'm not." I wipe away a rogue tear.

"But...how?" she murmurs. Then she looks even more mystified. "Why are you wearing that?" she asks.

I glance down at my staff shirt and look back at her sheepishly.

"Okay, I need to know what's going on." She shifts in her seat. "Now!"

I nod, moving towards the armchair opposite her. I slowly sit as she stares. I clear my throat. "What do you want to know?"

She scoffs, "Err, what the fuck has been happening behind my back, for a start," she replies.

I have to stifle a slight laugh, this is not the time to piss her off, but I suddenly find the whole thing quite amusing. She has all of these preconceived ideas and I'm going to blow them all out of the water. She thinks I cheated, I can convince her otherwise. She thinks I stayed away, I can prove I didn't. She thinks I don't care enough, I'll show her she is wrong. I've waited for the right moment, this is my time. She looks mad, I smile.

"You think this is funny?"

"No." I pull myself together and try to look serious.

"So come on..." she urges.

"Okay," I say, stalling while my mind races back through the past two weeks, searching for a point in the story I can pick up that will make sense to her. I shift nervously. "I called Max." I begin, knowing that this in itself will lead to more questions than answers. I should have called her, but I was too stubborn. "We were talking when you fell." Liv stares, she still can't process the fact that I'm here. "Max yelled your name and then the line went dead. I knew something awful had happened to you, I tried calling him back, but he didn't answer." I look at her, the thought of something worse happening to her still fills me with that same fear. I want to reach across and touch her face, but I know she doesn't want me to.

"I was with Jen at her store, she told me to just go to you. She booked my flight and I went home, packed my stuff and left for the airport. I was so worried. Jen kept calling Max, but his cell went off. I had no idea what was going on, I've never been so scared in my whole life." I fight back tears and take a deep breath. "While I was waiting at the gate, he called me. He said you were okay, he told me what happened. I was a total mess. I told him I was getting on a flight." I pause. She still hasn't tried to speak. I keep going, before she does. "He thought I should wait, but I was already checked in. I told him I was coming no matter what he said.

"I came straight here when I landed and dropped my bags. Connie gave me a ride to the hospital. You were in recovery after your surgery when we got there, so we just waited. It took so long, but finally they brought you back, still sleeping. I never want to feel like that again, you looked…I just never want to see you like that again." I sigh.

"You were there?" she asks in disbelief.

"For a while, Max didn't think I should be there when you woke up because he didn't want to stress you out. So Connie and I left. We came back here and fixed this place up ready for you." I say, gesturing at the remotes. Her eyes follow my hand and she stares at the remotes and then back at me.

"You did all this?" she asks, her tone softening slightly.

I nod and offer a small smile.

"And you've been working…in my bar?" she says slowly.

I nod again, afraid of saying the wrong thing.

"Why?" she whispers.

I hesitate. "Because, I had to do something. You wouldn't talk to me. They are flat out downstairs and I thought…I thought it would show you I'm committed." I sigh. "I love you, Liv. I will do anything to make you see that."

Fresh tears spring from her eyes and she looks away. She tries to compose herself and silently shakes her head in disbelief.

"So you've been here this whole time?…and everyone knows?" she asks, slowly piecing it all together.

"Yes," I admit, reluctantly.

Liv shakes her head. "I can't believe it."

"But only because I didn't want to push you while you were going through so much." I almost touch her again, I don't think she notices. It feels so wrong not to comfort her and find out how she is doing after the accident. I feel like it's none of my business, but I have to ask. "How are you?" I glance at her leg, which is still propped up and wrapped in a big bandage.

She looks at it too. "It's okay, I just have to keep it up as much as possible and I'm not allowed to put any weight on it at all…wait, I can't do this." She says putting her hands through her hair in frustration, revealing a huge bruise and a run of stitches close to her hairline. I wince. "We can't just sit here and have a normal conversation, we're not talking, we broke up." She sighs.

I wait, because if I say the wrong thing now, I could be finished. She finally looks at me again, so I seize my chance. Sitting forward, I look her straight in the eye. "If you tell me to go, I will." It's a gamble. But it will force her hand. She maintains my stare, but says nothing. All I can hear is the sound of my heart pounding as I wait for her to respond. She almost scoffs as if she thinks I have some nerve, but still, she says nothing. Then I decide she's had enough time to throw me out, I take the lead. "I'll get us some drinks then," I say with as much confidence as I can find. Then without looking at her I walk out the door.

As the door shuts behind me, I let out the breath that I've been holding. FUCK! I mouth. I'm playing with fire. But I thought a short break would do us both good before we talk. She needs to process this and I could do with some air. Pull yourself together Danny. I start down the stairs, a smile growing on my face and by the time I get to the door, I'm grinning from ear to ear. I head across the garden, resisting the temptation to whistle as I go. I collect some glasses that are in my path and drop them in the kitchen as I pass.

"Where have you been?" asks Max as I arrive behind the bar.

"Upstairs," I say, casually and watch with satisfaction as the disbelief engulfs his face.

His mouth drops open and while he deals with the information, I reach past him and take two glasses, fill them with ice and drop a wedge of lime in each. When I glance back at Max, he smiles an uncertain smile.

"How is she taking it?" he asks.

"Okay, well she hasn't told me to leave yet. I thought I would get us a drink so we can talk and I think she needed a break to process the fact that I'm here." I grab a bottle of rum from beneath the bar. "She can drink now, right?" I check, holding up the bottle for approval.

"Uh-huh." He nods and hands me two bottles of Coke, which I tuck into my pockets, I pick up a bottle opener and tuck it in with one of the bottles, then take two more Cokes and the rum in one hand and the glasses in the other.

"Can you manage without me?" I ask, knowing he wouldn't stop me even if they couldn't.

A huge smile erupts on his face. "Go!" he commands.

I roll my eyes at the suggestion he's making. "It's just talking Max, we are a long way from that."

The nerves set in again as I make my way up the stairs. I hope she'll talk to me. When I open the door, she is no longer sitting on the sofa. "Liv?" I call out, concerned that she's left. The bathroom door opens and Liv emerges looking more composed. She has straightened herself out, but I pretend not to notice.

I put the drinks down on the coffee table and get the bottles out of my pocket.

"Here, let me help you," I say, pulling her footstool aside so that she can sit down.

"It's fine, I can manage." She sulks. That's my Liv, she hates being fussed over. I remember when she had her tonsils removed when we were kids. She was a terrible patient.

"Took a guess," I say, showing her the rum.

"I haven't had a drink in two weeks," she says.

"Just a Coke then?'

"No, I'll have one."

While I pour, she says nothing, just watches, then I hand her the drink. She takes it without a word and takes a long sip. A satisfied sigh escapes as she enjoys the warmth of the rum so, for a moment, I just let her relax. This is absurd, we can't do small talk, but I don't know how or where to start. She hasn't even said I'm welcome as such. I'm just going by the fact that she hasn't thrown me out yet.

She surprises me by opening the conversation. "So why didn't you say you knew about this?" she asks, pointing at her leg.

I look down at my glass. "Because you made Max promise not to tell me, even though it was too late. He didn't want you to be upset with him too, with all you had going on."

Liv makes a sound, like pft. Shaking her head. "But you could have said something in one of your hundreds of messages." She accentuates the word 'hundreds' and rolls her eyes.

"By then I was already here and I knew you wouldn't let me help you. I thought it would be better you didn't know, so I could do stuff to help behind the scenes. Then I guess I just held out, hoping I could convince you to talk to me."

"So you think you've convinced me?"

"I'm not assuming anything, but you didn't throw me out...yet."

"Well the night is young," she says with this tiniest hint of humor in her voice. Then she forces a smile, which makes me laugh.

We sit for a while in silence, I was expecting a screaming match or something, but there is nothing.

"This isn't how I was expecting this to go," I admit quietly. She looks confused, so I continue. "I thought there would be yelling."

She kind of laughs. "I didn't think this would ever even happen." She shrugs. "So I really had no preconceived idea of how it should 'go'." The sarcasm oozes from her as she spits the words at me.

The silence once again descends. This is so frustrating.

"Seeing as you have the advantage and you have thought it all through, perhaps you ought to do the talking."

"How do I have the advantage?" I ask, mystified as to how she could think that I'm somehow winning in this situation.

"Well you at least knew you were here. I've been kept in the dark," she snaps.

I sigh. "I wasn't keeping you in the dark to get the advantage. I was waiting for the right time so that you didn't feel cornered."

"Well, just so that you know," she says, "you failed."

"Listen, you could tell me to leave." I remind her, trying to keep the frustration out of my voice. She shakes her head at me and scoffs, she knows I wouldn't leave without a fight now that I'm here, but I'm trying to make her feel like she's in control of how and when we talk.

She stares at an arbitrary point on the wall. Then she looks back to me. "You thought there would be yelling?" she wonders aloud.

"Sure."

"Why?"

"Because you are understandably angry." I look at her and she looks away. I summon all my courage. "So…the fact there is no yelling tells me one of two things." I wait for her reaction; she looks back at me and folds her arms. "Number one," I continue. "You don't care about us anymore, at all and there is nothing left to say." I take a deep breath. "Or number two, you believe me. But you are afraid to say it."

She watches me.

"So if it's the first one, you should tell me." I say as firmly as I'm capable of. This could really backfire…

"Why should I?" she challenges.

"Because, I'll never give up on us. But if you really have, then I need to know."

She rubs her forehead. "I can't deal with this."

My shoulders sag, have I gone too far? Wondering what to do for the best, I absentmindedly sit forward and reach my hand out to hers. She flinches as our fingers touch and I almost recoil when I realise what I'm doing. But she doesn't pull her hand away so I gently take her fingers in mine and stroke my thumb across the back of her hand. She begins to cry again.

"I love you so much," I whisper.

She sobs.

I feel awful for her. This is not something she can handle right now and I'm making it worse. "This is too much for you. It's not fair of me to burst in with no warning. I should give you some time to process everything…The problem is, I don't want to leave you alone like this." I reach into my back pocket and pull out my cell. Liv looks at me.

I text Max.

'Can you come up?'

I glance up at Liv, who is still watching me. "You need someone to hold you right now and as much as it hurts, that really can't be me. I'll go cover for Max and give you some space." She nods through the tears. "I really want to talk about this. But only when you're ready." I stress. "I'll lay off for a while, you need a break." I feel terrible about the way I've pursued her while she's in such a weak state.

After a quiet and slightly tense couple of minutes, I hear Max's footsteps on the stairs. I slowly get to my feet.

"Bye," I say softly.

Liv doesn't respond. I meet Max at the top of the stairs.

"How is she?" he asks. His voice lowered.

"In shock, I think. She really needs comfort right now and I'm not the right person to give it. Can you stay with her?"

"Sure. Are you okay?" he asks, his concern is genuine.

"Yeah, I'm fine. She didn't throw me out, that's more than I expected," I grin despite everything.

"You're doing well," he says slapping me on the back.

I smile. "I'll go back to work, look after her." I say with a hint of regret.

"I will," he says over his shoulder as he opens the door.

Just after midnight. Max joins me at the bar. "She's asleep," he says.

"Is she okay?" I ask.

"She's fine. Shocked is an understatement." He laughs. "But she'll be okay."

"What should I do next?" I ask, genuinely uncertain of how to proceed.

"See how she is tomorrow. Maybe let her approach you." He shrugs. "You may have to wait a bit, but you're not going anywhere are you?"

I nod slowly. I wish I could be certain she would approach me. It makes me nervous to think about not pursuing her. What if that's it? If she doesn't come to me, it would be over for good. I'm not ready to let that happen. But tonight I've made good progress. She knows I'm here and she didn't hit the roof. I should graciously accept that and try to build on it. I'll just have to see what tomorrow brings.

Eight.

I wanted your opinion on some wallpaper samples.

Danny.

My fingers type quickly. I'm using the morning to catch up on work. It takes my mind off the fact that Max and Charlie are having brunch with Liv, almost certainly discussing me, and I have to keep away. I'm no longer in hiding, but I want to maintain a respectful distance until she tells me otherwise. Until I'm invited, I will carry on with my previous routine. She will never know I'm here.

I yawn as I wait for a file to load. I'm so tired. I guess I haven't caught up with my jet lag yet. I've changed time zones so many times lately, I've no normal to try to return to. Before I came back, I was keeping terrible hours, working hard, trying to forget Liv. Then I was sick with worry and hit the ground running when I arrived. I've been doing two jobs, both with demandingly long hours and I'm spending every spare second attempting to get through to Liv. It has been exhausting. I hardly slept last night, going over everything in my head. My body aches from tiredness.

I push away from the desk, stand up and stretch. I look longingly at the cosy bed. I should try and sleep. I'm not needed anywhere and if Liv does want to talk later, I won't be up to it if I'm this tired. I look back at the computer guiltily, how productive am I really being? I've done plenty and I'm way ahead. I crash onto the welcoming bed but just lay staring at the ceiling. This is the problem. I go to bed but nothing happens. That's why I've been working so much, because if I'm awake I need to be occupied or I start to think, then I just beat myself up for the giant fuck-up of the past few weeks.

Here it comes… First, I kick myself for not being totally honest with Liv about Brooke. If I had, she would know I have nothing to hide and we wouldn't have a problem now. Next, I beat myself up for adding to the problem, by not admitting I'd made a mistake and continuing to hide more and more stuff about Brooke from Liv. That is why she doesn't trust me, it's totally my fault. Then I curse myself for being so self-centred that I couldn't or wouldn't see the real reason she left me. I wallowed in self-pity for a week and didn't give her feelings a single thought. I felt wronged so I wasted time. I should have been here and the accident would never have happened. Yes, the accident is my fault too and then, despite the fact that I rushed to be by her side, I've not actually had the guts to force my way back in. Max has been really supportive, but he's been insistent on me, giving Liv enough space. I should have been by her bedside when she woke up instead of sneaking out like a criminal.

I stare at the ceiling. The pity party passes fairly quickly, after all, I've been rehashing it all for days and days. I can go through the motions in record time now. But then I'm left empty. I feel no better for taking responsibility for it all. It means nothing unless Liv forgives me. If she won't, I've no idea what I'll do with my life.

I wish I could talk to Jen. She's well-practiced at the pep talk I need right now. She's been doing it every day, since I got here. She knows what to say to pick me up. She was over the moon last night when I called after my shift to tell her that I'd seen Liv. She thinks I did the right thing leaving her to process everything and she agrees with Max that I should let her come to me now. But it's eating me up, what if she doesn't? I need Jen to convince me again now, but she will be sleeping. God damned time differences. Why does life have to be so hard? I haven't questioned coming here to be with Liv. But now that I'm here and she won't see me, I miss Jen so much.

Max and Charlie have been so great. They've really welcomed me and that has made things easier. They've put me up and made sure I feel at home. I have a nice room, which is more like a hotel suite and you can tell that they love having guests to take care of. I think Max is a great friend to Liv, but he's become my friend too. It's meant the world to have him behind me through this ordeal. As my thoughts spin in their irritating circles, I finally drift into a distressingly anxious sleep.

Stirring awake, I suddenly sit up. I glance around the room, although for what I don't know. I feel like the whole atmosphere in here has changed, like while I was sleeping, someone came in and shook everything up. I jump up, in search of the source. What has changed? Charlie is working at his desk when I walk past his office.

"You're back?" I look at my watch. It's almost 16:00, of course he is back. "How is she?" I ask hesitantly, fearing his answer.

"She's okay," he replies just as hesitantly.

"What? What's happened? What did she say?" I feel the panic rising.

"We just talked it through," he says simply. "Don't panic." He smiles slightly. "Talk to her."

"I wish it were that simple," I say, running my fingers through my hair. "Where's Max?"

"He went back in early. Do you want something to eat before you go?" I give him a tight smile, I really appreciate his hospitality.

"I'll grab something there." I shake my head. "Thanks though." I wander into the living room. The air is different in here to. More positive I think. Maybe it's just having a sleep, but even as I think it I know that's not true. I've had dreadful, restless sleep with hopeless dreams since she left. I dream that she is just out of reach, different scenarios all with the same result play out every time I manage to close my eyes, so I know I can't thank any amount of sleep for making things feel lighter this afternoon. I shrug it off and pour myself a glass of water in the super-modern kitchen. I keep forgetting the ice-cold filtered water dispenser in the refrigerator door. I just go to the sink like a normal person.

I saunter back into my room to change my clothes for work tonight. I don't bother showering, I will need one later anyway, Saturday nights in the bar leave a stain or two. I slide my Lady Luck's shirt on and look at myself in the mirror as I pull it straight. It makes me feel close to her to wear this, I know that's ridiculous, but when I think about being part of something she created I feel proud, whether she wants me to or not. Also, the fact that I'm proving that I don't ever want to be anywhere but here with her, gives me a slight sense of satisfaction.

I pick up my keys and cell and say bye to Charlie on my way out, still feeling off balance because something I can't put my finger on feels different and Charlie seems cagey. Turning left onto the sidewalk, I begin the ten-minute walk I do every day, to the place where I belong. I feel more nervous today though, because Liv knows I'm here. My guess is, she will stay out of the way and I will just have to wait, like before. I consider texting her, but I promised her I'd lay off and I remember the advice of both Max and Jen. Wait, they both told me. Let her come to you.

I push open the door to the bar and breeze through to the back, completely at home now. I pass the bar and call out "Hey" to the guys. Toby stands closest to me and gives me a nervous look as I pass. Just as I'm wondering why, something catches my eye in the corner opposite the bar. I turn and see Liv sitting on the sofa, her leg propped up, watching me intently. I stop in my tracks and stare at her. She doesn't look the same as she did last night. She looks stronger. Her arms are folded across her chest, not in an angry, bossy way, but more for comfort. A half-empty glass of something sits on the table beside her cell and she just stares.

I don't know what to do for the best, my easy feeling has evaporated and rather than being completely at home, I feel like an unwelcome intruder. Having said that, she knows I'm here. Max must have told her when I was due in, so perhaps she wants to see me. I curl one side of my mouth in a shy smile. Her lips press together, an acknowledgement of my expression, but obviously she isn't in a smiley place just yet. Should I go over? I can hardly not.

I cautiously walk towards her and when I reach her she nods to the other sofa. I sit on the edge of the seat and eye her speculatively.

"I thought you weren't going to show," she says tentatively.

I frown. "You need me here, as if I wouldn't show up." I say defensively. "I won't let you down again, Liv. I'm here to show you that."

She looks confused. "Didn't you get my message?"

"Message?" I ask, reaching into my pants pocket for my cell. I flip it over and unlock the screen. There's a text from Liv. Fuck. I open it. Fuck, fuck! I call and I beg and I wait, then when she finally does contact me, I'm fucking sleeping. Shit!

'Can we talk? I'll be in the bar if you have time. Liv'

"Shit. Sorry, I was sleeping."

"I know, I saw," she says, cool and calm.

"Saw?"

She nods. "I came back with Max, but you were asleep."

"You wanted to see me?"

She nods again. We have totally lost our flow when it comes to conversation.

"Why didn't you wake me?"

She thinks for a moment and shrugs. "I didn't feel like it was my place." Her expression is sad.

"What? Of course it's your place," I bark, then I realise that sounded a little more aggressive than I intended. "Christ Liv, why would you think that?" I put my face in my hands then look back up at her. I shouldn't be taking this out on her, I'm just disappointed at the opportunity I missed while I was asleep. "So you came over to talk to me and saw I was asleep and just left?"

"I sat for a while," she says with an unaffected tone.

"You sat?" Jesus, this just goes from bad to worse!

"Well I'm a little unsteady on my feet at the moment." She scoffs. "I had to sit."

"Where?' I ask. Mystified at how this could have happened, I've hardly slept for weeks and she sits beside me the one time I manage some deep, unbroken sleep. The world is a cruel, cruel place.

"On your chair."

I sigh. "I don't believe it," I say shaking my head. "Wake me next time for heaven's sake."

"You looked like you needed the rest," she says with something bordering on fondness. Her guard is still very much up though.

"I haven't been sleeping that well and I'm keeping terrible hours. Still, I'm surprised I didn't hear you."

"I was quiet…It was refreshing to see you and not hear you. It gave me time to think." Ouch! I guess I've been hounding her.

"How long did you sit?" I ask, resigned now that I screwed up an opportunity.

"Half an hour, or so," she says, as if it's nothing. I was with her for half an hour, her choice and I wasn't awake. That sucks! I'm suddenly buoyed by this revelation though.

A) She came to see me.

B) She watched me sleep for half an hour.

And…

C) She text me asking to meet.

I may be disappointed that I missed her being in my room, but these are all good things that have happened.

"You watched me sleep?"

She reluctantly nods…YES!! This is perfect, you don't watch someone you hate, sleep!

I steel myself, I must not appear smug now, I'll blow all my chances, but I feel great. No wonder the air had changed when I woke up. Liv was there, watching me sleep. Blowing out a long sigh and trying to save face, I focus on the injustice.

"It's not fair." I huff.

She furrows her brow. "Not fair?"

"There have been plenty of opportunities where I could have watched you sleep." I pout. "But I wouldn't take advantage of you being medicated."

She laughs. "Well you weren't medicated and besides you have taken advantage of me being in this state." She points angrily at her leg.

"How?"

"You always called when I was at my weakest. Max was giving you the inside track. I've been well and truly played," she spits.

We stop trading barbs for a moment. This is exhausting.

"So what did you want to see me about?" I attempt to steer us onto a more productive path.

She laughs and shakes her head, raising her eyes to the ceiling. "Oh, you know, I wanted your opinion on some wallpaper samples…What do you think?" That's the first time she has really laughed since I can't remember when. It was pure sarcasm, but my God it's good to hear.

"You want to talk?" I almost whisper. My fragile state betrayed by my voice. She nods. I look down at my hands. "Good talk, or bad talk?" I know I sound pathetic.

She sighs and, instinctively I look up at her. "I want to hear it all. Start to finish, while I'm looking in your eyes. It's the only way I'll ever be sure."

"That you believe me?" I ask daring to presume this is what she means.

"We will see won't we?" Her tone is cold, but her gaze intense.

"So when do you want to do this?" I ask, thinking we would schedule some time.

"No time like the present." She shrugs.

"But…" I stutter, gesturing towards the bar. "I'm working tonight."

"It's not even five, you have time."

I was going to grab some food, but suddenly I've lost my appetite. "Okay, but not here." I look over my shoulder at the guys at the bar. "Can we go upstairs?"

"Yeah, I don't want to cry down here." She begins to shuffle herself to standing. Cry?…oh God! I know I can make this right, but I keep forgetting that she'll have to go to hell and back first. Once she is up, I feel I should help her in some way. It's so strange, I've been going through this as if I've been with her the whole time. I know every detail, every appointment, the cans and cant's. I know the physiotherapy exercises she has to do every day. But I haven't actually been near her, or tried to help her. I don't know how much help she even needs and now is not the time to get it wrong.

"Can I do anything?" I ask.

"No, I've got it. Can you bring my drink?" So, I pick up her glass and follow her out the back door, across the garden and watch while she puts the code into her door and wrestles it open, all without ever putting her foot to the ground. And that bandage looks really heavy. Ever the control freak. She hands me her crutches without a word and turns to sit on the first stair. Then she starts hoisting herself nimbly up each step.

"Shall I just carry you?" I ask before I think.

She shoots me a disgusted look. "God no! It's humiliating enough that you have to see me do it this way." Then she continues in silence, leaving me feeling terrible for humiliating her further. "I can do it you know... standing up." She's seething. I try not to watch her, I don't want her to feel worse. She continues her rant. "Mum's stairs were no problem, it's just these. They're really steep."

"Sorry," I whisper. She ignores me. After an excruciating couple of minutes she is on the top step. She holds out her hand for her crutches and uses them to hop up the last step. Once we are in I relax. I set her drink down on the table and wait while she settles in.

"Alright," she says as I sit in the armchair, "let's hear it." She looks at me with pleading eyes. Pleading me not to hurt her further. I can do that.

Nine.

It's not for nothing Liv, why can't you see that?

Danny.

"But you never showed up." I shrug, looking to Liv, as I finish recounting what turned out to be one of the worst nights of my life. "Then I found all your stuff had gone." I look away from her intense stare, fearing the emotions would consume me. "I was crushed." I swallow hard. Nothing will hold these feelings from the surface and I half laugh as I wipe the tears from my face. "Sorry."

I watch her, she too wipes a tear away but doesn't speak.

"I knew I'd lost you, I just misunderstood the reason why." I sniff. "I never would have waited if I knew it was Brooke. I would have chased you."

"So why did you think I left?" She croaks.

I shake my head. "Stupid insecurities," I say, hoping she won't probe any further. I'm not ready to talk about it, not with her.

She sighs. I wait for her to give some kind of verdict, she is impossible to read at times.

"I'm going to need more than that Danny. Whatever it is you thought I'd done was enough for you to wash your hands of me. I think I deserve to know what it is." Her eyes are hard with determination.

I roll my head, my muscles are so tense from the stress. I need to word this in such a way that she doesn't find out about the ring. She will never know about that, not until the day I finally give it to her and today is not that day. "I thought you left because you freaked out about our future."

She tilts her head, trying to understand. She waits for more.

"I thought you realised that we were about to start a life together and you got scared. I thought you just ran. I thought you didn't love me."

"What did I do to make you think that?" She sounds exasperated.

"You ran with no explanation. I guess it's a deep-rooted fear of mine." I shrug. "It's not rational, but how it ended with us before...it left me very insecure."

She shakes her head. "Apparently how it ended with us before didn't go how either of us wanted." She raises her eyebrows expectantly. "But it's the past. I want to talk about this, now." She points back and forth between us.

Hope swells inside me, she is talking like there is still an us.

"There is only something to talk about if you believe me," I say quietly. Laying it bare. This is the moment that it could all end. "Do you?" I whisper.

Her face changes. The hardness fades and whatever comes out of her mouth next is unimportant because her expression has just told me everything I need to know. We are going to be okay.

"Danny, I can't just go back to trusting you, even if I do believe your story. It doesn't work that way."

"That's not what I asked," I say quickly. "Trust has to be earned, I know that. But do you believe me?"

Slowly, without taking her eyes off mine, she begins to nod her head. Every hair on my body stands on end and I feel the wave of relief surge over me. I drop my face into my hands and sigh. It's a sense of comfort that I thought may never return. A single tear rolls down my face. I swipe it away as I return my eyes to hers. "Thank you," I whisper. Then I smile as my body relaxes. "If you believe me, it will be okay."

She hardens up again. "No, it won't Danny, I can't trust you."

"Yes, you can, Liv, I'll show you." I smile not convinced by her hard exterior.

"How?"

"Don't worry about it, it will take time, but I'm in for the long-haul." I carefully lean forward until I could reach out and touch her, but I hold off.

She stays put. "I will earn your trust back and we will be okay. I just want you to know that. I just need to know one thing." I reach across and touch her knee. "Do you still love me?"

She twists her fingers together and closes her eyes. When she opens them again, they burn straight into mine. She nods resolutely. She can't say the words, but I will take it. I smile as my tears start to fall.

I slide off my chair, drop to my knees in front of her and clasp both of her hands in mine, pressing my forehead against them as they rest in her lap. Briefly, I allow the emotion to overtake me. As a sob shakes my body, I feel her fingers slide into my hair. It's just comfort, nothing else, but it shows she cares. I didn't think I would ever feel her touch again. It's too much to take. I snap my head up and pull back. I want her, I want to be with her again, make us close again. But I can't. We have time to make this right...I want to do it right, not like this. We are both too fragile. I pull myself back into my chair and wipe my face.

"Sorry," I murmur.

She wipes her eyes with a tissue and hands me the box. We both compose ourselves. Minutes pass while we assess each other. I get a hold of myself, watching her for a clue as to what she is thinking.

"So what now?" she asks, a resigned look on her face. I was right not to take it any further just a minute ago, she's not anywhere near ready.

"I've to go to work," I say, forcing myself to think of the long-term goal, not some short-term gratification. In truth, I must get out of here before I blow it big time.

She frowns. "You don't have to."

"I want to. And I kinda do have to, it's Saturday and they're going to be so busy. They are all working so hard to compensate for you not being there, I have to help them...I want to help you."

She blushes and smiles appreciatively. I feel like I have an opportunity while it's congenial between us, so I swallow hard and ask.

"I was going to grab something to eat before I start. Do you want to come down and join me?" I feel sick from the anxiety and emotion of the last hour and eating is the last thing I want to do, but I can't waste a chance like this and I also can't work the next eight hours on only the cereal I ate this morning. She hasn't replied so I look at her hopefully.

'I'm not hungry, but I'll have a coffee," she says, with only a slight reluctance. I can't believe my luck and don't waste any time offering her a hand standing. I suffer through the rigmarole of her descending the stairs, but think better of offering to help this time. I feel great about how things have gone today, we are definitely on the right track.

I decide on a sandwich in the hope I can force it down and I give my order to Jake. He raises his eyebrows when he notices my companion and offers me an encouraging smile. I pat his back and laugh, heading out to make the coffees. Max has joined Liv when I get to the coffee machine, they look deep in hushed conversation, so I decide to leave them to it for a moment and glance at my watch. This is the perfect time to call Jen.

"Danny!" She greets me warmly. "I was just thinking about you."

"Cursing me for the mess I've left you to clean up, no doubt." I laugh. "How are you?"

"I'm good thanks. How are you though?"

"I'm great, really great!" I tell her with a huge grin. "I just saw her and we talked…she believes me, Jen!"

"Oh, Danny, that's fantastic news, I'm so happy for you. You remember to take it slow though."

"Don't worry, I'm not going to blow it. How are things there?"

"It's all done. Scott is over there with your dad now, they're just moving the bed over to his place, it's the last thing. Your cleaning lady is coming Monday morning and I hand the keys back Monday afternoon. That's it."

"And my stuff?"

"It went Thursday, should be a couple of weeks. I'll email you the documents. They'll transfer it to your storage facility when it arrives, they'll contact you to arrange that. You just have to sign."

"I owe you one, Jen. I don't know how I would have got through this without you." I smile at the love I feel for my friend. I still hope to be able to repay her one day, but that can't be my focus right now.

"Just be happy, Danny, that's all I want," she says softly.

"I know. Thanks."

"Did the transfer arrive?"

"I don't know, I've had a full-on couple of days, I didn't check. Should it be there?"

"Yes, yesterday. You should check on that, it's a lot of money."

"Yes, Mom! I'm sure it's fine." I laugh. "Will you thank Dad for me, he drives a hard bargain. Tell him I'll call him soon."

"I will. He has listed the truck, but that might take a while to sell."

"I don't care about that, whenever is fine." I say, glancing back towards the diner door. "Listen Jen, I should go, Liv is waiting for me."

"Go then! What are you doing talking to me?" She laughs. "Love you."

"Love you too." I smile as the line goes dead. It's all falling into place I think as I sit staring into space. Shit, Liv! I jump up and head in.

Both Liv and my sandwich are waiting when I get in and I order us two coffees before I sit in the seat opposite her.

"Sorry, I saw you were talking to Max and I didn't want to intrude, so I called Jen."

"How is she?" she asks.

"She's great, she's always great." I smile. "She's been really supportive, you know?" Liv nods, understanding.

My hunger has returned now that the mood has lightened and I take a bite of my sandwich as we sit together in comfortable silence. We have a lot of work to do, well, I do. But at last I feel like it will eventually be okay. Who knows, maybe it will be better, especially if we take our time. I smile to myself as I chew. Liv speaks, pulling me out of my thoughts.

"Has someone sorted out what we are paying you?" she asks, all business.

I frown, dropping my sandwich on my plate and my buoyant mood comes crashing down with it. I stare at her, hoping to find some sign that she is joking, but she isn't. "I don't want your money." I'm suddenly angry, offended.

"But if you're working here, which I'm assured you are, every single day, then you have to be paid for it like everyone else," she says. She possibly doesn't mean any malice but she sounds so cold. I'm left reeling.

"I'm not 'working here', I'm helping out and I'm not taking a cent for it." I can't believe this.

"But you need money, Danny, how are you living?" Her tone borders on concern, but I hardly notice in my fury.

"I'm fine."

"What about your work, aren't you supposed to be flat out with that right now?"

"I have time for both."

"I can't have you giving up your time for nothing."

"It's not for nothing Liv, why can't you see that?" My frustration gets the better of me as I raise my voice.

"But..." she begins, but I cut her off.

"Forget it, Liv, I'm not taking your money." I grab my half-eaten sandwich on its plate and storm into the kitchen. I slam the remains of my food in the bin in frustration and crash around. I grip the edge of the counter and pause for a moment, breathless. I drop my head and breathe deeply. It's going to be like this for a while I remind myself. I should expect disagreements and misunderstandings while we readjust our boundaries. I can't fly off the handle if I want her to forgive me and let me back in. I stand up and straighten myself out, snapping myself out of my dark mood. She has just said she still loves me, this is not the time to lose it.

She still loves me...She still loves me...She still loves me...this is my mantra.

I make my way back to her, but my face falls when I find the booth empty. I rub my face. Fucking, stupid asshole! I kick myself for ruining it.

She still loves me...why am I ruining it?

I double back hoping to find her somewhere and slam straight into her, knocking her off her feet. My arms fly around her instantly and I catch her before she falls. I pause, breathing hard, our bodies pressed together and our faces so close. I'm holding every inch of her tight against me and the feeling is incredible. I could just lean forward a couple of inches and our lips would touch.

She still loves me...don't push it.

I shake my head, not yet, I remind myself and gently stand her back up, releasing her once she is balanced. "Shit, sorry," I murmur regaining my senses. "Are you okay? Did I hurt you?" I suddenly panic, scanning her up and down for some sign that I've caused her harm.

"I'm fine," she breathes.

"I didn't know where you were." I offer as a feeble explanation.

She gestures at the counter, where two coffees are sitting, waiting. "Everyone was busy, I made us coffee. Can't carry them though." She shrugs and passes me, returning to the booth. I grab them and follow her.

"You shouldn't be doing that, get someone else to do it for you, it's what you pay them for." I frown then smile a tight smile, realising the irony of my point.

"I'm perfectly capable of standing up long enough to make a coffee." She scoffs. "Besides, I'm not paying you, so I couldn't ask you to do it now could I?"

I shake my head, but this time, in amusement. "You're so stubborn. I don't want money from you and that's final." I hold her stare, assuring her that I'm not budging. "It's bad enough I eat here and can't pay for it."

"You shouldn't be here if you have your own work to do though."

"It's fine. I do a little each day and I'm way ahead of schedule. I kind of threw myself into it after...um, when I had some time on my own." I correct. I don't want to dampen things discussing that grief-stricken time after she left.

"Okay." She concedes. "But please don't kill yourself."

Peace is restored and we talk shop while we finish our coffees. I help her back up to her flat and then, before I start work, I run down to the ATM to check my balance.

A smile spreads over my face as I slowly walk away holding the balance slip. I opened an account here last week and transferred my savings over. I've left just enough behind to pay off my final bills, credit cards and utilities. Jen is handling it all for me. The guy that valued the Shelby called me on the day of Liv's accident, which I ignored. But he was persistent, so eventually I called him back and it turned out he knew a collector interested in buying the old girl. I hesitated for a moment until he offered enough money to buy a house! Dad met with him on my behalf and negotiated in a way only Dad can. He threw in all the spares and tools I'd accumulated fixing her up and got a great return for me, which arrived in my account yesterday. It looks a little less in £'s but combined with my not-too-shabby savings, I have quite a nest egg.

I've worked really hard and made a name for myself in an industry that pays someone with my skills well. I've had very low living expenses apart from the Shelby, which turned out to be an excellent investment, so I've saved a lot over the last few years. That money on top of the car money will buy us a house. A nice one. It will pay for a wedding and a honeymoon. I may feel like I wasted my twenties not being with Liv, but heartbreak kept me unattached and with a strong work ethic that has secured our future. It's sad that the Shelby has gone, but she has paid the way to my life with Liv and I won't regret selling her for a second. Tomorrow, I'm going to buy a car – a sensible one – and get a cell phone. Then all I need is to get the girl. No going back.

She still loves me...

Ten.

I've never needed you more.

Danny.

She still loves me…

Ever since yesterday when I asked her the question, her burning gaze and affirming nod have played over and over again in my head. All through the evening at work, if my brain diverted for a second away from the constant stream of Saturday night customers, I would see those eyes, that nod.

She still loves me….

Max has stepped back now, leaving us to figure it out for ourselves. But I know I have a lot to thank him for. Although he isn't saying, I know he and Charlie gave Liv a stern talking to yesterday. Why else would she suddenly visit me and even watch me sleep, then ask to meet me in the bar? I'm certain he knows about our conversation yesterday afternoon and even if he didn't the look on my face must have given me away. But he isn't making anything of it so that Liv and I can quietly start repairing things.

She still loves me…so my new life starts here.

I survey the cars on the forecourt of the Land Rover dealership. I had it all planned out. As soon as I realised I would be moving here, I knew which car I would buy.

In LA, everything is big. I mean, lots of folks have succumbed to the lure of the hybrids and many celebrities are throwing their weight around about the whole issue. If they stopped to find out the facts about the massive environmental impact of actually producing these 'green cars' they might hush. Anyway…I've looked at Range Rovers before, but I had an adequate truck and I had my baby, so I couldn't really justify it. But I knew that when I came to buy my next car, this is where I would end up. Now that I'm standing here, however, in the UK, these cars seem so…big. Too big really. But I like them.

A couple of hours later I emerge with handful of paperwork. They had one in a dealership in the north somewhere, with all the specs I wanted. So I took the plunge, ordered it and it will be delivered in a few days. It feels indulgent, but I can't settle here yet, not like I want to, not without Liv, so I've indulged. So what? I know I will feel more rooted if I've something physical here and I can't wait. I walk back through town and head to the cell phone store.

She still loves me…

When I get back to the bar, I go looking for Max. I know he will love the car brochure I've brought back with me and I want to show Liv too. She'll be surprised I'm sure. She hasn't asked me what my long-term plans are yet, but buying a car here should show beyond doubt that I'm intent on sticking around. I'd buy a house too, but I couldn't do it without her, I wouldn't want to.

She still loves me…it will happen, in time.

Max isn't behind the bar, or in the kitchen. Liv isn't in the diner. I shrug and go back to the bar. I hear Max's voice coming from the store room.

"Of course, it's going to take time to get back to where you were. You just have to take things slowly, you'll get there.

It's what you want deep down and you know it." I freeze beside the slightly open door, then I hear Liv's voice.

She sighs. "I just don't see how I can get past it. How can I trust him after all this?"

"It won't happen all at once, you'll take it slow."

Then I can't quite hear what is being said, I hear the word 'trust' again, then it sounds very much like she says, "What if it's not what I want anymore?" Then more mumbling, followed by what I'm certain is this... "The thought of him touching me again..." and her tone resembles disgust. My heart feels liked it's being crushed.

More mumbling, followed by, "But you love each other" from Max. This I hear clearly, he sounds incredulous.

"It's not enough." She snaps. She may have said 'what if' at the beginning of that sentence, but I'm not sure about anything anymore. I'm just in shock at what I'm hearing.

"You're being ridiculous and stubborn." He snaps back. Then says something else I can't pick up.

"How am I being ridiculous?" Her voice is raised now.

Max says something in response and he is quite firm, but I can't tell what it is. Liv doesn't like it though.

"Don't you dare!" she says. "You have no idea how I'm feeling." The door flies open, fortunately concealing me in its wake. She storms away through the bar, as fast as she can on her crutches.

I stand frozen to the spot, destroyed by her words. Tears sting my eyes.

The door begins to swing closed again. Max is standing there with his hands on his hips staring after Liv. He shakes his head and turns around. His face when he sees me standing behind him adds to my desperation. Clearly I didn't get the wrong impression from what I overheard, his look is one of pity.

"Mate..." he says with a sympathetic tone.

I shake my head. I can't take whatever he has to say. I push past him, straight through the bar and out onto the street. I keep walking. Tears really threaten now. I can't let myself go. Not out in the open, I've some dignity. I've held it together this long and there have been many times when I felt like I couldn't take any more. I just keep walking.

She still loves me...but it isn't enough.

My cell rings. I ignore it. Then I pull it out of my pocket, I need to talk to Jen. A message from Max appears on my screen.

'Where are you going?'

I know I owe him more than a disappearing act, but I don't know what to say.

Its been like a pressure cooker since I arrived and the emotional ups and downs are exhausting. For the first time, I briefly consider a trip home. I know there is no going back, I have no home there. But maybe a few days with Jen would help me. I don't want anyone, least of all Liv to think I'm giving up though. That's not what it's about. I just feel like there is nowhere to hide here and I've never been so alone.

I don't do the math until the phone is ringing, but I figure it's past 8am in LA, so I may get away with it. Scott won't like it if I mess with his lazy Sunday morning, but hey. I breathe deeply, trying not to let the emotion get the better of me. Liv is entitled to her opinion, it's just crushing, that's all.

"Hello?" Jen answers, sleepily.

"Oh thank God. I've never needed you more." I say.

"Oh no, what's happened? I thought it was going well." She jumps into her role straight away.

"So did I, I thought she still loved me." I choke back tears as I cross the main road towards the park.

"Jesus Danny, what's going on, are you okay?"

"No, I'm not. I don't know what to do."

"Okay, you're scaring me. What happened, I can't help you if you're being cryptic."

This snaps me out of it, I realise I wasn't being clear and I would be so worried about her if the tables were turned. "Sorry. I'm okay, I just need to talk. I didn't mean to worry you." I make my way across the park and turn down the familiar path. As the tree comes into view I'm momentarily distracted by Toby from the bar walking past me to work. He smiles but quickly realises I'm deep in conversation, we pass with a nod.

"Danny, tell me what's going on," Jen insists.

I sigh. "I just overheard Liv tell Max that she doesn't want to be with me, I just needed to hear your voice."

"She said that?"

"Well, in a word."

"Exactly what did she say?"

"Just that the thought of me touching her ever again makes her skin crawl and she can't get past it or something."

"She actually said those words?"

"Oh I don't know, but that was the meaning. Max got mad at her and she stormed off. She doesn't know I heard. But Max saw me. I just walked out and before I knew it I was talking to you. I'm supposed to be working tonight, it's such a mess!" I drop myself down onto the trunk of the tree, trying not to think too much about the last time I was here.

"Okay, listen, Are you okay? Do I need to worry about what you are going to do next?"

"No, I'll be fine." I sigh. I guess I would feel the same, so far away. "Sorry, I didn't mean to scare you."

"So what are you going to do now?"

"Talk to you until you're sick of me, then probably get drunk."

"Does Max know where you are?"

"No."

"Do you know where you are?"

"Yeah, I'm fine. I'm at the park. Don't worry about my safety, just tell me what I should do. What am I even doing here, Jen? She was never going to forgive me was she?"

"Come on Danny, you know that's not true."

"But she can't stand the idea of me touching her ever again, what does that tell you?"

"She said it makes her skin crawl, really?"

"Yeah…I don't know…I guess…I got out of there as fast as I could."

"DANNY! Are you sure you heard it right?"

"I know what she meant from her tone and the way Max got mad. It's okay, Jen, I know I'm just going to have to get over it."

"You need to talk to her, or Max at least, and find out what was said. It could be a huge misunderstanding."

"No, there is nothing else she could have meant." I sigh. "Maybe I should just come home."

"No way. You haven't given it enough time."

"But when am I going to get the hint, that this wasn't meant to be? I've tried so hard, I'm giving her so much space. I don't know how much more I can take. I just wish I was there."

"There is nothing here to make you happy, your home is there now. You just have to keep trying."

I laugh a little to myself. This is ridiculous. I have nowhere to go. "I bought a car today, just trying to settle in a little. Ironic huh?"

"Come on now, don't be defeated so easily. You've held onto this for half your life. You're not giving up on it now."

I sit staring out across the view down the hill and sigh heavily. It all seems so hopeless. I don't know why I came to this spot exactly, nothing good ever happens to me here. It just has this kind of gravitational pull. My roots really are here.

"You still there?" she asks.

"Yeah," I reply.

"Go and talk to Max. Find out what she said for sure and if you still feel like this, call me back."

"Okay…thanks Jen."

"It's what I'm here for," she says and I try to imagine her comforting smile.

When I slide my cell back into my pocket and glance back down the path, Max is there. He's just standing waiting, with both hands shoved in his pockets, waiting for me to finish talking to Jen. My shoulders slump in response to his sympathetic gaze as he comes over.

"You had me worried for a minute. I didn't know where you'd go," he says.

"What gave me away?"

"Toby said he saw you. He said you looked angry."

A small laugh almost erupts at the thought of me 'looking angry'. "I'm ok."

Max shuffles his feet around in the dusty earth beneath the trunk. "Look, I'm really sorry you had to hear all of that, she can be so stubborn sometimes, she's her own worst enemy, but she is coming around."

"It didn't sound that way to me." I scoff. "She can't trust me…she doesn't know if it's enough…or even what she wants anymore, and the thought of me touching her again…" I trail off, not capable of finishing that sentence without crumbling.

"I think you got that a bit twisted." He laughs.

"It's okay. I know I'm wasting my time, she's never going to forgive me."

Max frowns. "Mate, she already has. Wasn't that clear?"

"Um, no, not exactly." I murmur, it's not exactly clear now either. "If she can't stand the thought of me ever touching her again, how can we be together?"

"Who said she couldn't stand it?" He looks bemused, but not as bemused as me. "She wants it…err, no, that sounded wrong! She wasn't saying she couldn't stand the thought, she was saying it was a lovely thought."

Okay, I'm so confused.

Max continues. "She doesn't know how to turn it around and say she can trust you and that she forgives you, but she does. I was telling her that I think she's being unfair keeping you at arm's length, she didn't like it that's all."

I rub my face, unsure how to deal with this about-turn. Did I really hear it so wrong? "But it sounded like she was writing me off."

He sighs. "She's trying to play it like she'll never be able to trust you again, but I can tell it's just an act. She wants to get back to how things were between you, she's tempted, but she needs a push to drop all the nonsense."

"This is your opinion." I point out. "Not fact."

"Oh it's fact," he says. "I know it, she knows it and if it wasn't concerning you, you'd know it too. Trust me."

"This is a real headfuck." I moan. "What do I do?"

Max laughs a little ruefully. Then pauses, trying to be diplomatic I think. "I should say you're on your own...that I can't get involved," he says. "But she holds all the cards and she isn't playing fair. So here's the thing..." He turns to face me. "You have to just make it happen."

I stare blankly at him, waiting for more than that vague directive. But he seems to have finished.

"How?" I ask, redundantly.

"Just don't take no for an answer. Push your way back in. But, at the same time, give her nothing. Make her want you, but make her wonder what you want. Show her how much you care, but with no affection." He grins. "It won't be pretty, but it's what she needs. It will take some time and it might feel like it's getting you nowhere, but in the end, she'll be putty in your hands, I promise."

"That sounds like something that would piss her off." I point out, but even as I'm saying it, I know he's right...and it amuses me too. I mean, I told her it would all be okay. That nothing mattered as long as she still loved me and believed what I told her about Brooke. I told her confidently that I would show her...and I meant something along these lines I guess. I meant that I would simply find a way of showing her that we had to be together. What I'd envisaged was slightly less devious. But I'm starting to think that being a bit more forceful might be the only way in.

She still loves me, I remind myself...and I'm going to get her back.

Max laughs with a mischievous look in his eyes. "And I know just where to start," he says.

Eleven.

I'm not a child...

Liv.

I drum my fingers on the table impatiently. Where is Max? He knows what time my appointment is. I check my watch, 13:35. We need to leave in ten minutes, he's cutting it close. I watch Danny restocking the bar. He's working really hard and I can't pretend it isn't having the desired effect. He's been pretty great actually, even though I'm not quite ready to admit it.

Since I saw him first the other day, he hasn't pushed me, he's stopped calling me every hour and has just stayed in the background. Which I know must be really hard for him. I try not to be too obvious watching him, but when he glances up, he catches my eye and smiles. Shit! Thankfully, he has a full tray of glasses to go out to the kitchen and he walks away. I blow out a long breath. It's harder not being with him than I thought it would be. Not that I could just magically trust him. But it still aches to be near him and not with him.

My mind drifts into an inappropriate daydream, which I quickly shut down. I can't allow these thoughts just because he's being helpful, I scold myself but not quickly enough to stop the hot flush from sweeping over me. I hope no one notices. I look up to see if I got away with it and find him standing over me with his jacket on. I frown.

He extends his hand to help me up. "I'm taking you." He explains when he sees how confused I am.

"Where's Max?" I ask as I allow him to help me up.

"Taking the day off," he replies as if it's of little consequence.

"But he said he would take me to the hospital."

"Well, I offered and he accepted," he says, all pleased with himself.

"And no one wanted to discuss it with me?" I feel furious all of sudden. "I'm not a child, Danny." I huff as I push past him with my crutches.

"Nobody thinks you are a child, Liv. I just thought it made more sense than him coming in especially."

I'm out the door, while he's still talking. Then it occurs to me, how are we going to get there? I turn to Danny to see him pulling keys from his pocket. Maybe he has borrowed Max's car. To my left, a swanky silver Range Rover unlocks and Danny scoots round me to open the passenger door. I've no idea what is going on, my face must be a picture. While he goes around to the driver's door, I try to smooth out my features into indifference. I'm still annoyed that they sorted this out without consulting me.

The new car smell is overwhelming. "Whose car is this?" I can't help but ask, as he climbs in.

"Mine," he says with boyish pride. "Like it?"

"You bought a car?"

"Uh-huh." He manoeuvres this monster out of the space.

My mind races through all the questions...

1) Are you staying then?

2) Are you that sure I'll take you back?

3) Have you already moved?

4) Where is your stuff?

5) Where will you live?

6) Should I be happy or furious that all of this has been decided without me?

I manage to run through this silently without a multitude of facial expressions, but I'm sure he knows what I'm thinking as he sits smugly beside me at the wheel of his new car.

"It's nice," I manage meekly. How much did it cost is all I can think. I don't know how much money he makes, it's none of my business, but he has two other cars already. Unless…no, he wouldn't sell her, would he? Not on the off chance we could get back together. I can't believe he's bought a brand-new car, here. He must be intent on staying. I've refused to ask him what his plans are, but I'd assumed that he would go home at some point. This says otherwise.

"Oh and this is my new cell number," he says, as he hands me a folded piece of paper without taking his eyes off the road. I silently accept it and glance at the number. It has no plusses or strange numbers in front of it. It starts with a zero seven…it's a plain old British mobile number. He has a UK mobile! Once again, I hope that none of these calculations and the questions they prompt are evident in my face as I try to maintain an air of indifference. I'm not asking him about it…I'm just not!

We ride in silence to the hospital and he parks the beast nice and close for me. It isn't discussed whether he will wait in the waiting room for me, or come in to hold my hand – metaphorically speaking. While I want to tell him not to come in, I'm slightly nervous about what they'll do, so I say nothing and wait to see what he does.

"Olivia Harper." The nurse calls from the door.

Danny's hand is in front of me before I can react and he picks up my jacket and bag as he follows me into the room with the nurse. I suppress a grin and chastise myself. But, like it or not, I'm a bit pleased that he thinks it's his place to accompany me.

The fresh air to my skin is the most surreal feeling. My leg is mortifyingly hairy, but what can I do? On either side of my ankle are four-inch angry scars that I can't take my eyes off.

"Whoa!" says Danny beside me in horrified wonder. He almost seems impressed.

"Yeah, Whoa." I agree. I can't believe it either. I've been so detached from this leg that I'd no idea what to expect, but this seems really dramatic.

The nurse sets about removing the stitches. Some are quite painful, but Danny's hand clasps mine as I suck air through my teeth. He seems to know just how to be. Max has been fantastic and he would do this for me, if a little green around the gills. But I have to admit, I've been needing

Danny's strong comfort since this happened.

"Wait here," he says, as we emerge from the entrance of the hospital. "I'll bring the car over."

"No, it's fine, this thing is light as a feather now, I can hop easily." I smile wiggling my new purple 'normal' cast in front of me. I feel so much better, even though it will be another six weeks before I'm allowed to put any weight on it, just being rid of that heavy bandage has made such a difference.

We walk back to the car together and he helps me in. I sigh as I watch him coming round. I feel it happening already. I must hold off, let him do what he needs to do to build my trust again. But it's hard. We haven't talked once about that night with Brooke since I gave him the chance to explain it to me. But I looked him in the eyes as he told me and I knew it was the truth. Not just because it was what I wanted to hear, I know him and I know he was being honest. Now I just have to figure out what more I want from him before I give in.

If I believe him, why haven't I fallen into his arms? I think I need more, some proof of his love. No, he is doing that really... It's more that I need proof that he loves me like I love him. I've spent so many years struggling with the imbalance in our affections, which left me utterly heartbroken. Now he's suggesting that he felt the same. Well I want to see it. I want evidence that he loves me as much, if not more than I love him. I don't want to feel like the weak one in our relationship anymore. I'm not sure if that's reasonable, but I don't care. It's what I need.

"You okay?" he asks, as I stare out the window.

I nod.

"Does it feel better, not having that big bandage?"

"Much. I just wish I could have a really good wash though." I'm unsure why I'm being so forthcoming. I could have kept that to myself. My cheeks flush from the embarrassment. "I mean, I can't go in the shower at home and with no bath, I just have to wash at the sink every day." I waffle. STOP TALKING! I shake my head, grateful that he can't see how embarrassed I am.

We turn off too early to be going back to the bar, I look at Danny quizzically. "Where are we going?"

"I thought you would want to show Max your new cast." He smiles. "Besides, I don't have to be back until six." He swings into Max's drive and switches off the engine.

He helps me out of the car and hands me my crutches. "Thanks."

"Max?" He calls out as we enter the hall.

"Yeah. How did it go?" He calls back. "Did she flip when..." He trails off as we walk through into the kitchen.

I narrow my eyes at him as he clamps his hand over his mouth.

"No 'she' didn't flip!" I quip. "But 'she' isn't a child and wouldn't mind being kept in the loop."

Danny chuckles as he switches the kettle on. I perch on a barstool and chat to Max about the trip to the hospital while Danny makes tea and potters around Max's kitchen. He seems at home here. Max really likes him. While we chat, Danny disappears.

Five minutes later he's back with a big grin. He holds out his hand for me and I take it. It's just becoming second nature again and my mind puts up no resistance to automatically placing my hand in his. I look at him for answers but he just leads me towards the back of the house, where he's staying in the downstairs guest room. I follow willingly until we reach the door, then I baulk at the suggestion that we are 'there' yet.

"Don't worry," Danny says, laughing. "It's not THAT!"

He leads me in and closes the door. I'm frowning.

"What am I doing here?" I ask.

He walks towards the bathroom and waits for me to look through the door.

Annoyed, I hop over and peer in. He has run me a bath. A big, steaming bubble bath! The bathroom is warm and humid and smells fantastic. I smile.

"Now the only problem is that someone has to help you in. Do you want me to get Max?"

I take a minute to figure out what he's saying. Oh, someone will have to see me naked! I get it. Yeah, maybe he'd better get Max.

I'm just about to say this, when my mouth betrays me. "No, you can do it." My tone is slightly reluctant, but I don't actually feel that reluctant. God, I feel like my body, mind, mouth and heart are all working for themselves. I need to get my shit together.

"If you don't mind that is," I add. Maybe he doesn't want to.

"I don't mind," he says softly and I can see in his eyes, he has no ulterior motive.

He leaves me for a moment to get undressed and when he goes I start to panic. Is this a good idea? I feel disgusting. Do I want him to see my body? There is no time for second thoughts when he gently taps on the door a few minutes later. I'm sitting on the edge of the big bath wrapped in a towel and he comes confidently towards me and scoops me up in his strong arms. I put my arm around his shoulders and grip tightly. He puts his hand under my cast and supports me while I stand on my good foot in the warm water. I slip my towel off and ease myself into the water as he gently places my leg onto a folded towel resting on the edge of the bath.

"Don't splash it," he warns as he wraps another towel around it to protect it from flying droplets.

The bubbles protect what is left of my modesty and I instantly relax as I lay back.

"Oh my God. Thank you." I groan with pleasure as I let myself go.

"Anytime." I can hear the smile in his voice even though my eyes are closed. "I'll leave you."

I open my eyes and look at him. "Stay...Talk to me." I know I'm dropping my guard.

"Okay." He sits on the floor with his back leaning against the cabinet.

I sigh into the bubbles, who else would really do this for me? I feel very cherished.

"So two weeks in that cast?" he asks to break the silence.

"Yes, then back again for more prodding and poking." I grumble.

"I'd no idea they could put so many screws in a human being!" He's referring to the x-ray he saw. He looked pained when he saw it, like he felt it for me and I know it's because he loves me.

"Well, I never do anything by halves."

"Are you okay?" he asks, concern etched on his face.

"Yes, this is lovely thanks."

"No, I mean in general." He sighs. "You've been through a lot recently…most of it my fault."

"Danny, this isn't your fault, it was an accident." I know I've felt like blaming him, but it could have happened anyway and I don't want him feeling responsible.

A silence stretches out between us.

"Do you have any shampoo?" I ask.

"Sure." He smiles and sits forward to open the cabinet behind him. "There are all kinds in here." He starts rummaging. "Here!" he says triumphantly as he pulls out my brand of shampoo and conditioner.

"Max likes to keep all of his guests happy." I giggle, secretly pleased he knew which was my favourite.

I try to sit forward and reach the shower head, but with one leg out of the bath it isn't easy.

"Would you let me do it for you?" He asks cautiously, kneeling beside me.

I look up to him and smile. I nod my head slowly, knowing I'm allowing an intimacy that I shouldn't be ready for, but it's too appealing to say no.

Danny sets to work adjusting the water temperature before he wets my hair. I grasp the handles either side of the bath to keep me sitting up and tip my head back. Danny tentatively smoothes my hair down with his hand under the jet of water. Then he turns it off and pours some shampoo into his hand. As his fingers begin to massage my scalp, I can't help the contented sigh that escapes me. It feels so good to be close to him again, I can feel my resolve weakening.

Danny rinses out the shampoo gently. "One more?" he asks.

"Mmmm. Please."

He dutifully does another shampoo and then once the conditioner is in he sits back and wipes his hands on a towel. I love that he knows I will want to leave the conditioner in for a while and I smile a little to myself.

"So you bought a car?" I say, for no particular reason. I don't know what else we can talk about.

"Yeah. I need to get around you know." He seems defensive.

"I know, but that's a big deal. A new car." I hesitate. Should I ask him if he plans to stay?

He speaks before I have to decide. "I've looked at them before, in LA. But I never really justified it to myself. I just thought, what the hell."

"It's nice," I say, bottling out of asking.

"Thanks. When I saw it, I knew you would like it." He seems a little shy.

I'm flattered that I was even a consideration in choosing his car, but it also feels like a lot of pressure on me to take him back. Silence again…I want to ask him where he will live if he is staying, but I can't, because I know he wants to live with me and I can't promise him that. I don't want to know his plans almost as much as I do, it's infuriating.

"Shall I rinse your hair?" he asks, sensing a need for a change of subject.

After he has finished rinsing it he gently wraps it up in a towel. "Do you want to get out now?" he asks.

"I think I should before I turn into a prune." I laugh.

Danny gets another towel ready, thank goodness for Max and his ridiculously over-dressed guest suite. It's like a five-star hotel.

"Now, when you stand up, it's really important that we keep this towel round your leg to stop all the water running into your cast.. So I'll hold it okay?"

"Okay." I'm amused by his efficiency.

He hands me the towel I will wrap around myself and wraps one arm around my back, under my arm and the other supports my leg and keeps the towel tightly wrapped around it. Just before he lifts me out of the bubbles, he says, "I'll close my eyes." He swiftly whips me out of the water and places me on the mat on my good foot, keeping his eyes closed while I cover myself.

"Okay," I say, letting him know it's safe. He blinks and then kneels beside me, lowering my leg and soaking up any drips. I keep my hand on his shoulder for support while he satisfies himself that my cast isn't ruined. "Thanks," I say. Danny picks me up in his arms without warning and I gasp. He takes me out into his room, sitting me on the bed. I look at him in shock.

He just shrugs his shoulders. "You can't use crutches and keep a towel wrapped around you can you?" he says as he walks casually to his wardrobe and gets himself a fresh t-shirt to replace the one I've made soaking wet. Then, to my surprise, he goes into the bathroom to change it. I'm left confused and disappointed, why would he go in there to change? Men go bare chested all the time and I've just bared all to him. Mostly I feel sad that I didn't get to see his whole tattoo. It's been teasing me under his sleeve for days. Every time I glimpse it, my insides do a backflip and I'm longing to touch it. Shit. No, I have to stop thinking like that, it's too soon.

I sigh and fiddle with the edge of my towel until Danny comes out with my clothes, neatly folded.

"I'll leave you to get dressed," he says with a small smile. But he's back to business again and the intimacy of the hair washing has all gone. I can't help but feel achingly disappointed.

He's quiet as he drives me home. I don't know what it means. For me, the day has been an unexpected step in a forwards direction and I know it has awoken feelings I was definitely trying to ignore. I've no idea what he's feeling, but it seems to have had the opposite effect on him. He has closed down if anything. I sigh, looking out of the window as the town passes by. When we pull up behind the diner, he helps me out of the car.

"Thanks for taking me today," I say trying to catch his eye, but he's looking anywhere but at me. "And thanks for the bath."

His eyes flit to mine and a tight, almost regretful smile appears. "Anytime," he says quietly.

Twelve.

Earth to Liv.

Liv.

I've spent the last couple of weeks snatching moments with Danny. He's so focused and I can't quite work out what it is he's focused on. Helping me, or rather, impressing me seems to be what was driving him. But I'm not sure anymore. He doesn't call me or text, he works and works. He has kept a respectful distance, with the exception of a few baths. I see him each day but only because I go out of my way to be downstairs when he is around. Occasionally, I catch him looking at me, but more often, he catches me looking at him.

I don't know what's happening anymore. We were so happy before, that looking back I think the bubble had to burst. It all happened so fast, we went from zero to forever in only a few intense weeks. I didn't see the wheels coming off altogether, but it couldn't keep going at the pace it was going. All I know is that when it happened, I was determined never to see or talk to him again. Things have obviously changed a bit since then, but now I don't know what is happening. I still feel like I should be waiting for something, some show or proof of his love and commitment. But the more time goes by, the less certain I am of what that should be. I'm beginning to wonder if I've pushed him too far.

He's finishing early today, so I make sure I'm sitting where he can see me, hoping he would stop and have a drink with me. Instead he calls out goodbye and leaves before I can open my mouth. I sit for a while absorbing the disappointment, until Max comes to my rescue.

"Don't look so sad," he says and sits down. "He just needs a night off."

"A night off from work, or me?"

"Both I think," Max says gently.

I sigh. "We have hardly spoken for days. Why are we going backwards?"

Max shrugs, but I can tell he knows exactly why. This is part of the problem, not only is Danny slipping away from me but we are sharing a confidant. This has led to me not really discussing it with Max for ages, so I feel all at sea. "Just let him go out, blow off some steam."

"Where is he going?"

"Some work party with Charlie to do some 'networking'." Max laughs. "Dullsville! I'm quite happy with him going in my place."

I digest this information and deal with the disappointment it brings. He is starting to have a life here and it doesn't include me.

"He needs some time out," he continues, reading my reaction. "He hasn't had a day off since he's been here. It's been a month, you know? Let him have this."

I stare into the middle distance. "Is it too late?" I virtually whisper.

"He's still here isn't he? The only reason for that is you. It's never too late, especially where you two are concerned. But you need to decide what you want and think about your part in making it happen." He looks at me with his most meaningful it's-all-on-you-now expression and I nod slightly in acknowledgement. "I know you've been hurt, Liv. But he was too and he is the only one doing anything about it. It's got to be soul destroying."

What he is saying is starting to sink in. I've watched in disappointment for a couple of weeks as he has become more and more distant, partly feeling defiant, because it's me that should be angry and distant, but a feeling I've refused to acknowledge has been trying to surface. Deep down, I know that I need to do something to change things.

My phone wakes me, I glance at the clock, 01:15 and I grab it and see

Danny's face on my screen.

"Danny?" I say urgently. "Are you okay?"

"Liv." He sounds drunk.

"Yes?" I say, anxiously. What is he calling about at this time of night?

"I've tried, you know?" he slurs.

"Danny, where are you?"

"You trust me enough to have me around. You trust me enough to work in your bar. You trust me enough to wash your fucking hair for God's sake…" He drifts off. "It wouldn't kill you to say it you know."

"Danny I…"

"Why are you still punishing me?" He sighs heavily.

I open my mouth to speak and the line goes dead.

I call him straight back but it goes to voicemail. So instead I call Max, he must still be here.

"Liv?" He answers quickly.

"Max, Danny just called me, he sounded really upset. I think he's drunk."

"Okay, I'll talk to Charlie," he says. "Call you back."

I sit in bed waiting. After a moment I try calling Danny again but I still get voicemail. I toss it on the bed, frustrated.

Suddenly, it rings and I grab it back quickly. "Danny?"

"No, it's me," Max says. "I just spoke to Charlie; Danny's had a skinfull and wandered off. Charlie is looking for him."

"Shit." I sigh. "What should I do? I can't get through to him, it keeps going to voicemail."

"Sit tight in case he rings you back. What did he say?"

"Oh, he was saying that it wouldn't kill me to trust him."

Max tuts, but stays silent.

"What?" I ask, knowing there is more to his silence.

"Nothing."

"No, come on, let's hear it."

Max huffs. "I just don't think you realise what a rough time he's having."

"He's not the only one!"

Max scoffs. "Liv, open your eyes, everyone is rallying round you, including him. What are you doing for him? He's far away from home, missing his friends and family, all for you, and you are like this great big, fucking brick wall."

"I didn't ask him to come..." I mutter.

"No, but you should be grateful he did."

I feel full of rage. "I can't believe this, can we discuss it when he isn't missing? I need to get off the phone, call me if you find him." I say, abruptly ending the call. "Huh!" I growl to myself. Seething, I try Danny again. Nothing.

I pull my laptop onto my lap. I need to email him and sort this out. He can read it in the morning when he sobers up, but I need to get it out now. My fingers hover over the keys while I decide what I want to say.

Danny,

You can't drift away from me for two weeks and then drunk dial, shouting at me.

No, I delete that and stare at the floor for several minutes. What do I want to say? My phone rings again.

"Danny?'

"No, it's Charlie. I've got him."

I blow out a long breath. "Thank goodness. Is he okay?"

"So, so," he says quietly, obviously in earshot of Danny.

"Can I talk to him?" Not really knowing what I want to say.

"I think he's a bit far gone for a deep and meaningful. Maybe you should leave it until tomorrow."

"Alright," I say reluctantly. "Look after him."

"We will. Night," he says.

"Night."

I hang up. I'm glad Danny has those two, but the sinking feeling inside me says that I wish it was me he had. I lay awake, my mind racing. He's right. It wouldn't kill me to say it. I shouldn't be punishing him still. I believe he's telling the truth about what happened, so this is all that is keeping us apart and after all he has done for me, maybe I'm being unreasonable. After a while I look at the clock again, it's 2.30am. Hopefully Danny will be safely in bed by now, but I wish we could sort this out. I reach over and pick up my phone, thinking about what I want to say. He wants me to say I trust him. I type a text.

'I do...I'm sorry. X'

I know it's not a full and frank apology, but I need to get my head round it still and I think I should actually talk to him about it, not text. I just want him to wake up tomorrow and see that the first move has come from me. I smile and try to settle back down to sleep. It isn't easy, but eventually I drift off.

I watch him making coffee for one of our regulars and, as he hands over the change, he glances at me. The corner of his mouth turns up in a smile and he winks at me. This kind of across-the-room flirting has been happening all day, but when he does come near me, he treats me like a nun. We haven't had chance to discuss what happened last night, he was here before I got up this morning. I imagine he has a monster hangover, but he's working through it...and it isn't my imagination that he's flirting with me.
"Earth to Liv." says Connie.
"Huh?" I tear my eyes away from Danny and smile sheepishly at Connie. "Sorry, what were you saying?"
She laughs. "You're not on the planet today."
"Sorry. I've got so much on my mind."
"It seems like there is only one thing on your mind," she says knowingly.
I smirk. "He called me last night, drunk."
"I heard."
"Of course you did."
"Why don't you talk to him?"
"And say what?"
"Tell him to pull his finger out."

I laugh and then sigh. "Oh, I don't know, Connie. I don't know what is going on. He hounded me until I let him talk and now he's backed off so much I've no idea what he wants anymore."

She leans across the table and takes my hands. "What do you want?" she asks with a meaningful look.

"I don't know."

"Really?"

I shake my head.

"You are as stubborn as your grandmother you know." She sits back in her seat and rolls her eyes at me.

"What does that mean?"

"Well, I remember when she was courting your granddad and they went through a bit of a rough patch, she had him jumping through all sorts of hoops to convince her he was worth a second chance, poor man."

"I haven't got him jumping through hoops!" I exclaim, insulted at the insinuation that I'm playing mind games.

Connie tilts her head. "Haven't you?"

"No!"

"Well, what is the holdup then?"

"I don't know." I sigh. "I thought I wanted him to prove something to me."

"What?"

"I think I wanted him to prove...that he loves me more than I love him," I say in barely more than a whisper.

"Liv!"

"I know it's unreasonable. But I wanted the security I never had with him before. He left me feeling like he never loved me as much as I loved him and after what happened in LA I just felt like I deserved the upper hand." Saying it out loud makes it sound even worse.

Connie shakes her head at me. "I'm surprised at you, Olivia." Oh God, I'm really in trouble if she is bringing Olivia out. "What makes you think you deserve the upper hand? He's been through just as much as you and you're torturing the poor boy over something I doubt he could prove to you anyway." She folds her arms. "I'll tell you something, no one will ever love you more."

"I know," I say hanging my head. "I see that now, but he has backed off. Nothing is happening."

"Well," she says, leaning in to me, "has it occurred to you that he is waiting for something too? Maybe it's him that needs the reassurance from you. Or are you too precious to make the first move for the ONLY man you will ever love? Honestly, I ought to bang your heads together." She shakes her head in disgust.

"I did make the first move!" She looks as though she doesn't believe me, so I continue. "I text him after he called last night," I say in a low voice. "He said that I was acting like I trusted him, so it wouldn't kill me to say I trusted him. Or words to that effect." She raises her eyebrows, clearly in agreement, which I try to ignore. "So I text him back saying I do and I'm sorry."

"You text him?" she asks incredulously.

"Uh-huh," I say, knowing what is coming.

"You think that will do? Do you? A text!"

I rub my brow in shame. "No, but he wouldn't answer the phone."

"Have you not discussed it today?"

"No, I thought we would but he's been busy all day."

She shakes her head. "Excuses, excuses! You're lucky he is still here. You have to do something about this before it's too late." Her tone is angry but her volume, mercifully low. "Only you can fix it, Liv."

"Oh this is such a mess." I sigh.

"Can I get you ladies a refill?" Danny chirps, taking us both by surprise. I guess from the look on his face that he didn't hear any of our conversation.

"Thank you." I manage and he takes our empties away. "Shit, that was close." I glower at Connie.

"It wouldn't be such a bad thing to have out in the open if you ask me." She grumbles.

When Danny comes back with our drinks, Connie excuses herself and helpfully suggests Danny sits and keeps me company. I flash her daggers for being so obvious, but she just smiles and heads to the counter.

Danny sits opposite me looking sheepish. "Hi."

"Hi." We exchange tight smiles.

"I'm sorry about last night. I shouldn't have called you so late," he says, without looking in my eyes.

"It's okay. I'm sorry you felt you had to." I know it's partly my fault after all. "How do you feel?"

He glances up at me briefly, a look of relief and hope. "Terrible." He laughs. My stomach flutters. "How about you?" he asks.

"Fine thanks." I blush. This is terrible, why can't I control my body?

Danny pretends not to notice. "You have an appointment tomorrow right?"

"Yes."

"Would it be okay if I take you?"

"Okay, that would be nice, thanks." I try not to seem flustered.

"What will they be doing this time?"

"I'm not too sure. A new cast I suppose." I shrug.

Danny nods. "Well whatever it is, I'll be there." He gives a shy smile. I get pathetic school-girl butterflies. Connie is right, he has shown me how committed he is to being here with me. So if there is something holding him back, maybe it's me. I haven't exactly been forthcoming.

"Thanks," I say, touching his hand. His eyes dart from our hands to my eyes. He is stunned. I give him a little squeeze and a smile plays on his lips. He tries to keep it under control, but it betrays him and suddenly I see what Connie was saying. Seeing his reaction to such a small gesture, I see that maybe he does need some reassurance from me too.

Then he clears his throat as if to snap himself out of his trance. "I have to get back." But as he stands to leave, he winks again.

Connie returns. "That looked like progress," she says.

"I think so. He's taking me to the hospital tomorrow."

"Oooh, how romantic."

"Alright! I know I have to make the first move. I'm thinking about it!"

"Well don't think about it too long, the poor boy has suffered enough."

"Ugh!" I huff. "Okay! I'll do better." I get up and hop on my crutches into the kitchen to find Danny. I'm acting like I'm cross with Connie for forcing me to do this, but in reality I'm grateful to her. I need this push and it's exciting to know we could be on the brink of reconciliation. I'm shitting myself. My stomach is turning over and my palms are sweating as I search for him in the kitchen. He is getting ice cream out of the freezer in the back. He turns around and stops abruptly when he sees me.

"Everything okay?" He frowns.

"Yeah, just checking on things in here," I say as casually as I can.

Danny glances around. "Are we doing okay?" he asks with a wry smile.

I laugh. "I don't think I need to call a meeting just yet. Oh! I got my date through for the second surgery this morning. 7th of August."

"That's over a month away!"

"Five and a half weeks."

He looks like he's in pain. "You can't even start to walk until then," he says almost to himself.

"I'm used to it now," I say, trying to ease his worry. "But I haven't used the wheelchair in a week and I can stand for a lot longer now."

"I know, but I just...you know. I hate seeing you suffer," he says quietly.

"I'm okay," I say taking a step closer. "I've great people looking after me."

Danny eyes me, feeling the change in my demeanour but maybe not allowing himself to believe the possibilities it could bring.

"We all want you back to your old self." His voice is slightly shaky from our proximity.

"Maybe after the hospital we could go out?" The words wander from my lips unchecked, but I go with it. "We could have dinner or something."

His eyes light up as he tries to suppress a smile. "That would be really great," he says, brimming with emotion. We stand a foot apart, I can feel the charging energy between us, it takes us both by surprise. I know he has lifted me naked in and out of the bath on several occasions over the last couple of weeks, but we have treated that like a separate world. It's not referred to. So this closeness we have now is the first of its kind since he came back. I take a deep breath. I wish he would kiss me.

"Danny." Someone calls from the door. "Where's the ice cream?"

Our spell is broken. "Sorry," he calls. 'Sorry,' he mouths to me, as he carries it into the diner.

I go back to the table and slump down opposite Connie. I sigh.

"So?" she demands after a pause.

"So, he is taking me to the hospital…and then we are having dinner." I smile, looking towards him again. "And I asked him, before you say anything!" I add.

"Well, it's about time."

I turn back to Connie and smile.

Thirteen.

Too scary?

Liv.

"Oh! That's amazing." I sigh as I relax with my whole body in the bath for the first time since, I can hardly remember when. "I can't believe they took it off!" I repeat for the twentieth time since we left the hospital.

To my surprise, they removed the cast today and didn't replace it. I still can't put any weight on it until I've had this screw removed, but the rest of my rehabilitation will take place cast free. The feeling of being under the water is both blissful and slightly unnerving. I gently flex my foot again as per my physio instructions, just because I can. The whole thing is just plain weird.

"I think we should celebrate," says Danny from his usual spot leaning against the bathroom cabinet.

"Okay," I say, excited about my evening with him. "Where shall we go? Remember I still probably can't wear a shoe!"

"Leave it to me," he says cryptically.

I sink back in the bubbles and relax. Things are starting to get better.

"You look beautiful," he says when I come out of my bedroom. I've admittedly gone all out and I feel a bit overdone, considering I don't know where we're going. But I haven't worn much more than a tracksuit for so long, I needed this. The crutches ruin any outfit, but despite that I feel sexy, just for having made an effort. Max was right, I did have one decent pair of shoes that fit my swollen foot and he has done a great job with the rest of my outfit too. It feels like that first night Danny came back into my life all over again. I smile to myself thinking about how that ended.

"Shall we?" he says, holding open the door for me. As I pass him and begin to hand him my crutches, he laughs. "I'm not letting you crawl down the stairs in that dress." He says firmly and sweeps me up in his arms.

"Whoa!" I cry.

"Don't worry, I won't hurt you this time." He says gently as he looks in my eyes. At first I think he is talking about my emotions and I freeze, staring intently at him, but then I realise he is referring to hitting my ankle on the door handle the first time he took me to bed. I blush, but then tuck my ankle in, just to be sure.

"Please don't." I implore.

Danny grins and we set off carefully down the stairs. Once I'm back on the ground, he holds open the door and we step out into the diner. A wolf-whistle comes from the kitchen as we pass and I stop briefly to chastise Jake for sexual harassment in the work place.

"Have fun kids." He laughs as he ignores me and carries on with his work.

When we get outside, a flashy car is waiting and the driver opens the rear door for us. It's not a limo, but is more like a limo than a cab. I think you would call it an executive car. I look at Danny in disbelief before sliding in and he gets in the other side, looking excited and nervous in equal measure. What is going on?

"Where are we going?" I whisper nervously.

"Surprise." Danny giggles.

"This is a bit swanky isn't it?" I say in disbelief.

"I thought we could both have a drink and I didn't want you squeezing in a cramped cab."

I smile at his thoughtfulness and my stomach flips over. As we set off, an image of Danny in my bed flashes into my head. Oh my God! What am I doing? I have to spend an evening with him goodness knows where and I'm thinking about him naked already. How am I going to get through tonight? I shake the thought out of my head and glance at him, grateful that he can't see my blush in the half light.

We drive for almost half an hour, chatting sporadically. Nerves getting the better of both of us. Then when I've absolutely no idea where we are, the car pulls up in a tiny village and Danny helps me from the car. We are standing outside an unassuming but undoubtedly classy brasserie. Danny opens the door for me and I smile at him as I pass. Danny gives his name and we are seated in a cosy corner.

"This is lovely!" I quietly giggle as we open our menus. "I wasn't expecting anything like this. I thought we would maybe try that new Thai place at the end of the road!"

"What? No! We're celebrating. You are one step closer to being back in one piece, I wanted to bring you some place nice" He smiles. "We can try the Thai place some other time though," he says with a twinkle in his eye, certain that this won't be our only night out.

We order wine and exchange a knowing glance as the waiter notes it down. Wine gets us both drunk, but in this kind of place, there isn't much else you can do, I would feel very uncouth ordering spirits, so we just go with it.

"Cheers," I say when the waiter leaves us alone with our wine, having taken our order. We clink glasses. "Thank you for bringing me here."

"It's my pleasure," he replies. "I've wanted to take you out for a while."

"So, why haven't you?" I ask cautiously, a little afraid that the answer will lead to a conversation that we can't have here. I do not want to cry tonight.

"Um, because I wanted you to trust me again and I guess I thought if it came from me, I would never know if you did."

I crease my brow. Not fully understanding.

"If I kept pursuing you, how would I know if you weren't just here to keep me off your back?"

"So this wait, it was to get me to ask you out for dinner?" I ask, trying not to sound irritated for appearance sake.

"Yeah, but not as a game. I just wanted us both to be sure when the time came, that it was mutual. I didn't want to push you too hard and now I know I haven't, because this was your idea." He smiles, picking up his wine glass again. I stare at him, unsure of how I feel about this. He looks up and reads my expression correctly. "Honestly Liv, it wasn't a game, I just wanted you to want it as much as I did."

A few simple words, but their effect on me is immense. He wanted me to want it as much as he did. A warm feeling floods through me, I think it's a relief and I feel it in every cell of my body. That, after all, is all I've ever wanted from him and now it looks like I have it, just like that. I laugh.

"What?" he asks.

"I think that's what I was doing in a roundabout sort of way." Although if I'm honest with myself, it sounds like his intentions were less selfish, he wanted me to feel secure, I just wanted him to make me feel good about myself. Right then I realise what a selfish bitch I've been. I could have helped repair this a lot sooner instead of sitting back waiting for some sort of fantasy grand gesture.

"Waiting for me to make the first move?" he asks.

I nod.

"Well we're here now." He smiles graciously.

"So what happens next?" I ask.

"I think we need to talk about the future."

I watch him as I sip my wine, hoping he will have something to say, because I don't know where to begin.

"Okay, I'll start." He smiles. "Where do we stand on the whole trust issue?" He asks knowing the answer.

"Well I asked you to dinner of my own accord didn't I?" I reply with a wry smile, taking another sip, but keeping my eyes on his.

He lets out a small laugh. "Yes, you did." He leans forward and rests his arms on the table. "But I'd like to hear you say it," he says and takes a sip from his oversized wine glass.

I laugh again. But I remember Connie's words. I lean forward too, holding his stare. "I trust you," I tell him with a smile.

I watch him closely as he experiences the same feeling of relief I just did.

"So what now?" I ask. Hoping he will know where we go from here.

He laughs out loud. "I don't know!" He says as he holds his hands up.

I laugh too, but it isn't so funny.

"Hey, come on," he says, seeing my face fall. "We can get past this, can't we?" He takes my hand across the table.

I watch his thumb graze my knuckles and I look up into his eyes. I love this man. So why can't I let go?

"We have to talk about that night," he says quietly.

"No, no! I believe you. We don't have to go through it all again." I don't want to think about it, let alone go through it in this lovely restaurant.

"Liv, whatever doubts you have are related to that night, if we can put them to rest, we can go back to how we were. Please. I've told you what happened to me, tell me what happened to you. It's like I only know half of the story. It will help us I promise." He looks so hopeful.

I try to take a deep breath to steel myself, but even that is shaky. I nod and sip my wine, for courage. "Okay."

"Why did you come back to the apartment?" he asks, to start things off.

I pause. "Erm, because I realised that I was punishing you for lying to me." I sigh.

He smiles. "I thought you were."

"I was talking it all over with Grace and I just suddenly realised how much I loved you. I didn't want to go to the party with all this bad feeling hanging over us. I just wanted to be with you." I think about what awaited me when I did. "I borrowed Grace's car and…" I swallow hard.

"So you came over? What did you see?" I know he has nothing to hide, I'm just not sure why we are reliving this.

"I hurried up to the front door. I was so anxious to see you and then I saw her."

"Did you go in?"

I shake my head. "The curtains were open a bit. I saw her standing there taking off her clothes. She was in her underwear." I look down at my fingers.

"I guess I was still in the shower," he says, shaking his head in disgust. "She was lying on the bed when I found her."

"She was smiling, I thought she was smiling at you. It killed me." I whisper as I bite back tears.

'God, I'm so sorry." He clutches my hand.

"It's okay," I say, trying to shake it off. If he is too nice I'm really going to cry.

"Why didn't you come in? You should have kicked her ass."

"I was too hurt." I admit. "I just ran away."

"Where did you go?"

"To that lookout point up by Jen and Scott's." I look at him. "I threw up." I add, with a small laugh.

"You threw up?"

I nod. "Twice." I shake my head at the recollection. "Once there and once at your place."

"Really?" He looks pained.

"Yeah. I guess I don't take heartbreak well."

"So what happened after that?"

"I sat in the car for a while not knowing what to do. Then I decided I had to get home. I didn't want to see anyone but Max. So I drove back to your place and waited until Jen and Scott came to get you. Once you had gone, I went in and got my stuff." I wince at his expression of shock.

"Shit. Why didn't you talk to me?"

"I couldn't, Danny. I was devastated. I watched you leave and it was like…" I gulp and just about manage to stop the tears brimming out of my eyes. I have to look at the ceiling to blink them back. One escapes but I catch it with my finger and then I'm okay again. "It was the worst experience of my life. I watched you get in their car, honestly believing I would never see you again." I sniff.

"I can't believe you were there," he says quietly.

"I went in, once I was sure you had gone, grabbed all my stuff and left."

"Just like that?" he asks as if it was the easiest decision of my life.

"No, not just like that. I was sobbing. I threw up in your bathroom. It was awful..." Then as I'm explaining it to him, it dawns on me. The jewellery bag. I hadn't thought about it for a while, but it was the kick in the teeth that let me know how little I meant to him and when I mentioned it to him before, he completely ignored it.

"What?" he asks with concern, seeing my expression change.

"There was a jewellery bag in the kitchen. It was empty" I say slowly.

Danny nods.

"That really twisted the knife, Danny. Did you give it to her?"

"It was for you." He frowns, hurt that I would think otherwise. "I had it with me."

I look at him; he's looking so intense. But it's the truth, with him I can always tell face to face. I feel that relief again, but this time it feels whole. I think that jewellery bag was the thing that was holding me back. Even once I believed what he told me about what happened with her, I think I still thought he gave the contents of that bag to her. "I'm sorry," I say, hoping it will be enough.

Just then our waiter brings over our starter, a big board of antipasti to share. My stomach contracts, I don't know how I'm going to force anything down with this conversation happening. We watch each other in tense silence as the waiter rearranges the table to accommodate the dish and refreshes our wine glasses.

"I still have it you know," Danny says once we are alone again. "The jewellery I bought you." He smiles. "I might save it for your birthday. It's only a few weeks away and it's the big 3-0!"

I smile back, but sigh. "I feel like I don't deserve it now. I should have trusted you."

"God, no. After what I did and then what you saw, you did what anyone would have done. Please stop beating yourself up." He reaches across to squeeze my hand. Then he looks at the table. "We should eat this food."

"I know," I say taking a deep breath. A couple of sips of wine help me and we start to eat. It isn't as difficult as I thought and the food is delicious. We make a good job of the starter and make some small talk.

Fortunately the restaurant is busy, so the buzz fills the silences and it's a while before our main courses arrive.

In the interval between courses, Danny picks up our conversation. "So do you feel any better now that we've talked about it in more detail?"

"Yes, I suppose I do." I smile. I feel a lot better.

"Do you want to talk about it anymore?"

"No, not really."

"So can we talk about the future now?" he asks with a tentative smile.

"I guess so." I smile. "You can start by telling me what your plans are," I say, regaining some of my confidence.

"What plans?"

"Well you jumped on a plane because I hurt myself and you're still in limbo at Max's a month later. How long are you planning to stay?"

He shakes his head. "Liv, I've moved here," he says simply.

I blink at him. "Even though we broke up?"

"I planned to come here to be with you, that's what I've done." He shrugs.

"Oh. So do you need to go back and get all of your stuff?"

"Nope, it arrived on Monday."

"You shipped it? Where is it?"

"In storage."

I look at him in disbelief. "So you aren't going back?"

"I hope not." He laughs. "My stuff is here, the apartment has gone, the truck is sold, Dad took my furniture and I cancelled my credit cards and cell. I think I'm better off here, don't you?"

"What if I didn't…what if we never got back together?" I stutter.

"I needed you to see how serious I was about us. It was a risk worth taking."

I breathe deeply as my heart does a backflip. I'm such an idiot. We are interrupted by our main course. Gah! Food again!

When we are once again alone, I continue. "So this is it? Are we starting again?" I'm a bag of nerves.

"I don't think we can start again, do you?" he says. "We've wasted too much time already."

"So we just pick up where we left off?" I gulp.

"Too scary?"

"A bit. Don't you think?"

"I don't think it is. Look at it this way, if LA never happened, we would be together, right? So really it's just a question of whether you can forget what happened in LA and simply be with me like we were." He holds my gaze. "You're on my mind 24/7 and I see you watching me, it's all still there, so it just comes down to this…Can we put LA behind us?"

I've been watching him and thinking about him too. I would love to erase the memories from my head, they have haunted me. But now I know the facts there is no point in going over it all ever again. I don't know what I'm afraid of. We have certainly been here before and despite all that has happened, I know a future without him is going to be harder than anything that comes at us when we are together.

"You told me once that you were afraid I would turn out to be just human and that I would hurt you. I told you then that I am just human and that I could be hurt just as easily. Well I'm still human…I'm still me and I know we could still destroy each other. But I don't care, because a life without you isn't worth living…I dare you." He whispers, with a cheeky tone. "Let me back in, you won't regret it."

I grin, he has such a way of making me believe. "Okay," I say quietly.

"But with new rules." He adds. "I'm never going to lie to you again and you are going to confront me if you think I have. Deal?"

"Deal." I smile.

He grins back. "Good, now eat your food."

We somehow finish our meal without taking our conversation any further, although my mind races with all of the possibilities. Will he kiss me? Will he take me home? Will he move in? Will we live happily ever after? I'm giddy by the time our plates are cleared. The waiter offers us the dessert menu but we unanimously decline, opting instead for coffee while the waiter calls our car back for us. Danny pays the bill and we head outside. There is no sign of the car yet, but we both wanted to leave the restaurant.

Danny is watching me when I turn to him and he steps towards me so that we are almost touching. He strokes my face with the back of his hand and moves a strand of hair away from my eyes. "I've missed you so much," he says as his fingers slip into my hair, bringing my lips to his. My lips part and his tongue explores my mouth slowly. I can't let go of my crutches, so I just stand there, locked in this unhurried reconciliation. I was expecting more urgency from both of us, but this has been a long time coming and it's worth savouring. Besides, we are a long way from home, so we can't tear each other's clothes off.

Our car pulls up and Danny breaks the kiss. He holds open the door for me then climbs in beside me. His hand finds mine in the dark as we set off for home and I sigh with relief as our fingers intertwine. I glance over at him and in the flickering light I see him smiling to himself too.

Fourteen.

I'm not afraid anymore.

Danny.

I direct the driver to the back of the diner, so that we don't announce to the world how well our date went. Liv goes ahead and opens the door while I pay the guy and I catch her up as she steps into her hallway. I wrap my arms around her waist from behind and kiss her neck, she moans softly. She lets go of her crutches as I turn her around, holding them in one hand as she wraps her free arm around my neck. I pick her up with ease and carry her upstairs. I stand holding her in the living room, reluctant to put her down.

"What is it?" she asks, wondering why I have let her go.

I blink back to the present. "I promised myself I wouldn't touch you until you were better." I say breathing harder, feeling the tension. "But I don't think I can wait that long to be with you."

"Neither do I." She drops her crutches and takes my face in her hands.

"I can though, it doesn't have to be tonight," I murmur against her lips.

"Yes," she breathes, "it does." She kisses me urgently and I respond, overwhelmed by how it feels to have her this close again. Even as our tongues caress, I can't help reflecting on what it has taken to get here. I feel like stopping for a second to text Max and Jen, just to say 'We did it!'. The feeling of triumph is amazing, but I'm afraid of pushing her too far emotionally or hurting her physically. We continue to kiss as I carry her into the bedroom and lay her gently on the bed. I switch on the lamp and lay down beside her. I'm so afraid to touch her that we just kiss.

"I won't break you know," she says.

I laugh. "How do you do that?"

"What?"

"Know what I'm thinking," I say as I trail kisses over her face.

"I can tell you're holding back." She smiles and strokes her hand through my hair.

"I don't want to hurt you."

"I'm not made of glass, we'll just have to do it old school. Can you cope with missionary?" She flashes me her beautiful smile.

"I'll take anything if it means I can be with you." I find her lips and lose myself in her.

Liv pulls at my shirt and untucks it from my pants. She pushes me up onto my knees and sits up, following me, not allowing our mouths to disconnect. Her kiss is full of longing, telling me that she has missed me too. Her warm breaths become groans as she licks and nips at my ear. I moan when she moves down my neck, she knows how this gets me. She pulls at the buttons on my shirt until they yield to her shaking fingers and when she slides it off, her goal becomes apparent. She groans as she runs her fingers over my tattoo, appraising it with hungry eyes before she begins kissing and tracing the lines with her tongue.

I laugh, easing her back onto the bed to do some exploring of my own. As I reach to peel her out of the dress that has driven me wild all night, her hand catches my arm and I hear her gasp. I freeze in realisation, pressing my lips together, I sit back on my heels. It has been almost a couple of weeks since I had it done and no one has seen it, and as it's mostly healed now, I kinda forgot about it.

"What the hell?" She recoils as she stares in disbelief at the side of my ribs.

I run my hand through my hair nervously, aware that I look like a total stalker. If I'd remembered I would have prepared her. But seeing it like this has probably just weirded her out.

I sigh. "I can explain," I say reluctantly as I pull at the bow of her wrap-over dress. Pushing the fabric away from her, I trace the words on her ribcage underneath our beautiful tree.

'You are always rooted here with me.'

"I never asked you about this," I say, glancing at her briefly, but returning my eyes to the beautiful words on her skin. "I was afraid you'd say it wasn't about me."

"It is," she whispers.

"I know," I reply. "I knew the moment I saw it, it's our place. When did you get it done?"

She shrugs. "A long time ago."

I laugh, shaking my head, more confident now. "You had it done four years ago, Max told me. Why is it so hard to admit that you have thought about me for years?"

She looks away from me. "Liv?" I bring her face back to mine with my hand.

"Because I didn't believe I could keep you. And I didn't want you knowing how heartbroken I'd be once you had gone again."

"Is that why you ran in LA?"

She nods, tears threatening to roll from her glassy eyes.

"You thought it was inevitable, so why fight, right?"

She nods again.

After a moment, I ask her again. "When did you get it?"

She thinks. "Four years ago sounds about right." She sighs. "Max and Charlie had gone off on their honeymoon. I'd helped them plan their wedding and once it was over I felt deflated. My dad had just died, it was before I met Mark and I was just low. I missed you. I'd tried not to for a long time, but with Max gone and everything feeling off centre, it really highlighted what was missing in my life." She brushes her fingers over my skin. "Do you remember our tree?"

I smile and nod. "Of course I do."

"I stayed away from it because it hurt too much, but at that time when I needed you, I went there and sat for a while, it made me feel like you were with me. I got this done because I wished you were by my side. Sometimes for me, this..." she waves her hand over her body.,"...is the only way of dealing with those kind of feelings. Everyone that has made an impact in my life, good or bad is represented here. Well everyone except you, because shutting it out was easier. Then those words came to me and I felt like doing this might be a cathartic experience."

"Was it?"

She shakes her head. "Not really." She half laughs. "Your turn to spill." She says sitting forward.

"Okay." I shift so that I'm sitting beside her. I touch her tattoo again. "I knew it was about me when I saw it, of course it was, that tree is like the symbol of us. I guess it helped me to know that you had been feeling exactly how I felt. I asked Max about it, because I was surprised that you'd been affected by me leaving enough to get this done. When he told me it was only for years ago, I couldn't believe just how recently it had still been affecting you. I mean, I've been out of your life for twelve years. Why didn't you look for me?"

"I had you married with kids in my mind."

"You're the only girl for me. You must know that by now," I say, stroking her face.

She grins. "I didn't then...and how is this explaining why we have the same tattoo?"

"Okay!" I laugh, relieved to see she isn't angry about it. "When I came back here after LA, it was hell. You wouldn't talk to me, you were hurt and I couldn't help you. I had to hide in the shadows every time you came downstairs. At times I felt like I'd lost you for good. Then one day I was upset and I just went for a walk and found myself there. It's still the same, I was surprised. I've struggled with the memory of it since I've been gone because that feels like where it all ended, but once I sat there in the peace and quiet, it wasn't like that. Like you said, it made me feel like you were by my side."

I glance down at my tattoo. I chose to reflect her wording. Mine says,

'I am always rooted here with you."

"Max helped get me an appointment again. He could see I was in a bad place. When I took the photos I had in to your guy, he remembered how yours looked but he said it wouldn't be exactly the same because he did it free hand. I didn't care, I just wanted to have it on me and I changed the words because yours are right. I will always be rooted with you, wherever you are.

"I needed to do this, either as a reminder to never screw things up so badly again, or…if I could get you back…a reminder that I had to keep you at all costs." I sigh. "I thought it would show you that we are just the same. All our crazy insecurities are bullshit, you know? We are supposed to be together and the only thing that has kept us from doing that is fear."

She stares while she takes in everything I've said.

"I'm not afraid anymore," I whisper.

After taking a deep breath, she smiles and runs her finger over the fresh ink. "Hurts there doesn't it?" she says, stroking the words.

"Like a bitch." I reply, moving in to kiss her again. "Apparently, you took it better than I did." I laugh against her lips, as my hand trails down her neck, pushing her dress off her shoulders and lowering her once more to the bed.

"It's the worst place." She breathes louder as my kisses fall lower and lower.

"It was worth it for you," I say against the skin of her hip.

She gasps as I pull her panties down.

"Have you really always felt that way?" she wonders aloud as I toss them on the floor.

I lift my hand to her mouth, spreading my fingers around her face and mashing my palm against her lips. "Liv, shut the fuck up and enjoy this." I growl, only half joking. A sound escapes her, as I pull my hand away; part laugh, part moan, but all pleasure. It's a sound that turns me on as much as she does and I waste no time moving my mouth between her legs.

She moans as my tongue works its way over her, turning circles and causing her to arch her back off the bed. I slide in my index finger at the same time as I land on her clit, which has the desired effect and she moans loudly, while her body shakes with pleasure. She is wet and ready, and my second and third fingers slide into her easily. She moans louder with my movements and I watch her, lost in the moment, her eyes closed.

I've thought long and hard about how I would play this if I got the opportunity. The last time we reunited it was mind-blowing, we each pulled out all the stops, but I don't want this time to be a pleasure-giving contest. I want to be in it together, beginning to end. So, unbuttoning my pants and leaving them at my feet, I crawl above her. She watches me as I reach for her drawer.

"No need," she says. "I'm still on the pill."

I grin, changing directions and settling between her thighs instead. We kiss slowly as I slip into her, savouring every inch of me pushing my way into her warmth, so slowly, until I'm pressed in all the way. I hold still inside her and we focus on our kiss, the effect is amazing, I'm hypersensitive to every fractional movement as I hold off from moving inside her. Even our breathing creates a rhythm I'm aware of. When I do move, very slowly drawing out, we both moan loudly. The sensation is heightened. Pushing back in at an agonisingly slow pace feels just as amazing and I keep this up for a while, watching her as she watches me.

I've never felt such a connection to anyone. "I love you," I whisper as I kiss her deeply again. Her eyes close at my words and I watch a single tear roll down her cheek. I know how she feels, but I don't want her to cry, not now. I kiss her face again and again, holding her tight as I increase the pace slightly. We need this to wash it all away, we should have never been apart. I grind into her and she gasps, our warm breath mingles as we begin to move faster and faster. She is panting beneath me, but when her eyes open she isn't sad, she wants it and she moves to meet me.

We stare into each other's eyes and I feel like I'm close. I don't know if she is, but I don't want to break this connection we have. Her mouth opens and her breaths become sharper.

"I love you," she gasps and then gives a low cry as I feel her convulse beneath me. It sends me over as her insides grip me.

"I love you," I groan breathlessly as I come inside her. "Oh my God. I love you!" I gasp as the waves keep coming and I can't stop this amazing feeling.

She pulls me into a deep kiss.

I stroke her brow as I lay beside her. We have barely moved for half an hour or more and we haven't spoken. We have just stared and dealt with our own thoughts.

"Do you want to talk?" I ask, breaking the silence.

"No." She kisses my nose. "But can you do something for me?"

"Anything."

"Can you get my crutches? I dropped them in the lounge and I really need the loo!" She giggles, knowing she has shattered the moment.

I laugh, scooping her into my arms. She shrieks and protests, but I don't care.

"I can walk, I just need my crutches!" She wriggles. "Danny you are not putting me on the toilet!" But it's too late, we're there and she puts her face in her hands as I sit her down.

"This is so embarrassing." She sulks as I walk away laughing. I go to the living room and pick up her crutches from where they fell.

"Here," I say propping them against the sink. I drop a kiss on the top of her head.

"Danny! Please, I'm having a wee!"

"I think we're past that aren't we?" I chuckle as I head back into the bedroom.

I smile when she appears in the doorway, naked, but on crutches. "You look funny." "Don't laugh at me." She scowls and sits beside me on the edge of the bed. She puts the crutches where she can reach them and gently swings her leg past me and onto the bed, settling against her pillows.

Silence descends for a second then I feel conscious. "Don't take this the wrong way, but should I go?"

She frowns. "I'm not sure what the right way to take that is? But why on earth would I want you to go?"

"Because this is the first night you've had no cast and I wasn't sure you'd want to share your bed with someone. What if I hurt you?"

She takes my hand and pulls me onto her. "I don't care if you break it again, you're not going anywhere." She kisses me. "Unless...you want to leave?"

I pull back and shake my head. "See, this is our problem. Insecurity. All the damned time." I climb onto the bed beside her. "I want to be here. I'm only leaving if you tell me to. Stop thinking the worst," I say, allowing some frustration to escape in my tone. "Tomorrow we are going to straighten this all out, but for now, we are just going to do this..." I plant my lips on hers and reach out to turn off the lamp at the same time.

"Oh!' she moans as the room falls dark.

Fifteen.

Easy tiger!

Danny.

I wake before she does and I watch her for a while. My cell buzzes in my pants pocket somewhere on the floor, so I slide myself away from Liv, trying not to wake her. I retrieve my cell and quietly slip on my boxers. It's a text from Max.

'Just bought you in a coffee… take it you are out for an early morning run…or some other kind of work out! ;-)'

I grin, he's going to be over-the-top happy about this. I text him back.

'I'll tell you all about it over breakfast!'

'You'll be at breakfast?…This I can't wait to hear!'

I slip back in beside Liv and she stirs, wrapping herself around me.
"Mmmmm." She smiles, before she opens her eyes. "I'm really hoping you weren't a dream." She says before opening one eye and grinning at me. "Hey."
"Hey." I pull her close. "How did you sleep?"
"Best sleep I've had for weeks," she says, stretching. She winces slightly.

"How's the leg?"

"Okay."

"I was really worried about hurting you all night."

"You'll have to get over it." She gives me a wicked smile, propping herself up on an elbow. "Do you have any plans today?"

"Work."

"No, not today. I'm the boss, you are taking a day off."

I push her back and raise myself above her. "No. I'm working, we're going to do this right. Part of our problem is having no normality. I was visiting you, you were visiting me. It doesn't work. I'm staying here for good now and until you are back on your feet, I have a job to do. So we'll have breakfast with the guys and spend some time together. But I'm working a two till two, no arguments." I kiss her when I've finished. "You can sit at the counter and distract me if you like. You're good at that." She sticks out her bottom lip. "I'm off tomorrow though," I say to ease things slightly. "Come on, let's shower."

"I can't," she says, but then remembers she has no cast anymore.

"Not on your own, but I'm here." I hold out my hand. She smiles and takes it.

Holding her body close to mine in the shower feels great. She obviously can't do it by herself, so I stand behind her with my arm protectively around her waist, while she washes. I've helped her bathe a few times but nothing like this. I kiss her shoulder as I slide my fingers between her legs.

"Danny! Not in here, I'm having a hard enough time standing up." She laughs.

"I've got you," I murmur into her wet hair.

She shakes her head and carefully turns within my hold, breaking the contact my wandering fingers had established. I pout. But then she takes her soapy hands and runs them down my chest, further down over my abdomen and grins as she does. I watch her, aching for her to finish the journey, but then she carefully parts her hands and continues down onto my thighs. I sigh with disappointment and even as she starts retracing their path, I know she will overlook where I want her most.

"Tease."

She just smiles and carries on washing.

"I'm guessing you threw all my stuff out," I say as I wrap a towel around my waist. "I'll text Max and have him bring me some clothes."

She looks sheepish and pulls open the bottom drawer. Everything I left behind is packed neatly away. "I couldn't do it," she mutters.

I laugh, picking her up and kissing her. "I love you," I say as I set her back down on the bed. I rifle through the drawer. "I only have sweats, I guess it's casual for breakfast."

"I thought it was black tie," she says sarcastically. "Do the boys know you're coming?"

"Well, they know I took you out last night and I'm not home, I think they'll put it together."

"Oh God, Max is going to be unmanageable!" She groans, flopping back on the bed.

"I'll handle him, don't worry," I say pulling her back up. "Now get dressed, the longer he waits, the worse he'll be."

Liv wears sweats too and we are having fun as we finish getting ready. I go ahead of her on the stairs and turn my back to her. "Hop on."

"What? No!" she cries.

"Hop on!" I insist and she gives in, laughing. At the bottom of the stairs, I don't stop to let her down, I push through the door.

"Danny, put me down!" she shouts hitting my back as we steam into the diner. Max, Charlie and Connie are waiting, with huge grins and knowing looks when I finally ease Liv down to the floor. "Bastard!" She giggles.

There is an exchange of congratulatory kisses and backslapping handshakes as if we have just got married.

"I knew you could do it," Connie whispers as she hugs me tight.

"I think you helped," I reply kissing her cheek.

"Hey! You two!" Liv shouts. "No whispering. I've had enough of all the meddling and scheming around here. From now on everything goes through me!"

We all laugh.

While coffee and juices arrive I duck out the back to my car. I grab the little red box from the glove compartment and put it in my pocket.

On the way back in, I text Jen. I wish I could call her but it's 5am.

'I have news! Call me later x.'

I grin as I take my seat beside Liv.

"So, are we celebrating something here?" asks Charlie.

"I think so," says Liv, looking to me.

I shake my head. "There you go again, with your insecurities! Yes we are." I confirm to Charlie and hold out my glass. We all chink glasses and I kiss Liv. Everyone makes approving noises around us, stopping short of bursting into applause. It's a little much, but I feel like these guys are my family now, our family, so it's great. Liv and I are so lucky to have them.

After breakfast, Connie leaves to pick something up from the dry-cleaners for Jack and Charlie takes Max shopping. So Liv and I have some time to ourselves.

"Come with me," I say to Liv once we are alone.

"Where?" she says getting up to follow me.

"You'll see." I smirk.

I help her into the car. It's not far, but I don't think she'd make it on foot. She frowns when we pull into the parking lot beside the park and she is even more confused when I lead her down to our tree.

"Do you remember the last time we came here?"

Liv hangs her head, then looks up at me and nods. It was that awful day. The day she made sure I would go with my parents. The day I told myself it was soon to be over and I just had to live with it.

"Why are we doing this today? I thought we were putting all of this behind us," she says with sadness.

"We are, but I have to do this first." I smile, hoping to put her at ease. "Do you remember that conversation?"

"Yeah, I wish I could forget."

"Did you know you'd been offered an interview at UCLA then?" I ask her.

She nods.

"Why didn't you tell me about it?"

"We've been through this Danny. I didn't think it was what you wanted." She's getting frustrated. "I was embarrassed that I'd taken it so far, when it seemed like it was the furthest thing from your mind. So I told you you should go, to make it easier for you."

"But you didn't want me to?"

"No." She sighs. "Can we drop this now?"

"No, because you're not letting me say what I want to say, just like that day. You went on and on and I thought I'd got us all wrong if you wanted me to leave so badly." I look out at the view, remembering how I felt when I walked away from here, it was the beginning of the end. "I came here that day to do something so stupid. I would have made a total mess of things, just so you know, so I think you did us both a huge favor. But I still wish I hadn't had to be without you so long." She looks at me, not understanding. "I was going to give you this." I pull the red box from my pocket and place it on her knee.

Her mouth falls open and she looks from the box to me.

"I'm not asking you now," I add. "Trust me, I'll do a much better job. But I was going to back then. I'm showing you because I just need you to know that you weren't the only one that came away from this in pieces."

"Are you serious?" she stutters.

"Painfully." I sigh. "I thought that you somehow knew what I was planning and you said all that stuff to stop me, so that you didn't have to turn me down."

She stares at me in disbelief. "I would have said yes," she whispers.

"I know. It's taken Jen over a decade to convince me of it, but I realise that now." I laugh. "But we were kids and it was twelve years ago, by now we'd have had kids, you wouldn't have your business, I'd be doing a nine to five, if we had made it this far, we'd hate each other. It was for the best."

She reluctantly nods in agreement. "I honestly had no idea," she says.

"I know, and I didn't know you'd thought about coming with me. We both did everything wrong, we could have saved each other a lot of heartache if we'd been braver. But who's to say we would've been happy? There's no sense in beating ourselves up. I just wanted you to know where my insecurities came from. When you left me in LA I thought it was happening again. I thought you saw the road we were on and freaked out."

"That's why you didn't come after me," she says almost to herself.

"I was a real mess."

"I'm sorry." She takes my hand.

"Don't be." I smile. "We're here now." I lean in and kiss her.

When we come up for air, she looks back at the box on her knee.

"I can't believe you left here with this still in your pocket. You must have felt like shit."

"No worse than you, I bet."

"God, we were stupid." She shakes her head again. But there's no point in dwelling. She snaps herself out of it. "Can I see it?"

"I want you to have it. But remember, I was eighteen, clueless and broke." I laugh.

She opens the box and smiles. "It's beautiful, Danny." She takes it out of the box. "Can I wear it? On a different finger, I mean."

"If it fits. I had no idea what I was doing." I take it from her and slide it onto the ring finger of her right hand. Amazingly, it isn't a terrible fit. She looks at it. It's a thin band of white gold, twisted like a rope and the threads of the rope are studded with tiny diamonds. It's no engagement ring, but it's so pretty and it looks better on her hand than I ever expected.

"I love it, thank you." She kisses me.

"I love *you*," I reply, holding her tight to me.

"Thanks for bringing me here today." She says after a while. "This means so much. We can put it all behind us now." I watch her twiddling her ring and think about the real one I have sitting in a box in my desk drawer. I smile briefly to myself, I can't wait to hit her with that.

I lift her hand and kiss the ring on her finger. "Let's get out of here. I need to go change for work."

I bring a crate of bottles out of the cellar and catch a glimpse of Liv through the doorway. I watch her showing Connie the ring, she seems so happy. I wonder if she has called her mom. Which reminds me, I should call mine! Not to tell her about the ring, I could never explain all that to her now. But she'll want to know that my big move has turned out to be worth it. With that, my cell vibrates in my pocket. I dump the crate on the bar and look at the screen, it's Jen.

"I need to take this," I tell Max showing him the screen and he nods as I head out the front door.

"Jen!"

"Tell me good news, Danny!" she says enthusiastically.

I laugh. "I've got her back." I sigh. The feeling of relief washes over me again, just being able to say it out loud.

"I knew you could do it." She squeals.

"I couldn't have done it without you." I can hear Scott speaking in the background.

"Scott says well done too."

"He's just happy he won't be hearing anymore about it you mean!"

"We're both really happy for you," she says. "So your night out was a success?"

"You could say that." I smile remembering what happened after we got home. Twice! "Oh and I gave her the ring." I add.

"*The* ring?" She gasps.

"Oh, no. The first ring. I told her all about it."

"And what did she say?"

"She was shocked. She told me she would have said yes."

"I told you!"

"I know, don't worry, I'm not that guy anymore. We talked about everything, it's a clean slate."

"That's fantastic, Danny. So…what's next?" She doesn't even try to mask her meaning.

"Easy tiger!" I laugh. "Give me a chance. I'm not giving her two rings in one day."

"Well when then?"

"I have a plan, but we've had enough excitement to last a lifetime. What I want is some normal for a while. Don't worry, you'll be the first to know."

"Good. So, are you moving back in?"

"I don't know, we haven't discussed it yet. I'm off tomorrow, we can talk about it then." I look up to see Liv sitting by the window, watching me. I wave and she blows me a kiss. "I gotta go, Jen."

"I know, I miss you," she says reluctantly.

"I miss you too. Talk to you soon."

"Okay, bye,," she says and cuts off.

I walk up to the window and put my hand on the glass, Liv smiles and places hers against mine on the other side of the glass. Smiling, I head back into the bar.

A kiss wakes me. I stretch and smile, wrapping my arms around Liv. This is bliss, I don't want to open my eyes.

"What time is it?" I mumble.

"Does it matter?" Liv replies. "You're not getting up today."

"Hmmm, I like the sound of that." I grin, prising my eyes open and turning to face her. "Good morning."

"Good morning. Sleepyhead. Why didn't you wake me when you came in last night?" "You were dead to the world." I smile, brushing her hair away from her eyes. "And I was dead on my feet."

"I tried to stay awake for you, sorry."

"It was just nice to come home to you, even if you were asleep." I lean over to kiss her. "What did you get up to while I was working? I hardly saw you."

"I know. Connie was giving me a hand with some stuff I couldn't manage on my own, in the afternoon."

"I could've helped you." I frown. "You shouldn't be overdoing it.'

"I have a broken ankle, the rest of me is fine!" She laughs. "Anyway, I saw you for dinner, so don't sulk."

"I know, I just thought I might see you in the bar."

She looks away.

"Hey, what?" I ask.

She shrugs one shoulder. "I just find it hard to be down there at night and not be part of it. It makes me feel pathetic."

I offer her a comforting smile. "It won't be forever."

"Yeah" she says quietly. "It's okay during the day because I have time for all the admin I usually have to cram in. But at night, everyone is heads down, working and I feel useless and lonely. I prefer to be away from it."

"I understand."

"So do you want to see what Connie and I did?"

"Sure." I watch as she gets up and goes to the closets on the opposite side of the room. I prop myself up on my elbows. She opens the double doors on the left side to reveal that it's completely empty. I frown. "Where did you put it all?"

"I got rid of most of it, and put the rest in here." She opens the double doors on the right. "For someone that only ever wears jeans and a work shirt, I had a stupid amount of clothes…and this…" she gestures grandly to the empty space, "is for you." She takes a small bow. Then a look of uncertainty crosses her face. "Err, for whenever you decide to come back…IF, you decide…no pressure."

I laugh. "Come here." She comes over and I have to resist pulling her on top of me. I have to keep reminding myself I could easily hurt her. She sits on the edge of the bed, apprehensively.

"You don't have to," she says. "I should have asked first, sorry."

"Stop it!" I say as I sit up and wrap my arms around her. "I want to. I'll do it today." I kiss her neck. "I thought you might want to wait a few weeks, slow things down."

She turns to look at me. "Perhaps we should, but you're going to end up being here every night anyway. What's the point?"

I nod in agreement. Looking at the empty closet a thought comes to me. "So when Mark lived here, where did he put his things?"

Liv smirks. "In the spare room." She laughs.

"Well I could put my stuff there, you didn't have to do this."

"No! Mark just lived at 'my' house, I want us to live together. Properly." She squeezes my hand. "But whenever you're ready. If you want to slow things down, I don't mind."

"You know I don't." I say kissing her again.

Sixteen.

You know what you're doing.

Danny.

It's over a month since I moved my stuff over from Max's place. Liv hired two new members of staff and I work less, so now we can spend some evenings together. I finished my project and I've been freelancing for Charlie's firm. I thought about taking a vacation, but that's artificial life again, we need normal, it really suits us. Liv's recovery has been on hiatus, due to this screw that still needs to be removed and that's the reason I'm awake so ridiculously early watching her sleep. Today, I have to take her to the hospital to have her second surgery and I'm worried sick about it.

She has been really anxious, she can't face a setback after so long. She's convinced that she will be worse off tomorrow than she was yesterday. But this has to be done so that she can get back to normal. I don't think this will set her back, that's not my concern. I'm just worried about handing her over for the surgery. The day of her last surgery was awful. Seeing her like that...well it's something I never want to go through again. I arrived in the middle of it all, while she was in surgery. Frantic with worry having been alone on a plane with no updates and when I did get to see her it killed me. Her face was all banged up and she was still unconscious. I stroked her face gently where she had no bruising and sat beside her silently. Then when she started to wake up, I had to leave in case she saw me. I didn't see her again for days, I just had to live with that image, while hiding away and taking rejection after rejection.

Well this time, I'm driving her, I'm sitting by her bedside, I'm bringing her home and I'm taking care of her. I think everyone understands what this means to me because we've had no interference from Max or Connie. They just accept that I will be taking care of her. My stomach turns over again at the thought of her being wheeled away and put to sleep. She'll be okay, I just don't like it. I watch her sleeping peacefully now, she is so beautiful. Then the silence is broken by the alarm.

"Hi," she murmurs as I shut it off. "How did you sleep?"

"Badly." I kiss her forehead and get up to run the shower.

"How about you?"

"Okay, considering." She stretches and turns to watch me. "I just want to get it over with and be home in bed with you watching films."

"By tonight you will be," I tell her as I return to the bed and scoop her up.

"Promise?" She smiles wrapping her arms around me.

"Promise."

I carry her to the shower and, as is now our routine, hold her steady while we help each other wash. I want her back to normal as soon as possible for lots of reasons, but I will miss this time, where she needs me.

We dress quietly, both lost in thought. Then we head straight out. Liv can't eat or drink and she has to check in by 8:30 am, so we have timed getting up to only leave time for a shower. We didn't want to be sitting around thinking about the surgery or food, we just want to get it over with. I haven't eaten since she last ate, partly in support of her, but equally because I'm too tense to eat anything.

At the hospital, she is luckily first on the list so there is no waiting around for her. I have to kiss her goodbye virtually at the door. Then it's just a waiting game. For almost two hours that seem like days, I read the old magazines and pace around, then finally I'm told she's been brought out and I can see her.

She is a sight for sore eyes. I pull the chair close and stroke her face. For a while she sleeps, but then she starts to come out of it, mumbling and drifting in and out. Then finally, she opens her eyes.

"Hi," she croaks.

"Hi," I whisper, holding her hand. I feel less tense immediately. I know it's irrational, of course she was going to be okay.

Before long she is sitting up, talking to her mom and Connie on the phone. Max brings us both sandwiches, fruit, coffees and sodas, which we both need badly and we eat greedily. He hangs with us for a while, but has to go back to work.

Then at 4:00 pm, when Liv is starting to get really restless, the surgeon does his rounds.

"Well, everything looks great," he says with a little too much delight. "You have healed nicely, so I'm happy to hand you over to the physio team for the rest of your care. Someone will come and see you shortly and then we'll get you off home. You need to wear the bandage for a couple of days and then see the nurse at your GP's to have the stitches taken out.'

"Okay," Liv says. "And when will I be able to put weight on it?"

"Now, today." He smiles. "I want you walking on it before you go home. Physio with go through the exercises you need to do, but from now on, you are working towards getting back to normal."

"Wow, okay," she says, wide-eyed.

"But I doubt you'll be wearing heels anytime soon," he adds.

I scoff and Liv laughs too. "Not really a problem for me," she says. "I'm not a heels girl."

"Oh, I see. Well, you are my ideal patient, in that case." He chuckles.

"When do you think I can get back to work?" she asks, casually, although I know this is her burning question.

"It depends how demanding your job is."

"As demanding as it gets," she replies.

"Oh of course, the bar and restaurant. I want you to take another two weeks off and then ease back into it. I think you will find it difficult to begin with, but stick to the physio and take it slowly. If it aches, rest, if it swells, rest. Keep up with the ice. It's a slow process, but I'm confident that you will be back to normal before you know it."

"Thank you." She sounds optimistic about things.

The surgeon leaves us and is soon replaced by the physiotherapist, who gets Liv straight out of bed and on her feet, both of them! They go for a walk in the halls and test out Liv's abilities on the stairs. Then she runs through some sets of exercises for her to repeat several times a day. I try to take in as much as I can, because I know Liv is overwhelmed by it all and I don't want her to miss anything.

"Oh my God!" she whispers as the therapist leaves to finish Liv's discharge notes. "I can't believe I'm allowed to walk on it this soon." She's grinning ear to ear. "I thought it would take ages!"

"You did so well. Did it hurt?"

"Not really. It's weird though." She laughs.

Once Liv is dressed, I hand her the soft canvas shoes she hoped she could fit on to wear home.

"I thought I'd be all swollen again, these are okay." She slips the shoe over the gauze that holds her dressing in place then fixes her crutches ready to leave.

I pick up her notes and bag. "Let's go home," I say with relief. It's still a long road, but we are done with this place."

We thank the staff as we leave and Liv smiles as we slowly make our way out to the parking lot.

"I feel like I should do something," she says as we cross the road.

"Something?"

"Yeah, something to celebrate."

"Liv, you have been out cold most of the day, I need to get you home to bed and take care of you."

She looks at me and smiles. "That'll do nicely," she says with a wink.

As promised an hour later she is all tucked up watching a movie with dinner from downstairs across her lap. We both are. I managed to sneak her in the back way and get her in bed before I went down to get us some food and tell Max she was home safe. I don't know why it seemed so important to have her to myself tonight, but I didn't even tell anyone that she can walk on her foot now. I just wanted it to be us and I knew Max would want to see her after such exciting news. I know it's selfish, but this feels like the last night she will really need me and suddenly I feel insecure about where that will leave me tomorrow.

"Stop it!" she suddenly exclaims.

"Huh? What?"

"Stop with the negative thoughts and the moping around and stuff. I still need you to look after me."

I frown, but I can feel my lips curling into a smile. How does she do that? "Stop with the reading my mind and stuff," I retort.

"I can see what you're thinking and I think it's silly that's all." She huffs. "You should be glad I'm nearly better."

"Oh my God, Liv, I am! That's not it. I just…I just, I've liked you needing me." I sigh. "You are so God damned independent that it's hard to feel indispensable sometimes, that's all. I don't want you be hurt or incapable, but taking care of you, well it's been nice for me…you know?"

"It's been nice for me too. But it isn't over, I still need you." She smiles softly trying to make me feel better.

"I know. I'm just worried about losing some of this." I say, gesturing to our feast in bed at 7 pm. "Soon, you'll be back at work and I'll be home alone."

Liv shakes her head. "That won't happen. I want this now."

"I know how badly you want to get back to it and I don't want to stop you." I interrupt. "I don't want you to change for me."

"I've changed because of you, not for you. My old life was what I needed, but now I need us. I couldn't go on forever working like that. The new staff aren't just for cover, they are permanent. I'm going to work like a normal person when I go back. There will be some nights, but you'll know where I am if you want to join me," she says with a shy smile. "Do you think you'll still want to work in the bar from time to time?"

"I feel like I'm part of this place now. I was trying to fill in for you, I just thought you wouldn't need me once you're back."

"I'll always need you," she says. "What you've done has meant the world to me and I want you to be part of it. I know you have your work, but this place is my world and you share it with me now."

I wrap my arms around her, ignoring the sound of plates clinking on top of our bed covers. "I love you," I whisper. I hold her tight to my chest.

I still need to hold her in the shower, but she can at least balance herself better now. I won't readily give up our morning ritual even when she can do it herself. I love the fact that I get to see her this way every day. It's nice to be back here again, now that she's had her stitches removed.

"Danny, I can feel that," she says, indignant, although I can hear the smile in her voice.

"I can't help it,," I reply, kissing her neck and pushing my erection against her again. "You do this to me. I'm trying to be good...but now you're just teasing me, rubbing back and forth."

"You are insatiable! I'm just washing."

"You know what you're doing." I laugh, turning her around and hitching up her leg, so that she is still standing on her good foot. She gives me an innocent look, so I push her back against the wall. She gasps at the cold tiles against her back, but I give her no time to think as I push myself into her, hard.

"Oh God!" she moans.

She knew what she was doing, she is so wet. So I give her what she so obviously wanted. I have her lifted slightly so that her foot is only just on the floor as I slam into her. Her arms wrap around my neck and her fingers grasp my hair as she desperately tries to gain some leverage, but I stay in control and don't let up for a second. This is going to be really fast.

I'm aware of my own moans mingled with hers as our mouths fight to connect, but I'm going too hard to keep her lips on mine for long. The water rushes between us, heating us up as I struggle to hold back.

Liv's cries are increasing, she is pushing away from the wall to meet me, grinding as she does. I feel like I can't fight it any longer, so when she says, "That's it, fuck me," through gritted teeth, I immediately start to come. I cry out and thrust through the intense orgasm, as hard as I can, wanting to take her all the way too. She digs her nails into my back and moans, then I feel it. That welcome grasping of her insides as they come crashing in around me. We moan and pant, I don't think we've ever been so loud.

I laugh, capturing her lips and kissing her deeply. I slowly withdraw and lower her foot back to the floor; I love the fact that I still can't let her go. I never want to let her go. I hold her close and feel her chest rising and falling rapidly.

"You okay?"

She exhales a shuddery breath. "I'm fucked!" She laughs.

Seventeen.

You should really have a bath.

Liv.

"You know, I was thinking," Danny says from the doorway of the bathroom as I pull on my jeans in the bedroom. "You should really have a bath."

I sniff my armpit sarcastically. "I just had a shower, what are you saying?" I laugh.

Danny laughs too, wrapping his arms around the bare skin across my stomach. "I mean, we should have a bath, not just a shower." He pauses, I notice a faraway look in his eyes. "You've really needed one all this time you were getting better." He frowns, like he has somehow failed me, by not providing me with this essential thing during my recovery. A recovery, he was forcibly absent for much of. The thought of our break-up still puts a dark cloud over me and I fight to shake it off before he notices.

"I assume a bath wouldn't fit, that's why Connie never put one in." I shrug. "I'm used to it."

Danny glances back at the bathroom. "Would you let me look into it?" he asks. He seems twitchy about something, I can't see why having a bath is suddenly all important. But I do like the idea of him putting some of himself into the flat. More and more it's becoming 'our' home, so if he wants a bath, I wouldn't dream of stopping him. A smile plays on his lips for a second and then his attention comes back to me, waiting for an answer.

"Sure." I shrug again. "If you think it can be done, I would love to soak in a bath with you." I twist in his arms and sigh with pleasure as his lips play on my neck.

Danny looks happy when I see him at his laptop in the garden later, content is probably a better description and he should be. I've come on nicely in the few weeks since I had the screw removed and things have settled down generally. He doesn't seem to have any regrets about moving here and while I know he misses Jen especially, he is making a special effort to stay in touch and he's really close to some of his new friends here. I occasionally marvel at how normal life is recently. After all the ups and downs of the last few months, it has taken no time at all for us to find a rhythm that suits us. We are better than ever now that we both know what went through the other's heads all those years ago. I know for sure now that he did love me as much as I loved him and the value of knowing that is immense, almost worth the heartbreak and all those years apart. Without it we wouldn't have what we have now.

I instinctively thumb across my ring. Looking at it, I smile. I have him, this is all I need in life. Well, almost. Before this all started to go wrong, he wanted to start a family. I wonder where he stands on that now? It's as if he never said it. Maybe so much has happened that he has reconsidered? My stomach tightens. I guess I'm not okay with that possibility. I just don't want to disrupt anything by bringing it up. I know that he wants to be with me forever, but as far as his thoughts on babies...and marriage, which I can hardly even dare to think about...I'm clueless.

I shake my head. I should be happy with what I have, God knows it was hard won. I turn back inside and force myself to get back to work. We will talk about it when he's ready, I shouldn't push things. I potter in the kitchen, humming along to the radio. This is okay. A happy, quiet life.

Danny makes me jump, slipping his arm around my waist and pressing his lips to the back of my neck. "I've to go out," he murmurs against my skin.

"Okay," I reply, sighing into his warmth. Then he withdraws quickly and I sag with disappointment.

"I won't be long," he says as he hurries away.

I wonder why he looks so pleased with himself.

A couple of hours later he's back carrying bags from the supermarket. He holds them up for me to see, so that I understand he's cooking me dinner and I smile. 'Seven,' he mouths to me as I hand some change to my customer. I smile and nod, then he disappears up to the flat.

I waste no time following him up there when the evening staff arrive at six and the aroma of garlic finds me halfway up the stairs. I find Danny in the kitchen listening to music and cooking as he so often is these days. We eat downstairs during the day, but in the evenings now, more often than not he cooks. Sometimes I beat him to it, but he loves it and I've no complaints. I know before I peer over his shoulder that we are having his legendary spaghetti and meatballs and as he turns to kiss me I notice the bottle of wine open beside him. I smirk, he is either trying to get me drunk, or force us to be more grown up so that we don't embarrass ourselves in restaurants.

"It smells yummy."

"Like you." He grins, wrapping his arms around me.

"Me? I smell like stale coffee. I'm going to have a shower before dinner," I say, stepping away.

"I'll be right there," he says, turning down the stove.

"I think I can manage." I reply without thinking, I'm doing fine now, so a shower shouldn't be that unmanageable. His face falls, like he is thinking the time has finally come that I don't need him anymore, just like he said it would. My heart melts for him. "But I don't want to chance it, are you sure you don't mind?"

His spirits lift straight away and he follows me into the bathroom.

"You can wipe that glum expression off your face. I still need you," I tease as he helps me step into the shower. "And even if I don't, I WANT you, which should count for more."

"I know," he sighs, holding me tight under the stream of water.

When I come out of the bedroom all dressed in my favourite chilling clothes, my black trackies and Danny's Guns 'n' Roses t-shirt, Danny is setting the table wearing only his grey sweats. I stop dead and watch him leaning across the table. Oh. My. God! I don't know what makes me weakest, the tattoos, the abs, his golden skin, the way his trousers hang low on his hips…it all does me in. Those grey sweats are such a turn on, he knows that. In fact I think he puts them on to guarantee he gets lucky. Although it's me that's lucky and I'm lucky pretty much every day!

I approach him quietly and when he stands up straight, he presses into me. He tenses for a split second, surprised that I'm behind him, but he instantly relaxes as I run my fingers around his sides and over his abs. I kiss his bare shoulder then run my tongue up his neck to the place behind his ear that always makes him shiver. I smile when a sigh accompanies the ripple from his skin and he tilts his head, willing me to continue. So I spend some time on that sweet spot he loves.

"Was it the pants again?" he breathes.

"It's everything." I sigh against his skin.

He twists in my embrace and catches my face in his hands, staring into my eyes. "I love everything about you too." He grins and then kisses me tenderly, leaving me grateful he is holding me up.

"I want you," I whisper.

He laughs. "You can have me later. It's dinner time," he says and smacks my bum as he goes back into the kitchen, picking up his t-shirt from the back of the chair and slipping it over his head as he goes.

I slump. "How do you have so much self-restraint?"

"I just know you're worth the wait," he calls.

I shake my head, following him to collect the wine and some glasses.

Danny turns to face me holding our steaming bowls of pasta and stops.

"What?" I say.

He shakes his head. "Nothing." He heads to the table.

"No, what?"

As soon as he's put our food down he turns to face me, catching both my wrists in his hands. He holds them tight and leans forward until our faces are almost touching, holding my gaze for a moment before leaning in to kiss me. I inhale through my nose as the kiss deepens and sigh when he pulls away.

"Did you realise, you haven't used your crutches since you have been home?" he says.

I look at my feet, conscious, because I know he's really insecure about me not needing his help anymore. I actually feel guilty and have to stop myself apologising. When I look back up at him, he takes the wine out of my left hand and the glasses out of my right. "You're getting better, at last."

I nod. But he frowns. "You don't seem pleased."

"I am." I sigh, sitting down.

"But?"

"But, I know you're worried about it."

"Liv! I'm not worried about it!" He shakes his head. "Is that what you think? That I don't want you to get better?"

"No, I…" I don't really know what to say, because that is what I think.

"I'm so sorry if I gave you that impression. I want you better more than anything. I just enjoy showering with you and it has been nice being needed. But there is so much I want to do that I need you better for, please don't think for a second that I would wish you a slow recovery." He grabs my hand and gives it a squeeze.

"I've changed," I say quietly. "I like things the way they are now, I like you doing things to help me. I won't suddenly stop wanting any of it."

"I hope not. But even if you do, I will still be glad you're better." He frowns again. "I can't believe you would think that I wouldn't."

"I'm sorry."

"No! It's my fault. I obviously gave you that impression." He curses himself.

This is going badly, I was so looking forward to dinner and a nice snuggle on the sofa, and now I've cocked it all up and made him feel awful. I sigh heavily. What a disaster.

Danny starts to laugh. I look up at him in shock.

"Sorry," he says covering his mouth with his hand. "It's not funny, but we are such a disaster!" He laughs harder.

Even though I don't really get it, I can't help laughing too.

"I thought we were getting better at this, but we still both think the worst all the time. It's funny."

I laugh more once I understand.

"Just to be clear. I want you better, I NEED you better. I want to get on with our life and I want you to be one hundred percent to do that." He takes my hand again, trying to look sincere as his laughter subsides.

I erupt now, I can't help it. He looks at me confused. "Well then I should tell you that I haven't needed my crutches for a week, in fact today I forgot to take one to work with me!" I laugh, hysterically now. "I didn't want to upset you, I hoped you wouldn't notice!"

Danny puts his face in his hands. "Oh my God! Look at us!" he mumbles from inside his hands, shaking his head.

"I know." I giggle. "I'm really sorry." I try to peel his fingers away from his face, but he holds firm.

"Why do we do this?" he says, finally looking at me.

"Do what exactly?"

"Assume the worst of each other." He sighs, trying to pull himself together, so I do the same. "Old habits die hard I guess."

I nod in agreement. It really is ridiculous, we need to stop this kind of thing from snowballing back into what we had before…doubt and insecurity. "Okay, I'm stopping as of now," I say decisively, then I tap him on the arm. "Hey, Danny," I say in an over-enthusiastic tone. "I don't really need my crutches anymore. I really feel like I'm getting better."

Danny sees what I'm doing and plays along. "Baby, that's fantastic, I'm so glad because now we can really get on with our future!" He grins stupidly. "We can still take showers together though can't we? I enjoy that."

"Of course we can, it's the best part of my day, I wouldn't change it for anything," I reply brightly. Then we both dissolve into fits of giggles. Danny leaps up and picks me up with him, twirling me around. Then, as he lowers me back to the ground, he tucks some hair behind my ear and leans in to kiss me. I sigh as my lips part and his tongue meets mine. The feeling behind the kiss is almost heartbreaking. No matter how much we love each other, doubt always gets the better of us. All because we were so young we couldn't express ourselves properly and it left us both so affected that even now, after everything we have been through, it still creeps in.

"We were too young," I think out loud. Danny, looks confused again.

"It wasn't our fault that we found each other so young and the fact that we were 'meant to be' just made it worse I think. We couldn't stop what happened to us because we weren't ready or able to really express how we felt about each other. Then that screwed us up so badly we weren't fit for anyone else and we certainly couldn't cope with each other again…It's a wonder we are so well balanced now!" I laugh and so does Danny, seeing the funny side.

"What did I ever do to deserve you?" He smiles, taking my face in his hands, his eyes burn into mine.

"I could say the same." I smile.

Eighteen.

I just don't feel worthy.

Liv.

I carefully carry the coffees into the garden, trying not to spill any into the saucers. I may have the use of both hands back, but I'm still stiff and have a slight limp, which makes transferring hot liquids a bit dicey at times. I walk up behind Danny, working at his laptop in the sunshine. Leaning around him, I place his coffee on the table and he looks up in surprise, then down to my hands. He's still surprised to see me walking unaided, he raises his eyebrows approvingly.

"Impressed?" I ask, doing a slight curtsey.

"You never stop impressing me." He pulls my face down to his and kisses me softly.

"Well at least I'll start being a little more useful round here, even if it's just one drink at a time." I joke, perching on the arm of his chair. "What are you working on?"

"I'm just playing around with something," he says, sounding cagey.

"What?" I ask peering at the screen.

"A new website for this place." He shrugs. "Yours is up for renewal and I don't think it's working all that well."

"We have an internet guy. You don't have to do that."

"Hi!" he says sarcastically, offering his hand for me to shake. "Internet guy! Nice to meet you."

"You know what I mean." I slap his hand away. "You don't have to do this, we pay someone to do it."

"Well I'm free and, frankly, I'm better." He smirks.

I raise my eyebrows. "Modest too!" I tease. But I love him for it. I know I used to have control issues, but I'm growing used to him calling some of the shots and I don't even mind. I no longer feel compelled to resist his help. "Thank you," I say, leaning over to kiss him and relish his confusion, he was expecting to have to fight his corner.

His look of satisfaction is rewarding for me. I've tried to take on board what he said to me after my last surgery. I was ridiculously over independent and I know how deep my need for control runs. It's a defence mechanism, a result of feeling the way I did when my dad rocked the boat in our lives so badly we were all seasick for years. I've tried not to depend on anyone since. Maybe Danny has always been the exception to that and, of course, Max. Although even with them I can still be a nightmare.

If Danny wants to build a new website for us, I won't stop him. I love that he wants to be involved. I shift off the arm of Danny's chair and take the one beside him, sipping my coffee.

"So where are we going?" I ask him, still intrigued about why he wanted me to keep this morning free and why he is radiating nervous tension that I'm obviously not supposed to notice.

"Bath shopping!" he says with a beaming smile.

I want to tell him that he can pick a bath without me, that I trust him and to me a bath is just a bath, but I can't because he looks so hopefully enthusiastic. Instead I smile back at him and get myself in a bath picking kind of place.

When Danny parks the car on Max's road, I'm baffled. But Danny looks so excited I try not to let my control freak streak get the better of me. He's practically giddy when he takes my hand and leads me to the opposite side of the road to a house I don't know. I frown, but he just grins. A man who seems to know Danny meets us and opens the front door and we step quietly into an empty house. I open my mouth to say something, but Danny stops me, leading me instead up the stairs, in fact we go up two flights into the loft space. It's a huge empty bedroom, within the eaves, but it's honestly so big up here you don't notice. Danny opens a door and takes me into an adjoining room.

We are standing in the swankiest bathroom I've ever been in. It puts Max's to shame and that is saying something. Danny looks terrified suddenly.

"What do you think of this bath?" he asks quietly.

"Um, I like it, but I'm not sure why you have bought me to…" I glance around as though the walls have ears and lower my voice, "…someone's house, to see it. Couldn't we just go to B&Q, like everyone else?"

Danny eyes me intently and almost smiles, but the nervous tension he was radiating earlier seems to have reached fever pitch. "I was wondering what you thought of the house?" he virtually whispers.

I blink at him.

"I'd like to buy it," he says clearing his throat. "For us."

I suddenly need to sit, so I perch lightly on the edge of this bath we are here to see. Danny crouches down so that he can look at my face and we stare at each other silently for a moment.

I muster the power of speech. "We haven't talked about this."

"I know," he says. "But I've been thinking about it. Do you hate it?"

"No," I say, glancing around at the glossy finishes everywhere. "It's amazing."

"Charlie told me about it, he knows the guy who has renovated it." He nods his head towards the door, he must mean the man downstairs. "It isn't on the market yet." He pauses. "I know it's a lot to take in."

I blow out a long breath.

"We need to talk about it I know, but the guy wants to put it on the market on Monday, so I wanted to show you, because if you want it, we can stop him."

I open my mouth to speak but words fail me.

"You don't have to answer right now, but I wanted to show you at least."

"Can we afford it?" This is all I can think right now, even though there are about fifty other questions forming a line in my head.

"Yes."

"But…"

"Questions later. Will you just look around it with me? Give it a chance? Then we will go home and talk it all through." He smiles so sweetly there is no way I could say no, even if I wanted to, which I don't. This house is amazing and Danny has just offered to buy it…for us!

"Okay," I say meekly.

"Great!" he says, jumping up. He lifts me to my feet and turns me around. "This is the bathroom," he says gleefully, "it has a bath AND a shower."

I take in the room. It's roughly the size of my bedroom. Every surface is covered in highly polished cream tile and when I say tile, I mean slab. The walk-in shower could house three of mine and the twin rainfall shower heads look like they pack a punch. Twin sinks line one wall and the spectacular bath looks plenty big enough for two. This is an indulgent bathroom and I hope we can buy this house because I don't think I would ever be satisfied with another bathroom again now that I've seen this.

Danny leads me out of the sparkly paradise and stands me in the centre of the huge bedroom.

"This is the master bedroom." He grins. "And this," he says opening the other door, "is the closet!" I step dumbfounded into the next room which has been professionally fitted out as a walk-in wardrobe. I absentmindedly open a cupboard door and the interior automatically lights up. I'm utterly speechless.

"What do you think?" he asks.

"I think I'm dreaming," I reply, trying to ignore the rising feeling of what seems like panic. This place is overwhelming. But I wouldn't be able to keep it looking like this.

Before I know it I've seen three more spacious bedrooms, two with small en suite bathrooms and a similarly equipped bathroom on the lower level. The quality of everything is insane. All the bedrooms have handmade, fitted wardrobes; every door is solid oak, as are the frames, skirting boards and banisters.

Downstairs the entrance hall is tiled like the high-gloss bathroom, but the floor becomes oak (which I've no doubt has underfloor heating) as we enter the immense open-plan living area. A huge open lounge area runs the length of the house and at the back a high-ceilinged, single storey extension houses the swanky kitchen. High-gloss everything, as you would expect and everything in trendy shades of nothing in particular. The kind of colours that you know are vastly superior to magnolia in every way, but equally un-intrusive. I feel very unsophisticated standing here in my work clothes, this is a house you need to dress up for. Now I start to panic. It's too good for me.

A study, a downstairs loo and a utility room later, I'm starting to hyperventilate. Danny whisks me around the garden and we thank the man. Danny promises to call him tomorrow. Then we're back in the car. I breathe a sigh of relief to be back in the familiar territory of Danny's car, but then I look around. This car would look the part on that driveway. More and more I'm feeling like I don't belong in Danny's vision of our life.

I don't care that it's still approaching noon, I mix two rum and Cokes and plonk myself on a seat in the garden. I lean my head against the back of the chair and close my eyes, sighing with relief to be back in the safety of my world. I don't know why I feel so freaked out, the house was lovely, amazing really. I was just a bit blindsided and then I started to feel unworthy. I know that's ridiculous and when I've calmed down I'll wish I could have focused on the house a bit more. For now I just breathe. I don't know what Danny is doing in the bar, but a couple of minutes to clear my head is just what I need, maybe he realises that.

The chair beside me scrapes on the ground and Danny sits silently beside me. I keep my eyes closed for a minute just enjoying shutting everything out. I know he will think I'm about to say something awful, it's what we do, we think the worst. I know we're both trying really hard not to, but I don't blame him after how I've reacted, I expect he thought it would go differently. My breathing has levelled out, so steeling myself, I lift my head and open my eyes.

Danny has his elbows on the table and his hands clasped round the back of his head. His forehead is almost resting on the table surface. I clear my throat and his head snaps up, concern in his eyes.

"I'm sorry, I freaked you out," he says straight away in barely more than a whisper.

I close my eyes and laugh. "You didn't freak me out," I assure him. "I kind of freaked myself out."

"How?" he asks nervously.

"Oh I don't know." I sigh, taking a long drink of my rum. "I'm such an idiot. I was just shocked by the whole thing really. It was the last thing I was expecting. Even when we were stood in the bathroom, I still didn't expect you to say you wanted to buy the house." I shake my head. It was obvious really, now that I think about it, I should have twigged on the driveway.

"It's too much, I'm sorry. I should have talked to you about it first. You like your independence, I shouldn't assume that we're just automatically going to buy a house together."

"No, that's not it at all. I love the idea, honestly, it just took me by surprise. Then we were in that walk-in wardrobe and I felt like a fraud. I mean imagine opening those self-lit doors and finding twenty-five of these," I say tugging at my staff shirt. "I mean come on, that place is way out of my league."

"I told you, we can afford it."

"It's not about the money, Danny, I just don't feel worthy."

"Worthy? Are you kidding me?"

"No! I can just picture my crap scattered all over that beautiful bedroom. A cracked floor tile in the bathroom where I dropped my deodorant and my makeup smeared around the sink. I can just see the burn on the kitchen counter where I accidentally put a pan down straight on the work surface without thinking...and the dust, Danny! I'm no housewife. I'm not worthy of it because I would drag it down just by being there! I would feel like a great, lumbering oaf!" I laugh, looking at my outstretched arm. "Do you think the person who designed that bathroom imagined the bathing beauty who would use it would be covered in these?" I ask, holding out my tattooed skin.

Danny smirks and shakes his head. "Are you finished?"

I shrug.

"A house is for living in, for us…just the way we are. You are more than worthy of it, you don't see how it would suit you. You would bring the colour it needs so badly." He says kissing a star on my wrist. "I was excited because I saw it on my own yesterday and I could really see us there. Liv, you have no idea, the sound system is all wired in and there is a projector. Imagine watching a movie on the sofa with me. It will be amazing. I'll get you a cleaner if that's all you're worried about. I had one in LA, I'm no housewife either, trust me. Max has one, we'll use her."

"Max has a cleaner?" I blurt.

Danny laughs. "Okay, um, I was supposed to keep that to myself!" He looks sheepish.

I sip my drink and think about the house again. It was beautiful, perfect really. As bad as I would feel for the house, it would be amazing to live there. A cleaner would help but…this brings me back to my first question. "How could we afford it?" I ask. "Do we need such a big place? Shouldn't we stay here and save some money first? I hardly have any savings, I put it all into here." Panic begins to rise again.

"Let's start again shall we?" Danny says, taking my hand and sitting straighter. "I shouldn't have started this with the punch line, I'm way too impulsive, sorry." He smiles his shy smile, so I try, really try, to relax my nerves and hear him out.

"I was thinking, maybe we could buy a house together, what do you think?" he says, carefully.

I nod slowly. "Okay, it might be worth some consideration." I smile, playing the game… "What did you have in mind?"

"Well I've seen a place on Max's street. It has been completely renovated. It's crazy cool and I really love it," he replies, his boyish grin returns as he pictures the house.

"Sounds expensive, how would we afford it? I've been putting all my money into this place and although we could probably get a mortgage, do we really want such high living expenses when we have virtually none right now?"

He positively beams. "Okay, well…I know how independent you are, but please hear me out." I tense, because I can guess what's coming. "I've been saving for a really long time. I'm an only child and my parents aren't short of a buck so I had no debts from school. I had a cheap apartment and simple lifestyle. My job pays well and while I've slowed down a little and just pick up a few big jobs a year now, I worked my ass off in the beginning. It has been kind of easy to put money away." He shifts in his seat. "And I sold the Shelby," he murmurs. I almost miss it. Then he adds, "and you wouldn't believe for how much."

I blink. "You sold the...Danny, you loved that car!"

"I love you more."

"But..."

"But nothing. I wasn't going to ship her and I'm not going back. Anyway, it turns out she was a great investment. I had my fun and now I have a nice pay out. Win, win. I have enough saved that we would only need a small mortgage to afford it, it would be manageable." He squeezes my hand. "That was until I talked to my dad last night."

I look at his eyes, they are wide with excitement.

"I didn't realise, but Dad sold his parents' place here after Pops passed away about four years ago...and he kept the money aside...for me!" He's giddy now. "We can easily afford it!"

"Whoa!" I breathe. I take a minute, I don't want to kill his buzz...but there is no way he's buying us a house solo.

Nineteen.

Two sounds perfect.

Liv.

"Danny, you know I can't let you use all of your life savings and bring nothing to the table. That's your money."

"It's our money, Liv." He gives me a stern look. "I'm serious."

"God Danny, you don't know what you're saying." I rub my forehead. "There's so much we haven't talked about. You can't just go off on the 'What's mine is yours' speech."

"Liv, think about why I have all that money, why I haven't settled down. Consciously or not, I was holding out for you. That money is our future, alone I don't need it. Without you I…I want to share it with you, that's it. Sorry, but like it or not, what's mine IS yours." He runs his thumb across my knuckles.

I watch him carefully, he's so serious, I almost want to laugh. I'm really trying to loosen up, but this..?

"I can't leave the money sitting there, it's too much, I need to invest it in something. A house is a reasonable investment isn't it?" He thinks for a minute. "If we stayed here forever, I would be living in a house you own. I want to have a home with both our names on the deeds. I want to do this for us, I've waited half my life for an 'us' to do it for." He studies his fingers, then looks up at me and seems more sure of himself. "Besides, how would we manage in the flat with a baby?"

My heart misses a beat. "I…I thought…I…I didn't know if that's what you wanted anymore." I manage to stutter out.

"Of course it's what I still want, you goof!" his shy smile reappearing. Then it falls. "Unless you've changed your mind."

I shake my head slowly, my own shy smile growing.

"Good. So you see why we need the extra rooms?"

"But four?"

Danny laughs. "Maybe two. We can keep the other rooms for Jen and your sister when they visit." He looks at me with such hope.

"Two sounds perfect." I smile. Danny wraps his fingers into mine and we sit quietly, digesting this new turn in the rollercoaster of our lives.

"Before, in LA..." Danny interrupts, "...when we talked about, you know, a family." He fidgets. "We said soon."

"Yeah, we did," I reply, feeling the flutter of nerves in my stomach begin again.

"That was almost four months ago." He hesitates. "So...is now too soon?"

My heads starts to shake slowly, involuntarily, before I even really process it. "Not really," I admit, although I've tried not to think about it too much.

"I was thinking now that you're getting better...I mean your body can probably spare the calcium." He smiles.

"Is that what you were waiting for?" I laugh.

"Yeah, well, I guess. I would have suggested it sooner, but your bones were healing. I figured it could wait."

"And now?"

"Now...I badly want to get you pregnant."

A thrill shoots through me and I'm sure my cheeks flush.

"Whenever you're ready, that is." He adds.

"I'm ready." And like that, I know I am. I want it all with him. I know I've forced myself not to hope too much, but this isn't a vain hope. It's being offered, something tangible and it makes me so happy. He still hasn't mentioned marriage, which feels okay with me. I tried not to think too much about that either, but the future together and a family, that is all I ever wanted with him. Marriage wouldn't make us complete, but I know a baby would.

"So will you let me buy us a house?" he pleads.

I turn to face him again. His eyes fixed on me in anticipation. He wants this so much. He wants to be the provider. Even my deepest urges to resist this can't deny him. "Okay." I nod taking his hand again. "But, you have to accept that it works both ways. What is mine is yours too." His smile is the most perfect I've ever seen.

He pulls at my hands until I lift up out of my seat and fall into his lap.

"I love you so much." He breathes into my ear as his arms hold me tight. A shiver runs down my spine leaving all of my hairs standing on end. If this is all it takes to see that expression on his face, he can buy all the houses he likes and I'll fill them with children. My stomach flips at this thought. It's primal and almost against everything I thought I believed, but I want so badly to be pregnant for this man.

He sighs long and loud. "You have no idea how happy you've just made me."

"I think I do. I feel the same way." I grin. A contented silence seems to fall on us. My thoughts wander to us in that glossy house. I'm not, well, glossy in the slightest, but I can envisage how it could accommodate my individuality…OUR individuality. I would enjoy the challenge.

"We can look at other houses if you like." Danny interrupts my thoughts.

"I was just starting to picture us there." I smirk.

Danny laughs. "Sometimes I don't know which way is up when I'm with you."

"That's how I like it. So are you going to tell me how much it costs?"

I pull back from Danny in shock, I can't believe a car could sell for so much money and I can't believe what he has saved. My shock deepens when I hear the price of the house, but once he explains that his inheritance from his grandparents' house will pay for almost half and he can more than cover the rest, I begin to relax. It will take some time for me to be fully at ease with a free ride, but he makes a compelling argument. Even after forking out for his ambitious furnishing plans, he will still have savings, which makes me feel better. All he wants is to make us a comfortable home and this will definitely be that.

"There's no chain, it could be ours in a few weeks." He nuzzles into my neck, inhaling deeply, then his lips make contact with the sensitive skin there. I begin to wonder if he wants to get started on the baby thing right away. "I need to come off the pill," I say, suddenly realising it was out loud.

He nods, not breaking contact with his lips as his fingers travel up my leg. I exhale when his tongue runs over my earlobe, rolling my head backwards. I manage to suppress my moan, remembering where we are.

"Danny...please." Although even I can't tell if I'm asking him to cut out it because we are at work or for the love of God take me right here.

He fortunately interprets the former and reluctantly withdraws his exploring mouth. Inhaling, then exhaling deeply to gain his composure, Danny seems to come back to earth. I go to stand up, but he grabs me back. "Give me a minute," he murmurs, then I feel the full extent of his arousal press against me.

"Oh!" I giggle, "Okay."

"It's your fault."

"How?"

"Apart from being the most beautiful girl a lucky bastard like me has ever seen you mean?" He grins. "You're going to stop taking the pill."

"And that's sexy, how?"

A lascivious look flashes across his face. "You're going to let me get you pregnant. Everything about that is sexy."

I shake my head in amusement, as I notice Max approaching us.

"Am I interrupting?" he asks, sitting before we answer. "You two look pleased with yourselves."

I catch Danny flashing him a look that says 'she went for it'. Max laughs when they realise I've rumbled them. "Am I always the last to know everything?" I moan.

"Charlie told me about the house," Danny clarifies. "It wasn't a conspiracy."

Chuckling, Max leans over to squeeze my knee. "So are we going to be neighbours?"

"Yeah," I laugh, "so we'll need the number of your cleaning lady!"

Max's face falls and he shoots daggers at Danny.

"Sorry man, it just sipped out!"

"Great, thanks." Max Laughs.

"Oh come on. I've lived with you remember. I didn't think YOU kept that place in order. I thought you had Charlie well trained!" I joke. "Your secret is safe with me."

"Charming!" Max says, standing. "I'm not hanging around here to be insulted by you. I'll leave you to your little moment."

As Max walks away, I turn back to Danny. "Now where were we?"

"I think we should save that for later," he says regretfully.

I raise my eyebrows. "Or we could just take it somewhere more private."

I groan as Danny presses into me. His hands planted on the floor either side of my head. We almost made it to the bedroom, but lust overcame us just inside the front door.

"Oh!" I gasp as his mouth closes over my nipple, just as his full length fills me once more. I run my hands over his back, scratching slightly with my nails. One of my arms is still in the sleeve of my top. My bra is yanked down to reveal my eager breasts and my jeans still cling to an ankle. Danny's are merely pushed down to his thighs in our hurry, although I did manage to rip off his t-shirt.

The soft bare skin against me reminds me of our purpose. I know I'm not going to get pregnant today, I've already taken my pill this morning, but it's symbolic of our decision. His flesh naked inside me feels more poignant than ever before and my senses seem heightened to the feel of him.

Danny is different as well. He seems to possess me as he stakes his claim on my body. Moving above me with such a purpose, he whispers, "God, yes." He drops to one elbow beside me, deepening our connection and offering me the friction I crave. Once his weight is supported, his other hand strokes through my hair, grasping through it to bring my face close to his. Our lips brush and we share ragged breaths as his thrusts become sharper, deeper.

I choke out a fresh moan, certain that I'm seconds away from an earth-shattering orgasm and Danny's lips press against mine. Our staccato breaths are more pronounced as our tongues complete our total connection to one another and Danny's muted cries come, unusually for him, with every stoke.

I always find it hard not being vocal while Danny makes love to me, but the intensity of this experience and the sounds Danny is making against my lips make it worse than usual. I would be screaming if I wasn't under the expert control of his tongue. However, the strangled sounds and the heavy, sharp breaths, sound almost animal and it's enough to send me spiralling as he drives into me one last, wonderful time.

He breaks contact with my lips to free his final sounds. "Liv…God…I love you."

"I love you too." I gasp, fighting for air as my climax grips me. "I love you…I love you…I love you." I whisper again and again, coming back to earth.

Danny showers my face with gentle kisses until he finally settles once more on my lips. They willingly part, inviting him in as I wrap my arms around him.

Once sanity has returned, I lift my hand to brush moisture from my forehead and giggle at the sight of my clothes hanging off my arm. "Look at us!"

Danny has a cursory glance and drops his head onto my chest, laughing. "What did you expect? I've dreamed of doing this for…ever."

"You know I'm not actually going to get pregnant today don't you?"

He shrugs. "Doesn't hurt to practice."

Danny is stood by the window in the living room wearing only his jeans. I stare at his immaculate body while I listen to his conversation. He's telling Jen about the house and I smile fondly at his enthusiasm. His smile fades slightly and I wonder why. His voice lowers as he rubs his forehead and then rolls his head to relieve the tension in his neck. Whatever it is they're discussing is making him stressed and I want to go over to him and ease his discomfort with my thumbs. But I feel like I would be intruding.

I wander back into the bedroom, pick up a hair elastic and sweep my damp hair up in a ponytail. Finding a fresh shirt in the wardrobe, I pull it on and reapply my eye makeup. It's going to be so obvious that we just came up here for a quickie!

Picking up our towels from the floor, I drop them into the laundry basket. Then I notice the contents of the bin beside it. Obviously, while Danny was dressing, he decided to trash my pills, they're in the bin, along with the other two months' supply from my bedside drawer. I grin stupidly. I love it when he calls the shots! Then I cringe at what I've become. Oh well, I guess this is happiness.

Danny's warm arms slip around me, his lips press into my shoulder. He peers over my shoulder into the bin. "I didn't think you'd need them anymore."

I simply smile and turn slightly to kiss his tattooed shoulder. Unable to resist, I sink my teeth slightly into his skin. Danny sucks in a sharp breath at the contact. "Come on," he says. "Let's go back to work." His voice is strained and I can tell it's a struggle not to start undressing me again. He forces himself away from me and shoves a work t-shirt over his head.

"Jen says hi," he says, lacing up his Converse.

I ruffle his hair as I pass him. "Everything okay?" I ask casually. "You looked stressed when you were talking to Jen, problems at home?"

He puffs. "This is my home," he says firmly.

"I know, sorry," I say, realising my mistake. "So what's up?'

He sighs. "Nothing really."

I realise straight away that this is to do with baby stuff. "How is it going with them? You know, when I...left." I hesitate to bring it up, but we have to move on. "They'd had tests, but they weren't really sure what they'd do."

Danny looks up at me and gives me a tight smile. "They're okay. Jen's on meds to figure out her cycle, or whatever. It's fixed her right up." He drifts off deep in thought.

I sit on the bed beside him, watching him. He is oblivious, I can tell he's there with Jen. I know it's hard for him being away from her.

After a minute, I take his hand and he comes back to me. "Sorry. I just..." he trails off again.

"You want to help her."

Danny's eyes widen. "I..."

"Danny, it's okay, you can talk to me about it."

"Really?" he asks, stunned.

"Really. It was obvious to me in LA that you were thinking about it. But it hasn't come up since."

He rubs his head again. "It's complicated."

"Well yeah. But not impossible."

He shakes his head and the corner of his mouth turns up into a reluctant smile. "Can I really talk to you about this?"

"You can talk to me about anything, you know that."

"Okay," he says looking relieved and he turns to face me, holding my hands.

"So when they first started thinking that they were having trouble, the doctors said they should just keep trying. But Jen started looking at all the different possibilities. I told her to quit it, but she can't help herself. She tortured herself with every possibility, so I naturally learned a fair bit along with her. Obviously we didn't know what their problem would turn out to be, but seeing it have such an effect on her, I promised myself that if it was a problem I could help with, I would." He pauses, thinking.

"So that night when you found out that they would need a sperm donor..." I prompt.

"Well I was all different by then. I had you." He lifts one of my hands to his lips.

"Different?"

"Well yeah, I was starting a new life, I wasn't the single guy that I thought I'd be when the time came."

"You didn't think you could discuss it with me?"

"It's a big ask, Liv. Oh honey, before we have our happy ever after, you don't mind if I impregnate my best friend do you?" he chuckles. "No way."

"But we didn't get to the happy ever after bit did we?"

"No, and that's where it gets complicated," he says. "See, after you left..." He swallows hard and thinks about whether or not to go on, I nod, urging him. "I wanted to put you behind me because I thought you bailed on us. I needed something to focus on. So I offered to be their sperm donor." He sighs. "They we were surprisingly on board, but I made them have a serious think about it first."

I listen patiently. "Then Jen told me that they wanted to go ahead...but only if I talked to you." He grimaces. "We had quite a fight. She had tried everything else to get me to call you and apparently she wasn't above emotional blackmail. She was convinced you must have had a good reason for leaving and she told me she couldn't take my first child if I still had a chance with you. She said if you really left because you didn't want me anymore, she would never mention it again, but if I wanted her to consider my offer I had to try. They would only go through with it if we were back on the right track, or if I was single for good." He exhales as he remembers the scenario. "That's when I called Max and found out about Brooke...that's when you fell. By the next day I was here. I haven't talked to Jen about it since."

"How do you feel about it now?"

"Everything is different now. I have you. We are going to start a family."

"Is it the distance? Did you see yourself being more involved?"

"No, I only ever wanted to be Uncle Danny. It's not that. It's us. I don't want anything getting in between us. I just wish helping them could be simpler, less significant, you know?"

"I know, but what you have offered to do is huge."

"Which is why I won't do it." He sighs. "Jen understands. I just wish I didn't feel so bad. Especially now that we are trying to make a baby. How will I tell her when that happens?" I watch him imagine that conversation in his head, it pains him.

"I understand what it is to love someone like you love her. Don't forget that," I say stroking his fingers. "I would want to help Max." I readjust my grip on him so that his hands are in mine and I dip my head to establish eye contact. "You should do it."

His face slowly changes from pained, to bemused and finally settles on amazed. "Why are you so wonderful?"

I laugh. "I just want you to be happy, I get why this is so important to you."

"But they won't have any trouble picking another donor. It would be less complicated for everyone." He argues.

"Now that you're here though, wouldn't you like that tie to them? We are kind of a family already. It doesn't make it that much more fucked up! You're essentially married to her anyway. You give yourself to her emotionally and I have no problem with that because I have it too. We healed ourselves by replacing each other, in a way that lots of people wouldn't understand. But now that we've found each other again, we are more than just us two...Do it. Make them happy, because by doing that you'll make us happy. I couldn't stand it if we had a baby and I kept seeing that pained look on your face, because you felt guilty."

Danny assesses me, looking for some sort of crack in me that shows I'm just saying this to do the right thing. There isn't one, I truly mean this. I want him to do it. When he is sure, he grabs me in his arms and squeezes me tight. "Thank you," he whispers and I squeeze him back.

Twenty.

Happy birthday, baby.

Liv.

Okay, where is he now? I'm starting to get a little ticked off. Every time I turn around these days Danny has nipped off somewhere. What is worse is he keeps taking Max with him. I don't mind sharing, but it's getting ridiculous. Ever since our offer was accepted on the house, he has been running around like a blue-arsed fly. I don't even know what he gets up to. It's an hour here, a couple there, but it's every day. If he's picking stuff for the house, I'd like to be involved. If he's meeting the solicitor, I should be there…If he's freaking out, I should know!

He is fidgety, even in the evenings, he is constantly checking emails and sending texts. He's not troubled, he seems happy and he's being really attentive too. Our 'baby practice' is going well, he can't keep his hands off me. If I'm not carrying triplets right now, I'd be really surprised! I'm not, by the way. But we are working on it. I'm impressed with myself for not thinking the worst. The potential meaning of the fact that he is missing a lot, sending private texts and being overly attentive in the bedroom, isn't lost on me. But I have no doubts this time, it isn't even a consideration. Danny is all mine and mine alone. I would just like to know what he is up to.

I run into Max locking up the store room. He looks really guilty.

"Hey, where's Danny," I ask, pretending not to notice. I cut him a little slack today, it's my thirtieth birthday tomorrow and they may well be planning something. That doesn't account for almost a month of this weirdness, but I'll let it go today.

"Parking the car, I think." He shrugs.

"Oh." I mutter turning away. I catch Max's look of 'Phew-that-was-close' and I round on him. "I will get to the bottom of whatever it is you two are up to!" He pulls a face, but says nothing and I walk away feeling satisfied. I just wanted to put the wind up him, not ruin a surprise.

Danny is walking through the back door when I cross the garden. He looks up from his phone and grins, shoving it deep in his pocket.

"I've been looking for you again!"

"Sorry, I had to go out, what's up?" he says casually as he wraps me up in his arms, distracting me with a deep kiss. This is what keeps happening. If I show any interest in what he's up to I get the disarming, full-mega-watt Danny.

"My mum's here, she wants to take me out for the day. I just wanted to let you know."

He grins. "Perfect. Have fun." He kisses the end of my nose and lets me go.

Huh! I think as I walk away, nice, I'll miss you too! I grab my bag and find Mum and Connie chatting in the diner. It's nice that she has come up to see me for my birthday. I haven't really seen her much since I've been back to almost normal. She is so sweet coming today so that I can have tomorrow with Danny.

"Okay, we can go." I huff as I approach them.

"Everything alright darling?"

"Oh, yeah," I say shaking my head to let her know it's nothing really. "Danny is just very distracted with the house and stuff. I know he and Max are up to something, it's probably my birthday present. But I'm hoping he will come back to me once this is all done." I sigh. I haven't told her he is also planning to fly to LA in a few weeks to donate sperm for Jen and Scott. He hasn't even told them yet. Apparently he just wants to sort the house out first, but it sounds like an excuse to me. I think he's leaving it to sink in a bit, to test how I really feel. But I know how I feel won't change. I fully support him in wanting to do this and when he goes,

I'm going to go with him to prove it.

Mum smirks. "Don't be on his case about your birthday. You know he will want to spoil you rotten. Don't you dare ruin it for him."

"I won't, Mum."

I feel a tiny bit tipsy when I get home. Mum and Connie took me to a spa as a birthday treat. We had afternoon tea with champagne and then we ordered more bubbly and sat around by the pool lazily, knocking it back. I've had a full top-to-toe and I feel like I'm floating. Mum went to town treating me and after having the works, they insisted we all have our hair done. I feel a bit overdone for a night on the sofa with Danny, especially as I return home to an empty flat. I was expecting Danny to be home, but he's obviously in the bar. I turn back around to go downstairs and find him, when my attention goes to the door.

Hanging on the back of the door is a garment bag with an envelope attached. Written on the envelope is my name in Danny's writing. I reach for it slowly, not sure if I should have seen this before tomorrow. He surely wouldn't have left it here if I wasn't. I open the envelope and pull out a note on heavy white paper.

Liv,

I hope you had a wonderful time at the spa, you should be feeling pampered and relaxed. I know I've been very distracted lately and I want to make it up to you.

Please put on this dress and meet me in the garden at 7pm.

Danny x

I read it again. Did Danny ask Mum and Connie to take me out today? Have I been played? Oh well, I had a great time and now Danny has bought me a dress and wants me to meet him. I wonder what he's got in store? I carefully slide the zip down, revealing a flash of deep-purple silk. I gasp. The colour is beautiful.

I slide the cover off the dress and step back to admire it. It's a fifties-style dress. Knee length, big skirt and nipped in at the waist with a belt made from the same fabric. It's beautiful. The neckline at the front and back are deep V's and I just know it's going to suit me before I even try it. Danny is a genius!

I take the hanger off the door and go into the bedroom, checking my watch. I have half an hour and butterflies are forming in my stomach. I try to concentrate on what I have to do, instead of thinking about what is in store for me.

My hair is loose and falling in shiny waves thanks to the expensive blow dry, but this dress demands an up-do. I twist and pin and artfully arrange it so that the glossy tendrils are piled loosely on top of my head. Next I apply my usual smoky eye makeup and a hint of deep pink lip gloss, then I seek out my sexiest underwear, grateful that I showered at the spa as I slip it on. I pull out my glittery, beaded black ballet pumps. I sigh that I can't wear the heels this dress probably deserves, but I hated them anyway and I'm not taking the chance now. Danny will understand.

With only a couple of minutes to go, I slide the zip up the side of the dress and fasten the belt. I turn to the mirror and freeze. This dress is perfect, just perfect. I bite back a tear thinking how lucky I am that he loves me so much. Then without another thought, I go to him.

The diner is pretty deserted when I open my door, but I'm too anxious to care. Opening the staff door to the garden I see Danny. I feel a thrill. He is beautiful. I take him in quickly as I walk towards him, he's wearing dark grey trousers and a matching waistcoat, shirt sleeves are rolled up and his tie is perfect. His hair is kind of slicked over in a style he doesn't normally wear, he looks like a casual movie star. I swell with fondness when I notice his black Converse. It's these touches that make us perfect together, the fact that even dressing up doesn't have to mean selling out.

He doesn't take his eyes from mine, but I'm momentarily distracted by movement beside him as I round the corner into the garden. Max is there, so is my mum. It's then that I notice that know every single face in the crowd filling the garden. I gasp and step back behind the protective wall of the diner, my hand goes to my mouth and my eyes return to Danny.

He beams at me. Chuckling to himself, he steps forward and takes my hands. "It's okay," he whispers. Pulling me gently out into the open again. The crowd erupts into a cheer as he pulls me tight to his chest. I can't believe this, a surprise party!

"You look beautiful," Danny says tenderly against my ear.

I blush. "Thank you for the dress," I reply. "What's going on?" I look to his face. He looks shy and happy at the same time. He is hoping I like this surprise, but he secretly already knows I will.

"Surprise!" He laughs as he releases me and turns me to see everyone that's here.

My mum rushes forward and squeezes me. "Surprise darling," she says with a knowing smile. Dave joins her, hugging both of us as I start to feel overwhelmed. Over her shoulder I see Grace, holding Mia and Andy clinging onto Matty's little hand. I gasp and look back at Danny in disbelief.

The next few minutes are a blur as I hug my sister, kiss my way through the rest of my family and friends and then find that Danny's parents, and Jen and Scott are also here. I didn't realise I was crying until Max slips a tissue into my hand. This is completely overwhelming, what are they all doing here? I think I say that out loud to a few people, but no one really offers me an explanation. Then I'm passed back to Danny.

"What is everyone doing here?" I ask again, while Danny catches a stray tear with a fresh tissue.

"They came to see you." He soothes. "Do you need a minute?" A glass of champagne is put in my hand by someone.

I need a week, I think to myself. But I shake my head. I breathe in deeply and let it out in a long, juddery whoosh.

"Okay," he says, taking my hand. "Come with me."

What I didn't notice in the chaos and confusion, is that our modular stage that we have in the bar for live music, has been set up in the garden. Danny leads me onto it and I follow in a daze. I turn and gasp again when I see just how many people there are.

Danny casually takes a microphone from its stand and flicks it on.

"Good evening everyone," he says, causing a hush to fall over the crowd. "Thank you all for coming and for helping me keep this secret."

He laughs. "Liv is not an easy person to hide something like this from, so well done for all the lies, but remember it's not over yet!" Laughter ripples through the garden. I frown at that, but Danny carries on. Turning to me, he smiles. "Liv," he says raising my hand to his lips. "You take my breath away." He almost whispers. He says it just for me, but shares the thought with everyone via the microphone. Lots of people cheer and I hear a few whoops and words of agreement. I'm not shy, but this is beyond doubt the most embarrassed I've ever felt and yet standing here with Danny, I don't want this moment to end.

"Happy birthday, baby." Once again the crowd erupts as Danny picks me up and turns me around, kissing me briefly as he returns me to the floor waiting for everyone to settle down. He continues. "This has been the best and worst year of my life. I started the year thinking it would be just like every other…Without you." He sighs as fresh tears spring from my eyes. "Then a surprise message from a good friend," he smiles down at Connie, "changed everything." He swallows back his own emotion. "From the very first time I talked to you again, I knew my life was never going to be the same. I've always loved you."

"I love you too," I sob. Some 'ah's' come from around us.

Danny steps over to Jen at the side of the small stage and Jen hands him something. When he turns back to me I see it's the crumpled jewellery bag from his kitchen in LA. I watch him hold up the bag. "Remember this?"

I nod. Unsure of its significance now and wary of its connection to that horrible day.

He looks into my eyes. "I asked everyone to come here today, to shock you into silence so that I could finally get these words out." He laughs. "I've waited a long time for this moment, I hope it's third time lucky!" He pulls something small from the bag. I watch it fall and then look back to him in time to see him sink to one knee. I gasp and my hands fly up to my mouth.

Steadying himself with a long breath, he finally speaks. "Liv," he says sincerely. "You are the most beautiful, vibrant person I've ever known. I've loved you since I was six years old and I know I'm never going to stop, so please…will you marry me?" Then he opens the tiny box in his hand and shows me the most amazing ring I've ever seen.

"Yes!" I whisper. His eyes fill with tears and he jumps up to hold me. His lips press against mine and then several other places in the chaotic, emotional embrace. He picks me up again and holds me so tight. "Yes?" he whispers in my ear. Checking he heard me correctly.

"Yes," I repeat, louder. I'm dizzy now and no longer aware of my surroundings. "Yes!"

Once again the place erupts, but this time the sound continues, whistles can be heard and I'm aware of some crying too. I know I am and Danny is having real trouble keeping it together. He sets me down once more and takes half a step back to get the ring, which he slides onto my finger. Oh my God, it's perfect, it's grey, or at least it looks it in this light, its beautiful and unusual, and huge! We both stare at it on my finger. I don't know what to say, my hold on my senses left the building a while ago. I throw my arms around Danny's neck.

"Thank you," I whisper.

We descend the steps and into the waiting arms of first Jen who is sobbing, followed by Max, who is also very emotional. Then just as overwhelmingly as the first time, almost everyone here comes to greet us, offering their congratulations. I've no idea how long this takes but at some point a strong rum and Coke finds its way into my hand, the other hand never leaves Danny's. He holds onto me like I'm oxygen. I've felt his love for me before and it was nothing like this, it's as if he is finally free to show how he really feels, no holding back.

After some time talking to everyone, Danny turns to me and pulls me close. "Are you ok?" he asks.

I smile, shivering but not from cold. "I'm perfect."

"That dress looks amazing on you." He grins.

I look down. "I love it, Danny, thank you so much."

"And this does too," he says, lifting my left hand to his lips and kissing the ring on my finger. He sighs with contentment and holds me close, then I feel him laugh to himself. "There is one other thing," he says and takes my hand again, pulling me once more up to the stage. I'm bemused, how can there be more?

"Um, ladies and gentlemen," he says into the microphone, waiting for the hush to fall. "As you know, there is just one more thing. Thank you all so much for keeping this secret for me." He turns and grins at me. "I suppose I should tell my fiancé!"

I've no idea what is going on as I just stare at Danny, helplessly.

"As you can imagine," he explains, "it wasn't easy getting everyone together in one place at the same time." He waves a hand at Jen and his parents in particular. "So doing it twice would be damned near impossible."

I nod as if I understand but I'm so confused.

"So I was hoping you would do me the honor of marrying me..." I frown, I've already agreed to that. He looks worried as he says the next word. "...Tomorrow?"

I blink. "Tomorrow?"

"Tomorrow."

"I...But..." There are no words.

"Do you trust me?" he asks close to my ear.

I nod, this I'm certain of, now more than ever. "But...how?"

"It's all taken care of." He grins at Max. "Everything is in place. All you have to do is say yes."

I look at Max. He gives me the thumbs up. I realise that this is what they've been up to for weeks, in secret, working hard on this whole plan. I couldn't deny them this, either of them. "Of course I will," I say. Danny once again swamps me in his relieved embrace.

"She said yes everyone," he says triumphantly to the crown when he lets me go. "You are all officially invited!"

We once again dismount the stairs to rapturous applause, it's getting a bit embarrassing. I have a million questions and before anything else comes up, I need a word with my husband-to-be. I get goose bumps just thinking that he is so soon to be my husband. But, intent on finding answers, I grip his hand tightly and pull him towards the back of the diner. Danny smirks as I punch in the code to the flat and lets me tug him through the door, misunderstanding my intentions.

Once in the relatively tranquil environment of the hall, I sink to the bottom stair, rubbing my head with my fingers, just taking a minute to readjust to all this new information.

"Liv?" Danny says. I take a deep breath, there is so much to ask I don't know where to start and I'm really enjoying the peace for a minute.

"What's wrong?" Danny drops to his knees in front of me. I'm still trying to formulate a coherent sentence in my head when he cuts in again, his tone more like panic now. "Liv, no, please…"

My eyes shoot to his in alarm, "What?" I ask, confused.

"Don't back out now," he says quietly. "It'll kill me."

"I'm not backing out!" I'm stunned that he would think I could.

"But you look like you're getting ready to tell me something really awful."

"No! Not at all. I have so many questions and I just wanted a minute alone with you that's all." I stroke the side of his face. "I'm just a bit overwhelmed, it's a lot to process."

"You're not going to tell me it's off?"

"No way." I frown. I suppose I did act a bit like that. "Sorry if I scared you, but it's so calm out here I just shut down for a second." I grab his hands. "I'm so happy, honestly."

He studies me, sagging with relief once he sees the sincerity in my eyes. "I did it again didn't I?" He sighs, joining me on the step.

"Did what exactly?"

"Blindsided you."

"It's becoming a habit, but I love you for it."

"I'm sorry, I just get so caught up in how to show you just how much I love you."

"You can stop now." I laugh. "I believe you!"

He nods solemnly. "Do you still want to marry me?" he asks, his voice so small.

"More than anything." I grin and look at my ring. "This is so beautiful." It's grey, I can see it properly now. I've never seen anything like it, I think that was probably the point. I never really imagined this milestone in my life, because I was nonplussed about all the usual girlie details. I couldn't see myself picking table centres and things. But if Danny's choice of ring is anything to go by, I think the wedding is in safe hands.

Danny runs his thumb across the ring. "I knew it was for you the minute I saw it."

"When did you buy it?"

"In LA. I was going to give it to you at the party the night it all fell apart."

"So I've left you hanging with a ring in your pocket...twice?" I sigh and touch my thumb to the tiny band on my right hand.

He regretfully nods.

"I'm so sorry."

"Hey, it's done now. We made it," he says softly. "Just marry me tomorrow and I swear we can just get on with our lives. No more drama."

"Are you sure?" I laugh.

"Positive."

"I love you so much," I say touching his newly styled hair. "I like this a lot," I tell him, leaning forward to kiss him. I pause before our lips touch. "You look lovely tonight."

His sharp intake of breath as our lips meet fires up my insides.

"You look amazing," he murmurs.

"You picked the dress. It's perfect. Thank you." I glance down at the fabric and realise with a smile that the colour matches my nails. I suspect that this was carefully orchestrated and it explains my mother's enthusiasm for the shade when she was urging me to get my fingernails and toenails painted today.

"I'm glad you think I picked well." He smiles. "Because I've picked you one out for tomorrow too."

I giggle. "That answers one of my questions."

"I know." He smirks. "This must be killing you!"

I hang my head in shame.

"Do you think you could not ask me? Just trust that I've thought of everything."

I take a deep breath, hoping I can do what he has asked. "I'll try."

"Tomorrow is going to be…just…it's so 'us', Liv. I can't wait for you to see it." His smile is infectious.

"Where is it?" I ask, not thinking. Then I clap my hand over my mouth, realising my mistake. Danny gives me a raised eyebrow in disapproval. "Sorry," I whisper.

He shakes his head, laughing. "Just one thing," he asks. "I don't know how you want to do this. I was going to stay at Max's and have one of the girls hang here with you. You know, if you want to do the whole 'not seeing each other before the wedding' thing. But if that doesn't matter to you, I could stay here. Your call."

"I suppose, we should do this properly."

"Really?" He chokes, trying to mask his disappointment.

"No, not really you fool!" I laugh. "Since when have I been the traditional type? Stay with me, please."

"Wow, that would have made tonight the hardest night of my life!" He breathes a huge sigh of relief, but his desire shows through the bravado.

"I didn't say I'd let you touch me," I whisper, leaning in to kiss him.

"We'll see," he replies, grabbing the back of my neck and closing the distance. I groan as he claims what is his. Me.

Just then the door opens. "Oh! There you are!" Max exclaims. "People are looking for you. You'd better pack that in and get out here."

I wipe my lip gloss off Danny's mouth and smile up at Max.

"Everything okay?" he asks.

"Everything is perfect," I reply.

Twenty-one.

Awkward boner.

Liv.

The delicious memory of last night makes me tingle before I open my eyes. In my half-sleep state I can almost still feel Danny's hands all over me. I shudder remembering how he took me beyond anything I'd ever experienced before. I reach out for him now and find the bed empty. That's when I realise with a start that today is my wedding day. My eyes fly open and I scan the room, but I'm alone. A girlish giggle drifts in to me from the living room and I notice other voices too.

My bedroom door is closed, which it definitely wasn't when I fell asleep, but it's a good thing because under the covers, I'm naked. I sit up in a slight panic about who is out there and where Danny could be, when my foot bumps a black box at the end of my bed. I pull it onto my lap and shake my head. The box is tied with deep-purple ribbon and a card is tucked under the bow. Already I know that today will be full of surprises, so I relax and go with it. Pulling out the familiar white card, I smile with excitement at Danny's message.

To my beautiful fiancé (This is my one and only chance to say that to you!)

Happy 30th birthday!

I'm sorry I can't be there with you. I have things to attend to, but we will be together soon, I promise.

I know I owe you a Bachelorette Party (Hen Night I think you'd call it) but this is the best I could do…Please get up and wear what's in the box. Your bridal birthday breakfast awaits!

You must be itching to know about today, so I'll tell you what's happening…You are going to become my wife!

Sorry, but that's all you're getting for now, except that I will see you at 2pm.

Try not to be too late, I want to start my life with you as soon as possible.

I love you,

D x

I pull the ribbon off the box and lift off the lid. Under the tissue I find a silk camisole and French knicker set edged with lace and a silk robe, in the seemingly obligatory purple that I now realise will be a feature of today. I smile at the thought of Danny choosing this and pull the covers back to put it on. I turn to look at myself in the mirror, Danny will love this, so I quickly snap myself with my phone camera and text him the shot with the message 'Thank you x'. I put my hair up in a ponytail, then finally tying the sash on my robe, I'm ready to face whatever waits for me on the other side of the door.

I open the door and gasp. It's a proper girlie affair – almost! Mum, Grace, Connie, Jen, Danny's mum, Pam, and, of course, Max are all milling around drinking champagne along with Ali and Carla, who are arranging a breakfast buffet on the table. I smell coffee and waffles. It all looks amazing. There are fresh flowers, like the first ones Danny gave me, which makes me smile. I cover my mouth with my hands while I take it all in. Max notices I'm up and grins stupidly as he comes towards me.

"Morning chickadee," he says and plants a kiss on the top of my head. I slip my arms around his waist and squeeze him tight, I'm so glad he's here. I'm overwhelmed already, but I just need to get used to it. From here on, everything that happens today is going to blow me away, I need to stop reeling from each thing and just enjoy. I'm greeted by everyone else in my little party, with birthday wishes and wedding day excitement. Then, before I've time to think, I'm ordered into the shower before breakfast is ready.

When I slip back into my gift from Danny, I grin and check my phone.

'Happy birthday baby! That just made my day, but no more, I just had an awkward boner! X'

Then it buzzes again.

'I love you x'

I hug my phone, I wish he was here. With a towel wrapped around my hair, I join everyone in the living room. Since I've been gone breakfast is ready and I pick up a strawberry and a glass of champagne and wander around to a seat on the other side of the table. Jen is helping herself to a waffle and then she passes them to me. I feel a little shy as I realise that although I know her like she is part of Danny, I've never been with her without Danny. It's fine, but strange.

"Thanks for coming," I say to her as I pour syrup on my waffle.

"Like we were going to miss this!" She smiles.

"No, I mean this morning, it means a lot that you're here."

She shrugs. "It means a lot to be here," she says touching my arm.

I giggle. "I feel like you should be giving Danny away or something."

She smiles and shakes her head. "He has always been yours, trust me."

Grace joins us and I realise quickly that they have obviously met properly already and seem to be friends. It's satisfying to know that our combined family in LA are forming connections, because it will make visiting all the more fulfilling if we can all spend time together rather than splitting it between them.

"So is anyone going to tell me anything?" I ask.

Jen and Grace exchange glances. "Our lips are sealed," Grace says and giggles.

"Oh come on! You must be able to tell me something. How long have you been here?"

"We got in yesterday," says Jen.

"We've been at Mum's since Wednesday," says Grace.

"Where are you all staying?"

"Connie's," replies Grace. "Mum and Dave too."

"And Max and Charlie are graciously putting us up. Along with Danny's parents," she says, nodding at Max in appreciation.

The mums and Connie are chatting away excitedly and a strange thrill goes through me again. I keep remembering it's my wedding day! I look down at my beautiful engagement ring.

Grace sees me looking at it and takes my hand to inspect it herself. "I couldn't really see it in the light last night," he says, eyeing it greedily. "That's a hell of a diamond...It's a diamond isn't it?"

The thought hadn't occurred to me, I certainly didn't ask Danny. I just thought it was beautiful. I shrug in response, it doesn't matter to me what it is.

"It is," interjects Jen. "It's very rare." She gives us a knowing smile that says she was with him when he chose it. I smile back warmly, conveying my appreciation.

"And what about you?" I ask Max across the table. "Can I assume you've had a hand in all this?"

He holds up his hands in surrender. "I was just the errand boy, it's all Danny. You'll be impressed, I promise. I was."

"Does everyone but me know what's going to happen today?" I ask, feeling the frustration bubbling up.

"I think only Danny holds all the cards," Jen laughs. "Max is the deputy, we all have our instructions." She squeezes my arm. "It's going to be fun!"

Then, after a relaxed breakfast, Suzie, my usual hairdresser, arrives to do my hair and help everyone else with theirs. Danny has thought of everything. We discuss options briefly, but as I don't yet know what my dress looks like I can't really comment, so I'm led by Max and my sister and go with a relaxed up-do. I'm glad I don't have to have something severe, it hints at a relaxed atmosphere for the day. I have to take these little tit-bits, they are the only clues I get.

My hair looks beautiful, I'm really pleased with it. While Jen and Grace are deciding on their hairstyles, I go into my bedroom and close the door. I just want five minutes to myself. I feel a bit spacey, it's probably just nerves. I don't feel nervous about forever, I just feel nervous that I don't know what's coming. But as Danny's note said, what is coming is that I'm going to finish the day as Mrs Morgan. I don't really need to know anything else.

I get all my makeup out and sit at my little dressing table. I stare at myself in the mirror for a long time. I can't believe I'm here. This is all so much to get my head around. We have never discussed marriage, like never! We both want a family, we have sorted all of that out, but I never thought all of this meant anything to Danny. I honestly thought after we agreed to try for a baby, that he would have said something if he wanted to do this. He was obviously thinking about it secretly all along.

Evidently he has done more than just think about it. I chuckle and shake my head. Danny, the king of the grand gesture. My life has been a whirlwind ever since he re-entered it, I never know what to expect. He's always finding the ways to make maximum impact. I'm glad that getting pregnant is something I will have a heads up on. When and if I do, I will know first. Maybe I can surprise him for once. If it was in his hands, I would be half expecting to be told via a billboard or something.

A gentle tap at the door pulls me from my thoughts and Connie peeps in. "Are you alright in here?" she asks trying to cheerfully mask her concern that I might be having second thoughts.

"I'm fine," I reply. "More than fine."

"I was just worried that you'd shut yourself away."

"I just wanted a second that's all."

"You're not having a wobble are you darling?"

I smile at her fondly. "Not at all."

"Good." She kisses my cheek. "You deserve to be happy and I know he is the right person for you."

Thinking about how she started this, I realise that even her overactive imagination couldn't have foreseen this all happening so soon. "Thank you," I say. "We needed you."

"You needed a boot up your arse!" She scoffs.

"Connie!" I giggle.

"I'm just glad you got there in the end. Now come on, get that face done, we have more surprises out here for you." She looks back as she leaves me and blows me a kiss.

I put the finishing touches to my makeup. I haven't done anything very unusual with it, I want to feel real today. I don't need a mask. Perhaps I've gone a little heavier, for the photos. I assume there will be photos. I've applied my perfumed body cream and changed the small stud I wear in my lip from my plain silver one to a tiny sparkly one that I only wear from time to time. The one in my nose is always sparkly. I feel as ready as I can be. I feel more relaxed for having a moment to myself, so I open the door to the living room.

"There she is!" my mum says. "You look beautiful."

"Thanks, Mum."

"Now come and sit down, we have instructions to follow." She leads me to the sofa. "Danny asked us to give you some things."

Connie hands me a small box. "Something old," she says softly. I stare at the box. I know what this is. I open the old box carefully, and smile at my Grandma's diamond pendant. I know she wore it on her wedding day, as did my mum and Grace. It's very special.

"I've just done my makeup!" I laugh, dabbing my eyes with the tissue immediately offered by Max.

"It's only going to get worse," he says as Mum and Connie secure it around my neck between them.

"Now, something new," says Mum, handing me another small box. I open it and a little card sits on the top. 'D x' is all it says. I lift up the card to reveal small diamond drop earrings that match the pendant so well. I take out the small silver hoops I wear and put them on.

My sister is itching for her turn. "Something borrowed!" she exclaims gleefully. I cringe, imagining it to be her garter. I really don't think I'm 'that' girl. I can't imagine Danny putting me through the grossness of that particular ritual, but my sister is a sucker for all that nonsense. She surprises me by unclasping her diamond bracelet and slipping it around my wrist. "Don't lose it though!"

"Thanks," I say, giving her a squeeze.

"And something blue," says Jen handing me a large bag...with a giggle.

Inside the bag I find a box and once I've removed the lid and swiped away the tissue, I see the reason for Jen's amusement. Danny has chosen me the most beautiful lace underwear in a delicate powder blue. A card tucked in with it, makes me grin.

"I can't wait to see this on! X"

I blush, but only because his mum is here. She's smiling though then she hands me something, a coin.

"And a silver sixpence for your shoe," she says and this sounds funny in her American accent. "Bob's mom handed it down to me on my wedding day, she was very traditional. It's yours now."

"Thank you," I say quietly. "I'll keep it..." I almost say 'for our children' but none of them know we are already trying and I don't want to open that can of worms this morning. Max and Jen exchange a look...they know, clearly. "I'll look after it," I clarify. Anyway, I think everyone realises what I'm trying to say, I'll keep it for 'future generations' whenever they may come.

"Okay!" says Max taking the heat off. "That just leaves me." He gets up and holds out his hand. I take it and stand to follow him, goodness knows where. Everyone follows as he stops at the spare room door. "Close your eyes,' he says giddy with excitement. Then he opens the door and leads me in. I'm positioned in the middle of the room and I stand perfectly still.

"Open," he says.

I blink and set eyes on my wedding dress.

Both hands cover my mouth as I gasp. In fact, collectively, everyone gasps. Hanging beside it are purple dresses for Grace and Jen, which are very like my dress from last night but in a floatier fabric with less full skirts. My dress is beautiful. Again, very like my dress from last night. Very fifties. It's ivory silk with a lace overlay and a full netted skirt. It's short, I'm guessing below the knee and it's belted with a purple bow. The neckline is a flattering deep V, it's just perfect and obviously a style Danny likes.

I step forward and touch it while everyone watches me silently. I never even started to imagine what sort of wedding dress I'd choose, but I would like to think, given the choice of any dress, this would be the one I would pick. Seeing it now, as the dress Danny thinks is perfect for me, I can't imagine I would want any other dress. Max's hand squeezes my shoulder.

"What do you think?" he whispers.

"It's perfect," I say in wonder.

A collective sigh of relief is released and I laugh as I turn to look at them all. My mum is dabbing her eyes with a tissue.

"Oh and these are to go with it," Max remembers, now that the big reveal is over.

Inside one box is a small ivory net veil. It's not really a veil as such, but one of those net things that will just cover my eyes. It's held in place by an ivory flower, it's perfect for the dress and the hairstyle I have. The other box must be my shoes. My stomach turns. I know Danny gets my shoe issues, even before the accident, heels were not my thing, but this dress deserves heels. I open the box with trepidation, but the love I feel for Danny is immeasurable when I lift out a pair of purple Converse. Everyone laughs but it just finishes me off, I'm in pieces before I know it, with Max soothing me and trying to remind me about my makeup.

Max produces an envelope and I just about pull myself together to read the note.

I know picking shoes for this dress would have really stressed you out. But you are the girl I love and it's you I want beside me today, so I've chosen shoes that are you through and through. I wouldn't want you to try and be someone you're not, especially not today.

I just can't wait to see you.

Dx

He really gets me. Oh my God, I have to stop crying!

Significantly more composed and with my makeup retouched, I let Max help me get dressed.

"Wow!" he sighs as he finishes primping the purple bow. He pulls me in front of the full-length mirror and I take it in. It's just perfect. I never could have chosen this well for myself. I turn and look at the back, over my shoulder. The deep V almost frames the large peacock tattooed there perfectly. I'm sure the person who designed this dress never imagined a bride like me wearing it, but I like the way my bold skin contrasts with the delicate lace, and the statement of the sash brings the perfect balance. I sigh. It's all so me.

I'm not aware of the time, just that we are moving forward, but when I come out of the spare room all dressed, I'm surprised to find everyone ready. My mum looks beautiful in a lilac dress and jacket, with a feathery fascinator. Danny's mum is wearing a smart but feminine indigo suit, her headdress is more a hat than a fascinator. Her signature style, a suit and pearls has remained since I was young. Seeing her like this for the first time since our reunion is a reminder of how much history we have.

I kiss them both and we all gush over how beautiful the other looks. Grace and Jen too, their dresses are lovely. I wonder if perhaps they met in LA to choose them together? It would explain how they seem to have got to know each other. While the living room is a flurry of compliments, Max reappears, having quickly put himself together. You'd never know it only took a few minutes, he looks devastatingly handsome and immaculate in his dark grey suit. The shirt is the faintest lavender and the tie is a few scant shades darker. He raises an eyebrow and looks down at his feet to draw my gaze. Black Converse.

"Don't you look handsome!" purrs Connie.

It always makes me smile to see Max dressed up. Because formal wear covers almost all evidence of the fact that he is just like me. Max has gradually allowed tattoos to peep above his collar and under his cuffs to compensate. I show more of myself than usual when we dress up like this, so I never have that problem.

"He always looks amazing." I grin and kiss his cheek.

There is a knock at the door and Mum lets Ali in, she's dressed now too and is carrying a box full of flowers. My bouquet is a riot of orchids in every shade of purple and pinks. It's stunning. The flowers for the bridesmaids are less riotous, but no less beautiful. My mum pins a buttonhole on Max and I scan the room.

"I can't believe Danny did all this!" I exclaim,

Max grins and winks, telling me that he had a little help from the master.

'Thank you,' I mouth.

"Right, let's get this show on the road," says Max clapping his hands together.

Twenty-two.

I promise not to go up any more ladders.

Liv.

I laugh hysterically when we walk through the deserted diner and see the cars that are here to collect us. A traditional London black cab for the mums and a vintage yellow NYC chequered cab for Jen and Grace.

Ali locks up behind us and she and Carla jump in the car with Ali's boyfriend.

Max and I wait on the curb as the cars pull away.

"Did you close the diner?" I ask with mock disapproval.

"Sack me." Max shrugs. I laugh.

Just then a throaty roar can be heard and I look up to see a Mustang approach. I look at Max aghast.

"That's not…?" I stutter.

"No," confirms Max." "Hired for the day, but he thought it would be a fitting tribute as she paid for the whole thing!"

I look up and down the car as it pulls up beside us. It's unbelievable, the colour, every detail. It could be the same car.

"The whole day?" I ask just realising what Max said.

"It could have paid for it ten times Liv."

I whistle.

Max offers me his elbow to help me into the car, this is when I realise that he is escorting me. I panic slightly, what about Dave? He gave Grace away, won't he be upset? Before I get to articulate any of this, I shut it down. Danny will have it all covered.

While we're driving along, I start to get twitchy about where we're going. I haven't ever thought about getting married it's true, but I definitely know I would have a hard time settling for a hotel with a per head price, drab decor and mediocre food. I try not to let this play on my mind. I know from when Max and Charlie got married, there's not much around to satisfy us, which is maybe why we run the type of place we do. If it was my choice, I know what I would do, but Danny is in charge of this. Whatever he has chosen, I'm sure I'll love it.

Max shifts in his seat beside me and I see him pull an envelope from inside his suit jacket. "This is the last one," he says, handing me Danny's note. I start to shake inexplicably. I know it won't be bad, but I can't cry here, I can't. My makeup can't be redone again. "Don't worry," says Max, seeing my panic. I open the envelope cautiously.

Dear Liv,

I hope you like everything. I've had the most fun getting this day ready for you!

This wedding that I've planned for us is exactly how I've always seen us promising each other, in front of everyone, that we will love each other forever. But because I really wanted to surprise you, I'm afraid it isn't going to be legal. I've really battled with this, but I really wanted to do this for you, so I decided to risk it. After we have done this today, you will be my wife and I will be your husband. But we will still need to go and get the paperwork done. Today is your birthday, but it will also be our anniversary for evermore, no matter which day we get the stamp on the certificate.

Everything about today will look and feel real and only you and I (Max, Charlie, Jen and Scott!) will ever know any different. I'm sorry it has to be this way, but they make you attend in person to apply to get married! Bastards!

We've come such a long way to get here, I can hardly believe it's real. I can't wait to see you and, just so that you know, because I know I'll be too emotional to say it when you arrive…you look beautiful (I know this without even seeing you!) and I love you with all my heart…

D x

I take a shuddery breath and Max offers a tissue, but I hold my hand up and smile, shaking my head. "I'm good." He has done an amazing thing. I wouldn't care if we were never actually legally married. I never did. As long as we have each other, that's all I want. Now I just can't wait to get to wherever we're going, I need to be with him.

When the car pulls into the park, I look questioningly at Max. He shakes his head and I don't ask. The car stops and Max jumps out. He opens my door and helps me out. Then he offers me his elbow. "Shall we?"

I can't think anything except 'we're at the park' but I take his arm and follow him. We start down the shaded path and an arrow staked in the ground points the way. As we follow a trail of white petals along the edge of the footpath it suddenly dawns on me where we're going, even though I've figured it out, I can't help the gasp when our tree comes into view.

Everyone we know is seated in a semicircle around our beautiful tree and standing in front of them is Danny. He looks amazing! Scott is beside him and I see him squeeze Danny's shoulder and tell him I'm here. Danny slowly looks up and his eyes meet mine. It's like no one else is here. Like we are kids again, meeting at our place to hide from everyone else. Right from the moment I met him, he was all I ever needed and this place is the symbol of that. It was just ours. A secret forever. Now he's chosen to share our secret with everyone, because it means so much to us.

"This is it," Max whispers excitedly as he stops us at the top of the aisle in the middle of the seating. "Well done, you made it!"

I clasp his arm tightly. "I love you," I whisper.

"I love you too."

That's when music starts, I couldn't tell you what it was though. I'm more or less unable to process anything as, in slow motion, Max steps forward, leading me and then kissing my hand, he passes me to Dave who is waiting at the end of the aisle with a huge smile. I'm only vaguely aware of any of this, because at this precise moment all I can see is Danny. He stands at the front, watching me intently. His face full of emotion. We inch our way towards him. All else has faded from my consciousness. All I see is him.

Once I reach his side, Dave kisses my cheek and steps away to join my mum, Danny takes my hand and I breathe again. Although it has only been a few hours that we have been apart, it feels like forever, as if I've just completed the longest journey imaginable and finally reached my goal. Danny shuts his eyes tightly before returning them to me. He smiles.

"You're beautiful," he whispers and I can tell that he has only just managed to get that out. I won't be so successful holding it together if I try to speak, so I squeeze his hand and smile.

A smart lady at the front clears her throat and draws our attention. She begins by introducing herself and welcoming the guests. I'm vaguely aware of the people behind me, but I can't look now. Instead I look down at my feet and that's when I notice Danny's Converse, crisp and new and black just like Max's. A stupid grin threatens to grip me and derail the moment, so I keep my eyes low. But Danny's fingers brush mine to get my attention so I have to look up at him. Frowning at not knowing what I'm finding funny, he holds my gaze. I mouth 'It's perfect' and he's almost bashful and looks away. I squeeze his fingers to force him to look back. 'I love you,' I mouth. His eyes fill with tears and suddenly I fear we are both going to crumble in front of everyone.

"In normal circumstances," the celebrant says, interrupting our silent torment, "I would have got to know the couple before me already. But I understand that this is no ordinary couple." A ripple of laughter comes from behind me and I smile that she has rescued us. "When I meet a couple I am to marry, it's quite normal to hear most of the information from the excited bride, while the groom takes a back seat. However, I've had the privilege of dealing solely with the groom on this occasion and it has been wonderful to learn about the love they have for one another through his eyes."

Okay, I'm going to cry! I'm very grateful that the last thing Max did was press a folded tissue into my hand as he kissed it.

She goes on to say some touching words about our friendship as small children and how it blossomed into love in our teens. She speaks about our separation, glossing over the gut-wrenching heartbreak, instead issuing wise words about sometimes needing a second chance, because sometimes we are not ready when fate hands us the first chance. I dab my eyes throughout. She enthusiastically describes how we reconnected. Again managing to side-step all talk of the devastating break-up, but making sure she covers the point that we were so in love that our fear of losing each other again almost threatened our future. Then she rounds off her brief history by saying that we have learned from the troubles we've had, never to underestimate each other's love and commitment. It's all just perfect.

"Now the bride's best friend, Max, would like to read a passage." I watch Max come to stand at the front and unfold his paper, I marvel at how calm he looks. He faces the audience, but turns his stare to us, as he confidently recites the words without once looking at the page.

It's a beautiful passage by Richard Bach. I almost read it at his wedding, but we found something more appropriate for them. But it suits Danny and me perfectly. It's about keys fitting locks and when we feel safe enough to open the locks we can be who we truly are. I'm not completely taking it in right now, but I can remember thinking it was beautiful.

Every one claps as Max sits back down. I wipe my eyes as delicately as I can. Then we move into the formal part of the ceremony.

She asks us the important questions... "Daniel, will you take Olivia to be your wife? Will you love her, comfort her, honour and protect her and forsaking all others, be faithful to her as long as you both shall live?"

"I will," replies Danny, never taking his eyes from mine. A shiver runs down my spine. I want to look away, it's too emotional, but he wants our eye contact, it's important and if he can do it, so can I.

"Olivia, will you take Daniel to be your husband? Will you love him, comfort him, honour and protect him and forsaking all others, be faithful to him as long as you both shall live?"

"I will," I reply, expecting to be overcome with emotion as soon as I try to speak. Instead I feel a thrill of excitement. We are really doing this and nothing is stopping us, not the universe, not psycho exes, not even our own insecurities.

"Will you, the friends and family of Daniel and Olivia, support and uphold them in their marriage, now and in the years to come?"

"We will." They all answer collectively and I physically feel their warmth and love as they speak.

Danny and I are asked to hold hands and face each other. "Olivia, Daniel hopes you won't mind that he has made the vows more personal for you." Danny grins sheepishly. Then she recites his vows and he repeats them, line for line.

"I, Daniel, take you, Olivia, to be my wife.

To love you from this day forward, as I've always loved you in the past,

For better, for worse and all that other stuff that doesn't matter as long as we are together.

I promise to be honest with you and never doubt your love for me, whatever life throws at us.

I will always support your individuality and be grateful you don't like Jimmy Choos.

I promise to be your tech-support, watch chick flicks with you and rub ointment on your new tattoos."

We all giggle. A big, fat tear rolls down my face, I hope this mascara holds up. Then he takes a deep breath and finishes with a line that threatens to send me over the edge into a sobbing mess.

"Like this tree, we stumbled and fell, but something so strong cannot be wiped out in one moment.

I'm always rooted here with you and together we are too strong to fade away.

I promise we will continue to grow together even if there are more storms to come."

I just manage to hold it together, I don't know how. Most people here won't understand the reference, but I'm so glad he included it. Those words are so special to us.

I wonder what I will have to say? Danny winks, knowing I'll think it's funny. Then it's my turn to repeat the words.

"I, Olivia, take you, Daniel, to be my husband.

To love you from this day forward, as I've always loved you in the past,

For better, for worse and all that other stuff that doesn't matter as long as we are together.

I promise to be honest with you and never doubt your love for me, whatever life throws at us.

I will always let you do things for me, even though I'm a control freak.

I won't object if you decide to restore another classic car and I promise not to go up any more ladders."

Waiting for the laughter to settle before she continues, the celebrant has no idea that she is letting my poor, frayed emotions build up before I say the very thing I'm not sure I can say out loud. I inhale a calming breath as she says it first, then I release it before I speak.

"Like this tree, we stumbled and fell, but something so strong cannot be wiped out in one moment.

You are always rooted here with me and together we are too strong to fade away.

I promise we will continue to grow together even if there are more storms to come."

I finish my vows, in pieces obviously, but grinning at Danny's cuteness along with everyone else. He looks so pleased with himself.

Next the rings are presented by Scott who stands behind Danny. The celebrant asks us to hold both hands in front of us while she reads the Hands Ceremony. Whatever that is…it sounds American.

"These are the hands of your best friend, young and strong and full of love for you, that are holding yours on your wedding day, as you promise to love each other today, tomorrow, and forever. These are the hands that will work alongside yours, as you build your future together. These are the hands that will passionately love you and cherish you through the years, and with the slightest touch, will comfort you like no other. These are the hands that will hold you when fear or grief fills your mind. These are the hands that will countless times wipe the tears from your eyes; tears of sorrow and tears of joy. These are the hands that will tenderly hold your children, the hands that will help you to hold your family as one. These are the hands that will give you strength when you need it. And lastly, these are the hands that even when wrinkled and aged, will still be reaching for yours, still giving you the same unspoken tenderness with just a touch."

When she says that thing about holding our children, my insides literally clench. Now that it's in our immediate future, I've begun to feel it like a dull ache, which flares up whenever my attention is drawn to it. I never saw myself this way, but the reality of making a family with Danny has had a strange effect on me. She turns to Danny and offers my ring. He places it on my finger and repeats the words she reads.

"I give you this ring as a symbol of my commitment to you. It has no beginning and it has no end. Let it always remind you of my infinite love for you." Danny slides a perfectly plain platinum band onto my finger and I smile. It will look just right with my far from plain engagement ring once I put it back on after this.

Then we repeat the process and I say the same words, sliding a matching ring onto Danny's finger.

Then the moment we've been waiting for.

"I now pronounce you husband and wife. You may kiss the bride."

Danny leans in to kiss me and everyone cheers.

Then in a whirlwind, we sit and sign some kind of declaration that I know is not the legal stuff, but it's for appearance, I love him for the lengths he has gone to. Max and Jen witness. Some photos are taken, but it's a bit of a blur.

The next thing I know, drinks have appeared from somewhere and everyone is milling around chatting. I'm scanning the scene and taking it all in, when my hand is taken and Danny pulls me quickly beneath the tree's canopy.

He presses me against the reclining trunk, exhaling a deep shuddering breath as his lips find mine. He kisses me with more passion than I've ever been kissed. To start with it's almost violent, but as we melt into it, it becomes a more loving passion. He draws away reluctantly and grins.

"Happy birthday, Mrs. Morgan!"

I laugh. "Thank you, Mr. Morgan."

"You look amazing." He adds stepping back to look me up and down.

"I've a great stylist." I grin pulling him back to me. "You look pretty good yourself." I murmur, bringing his lips to mine again, this time for a heart-stoppingly tender kiss. I pour everything I feel at this perfect moment into it.

"I've missed you today," I whisper. "It feels like I haven't seen you in weeks."

"It was so hard leaving you asleep this morning."

"But it was so worth it." I sigh. "Thank you doesn't seem enough for what you've done."

He gives me his shy smile. "Sorry it isn't official." He shrugs. "I just got this whole surprise idea in my head and then I got so far and found I couldn't do it legally."

"Danny, its fine, I don't care if we never do it. This is enough for me."

"Oh hell no! We are doing it in two weeks, don't worry, I've got it covered."

I laugh, of course he has it all planned. "I love you."

"Oh my God, I love you too." He lunges at me again. Holding his hands tight to my back, I can feel that he wants to run them all over me, but I'm so made up and literally everyone we know is on the other side of a thin covering of leaves. He forces himself away before it's too much.

"Shouldn't we get out there?" I ask.

"Screw them." He laughs and then sighs, knowing I'm right.

We slip as discreetly as possible into the throng, but straight away we garner suggestive comments and raised eyebrows for our absence.

"I just needed a moment alone with my wife," exclaims Danny loudly, attracting even more attention and everyone laughs and makes 'aw' noises or other more suggestive things.

"We need to get out of here," Danny murmurs in my ear and starts to lead me towards the path we came in.

Why are we leaving everyone behind? Where are we going? How will they all get there, wherever it is? As if I'm broadcasting these question buy loud speaker, Danny says, "Try not to ask." I flash him a 'give me a break, I need to know something' look and he chuckles. "All will be revealed."

He takes my almost empty glass from my hand and hands me my bouquet, then taking my hand, he leads me back up the footpath. No one follows us. I laugh out loud, as I'm faced with two old Route Master buses, marked 'Wedding Special'. But as I walk towards them Danny holds me back.

"They're not for us," he says. Leading me past the first bus to where the Shelby is waiting.

"Danny, where are we going?" I beg as the Shelby pulls out of the car park, leaving the buses behind, waiting for their passengers.

"You'll see." I huff beside him. "I hope you like it…I just thought that the whole hotel thing wasn't really our scene. You don't want a stuffy three-course meal with half a bottle of wine per head do you?"

I shake my head, wondering how I managed to find someone who just got it.

"So, I have something better lined up."

We chat about the day so far as the car whizzes along, but I'm barely concentrating, trying to imagine our destination.

"This is eating at you isn't it?" he teases.

"Stop it, Danny." I sulk. "Just give me a hint."

"Come on now, you just promised in front of everyone that you would let me do things for you, even though you're a control freak!"

I press my lips together, then we both burst out laughing.

Twenty-three.

This ain't no ordinary shindig!

Danny.

"You are just perfect, do you know that?" Liv says, grabbing my face and kissing me. The car has just come to a stop outside our venue. I help her from the car and one of the two photographers is already at work capturing her reaction. The other guy is on one of the buses.

"How did you know?" she asks incredulously.

I smile, I'm so happy she likes the idea. "It was obvious I guess." I shrug. "It wasn't about the money." I'm suddenly worried she'll think I'm mean. "I looked around at what was available and nothing suited us. I just knew you'd want to have it here." I stop and kiss her lightly. "Are you happy?"

"Ecstatic!" She beams.

"Me too." I lead her through the open gate, past the sign saying 'LADY LUCK'S IS CLOSED FOR A PRIVATE FUNCTION' and into the garden.

Home.

"Wow," she whispers as she soaks up the scene. We kept her out all day yesterday and then when she came home she went upstairs and then only came out into the garden, she didn't see anything in the bar and I had people on standby to stop her if she had tried to go in. The staff worked late on the decorations and started again early this morning. Most of them came to the service, but a couple were here finishing up.

They come out to greet us and we let Liv have a good look at what we've done. The stage is back inside, set up for the live music. All the doors of the bar are open and both inside and out the tables have all been decorated with flowers and candles. There are no table settings or place cards, and there is plenty of room for milling around. It's a really casual affair.

A table is set up inside with our cake, a huge pile of doughnuts. Jen has made tiny flags to stick all over it indicating which ones have jelly and which ones have jam. Liv thinks it's great. I love watching her laugh as all over the place she is finding the little touches that make today so personal to us. On every table, tucked in the flowers, Jen has printed cards with all the movie quotes I gave her. All the classics, like 'Nobody puts Baby in a corner.' (We put that one in a corner!), she loves it!

We have a real old-school photo-booth set up for some fun shots later, because it reminds me of our teens. In fact, on an easel beside it there is a grainy, enlarged strip of Liv and I. We must have been about seventeen and we're kissing, sticking out our tongues, laughing and then kissing again. It's one of the few things I allowed myself to hold onto.

"Oh my God, look at us!" she squeals.

The buses will be here any minute and I just want her to myself for a moment, so I pull her over to Baby's table in the corner and sit her down.

"Okay, here's the deal," I say hurriedly. She frowns. But I have to get this out before everyone comes. "I chose to do this here because there is nowhere more perfect for us than this world you have created. You made it like this because it made you feel at home, but without knowing or realising, you built me into it as well. The two of us are all over this place and I wanted to celebrate us, in our home. But I know you, and you need some rules. So, the conditions are: You don't work here tonight, you're here as the focus of everyone's attention, the guest of honor. Everyone knows what they're doing, you don't need to help. You are mine tonight and I won't share you with a bar. Everything is paid for, we won't be discussing that again. I have everything under control. It's all planned. Don't interfere. Do you understand?"

She visibly shudders. "Uh-huh." She mutters as she lunges at me. Our lips lock and I feel her tongue brush against them. I succumb for a moment, parting them to allow her exploration. Then I hear the damned buses pull up.

"Liv." I halt her. "They're here."

"Shit!" She giggles. "You got me all turned on and now I can't have you."

"How did I get you turned on?" I ask, pulling her to her feet.

"You don't know what it does to me when you lay down the law!" She laughs, not quite believing it herself.

"Sometimes with you, it's the only way." I tug her hand so that she is pressed against me.

"Well, it does things to me." She laughs ruefully. "You've messed with my brain Danny Morgan. I've changed."

"Things?" My face moves close to hers until we are sharing air. "What things?"

She nods. "Rude things."

I run my fingers up her back until my hand is at the back of her neck, poised to make her close the remaining inch between us. "I'll have to remember that," I whisper, breathing harder, just from the closeness.

Just then, Scott and Max walk into the bar. "Get a room!" yells Scott.

I close my eyes and sigh. "Later Mrs. Morgan," I say kissing her forehead instead and prising myself away. I don't let go of her though, we hold hands all night.

She seems to love everything. I've arranged an American feast from our American diner. Jake has done all of the best stuff they do here in smaller versions and it's being served canapé style. Except these canapés will actually feed you and I've told them just to keep it flowing. No half bottle per head here. Everyone is enjoying it, it's way better than a sit-down meal.

We manage to take some group photos. I didn't ask for all that formal stuff, but having everyone together like this it seems ridiculous not to. But they are not the posed, stuffy kind. We are all laughing at each other and having fun. I know the shots will be animated and full of life. The photographer gets a great shot of me and my groomsmen showing Liv our matching shoes. Then one of just Liv and I with our 'his and hers' shoes. She loves the shoe thing best of all I think. Every photo I'm aware of (and I'm sure there are so many I'm not aware of) makes me think of the house that we will fill with them. I can't wait to be living there now, with any luck we'll sign the papers before we leave on our honeymoon.

Liv is laughing with Connie about Dave and Connie's husband, Jack, wanting to be 'down with the kids' and insisting on getting Converse too. I wasn't planning on it becoming a feature, but as I'd mentioned it to lots of people, everyone seemed to get involved. I would say over half of the guests are wearing them or at least pushing the accepted formal footwear boundaries. I've seen some Vans and one friend of Liv's is wearing velvet Doc Martins. This is just what I wanted. No pretences, just us.

I spot Ali and Carla coming out of the diner. Ali nods to confirm their job is done. I asked them to fix up the flat for me. When I decided to have the wedding here, I also gave our wedding night some thought. Although it would be nice to go to a hotel, then we'd have to leave the party. I decided Liv would prefer to be at home, so I asked the girls to tidy away all the traces of everyone getting ready there this morning. They said they would make it romantic for us, I trust them, they seemed really into the idea.

Max taps my shoulder and tells me it's time for the speeches, so I gather Liv and some drinks and head inside to the stage. Everyone either files in or finds a spot in the garden where they can see. Liv and I step up onto the stage and join Max and Jen.

"Hello everyone," Max says into the mic, to settle the crowd. "Where are the bride and groom's parents?" We wait while they position themselves either side of us. "I think we'll start with Dave."

Dave gives a wave as friends cheer. "Thanks!" he says. "I only want to say a few words about this wonderful girl. She was ten when she came barrelling into my life. I was already in love with her mum, so I knew I would love her girls easily. We have certainly had our ups and downs, becoming a family. Being a step-parent is a constant test. Some days you pass, some days you don't. But Liv is one of those people that doesn't make things more difficult than they need to be and I'm very grateful to have her as my daughter. She has made her mother and me so proud with her accomplishments. We've watched her grow into a superb business woman. She has a rebellious streak, sure. But we've never needed to worry about her. We're so happy that she found Danny again, because we have always known that they are perfect for each other. Danny doesn't need to be welcomed into our family, he knows he has always had a place with us. So let me just say, we're glad you're back where you belong. Please raise your glasses to our girl and her perfect man." Everyone, murmurs 'to the bride and groom' as Liv hugs Dave and then her mom.

I'm slightly surprised to see my dad then step up to the mic. We hadn't planned for him to say anything.

"Hi everyone, I know it's unconventional for the groom's dad to join in, but hey, I'm in unconventional company. I just wanted to add a few words about Danny, while we are doing the proud parent thing. I hope you don't mind?" He looks to Dave as he says this and Dave laughs and signals that the floor is all his.

"Most of you know that Danny is an American, which may or may not have inspired Liv's path in life," he says waving at the surroundings. "But you may not know that I was born here, a couple of roads away as a matter of fact. Like Liv, I too know what it is to be infatuated with all things American, so I decided to study there. I met Pam in the library at Stanford and the rest, as they say, is history. But when we were given the opportunity to come back here, I jumped at the chance to bring our boy up in my hometown. He settled in straight away, no doubt because on his first day here, literally his first day, he fell in love. We always knew we would go back to California eventually, but we didn't fully appreciate how difficult that would be for Danny. We are so proud of the difficult choices he's made. He followed us home when we suspected he might refuse and took the opportunity to get the finest education and become an expert in his field. But we always knew his heart got left behind. So we are so pleased that he has finally made himself whole again. Being so far from your child isn't something you necessarily want as a parent, but we have divided our life between two places, so as far away as it is, at least it's home. Danny, we are so proud of you for coming home." I bite back tears as my parents hug me. I really need to keep my shit together, I still have to speak.

Next Jen and Max step up together. Jen goes first.

"At this point we usually hear from the best man. But as you already know, this ain't no ordinary shindig! Max and I are totally used to explaining the relationships we have with these two by now, so just to clarify, I'm Jen and I'll be your best man today and the lovely Max will be your Maid of Honor!" Cheers and whistles erupt as the whole room laughs. Jen lets it settle then continues.

"Danny and I were babies together, our parents are best friends. But he moved here when we were so young I hardly had any memory of him. When I heard he was coming back, I thought, oh no! I just knew straight away, I would be expected to show him around, have him come out with my friends and knowing our parents, eventually marry him! I didn't know him but I knew he was an eighteen-year-old boy, how hard are they to figure out? Well...what I got was not what I was expecting. For a start he was gorgeous! But he wasn't like other eighteen-year-old boys. I dragged him around to parties and the movies, but he only went to keep everyone off his back. Hell, I only took him to get everyone off mine!" She giggles.

I laugh. "Thanks babe, I love you too!"

"It took me a while to realise and an even longer time to get him to admit that he had a broken heart. But once he opened up, we instantly became friends. Then it wasn't a chore to be with him at all. I like to think I helped him to get back on his feet and get back out there. But even though he forced himself to forget, he never really did get back out there. He has great friends and was enjoying life, but no one ever came close as far as love was concerned. I was getting worried that this would go on forever, when Liv landed in our lives with a bang. All I can say is, on that day, Danny came alive. It was like someone switched him over to HD.

"Danny has been my best friend for twelve years. I'd never been friends with a guy before, but Danny wasn't a guy, he was Danny. He has looked out for me, laughed with me, cried with me, even found me a husband. He has been the most loving, supportive, generous best friend a girl could ever have. I love you, Danny," she says directly to me, lifting her glass.

"But Bob was right, he left his heart here and although it sucks that you left it so far away, Danny, I'm glad you came to find it." Murmured agreements come from all around as I wipe tears from my eyes. Liv dissolved ages ago and is on her third tissue. "I'm so glad you're finally happy," she says rushing into my arms as she too gives into the emotion.

Once we've composed ourselves, I go back to holding Liv's hand, but I keep hold of Jen's too. Max steps up.

"Hey everyone. I'm not sure about this Maid of Honour business, but...'I am what I am, I don't want praise, I don't want pity'..." Max croons.

"Oh God! Don't sing!" groans Liv beside me. Everyone laughs.

Max rolls his eyes, "Alright, I won't steal your limelight. I'll make it about you," Max tells Liv, ignoring the crowd. Then he turns back to the room and shakes his head.

"Like Jen, I met Liv straight after Danny's departure...and like Jen, what I got was a broken heart. She was a mess." He turns to Liv and shrugs. "Sorry, but you were!" he continues. "It didn't take me any time at all to get the whole story out of her though, Liv is a sharer! She tried very hard to put it behind her and move on, but most of it was just for show. She never got over him. So instead she started to reinvent herself. Liv was up for a bit of self-discovery and I was into that too, some might say we overindulged! But we found ourselves together and I will love her forever for being part of my journey. When the chance came to start this place, I was IN, no question and it has been the best job ever, doing something I love beside my best friend. I'm so proud of her, for everything she has done and I'll be behind her wherever she goes from here. I love you Liv, but you know that." Then he calmly picks her up, twirls her around and kisses her before he sets her down, to rapturous applause. He's so cool despite the crowd, but then this is his crowd.

"I haven't finished!" he shouts and most people quieten down to hear him out. "I just wanted to say that, while I may have been part of the conspiracy to get these two talking again, my co-conspirator and I could not have predicted the impact Danny would have on all our lives. The love these two have for one another was one thing on paper, but seeing them lay eyes on each other for the first time in twelve years stopped me in my tracks, I even dropped table three's burgers! It was electric, you could feel the atmosphere change in the room. I realised then that nobody could have ever filled the space left by Danny, but Danny."

He focuses on me now. "Danny, I feel very lucky, you see, when you have a relationship like Liv and I, it's rarely understood by partners. But you didn't just get it, you enriched it. We have been through a lot, you and Liv and I. So now I'm not just able to say I like my best friend's husband, I can say I consider him to be one of my closest friends. I wish you a lifetime of happiness together and I know I'm going to be there to share it." He raises his glass. "To my best friends," he says and the crowd responds. "Danny and Liv." He pulls me into a hug and claps me on the back.

Now it's me. Taking a deep breath, I hold Liv's hand and pull her with me to the mic. I've a speech written in my pocket, but after those, it just seems too stuffy. I don't even get it out, I'm going to wing it. "Whoo!" I breathe, just to let everyone know I'm struggling.

"Okay, this is harder than yesterday!" I glance at Liv, she is quietly drying her eyes. She gives me a look, like, 'come on, you can do this'. So I suck it up.

"I just want to say thanks. Thanks to everyone for whatever you did to help me. For a month, people have done favors, kept secrets, lied, hidden things, travelled in secret, put people up secretly who have travelled in secret! The list of things to thank you for is endless. So thank you all for making today happen for us. I had to do it this way because this girl WOULD NOT let me propose to her." I laugh trying to make light of the facts, but I do want to talk about it because it's our story.

"I've nearly missed out on this future twice in my life, so it was very important to get it right this time. I couldn't leave it to chance. You see, I was only half living without you," I say, turning to Liv. "I'm certain it was the same for you." She smiles in agreement.

"As we've already covered, I fell in love with you the moment I saw you. You were sitting on your front step, brushing your Barbie's hair. You were so beautiful I couldn't speak, but you just waved like it was nothing. I've never been the same again. I tried being without you, life is nothing without you."

I swallow hard, desperate to finish before this emotion takes over. "Thank you for giving us this chance, Liv, you'll never regret it, I swear." I draw Liv in for a lingering kiss, while people clap and make approving noises. "I love you," I tell her. Then I turn back to the mic. "Now, I'm going to dance with my wife!" I start to move off the stage but Liv pulls me back.

"Hold on!" she exclaims, pulling the mic out of the stand. "You didn't seriously think I would say nothing did you?" She grins. I shake my head in wonder. She's incredible.

"Hi everyone." She waves. "I just wanted the chance to speak...I can't believe this. Yesterday I was wondering what Danny would cook me for dinner tonight and if I should clean the bathroom today, or let him do it as it's my birthday. Now here I am at my dream wedding with my one true love." She looks at me and laughs when she sees me no longer able to hold it back. She hands me her tissue.

"Danny said that he's loved me since we were six years old. Well, of course I have too. But let me tell you, it's hard when you find your soul mate so young. Circumstances pulled us apart before we found our voices and although we both tried to make a life apart, something was always missing. We needed a second chance because we just weren't ready for the first one." She wipes a tear with her finger and smiles softly at me. "Okay, so perhaps we needed a third chance too. You see we did doubt and we did underestimate and we did believe the worst, but only because we were too young the first time and too hurt the second time.

"But we've changed and if we're not the same, things can only turn out differently." I swallow hard, she's going to finish me. She takes my hand again. "Thank you for offering me this chance, of course I know I'll never regret it. Thank you for this perfect day and for knowing me inside out. I always knew you were perfect for me, but today proves it beyond doubt." She laughs and adds, "I didn't know that you'd planned a first dance and we've never had an 'our song' but I've had the perfect one in mind since I was seventeen. I just asked for it to be played... and I was informed that we've picked the same song!...So please will you dance with me to our song?" she asks leaning in to my chest as I wrap my arms around her.

"Did you seriously pick the same song?" I ask in disbelief, as everyone cheers.

"Uh-huh." She grins. I lead her down the steps as people move off the small dance floor in front of the stage.

"Why?" I ask, wondering if she would realise why it's significant, we never discussed it.

"You know why," she says close to my ear.

The music starts with the word 'Wonderful' and I hold her close as the bass drum sounds once. 'Some kind of wonderful' by The Drifters, fills the bar and Liv and I dance as if no one else is there. She looks in my eyes as we move. We aren't great dancers, but it doesn't matter.

"Why?" I ask her again. "Say it. I need to know that it means the same to you."

"Because it was playing the first time we...our first time," she replies, her smile glitters. I close my eyes and pull her tight. I never realised she even knew that, let alone remembered it. It was always on in her room, the 'Dirty Dancing' sound track, it was just chance that that track was playing. But I've never forgotten and apparently neither did she. While I'm lost in thought, her lips find mine.

Twenty-four.

I love you too.

Danny.

"Come to bed with me," I whisper in Liv's ear as she stands watching her sister and Jen tear up the dance floor.

She giggles. "We can't just leave the party."

"Half the guests have left since midnight, I'm getting impatient and those two could go on for hours."

She looks like she's considering it. "I should say goodnight," she says.

"No! That'll take forever, please just sneak out with me."

"We can't!"

"Sure we can." I grab her and scoop her up in my arms. Then I yell, "Night everyone!" I see people turn towards us but I don't hang around, I take my wife inside as fast as I can. She's giggling, while telling me off for being so rude to our guests.

"Relax, everyone important will be here for breakfast in the morning, my treat. We can apologise then. Right now, I want you and I don't care about them." She punches the code while I hold her. I won't let her down in case she escapes. We're kissing as we step into the hallway and I let her feet back down to the floor once the door is firmly closed behind us. Our kiss is hungry and we stumble slightly, trying to make progress on the stairs while greedily consuming each other. Eventually I step back and fall onto the step behind me. Liv climbs on top of me and I groan as she presses herself against me. I'm painfully hard. She has on that dress and I've been watching her all night, imagining taking it off, I can't stand it anymore, I have to shift her off me. As I do she glances up.

"Oh God, Danny, it's beautiful," she says.

I turn to see what she's talking about. The stairs are strewn with white rose petals.

"It wasn't me," I admit. "Ali and Carla cleaned up after you got ready so that it was nice for us to come back to. They must have done it." She smiles fondly at having friends that would do this for her. "Come on," I say grabbing her hand and leading her upstairs. I'm slightly glad something interrupted our moment, the discomfort has eased now and I'm at least able to make it up the stairs without exploding. As I open the door, I scoop her up again, carrying her across the threshold. We notice instantly that they have done more than just tidy up, everything is perfectly neat and the petals lead straight into the bedroom, where the lamp is on, welcoming us. We cross the living room and stop at the bedroom door. It's as if we are in a hotel. The bed, freshly made in what looks like new linen, has been turned down. Two fluffy white robes tied up like parcels sit on the covers. Petals surround the bed and on the nightstand is a basket.

A note tied to the handle reads 'Congratulations Liv and Danny. From Lady Luck's Staff x' and inside is a wedding night care package. Champagne glasses, a bucket of ice (they must have added this not long ago) containing some expensive champagne, chocolates, some painkillers, bottled water, I stop looking at that point and turn back to Liv, she's standing beside the bed staring at me. I reach out and pull her to me looking at her in that dress. I don't want her to take it off, but I know it's just a moment in time, she can't wear it forever. Besides, I want to see what she's wearing underneath it even more.

I take the ends of the purple sash and slip the bow open, like I'm unwrapping my gift. I slide my finger beneath the knot and ease it open, holding eye contact with Liv the whole time. Then I pull on one side of the sash to pull it free of her body. Tossing it on the bed behind me, I return my hands to her fabulous body. "I feel bad being the one with the gift to unwrap, it's your birthday."

"Not anymore." She shrugs.

I trail kisses around her neck, catching her necklace. I unclasp it and place it carefully on her nightstand, to keep it safe. I know what it means to her. She watches me. "Something old," I whisper, touching the diamond dangling from her ear. "Something new." I continue, unhooking them both and stashing them with the necklace.

"Something borrowed." She joins in, lifting her wrist to show me. I do the honors. Then I run my finger down the sharp V of her neckline and follow its path, sinking to my knees. I unlace her shoes and slip them off her feet, then start back up again, keeping my hands on the inside of her dress, running my fingers up her silky smooth legs. When I get to my feet again, I've let go and allowed her dress to fall. But as I explore her neck with my mouth, I find the zipper behind her and start dragging it down.

Liv lets out a moan when my tongue slides up behind her ear and I take her earlobe between my teeth, at the same time that my hand travels along the bare skin of her back. I deftly send her dress complete with its full petticoats to the floor and gasp as I step back to see her in her powder-blue lingerie. "Something blue," I breathe, taking her back in my arms. I gasp as she brings her hands around my belt and brushes her hand lower over my zipper. I try to focus, I need tonight to last.

She begins tugging at my shirt as I stroke the smooth skin of her lower back. "Wait, wasn't there supposed to be something in your shoe?" I ask absently, trying to distract myself as her hands find my skin.

"Oh! Yeah." She giggles, reaching into the cup of her bra and pulling out the old coin. "It was killing me and that dress doesn't have pockets!"

I grab her, laughing and lift her legs to wrap around me. The coin falls amongst her clothes on the floor, but I don't care. I lay her back on the bed and stand above her, between her legs, loosening my tie, my jacket and vest long gone. I unbutton my shirt, watching Liv. She is alive with need, I can feel it. She can hardly keep still, her toe strokes up my inside leg. Removing my shirt slowly, I keep her waiting. I'm killing myself, but watching her makes it worthwhile. She can't stand it though, her hand drifts across her stomach and brushes across the lace of her panties, she sighs and draws back, sliding her fingers under the fabric.

I can't just watch while she does that when I need her so badly, so I quickly divest myself of my pants and underwear and bend to my knees. I pull her hand free and pin it to the bed with mine. She moans and wickedly pushes her other hand in its place. I tut tut, shaking my head and capture that hand too, pressing them both down with my weight so that she feels restrained. Then I lean forward and kiss the spot just below her belly button. She sighs. I kiss two more spots on the way to her underwear and then I run my tongue over the fabric.

Liv cries out when my tongue passes over her swollen clit, even through her underwear, the impact is incredible. I kiss my way back to the top of her panties and pause, watching her squirm. She tests the strength of my fingers at her wrists and realises I'm not letting go, so she surrenders to it. I take the delicate panties in my teeth and move them down as far as I'm able. It's not enough to reveal where she wants me to go, but enough to tease her some more.

When she can't take it anymore, I release her and slide her panties off, then I glance at her nightstand and spot the ice. I grab a piece and hide it in my mouth while she's distracted, reaching to touch herself again. She is deliberately trying to get me to restrain her again, I know it! She liked it, so I grab both of her wrists in one hand, pinning them lightly above her head and pull down the cup of her bra with the other. She cries out as my icy mouth closes over her nipple and she writhes beneath me, almost trying to get away, but not convincingly enough.

I turn my attention to her other nipple, which gets an equally impressive reaction. I release her hands and they go straight to her shocked nipples, her back arching at the sensations. Then with the ice between my teeth, I slide my way across her heated skin, slowly all the way down until I reach her thigh. I move the ice over her and she gasps as I come close a couple of times, but I make her believe I won't go where she is begging for me to go. Then just before I start the journey back up, I flash the ice right over her clit. She virtually leaves the bed, crying out a throaty scream of pure, unrestrained pleasure.

I trail the ice straight back up, all the way to her throat. She's still panting when I brush the ice across her lips but she comes back from her high at its touch and grabs me, kissing me with abandon, forcing the half cube of ice into her own mouth. She gives me a lascivious grin and pushes me off her. I fall beside her willingly and watch her remove her bra. She bends to drop icy kisses over my stomach and chest. I suck in a sharp breath as it skates over a nipple, but it doesn't linger.

She turns so that her back is to me as she works the diminishing ice down over my abs, the fact that I can't see what she is doing only adds to the sensations. Suddenly, with no warning, she plunges her icy mouth straight down over my whole length. I'm sure the remaining wedding guests must have heard my cries. The feeling is phenomenal. The ice has gone, but every recess in her mouth is cold and my burning cock is engulfed. The contrast is shocking, but I don't want it to stop. I can't help my loud moans as she relentlessly works her freezing lips up and down. She takes me so deep, she is so good at it and the sensation changes again, as she takes me through the icy cold and into the tight warmth of her throat. Again and again...I have to stop it.

"Oh, yes...Liv...oh...please...stop...please." I'm not sounding convincing, I have to stop her. I don't want to use my hands, if I touch her I could very well push myself further in, that won't help, even though she loves it. I have to stop now!

"STOP! Please, stop..." and she mercifully does. I lay panting.

She raises an eyebrow and laughs. "Sorry, I got carried away."

"I'm not coming in your mouth on our wedding night." I gasp. "Not while we're trying to make a baby." Liv smiles at this and turns back to kiss me, slowing the tempo right down. Now we lay side by side, kissing and touching for an eternity, making the most of this time, not rushing it. I glide my fingers down her body until they are playing against her swollen clit, she gasps. I continue to stroke her and she builds back up quickly. I know we can both come now with little effort.

I roll us over, so that she's beneath me. Staring into her eyes, I smile. I push against her and she moans. I push again. I nudge her legs apart with my knee and position myself. She stares. We both know that as soon as we are joined it will be fast. She kisses my jaw, my cheek, my neck, then she reaches my ear and whispers. "I love being married to you." I groan and sink into her, then pull back and push in again. Slowly and steadily with a lingering rhythm that belies my desperate need, I move inside her.

Her legs wrap around me as she moves with me and once again I'm sure, the remaining guests must be able to hear our fevered cries. I can tell she's close, she always does this pre-emptive gasp.

"Open your eyes," I plead. "I need to see you come." She blinks back to reality for me and our eyes fix on each other as I thrust just a few more times into her and finally feel her explode.

She keeps her eyes on mine and makes a croaky sound of ecstasy. "I love you," she whispers, hoarse from her cries and I come long and hard into her. I manage not to close my eyes and I find the words. "I love you too."

I wake with a start. A panicked feeling like I've missed something. This has been happening more, the closer we get to the wedding, I must be subconsciously worried about forgetting something or being late. Then the warm memory of yesterday floods over me. We did it! It's done, I can relax, she said yes, nothing got in our way, she is my wife. I sigh with relief and drop my head back to the pillow.

"You okay?" Liv murmurs next to me.

I turn to face her. We're so tangled it's difficult, but I manoeuvre so that we are face to face. "Good morning, Mrs Morgan." I grin, kissing her forehead, then the end of her nose.

"Morning my husband," she purrs, closing her sleep heavy eyes again.

"I love hearing you say that."

"Get used to it," she says forcing her eyes to get with the program. "Why were you sighing?"

"Oh, I've been stressing a little in my sleep lately, but I just woke up and remembered it all paid off! It was a contented sigh."

She thinks for a moment. "Thank you for everything. It was the most perfect day of my life."

"I'll do anything for you."

Now she sighs contentedly. Then I see a flash of recognition in her eyes. "Is everyone really coming for breakfast?" she asks.

"Yeah, but not yet, it's still early." I glance at the clock. "We have a couple of hours."

"Hmm." She hums, snuggling in to me. "What can we do with a couple of hours?"

"Plenty." I kiss her. "But I have to pee!"

"Me first," she says suddenly and leaps up.

I fly after her and catch her at the bathroom door. "Oh no you don't!" I grab her around the waist from behind and pick her up, she shrieks and slaps me, but I put her down on the other side of me so that I'm in the lead and easily win the race.

"You're such an arse." She sulks, hopping from one foot to the other behind me.

"Hey, you married this ass!" I chuckle, making her wait.

"Well, this marriage will work better when we have two bathrooms." She teases as I finally step out of her way.

"Don't worry, we'll soon have more bathrooms than we can use," I say walking back into the bedroom. I throw on some underwear, sitting on the edge of the bed, then I pick a bottle of water out of our basket. Opening it and taking a swig, I leaf through the contents. It was so sweet, but we were too distracted last night to use any of it. Well apart from the ice, I must be sure to thank someone for that! I pull out the paracetamol, I don't feel too bad and I don't think Liv drank too much either. It was a kind thought though. I notice that beside the chocolates are some other snacks in case we were hungry last night. I was, but not for an energy bar. I lift the ice bucket out. It's now a bucket of warm water with an expensive bottle of champagne floating in it. I'll put it in the refrigerator and we can open it in the new house. Tucked behind the bucket is an envelope marked MR & MRS MORGAN.

Liv wanders in wearing the silk robe I gave her yesterday. "Look." I hold out the envelope.

"What's this?"

I shrug. "A card I guess, it was in the basket."

"We've got loads of these downstairs...and presents. I hope they're okay. You whisked me away!" She grins, tearing open the envelope. She opens the card and some paper slides out. I catch it and hand it to her. She frowns as she opens it and then gasps.

"What?"

"They've got us a night in a really posh hotel, in a suite! Wow, this must have cost a fortune."

I stand to look at the voucher over her shoulder. "Nice." I say kissing her bare skin.

"We could use this after we do the legal stuff to make it official. Like a second wedding night."

I smirk and scoop her up. "Can't," I respond. I hope she's still naked under that robe. "Got plans." I lay her back on the bed and crawl over her.

"Plans?" She stops me as I start to pull on the belt. She fixes me with a look that says that she won't be kept in the dark over everything. Not happily at least.

I laugh. I suppose I'm going to have to tell her. "Don't do your evil laugh, tell me what's going on!"

"Alright, I'll tell you!"

"Everything?"

I screw up my nose, maybe not everything.

"Danny!" She slaps my chest.

"Okay!" I roll off her and hold up my hands defensively. "Okay." I prop myself up on one elbow. "We're going on our honeymoon, but not yet. I wanted us to spend time with our families for a few days as they have come such a long way. So we're leaving Friday."

"A honeymoon?" she says with a big smile. "You didn't have to do that, you've done more than enough."

"You get married, you have a honeymoon. Of course we're having one. Besides this one's on my parents so don't sweat it."

"Wow, really?" she muses. "Everyone is being so generous, are you sure we should accept it?"

I frown. "Damned right we accept it, are you nuts? My parents know how to do the vacation thing like nobody else, so if they are buying I promise it's going to be great. Just relax."

She nods, then smiles again. "So where are we going?"

"Do I have to tell you?" I ask but with resignation in my voice, so she knows she can win.

"Danny!" she moans because I'm driving her nuts.

"Mexico, okay. We're going to Mexico. We fly out Friday to Cancun for five nights and then we fly on to Cabo for five nights. They want us to see the sights in Cabo, as they're going to be making it home for half the year soon and they'll want us to visit them there." I hesitate, but I should at least tell her some of the rest. "Then we're visiting LA for a few days or so before we come back so that I can look into doing that thing, you know for Jen and Scott. If that really is still okay with you." I don't know why it's taken me so long to check back with her about how she really feels, I guess I'm just afraid she'll say yes, but mean no. Or simply regret it later. I can't have this affect our marriage or our future.

She strokes my face. "It really is still alright with me. I was going to come with you, whether you liked it or not, but this is perfect."

I wince. "Is it okay to visit a sperm bank on our honeymoon, or is it just too weird?"

She laughs hard. "It's a little weird I suppose, I doubt most people would get it, but surely we're just weird enough to pull it off? Besides who will know other than us? You should do it and I support you completely."

"I promise I won't go ahead until we have our family. They will completely understand, Jen said as much herself."

"It's okay." She rubs my shoulder. "It will be fine. You'll donate and it will be kept until you say so. Do you know how many times you have to do it?"

I sigh. "I've read so many different accounts. But I think they will need a few because it's only half as effective if its frozen. I just need to get out there and meet with them to find out more." I smile at her. "You are a wonderful person, letting this happen, you know?"

"Me? I'm not doing anything, it's you doing the wonderful thing."

"You know what I mean. Most people wouldn't be okay with this."

"Well I am," she says, putting an end to my fears. "Have you told them yet?"

This is my other problem. I shake my head, twisting my fingers between hers. "It feels like too much pressure. The odds aren't great. I don't want to build their hopes up. I'll tell them once I know more."

"It will be fine, I promise." She kisses me gently. "Three weeks huh? You spoil me."

I managed to shake off my funk and find a pleasing way to pass an hour or so with my wife. I hand her a towel as she steps out of the shower. I should never have worried, she loves our morning ritual as much as I do and we still shower together almost every day, even though she doesn't need me to help her anymore.

She looks fantastic in her long black dress, so cool and casual, with her sneakers and her hair loose and still wavy from being twisted up yesterday. She picks up her sister's bracelet from the nightstand before we head down and I hand her her shades as I hook mine on my shirt. It looks bright out and we're eating in the garden.

Everyone is here already when we get outside, my parents, Liv's parents, Connie and Jack, Grace Andy and the kids, Jen and Scott, and Max and Charlie. Our family. They all greet us warmly and then some light-hearted ribbing about our disappearance last night gets a wolf-whistle from Scott. Jen slaps him and it settles down.

They have configured a long table and Liv and I take the last two spaces in the middle. Everyone is chatting and drinks are passed along the line, orders are taken, Matthew is hopping from one grown up to another, making the most of all the attention. Jen is holding baby Mia, which makes my stomach clench tightly. I want that so badly for myself right now but the responsibility I feel for her to have it too is almost overwhelming. It just isn't fair that it's so hard for her. I can remember a time when *not* getting pregnant was her only concern in life and now…this. It sucks. I'm going to do everything in my power to help her.

I'm intrigued with this new friendship between Grace and Jen. I guess they spoke a few times on the phone when Liv first left me and then again while we were planning this whole week. It's nice, just weird, considering what Grace used to be like. Jen spies me watching her with Mia and gives me her best 'I'm okay, really' smile. I respond with mine that says 'I'm just concerned that's all'. She laughs a little and then turns her attention back to the baby.

After a predictably awesome breakfast, the crowd disperses. Some are going shopping, some are just heading off to relax. Liv and I go back to bed! Hey, it's our first day as husband and wife and I don't have to abstain from anything yet.

Twenty-five.

Funny and wonderful.

Liv.

"Typical, just as I'm getting on a transatlantic flight!" Jen says as she holds up a tampon. I roll my eyes in empathy then feel a pang of sympathy. It must be awful when you hope so badly that something will happen month after month and then you get the flat out no, in the airport toilets of all places. I can't imagine the disappointment. I hope I never have to feel that disappointment. I'm not expecting to fall pregnant instantly, but month after month it must be awful, the hope building up and then crashing down. They've been trying for over two years. At least now they're working on a solution.

When she emerges and uses the sink beside me, I casually ask. "How is that all going anyway?"

"Oh, you know, it's going." She smiles, it's obviously a practiced smile. "It's a lot easier since we know what the problems are. I'm ovulating like clockwork now and we are timing our attempts to coincide as precisely as possible…and the days either side too. I'm killing Scott in the process, mind you. I know it's unlikely to happen, but the doctor said it couldn't hurt to keep trying. Especially as we know I'm in full working order now and I'm keeping track. You never know, one of his swimmers might get lucky if we give it a helping hand." She laughs then wrinkles her nose.

"It's disappointing when that happens every month, but I guess we're used to it. I won't tell Scott it's happened again just yet, I'll wait until we are home. Besides, when I do, I see the look in his eyes, it's dread more than anything, he makes a mental note that in a couple of weeks I'll have him on call for days. The fun has well and truly left the building, he almost looks afraid!" She giggles, so do I at the mental image of Scott, running and hiding. I admire her strength for being able to laugh, when it's far from funny.

I wish I could tell her that Danny is going to help them, but it's for him to say not me. I need to let him do it however he feels comfortable. I just can't help thinking there must be an easier way than the whole freezing thing. But the only thing I can come up with, would involve my new husband crossing a huge line with his best friend during our honeymoon...So freezing it is!

We meet the boys back out in the terminal. Danny's parents flew home early this morning, but as we are only flying an hour before Jen and Scott, we decided to come to the airport together. It has been nice mooching around the terminal with them, but it's time for Danny and me to go to our gate, so we hug them and say our goodbyes. We will see them in ten days, so it's an easy farewell.

I buckle my seat belt and settle into my large, comfy seat. We are in Premium, so the seats are bigger and there's more leg room, but best of all, the seats are in pairs, so we don't have to share space with a stranger for hours. Danny flips through his magazine beside me, his wedding ring glinting in the light makes me smile.

"Don't!" he says, snapping his magazine closed.

"Don't what?" I frown.

"I saw you smirking at me. I'm excited about the house that's all, if I want to look at an interior design magazine, I will. I'm comfortable with who I am!" He says, stifling a laugh.

I burst out laughing. I didn't notice he was reading *Living etc*. I press my lips together to prevent a mocking remark escaping. He narrows his eyes. "I was smiling at your wedding ring, I like looking at it. God, touchy!" Then I can't contain my laughter.

He's so excited about the house. I'm relieved it was all finalised before we left because it would have eaten him up. It's bad enough we are both thinking about Jen and Scott so much. I know it's our honeymoon, but it's dominating our thoughts. I'd not fully appreciated how much it was affecting Danny and since talking to Jen at the airport, now it's all I can think about too.

I promise myself a little alone time with the laptop as soon as I can. I want to support Danny, but I need to know more in order to be of use. Until now I've just gone along with what he told me, but if we're going to do this, then I want it to be together. I'll always support him and he needs to know that now more than ever. He is taking a huge risk with our fledgling marriage and far from worrying me, it has shown me the faith he has in ME. He's taken me at my word and believes that I support him in something many people would think of as unacceptable. Especially in this early stage of our life together. I'm going to show him that his faith is warranted. Wow, we've come a long way.

We're offered champagne and then it really feels like our honeymoon gets started. From then it's a whirlwind. Cancun is beautiful, we hardly see any of it though, because Danny's parents have stumped up for the honeymoon suite in the most spectacular hotel I've ever seen, and… because they/the universe gave me Danny to share it with.

The food was fabulous, I must have gained at least a stone. I notice my jeans are tighter when I put them back on to travel, but this is no surprise, there was buffet after buffet. There were snacks and cakes and hors d'oeuvres…We ate on the balcony, in the bath in the centre of our plush suite, in the pool, by the pool (and it wasn't just gratuitous eating that we did in all those places either). Danny and I have simply lazed in each other's arms, for a blissful week.

We'd agreed to try and do more this week, in Cabo. Partly because his parents have assigned things for us to see, like the place they're buying and the surrounding area. Of course we did this dutifully, but it isn't our fault that they got us another insanely luxurious suite that we never want to leave.

"Come on, Danny." I sigh as his arms fold around me and his warm breath stirs the nerves of my neck. "We have to get dressed for dinner."

"Why? Let's get room service again, I have everything I need right here," he murmurs, pulling me closer.

"We haven't seen the light of day today, don't you want to get out?" My pale blue, wedding night underwear presses against his bare golden skin. I put it on for him because it turns him on, and on this occasion he can leave it on me and admire it. We're going out for dinner…if he ever puts some underwear on!

"We did, we were on the balcony for ages and we went for a swim." He softly croons in my ear as his hands snake their way over my body.

"Danny, sex on the balcony and then in the hot tub for three hours, is not seeing the sights!" I giggle trying to extricate myself from his grip.

"I saw some sights," he smirks. "Now I want to see some more."

I'm determined to go out tonight, but he's making it so hard. I turn in his arms and face him. He's impossible to resist. I gasp as his hand slips inside the delicate lace of my underwear and shudder when his finger brushes my clit. I kiss him, slowly, as his fingers enter me. I know we're not leaving this room tonight, but I keep up the pretence for a minute longer. While I'm lingering around his ear, I whisper what I wish he could do to me if we weren't going out to dinner. He moans, turned on by my explicit words, so I continue, telling him what I wish I could do to him. Then, what I say to him turns him on so much it almost gets him there.

I whisper. "Oh, screw it. Use me…don't hold back, take what you need."

"Oh God, Liv." He groans as I sink to kneel at his feet.

I take him in my mouth, running my tongue all the way around him to ease my path. He sighs at first but as I move, his sighs become whispers, the whispers become moans. Then as I begin to accept him deeper and deeper, his hands appear, ready to do what I asked. To use me and take what he needs.

He is never rough, but I love it when he takes control. That first night we were together, it happened by accident, but the effect on both of us was amazing, it's something he knows I love now and he doesn't feel bad about it. He forces himself into my mouth, over and over again, while my fingers dig into his thighs. My hands give an indication to him of just how much I can take. Occasionally they twitch up, almost at the point of asking him to stop, but I never do. I can take it, but it drives him crazy, thinking I'm on the verge of begging him to stop.

I make that low throaty moan he loves and he gasps.

"Jesus, Liv." He hisses. "Touch yourself."

A thrill goes through me and I willingly oblige, sliding my hand under the soft lace of my underwear. He can't see, but he knows I'm doing it. I moan to let him know I've hit home and he seems to lose control at the thought. Focusing hard on his goal, he uses long, slow strokes. I roll my tongue around him every time he almost withdraws and accept him back as deep as possible each time he pushes in. His jagged breaths tell me he's getting close and my fingers bring a stifled moan from me that seals the deal for him.

"I'm gonna come." He moans desperately. I simply allow him to use me to get there, I love it when he really lets go "Oh God." He gasps as his body tenses, then releases into my willing mouth.

He shudders as he finishes. Looking down at me, he laughs.

I'm breathless and weak with need, but I'm happy on this occasion to make that all about him. It's one in the bank for me later, not that we're keeping score. Trembling a little, I stand and wipe away the tears he forced from my eyes with his deep thrusting.

"Can we go to dinner now?" I smirk.

"I don't think you were finished." He grins, trailing a finger along the fabric of my knickers.

"Later." I say firmly, moving his hand away.

"No, now!" He demands, lifting me suddenly.

I shriek, "Danny! Put me down!" Which he does, on the bed, with a thump. He yanks my underwear to the side and sucks in my clit, before I know what has happened.

"Oh, God!" I cry as his fingers push inside me. He's unbelievably talented, my husband. He takes me straight to the edge and holds me there longer than I can stand it. I'm begging for mercy within minutes as he relentlessly sucks and licks and occasionally bites. I hiss as his teeth once again close over what, right now, feels like the centre of my being.

"Danny, please…"

"Uh, uh." He shakes his head.

"Please…" I whimper.

He sucks me hard again.

"Fuck! Please give it to me…please let me come."

Then his fingers twist inside me and his free hand reaches up and pinches my nipple…and I'm gone. Shouting his name, I crash out of control into a mind-blowing orgasm.

Panting, I lay tangled in the sheets. Danny flops down beside me looking very pleased with himself.

"Ready to go to dinner then?" He laughs.

"Fuck you!"

"Hey! That better not be an empty promise." He pulls the sheet over us and tickles me until I can't breathe.

"Danny, stop!" I beg. "I give up!"

"Give up what?"

"We can stay in and get room service." I giggle, his hands still making me squirm.

"Yeah!" He yells, fist pumping the air.

"You're so funny!" I wipe a stray tear and lift the sheet to peep at him. He laughs and pulls me in, hugging me tight.

"Funny?"

"Funny and wonderful," I say, lovingly stroking his face.

"You forgot hot."

"Funny and wonderful and hot.' I correct myself.

"And virile, don't forget virile."

I raise my eyebrows. "How virile?" I ask as his mouth hovers over mine. He looks at me suggestively and then shows me. My God, he shows me.

I still can't quite believe he managed it. It took him so long to build back up to it that I was completely wrung out by the time he reaches his second and I reached my fourth climax of the night. A record for both of us. Virile hardly covers it!

I'm actually aching from the things we've done to each other. I'm afraid to even calculate the number of orgasms. But if the average is once per new surface and at least twenty per hot tub, I'd say we were in the hundreds. Danny is behaving like we will never have sex again after today, I know we're staying ay Jen and Scotts but we don't have to stop, we just have to learn some restraint. I sigh as I cross my legs and feel the familiar tenderness from our overexertions this morning. Determined to have me while he still could, we had a lovely long shower. My fingers are still pruney.

Sitting in the departure lounge in Cabo, I hold his hand. I can feel the anxiety building in him. Heading back to LA to do his best to help his friends has begun to take its toll on him. The pressure he's putting on himself is immense. Our flight is called and he gives me that 'here-goes' look as he stands and picks up our bags. His foot begins to tap as we push back from the stand and I touch his knee gently to steady it. I try to offer him a reassuring smile, but he's lost in the tension. We've talked so much about it now, that I know his biggest fear is it never working. The odds are stacked against them, given the restrictions of time and distance and he just doesn't want to let them down.

Jen wanted to pick us up from the airport, but Danny said we'd need a car anyway, so he has arranged a hire and we make our own way. I smirk at the Range Rover. Boys! It's strange to be here again. Only five months since I fled, life looks a whole lot different cruising along the freeway today. I stroke Danny's leg. He's still tense, but being home seems to have settled him slightly and when we pull into the driveway at Jen and Scott's and Jen bowls out to greet us, he visibly relaxes.

"Long time!" She teases.

It's mid-afternoon on a Monday, so I'm surprised when Scott appears in the doorway to help us in with our luggage.

"What are you doing here? I was told you never stop working," I say and kiss his cheek.

"Well, I don't know how often I'll see you two now, so I took a few days off." He says and softly kisses me back.

"We're honoured." I grin.

"Come on, let's get your things in the laundry," says Jen. She had very helpfully suggested not packing too much for the long trip as we could use her washing machine. A genius idea and it prevented me from having packing melt-down.

"You're a star!" I say, linking my arm through hers, leaving the boys to bring in the bags.

We round the corner into the open-plan living area and I'm stunned to find Max and Charlie relaxing on the large corner sofa.

"What the hell?"

Max laughs and jumps up and still holding his cold beer, he squeezes the life out of me.

"What are you doing here?" I ask, though my question gets lost, or ignored, amid the hugging and backslapping of our group. It's obvious at once that I'm the only person not in on this surprise. I stand hands on hips, waiting for someone to fill me in and when everyone notices, they all laugh.

"Come and sit out in the garden, I'll get you a drink and we'll tell you everything." Danny smirks.

"Hmm." I huff.

I follow Max and Charlie into the garden and sit with them, looking between them, all I get are shrugs and grins.

"Okay," says Danny, bringing a tray of cold drinks out, with Jen and Scott in tow. He hands them out and sits beside me. I look at him, waiting. He gets the message and spits it out. "I invited them," Danny explains. "You and I still aren't legally married and I wanted to put that right as soon as possible, so we're all going to fly out to Vegas this weekend to make this thing official." He shrugs. "I just thought it would mean more to you if our friends came too."

I shake my head and laugh. "You are something else, do you know that?" I say looking at his perfect face. I lean over the arm of my chair and kiss him. I get up and hug everyone. "So this is what you meant by having plans?"

"Yeah," he says lovingly, pulling me into his lap.

"It's brilliant, thank you. And thank you guys for coming out here. It wouldn't be the same without you." I kiss the top of Danny's head. I guess I'm growing accustomed to his constant surprises. It feels much easier to just go with the flow.

"Aren't you going to fret about how I've covered us both being away?" Max teases.

"No!" I shoot back. "This is a new me, get used to it. You are the manager, I trust you. I'm relinquishing control."

Max raises his eyebrows. "I'm very impressed."

I did tell Max before we left for Mexico that Danny and I are trying for a baby and obviously once that happens, my Rottweiler-like grip on the business would have to ease. He knows he will be running the show, it's why he's on board. We've always been more of a partnership really and Danny and I are looking into ways to make it more rewarding for him, but I know he doesn't expect it.

"Seriously though, is this it now? There's nothing else you are keeping from me?" I ask Danny.

Danny really has to think about it. "Nope, I think then we're done."

"So no long-lost siblings I'm about to be reunited with? I'm not getting punked? This is really it?"

Danny laughs. "Yes, this is it, I swear. I'm done blindsiding you." He strokes my shoulder.

"Good," I say. I smile inwardly, the next time someone get blindsided, I can safely say it won't be me and I'll be the one holding all the cards…I can't wait.

Twenty-six.

I'm calling a meeting.

Liv.

With Danny and the boys at the beach and Jen gone to check in on her shop, I'm grateful that the house is empty while I digest what I now know. We've only been here a day and it's been lovely, but Danny can't relax and I've been feeling it too. I know Jen is constantly thinking about Danny's original offer and, to be honest, it's become the elephant in the room. Danny talked to the clinic earlier and, when he's ready, he just has to make an appointment for blood tests then he can donate. He wants to wait and come back to do that when we're ready.

I'm just coming out of the bathroom when I hear Jen come home. I breathe deeply, my hands are shaking and I need to calm down before I go out there, or I could blow my cover. I can't believe how it's coming together. I'm virtually giddy and I would hug myself if I could.

"Hi." I call out across the living room, to Jen in the kitchen. I hope I don't sound like I feel.

"Oh, hi. I thought everyone was out."

"I just got back."

"I'm having a coffee, do you want one?" she asks.

"Actually, I was just going to have a juice, if that's okay?"

"Orange?" I screw up my face and shake my head. Jen chuckles, reaching for the apple juice. "You and Danny are made for each other!"

"So how are things going now?" I ask casually. "You were saying at the airport that you'd have Scott on call twenty-four-seven after a couple of weeks."

"Ha!" Jen blurts. "He's wise to me. Do you see him anywhere around? He's afraid to be left alone with me."

"Hmm, it won't be ideal for you with all of us here, just at the wrong time." I look at my hands, suddenly feeling guilty for being so inconsiderate. "We could go to a hotel if you like."

"Don't be silly. A month off won't kill us, it's a damned near impossibility anyway. It just can't hurt that's all." She sighs.

"So what's next?" I ask. I'm looking for a way into a sensitive conversation I've no place in. But Danny hasn't talked to them yet and time is ticking. He has an appointment at the clinic in two days and I need to state my intentions before then.

"Well, we need a donor…but that's been…on hiatus." She suddenly looks as awkward as I feel.

A silence spans between us. Oh God, I'm just going to have to bring it up and hope Danny won't be angry with me for getting involved. "I know Danny wants to help you," I say quietly. Then, seeing Jen's blanched face, I realise that came out like I hate her for it. "We've talked about it and I really support him…all of you. I want him to do it."

She frowns at me, probably because she doesn't get why I would support it.

"I…I didn't want him to jeopardise anything between you two, he offered when he thought…" She drifts off before she finishes saying that Danny offered this when he believed all hope of us having a future was gone.

"It's okay. He told me everything. I really appreciate what you did for us. We wouldn't be here if you hadn't. But…it's really important to him and I know why. I'd be the same for Max. I just wanted you to hear it from me. I'm okay with it, really."

I realise that her eyes have welled up, so I step towards her and put my arm around her. "You don't have to say it's okay. I knew it was a long shot. We can go through the normal channels." Tears roll down her face.

"No, Danny badly wants to give you this. Please let him."

Just then we hear the boys pull into the driveway. Jen quickly wipes her eyes and laughs a little at her wayward emotions. She doesn't know how close I came to joining in, but we pull ourselves together just in time and the boys find us sipping juice. That was close, I need to talk to Danny; the weight of what I have to say to everyone suddenly becomes unbearable.

Danny frowns from across the room as soon as he walks in, he can see something is wrong. He comes straight over. "What's wrong?" he whispers.

I smile. "Nothing's wrong, everything is so right in fact." I slip my arm round his waist. "But I think we should have a talk with Jen and Scott."

"Not yet," he mumbles.

"No, we have to say something, all this not saying is eating away at our time together. Please?"

He nods, he feels it too. "Okay."

I grab my chance. "I'm calling a meeting," I say to the room. Five faces turn to me with varying degrees of uncertainty, ranging from Charlie's general surprise, to Danny's horror that I'm just running with this now, no further conversation. "Please, it's important. Can you all just sit down?"

"What are you doing?" Danny hisses.

"The right thing," I state simply and push past him.

"Wait, Liv we have to talk about this. I don't think I can go through with it...I'm not ready...I need to be sure you can deal with it."

"I can deal with it." I look into his eyes, trying to will him to have the confidence to believe me, find the faith I know he has in me underneath this momentary lapse. "Do you trust me?"

"Without question."

"Then come with me and listen to how on board with this I really am." He hesitates and then follows.

Everyone else is sitting round the big table between the living room and the kitchen, waiting to know why they are there. Max looks like he ought to know what this is about, but can't put his finger on it and it's bugging him. Maybe we should do this without them, but it sort of involves them too.

"Alright everyone. We need to talk about some stuff and unless someone speaks up, the wondering what will happen is going to affect everyone." I take a deep breath. "Max, Charlie." I turn to them. "Jen and Scott are trying to conceive and Danny has offered to help them by being their sperm donor." Danny cringes. Max nods, he knew about their fertility issues.

Charlie begins to stand. "We should let you discuss this in private" he says sweetly.

"Sit down." I say, a lot more forcefully than I meant. Charlie looks shocked. "Sorry. It's just that this concerns you too, If you two ever want children, I'm helping you, so you may as well be involved in this." Charlie is taken aback. Max half smiles. I always said I'd have his baby for him one day, but this is real. My asking them to join this conversation is a future offer, he knows I'm serious. "If you don't want that, then your support on this is still appreciated."

"Okay." I take a steadying breath. "So Jen, Scott... Danny has been tying himself in knots over helping you. He wants to do it so much it aches, I can feel it. I've told him I think it's great. I've talked about it with him until I'm blue in the face. But deep down he's terrified that once it's done, it will somehow come between us." I turn to Danny. "Is that about right?"

Danny nods.

"Good. At least we all understand each other. For my part, I wholeheartedly support him in doing this and I want to make a similar offer to Max and Charlie. For years I've said that if Max wants to be a dad, I'd carry his baby. I don't even know if he wants it anymore, but if at some point in the future you wish to explore the options." I turn to Max and Charlie, so they can see I'm dead serious. "I would need to discuss it with Danny fully, but I would be open to talking about it." A few cautious nods follow. Danny is wide-eyed, but the support for my sudden and frank offer shows on his face.

"I just can't stand this anymore. The pressure is getting to Danny right at a time when I need him most. So tell them Danny, tell them you're helping them."

Danny sighs but then he gives me a tight smile and takes my hand for support. "Okay, I called the clinic and I have all the information." He shrugs. "So once we're ready, you know, once we've started our family, I want to get started. I'll fly back and make the donations until you have however many you need."

I shake my head. "Actually, I called them back. You have an appointment for tomorrow."

Danny looks at me, stunned.

"Liv, we talked about this, not until we have our own family."

"No way!" says Jen. "We told you, we are not taking Danny's first child."

"We can wait," says Scott quietly behind her.

"Liv, you should think about this," Charlie interjects.

Max just eyes me quietly. I hold his stare and I know he sees what is at the centre of this. A ghost of a smile crosses his lips.

I hold my hands up to stop everyone, someone is going to have an aneurism if I don't calm this down. "Stop, please just hear me out."

"Liv, no!" Danny erupts beside me. "I know you want to help, I do too, but not like this. We come first." He gives Max a pleading look. "Max, will you talk to her?"

I stand and slip my hand in my back pocket. Pulling it out, I hand him the white stick.

Danny looks at me, eyes wide, his mouth twitches, he blinks and then looks back at the stick. He takes it gently from my hands and looks at the display. Slowly he looks back at me. I've never seen him so stunned, then the lights come back on and he leaps to his feet. The happiest, most confused, delirious smile I've ever seen, spreading across his beautiful face while he is in motion. He grabs me and lifts me clear off the ground, spinning me around and laughing. I'm suddenly aware that we're both laughing. Tears roll down my face and when Danny finally puts me down, his lips are on mine before I even get a proper breath in.

"Are we having a baby?" he asks as he lets me up for air, his eyes shining with unexpressed emotion.

"Yes," I whisper.

The others gather around us and I'm aware of congratulatory hugs and kind words, but, after Danny, my main focus is Jen. Our eyes meet. She's crying, but they're happy tears. There's not a trace of resentment in her eyes and I know then that she is a true friend to Danny. Only the most pure friendships can withstand such landslide moments and she is unquestioningly happy for us. I smile at her and she smiles back. Danny lets go of me for a second and grabs her and I watch while they share this fantastic news together. Max envelops me in his arms.

"I'm so proud of you," he whispers. "Congratulations." I wipe my eyes as Danny turns back to me and Max relinquishes me to my husband.

"When did you find out?" Danny asks.

"Today. I'm due on in a couple of days, but I feel different, my jeans are tight. I've felt like it for a week. So I did a test." I gasp as he slides his hand over my stomach. We've had some heartbreakingly tender moments over the years, but this tops them all, hands down.

A tear rolls down his cheek. "Thank you," he says. I smile softly.

"You see why I think we should do this now?" I say quietly to him while everyone else is giving us a little distance for our moment.

"Yes." He sniffs. Then he smiles. "You are a very special person, you know? You don't even stop to savour your own moment without thinking of someone else."

After we have composed ourselves, Jen suggests tea and coffee as we are unprepared and have no champagne. I help her make it. For a minute or two we work in silence and then I catch Jen looking at me.

"I'm so happy for you," she says .

"I know you are," I say and hug her.

"I just...I don't want you to think I'm just saying it. I'm so happy for you both, you will make wonderful parents. This is Danny's dream, I love him, I know you understand that, so you must know that I wouldn't have to fake this."

"I do, I get it. Thank you." We hug again. This is fast becoming emotionally exhausting!

After a pretty heavy afternoon, we all relax and digest the new turn in our lives. I watch in awe as Jen and Danny make us all dinner. They move around the kitchen like they are two parts of the same whole. They are so in sync and their bodies touch with practiced ease, it warms my heart and makes me feel smug at the same time. I doubt many spouses could stomach it. Scott is an understanding guy and came into this knowing their friendship…and me, well, just as I'm watching, Max comes up behind me, wrapping me in his arms and kisses my cheek. We're just…different…and today has proved just how different we really are.

Weary from an emotional and mind-bending day, we all turn in early. Tomorrow, Danny has his blood tests and will make his first donation. I sigh contentedly as I flop onto the bed. Danny closes the door behind him and stands watching me. I look up to see what he's doing after there is silence for a minute and realise that he's just staring. I raise up onto one elbow to look at him properly and he moves towards me, not breaking the intense stare, he drops to his knees beside the bed.

He continues holding my gaze as he gently runs his hand across my midriff. It still makes me gasp even though he's been doing it repeatedly all afternoon. I guess it'll just take a while to sink in for both of us. He's asked me how I'm feeling about fifty times and I haven't lifted a finger since I told him, giving me some insight into how he's going to be for the next eight to nine months. I honestly expected him to insist on carrying me the few feet to our guest room, fortunately, he let me walk.

Still with his hand on my stomach, he turns his eyes there too. I don't know what he thinks he will see, but the look on his face is pure joy and I won't take that away from him. I stroke my fingers through his hair and just watch him, lost in his moment.

He blinks and returns his eyes to mine, a smile lighting his face. "Are you feeling okay?" he asks again softly.

"Yes!" I giggle, a slight amused exasperation apparent in my tone. "I feel fine. Are you okay?"

He nods and that look of delirious joy comes over him again. I burst out laughing.

"What?" He frowns, although even that looks giddy with happiness, which makes me laugh harder. "Hey, what?"

"I blindsided you!" I laugh, pumping my fists in the air. "I did it!'

He laughs. "You did." He smiles with adoration. "You really did. Thank you."

"You've made me so happy," he whispers.

I woke this morning with Danny in my arms, exactly as he fell asleep. I stare at him, his peaceful face, utterly relaxed, the past few days he has been the happiest I've seen him. He's getting used to the idea that we have our dream come true and now that he is actively doing something to help Jen, he feels so much better. He has made a couple of donations so far. His last one for this trip is today. Unable to resist, I kiss his forehead and he stirs. We both stretch and he immediately reaches for me and then opens his eyes when he realises we are pressed together already.

"Morning." I smile, snuggling into him tighter.

"Morning. How are you feeling?" His now standard question.

"Great thanks, stop worrying. You'll be the first to know if I start feeling sick."

"I know, I just want to take care of you."

"Grace didn't get morning sickness, neither did my mum, it could be a genetic thing. I might be lucky."

"My mom got so sick, it's the main reason I'm an only child," he says regretfully. "I hope it's not genetic, I could have just cursed you to a full nine months of not being able to stomach anything."

"Well I feel fine so far, let's just hope this baby has my genes."

"That is what I'm hoping. She'll be perfect just like her mom."

"She?" I frown.

"Um, I don't know, that just came out," he says embarrassed. "I don't care, as long as you are both okay."

He squeezes me tight, this is still so hard to get used to; I feel almost silly claiming to be something as monumental as pregnant. Apart from tight jeans and an odd feeling of my body being on overdrive at times, I really don't feel any different. I feel like a bit of a faker. I even secretly did the spare pregnancy test yesterday to make sure. It was definitely positive. We've decided not to tell anyone else yet though. It's not my normal MO. I'm all for full disclosure, but with this whole Jen thing going on, it might be best if we wait. Nobody knows we aren't even properly married, what's one more secret?

But we're fixing the marriage thing, we're flying to Vegas today.

"We should get organised," I murmur, trying to ignore Danny's insistent lips on my neck.

"Really?" He tries his husky whisper on me.

"Really...Or don't you want to marry me?"

"I'd marry you every day if I could. But I just want five more minutes in bed with you first." He slides his hand up my camisole and caresses the sensitive skin under my breast.

"Okay, if you think five is all it will take, I'll get the cup." I smirk.

"Shit." Danny huffs, rolling over.

I sigh and turn to him. "I know it's been full-on, but you only have to do it one more time before we go, then you're all mine." He just has one last appointment before we leave, but I think he's starting to feel like a performing monkey, although he would never say it.

He turns suddenly and pins me beneath him. "I just want inside you." He growls, kissing me hard.

I smile against his lips and he begrudgingly releases me. "You can have me any way you want me when we get to Vegas," I purr.

He raises his eyebrows. "Any way...?" I laugh and push him off me.

"Come on, you have a date with a cup!"

Danny groans.

The afternoon sun on the strip is intense and so is the heat. You can never underestimate the cooling effect of being near the sea and out here in the desert, everything is so exposed. We pull into the Bellagio and our bags are loaded onto a bellhop's trolley and my wedding dress, kindly flown out by Max and Charlie, is placed on top. I can't wait to wear it again. Once we've checked in, Danny and I leave the guys and hop in a taxi to the Marriage Bureau, to get our marriage licence. I've been good and I haven't asked a lot of questions. I know Danny has fixed everything and I'm loving the freedom. I've been told the wedding will be happening tomorrow evening. So for now, we head back to the hotel and shower before meeting up for dinner.

The Bellagio buffet is extraordinary, then we hit the strip. I must say I never expected to spend my first trip to Vegas sober and watching both what I eat and how I take care of myself. But Jen is taking it easy, so that makes it easier. We do a whistle-stop tour of Caesars, The Mirage and Treasure Island, in the warm evening air, stopping at all the attractions. This place is like a giant Disney for adults; it's great fun. We go back towards the Bellagio on the other side of the strip and call in at the Venetian to wander around the canals and take a gondola ride, then after stopping briefly in Paris, we cross back and watch the fountains do their show before retiring to our hotel for the night. We walk through the casino with only mild interest and stroll through Via Bellagio window shopping the designer boutiques, then settle in at the Lily Bar for a nightcap.

Exhausted, I smile at Danny laughing with his friends. He smiles softly back at me and finishes his drink.

"I think I'm going to take my beautiful wife up to bed," he says finishing his drink.

"She's not officially your wife yet buddy," teases Scott.

"Hey, watch your mouth!" Danny snipes back with a wry smile, but I can tell he'll be happier tomorrow when Scott can't say a word. "Ready?" He offers me his hand and pulls me out of the oh-so-comfy seat.

We say our goodnights and find the lifts. I really am tired, it hit me like a ton of bricks as soon as we stopped moving. I stifle a yawn as we wait and Danny wraps his arm around me.

"Tired?" he asks, trying to conceal his real question, it's been days.

I nod as we step into the waiting lift. I see his shoulders sag slightly from the corner of my eye and smirk. I may be on the verge of sleep, but for him, I'll always find reserves. As soon as the doors close, I turn to him, deliberately and quite aggressively palming his crotch as I probe his lips with my tongue. He groans, surprised and overwhelmed, gasping when I break my seal of his mouth. "Jesus." He rasps while I tease him through his trousers. The lift dings and I turn away from him, allowing him to pull me close to cover his obvious erection.

I nod at the older couple who join us in the lift and Danny does his best to look un-phased, bless him. He has his arms slung casually around my waist and my hands rest over his, only I can hear his laboured breathing as he pants softly in my ear. The couple are to our right and slightly forward, so I press Danny further into the back wall and swivel my hips against him.

"Fuck," he whispers.

I turn and give him an innocent peck on the cheek. The lady beside me smiles, warmed by our 'young couple in love' cuteness. Maybe she wouldn't be so amiable if she could see the rock-hard bulge pressing against my arse and my wandering hand, the one she can no longer see, teasing Danny into near insanity.

He sucks air in sharply between his teeth and grunts slightly when I grasp him almost too firmly. He tries to cover it with a cough, but the man has already glanced at him.

"Please." Danny begs almost silently. He's begging me to stop in front of these people, but the edge in his voice is also pleading me to keep it up. I don't think he'd even be able to say which he really means, but I do ease up...a little.

The lift stops at our floor and Danny muscles me out, still clamped to my back. The couple eye us suspiciously, I'm near hysterical.

"Are you trying to get me arrested?" he growls, I laugh but he shuts me up by pressing me into the wall as the doors finally close. His mouth on mine settles my giggles and his iron crotch digging in to me reminds me that I've started something that needs to be finished. On the other side of us the lift dings as the other car arrives on our floor, worried that it could be our friends, Danny hustles us along the corridor to our room.

While he fumbles for the key card, I turn in his arms to face him and glance beyond him. It's just a couple of guys making their way down the corridor towards us, I wrap my arms around his neck and draw him in to a kiss, not caring if strangers see. All the while he is still trying to engage the card in the lock. The men mumble some crass comment as they pass and finally I hear the lock click behind me.

"Thank fuck!" Danny gasps picking me up and hoisting my legs around his waist. He steps through the door, his mouth on mine and bumps me against the wall of the entrance hall while he kicks the door shut behind him.

"Are you going to fuck me into another hotel wall?" I ask.

"I'm tempted." He says breathlessly, kissing and biting all of my exposed skin. "But I haven't been inside you in days…" His teeth capture my bottom lip and I groan. "…And I want it to last more than thirty seconds."

Twenty-seven.

You're everything to me.

Danny.

Lying awake behind her, I stroke my hand lightly across her stomach and leave it in place. I shake my head at myself as I bite back tears, again! This keeps happening, surely it should be Liv overcome with emotion, I can't even blame hormones. But the last few days, whenever she sleeps I lie awake and do this. This morning, the Las Vegas sunshine woke me as we forgot to close the drapes after…God, that was amazing last night.

She gave me head in front of the floor-to-ceiling window of our room overlooking the Bellagio fountains. If they attracted the usual crowd, we most definitely had an audience. I suppose the windows are probably tinted, but not knowing for sure didn't stop her. Then when I bent her over the desk beside the window, it didn't stop me either.

I pull my mind away from thoughts of last night before I start thinking about waking her up. She is so beautiful sleeping. It's just so unreal. This thing I've wanted since I was so young, since before the knowledge of what I wanted was even fully formed. She's here in my arms and I can't believe it. She is the love of my life, she's taken me back, she loves me exactly like I love her, she is my wife and now she has made it all real, she is having my baby.

I give her a gentle squeeze and she stirs.

"Whoa, it's bright." She winces burying her face in the sheets.

I chuckle. "We forgot to close the drapes after your little show," I tease, kissing the back of her neck.

"My little show? What about you? You actually swept stuff off the desk!"

"Sorry, next time I'll just let you get the brochure stuck to your face."

"Hmmm, next time, when will that be?"

I laugh as she turns to me, still squinting at the bright light, but I know that look. "You are insatiable." I grin, kissing her. I'm the luckiest man alive.

"I've missed it that's all, I've been sharing you with a cup for the last week."

"Well, I'm all yours now." I move over her and press against her until she groans. I nudge her knees apart and sink straight into her. She moans loudly and pulls me down on top of her, our bare skin pressing together as I start to move. Her fingers dig into my back, keeping me close while she raises her hips to meet me. I start to worry that I'm putting too much weight on her and I hesitate for a second giving my thoughts away.

"You were thinking about the baby again weren't you?" She sighs, throwing her hands back against the pillow in frustration.

Last night when we burst through the door, I had only one thing on my mind, fuck her hard. But the now constant thought in the back of my mind stopped me.

She is carrying our baby.

I'm realistic enough to know that sex won't do her or the baby any harm, but she's also delicate. I have to take care of her, I can't go throwing her around. But as hard as I try to be rational about nothing changing, I start feeling like the word 'fuck' should no longer be applied, she's growing a child inside her, my child, she should be revered, not fucked. She busted me thinking it last night and gave me a stern talking to. She's right, I just have to find the balance.

I'm processing all of this when I realise Liv is still looking at me.

"Danny, don't you go all weird on me."

"I'm not weird, I just want to make sure you're okay."

"I'm fine," she says firmly. We're about to lose the moment and I don't want that to happen.

"Good," I say, leaning forward and kissing her with enough force that she lets out a sound of pleasure. While my tongue reminds her that I know she can take it, I press forward inside her and she moans again into my mouth. I grab her wrists and hold them together above her head, pressing them into the bed with my weight while I pick up the pace. She gets really into it and is pushing against my hands, not struggling, just testing. It feels amazing, holding her down, invading her mouth with my tongue and owning her everywhere else as well.

She groans when I let her breathe and then she kind of yells involuntarily when I shift slightly changing the angle of the friction between us. "Shhh!" I hiss, aware that Max and Charlie are next door and while that didn't stop us last night, it's early and sound will carry further in the quiet of the morning. Liv gives me a flick of her eyebrows, a challenge, like she's saying, if I want her quiet, I'll have to shut her up, then with an impish grin she moans loudly again. I flash back to that night in her parents' guest room. She got really turned on when I made her shut up, maybe she wants me to do that again.

I push into her harder than before and she moans, "Shhh," I whisper. She moans again. "Quiet!" I say with as much authority as I can muster. "I'll have to stop if you can't keep it down." In response, she does a kind of hip swivel that nearly has me shouting out. "Fuck," I manage to say quietly. Then, still holding her hands captive, I slip my free hand between us and touch her in a way I know can only result in her being loud.

"Oh!" she cries.

I stop myself grinning triumphantly as I release her hands and plant my hand over her lips. "Shut the fuck up!" I whisper in her ear, getting a little carried away. How we got to this from me being worried about the baby, I'll never know, but it's working for her.

"Oh. My. GOD!" She breathlessly mumbles from behind my hand. Her eyes roll and I know if she had been standing she would have crumbled. Her hands stay firmly planted like I'm still holding her down, and while I keep her mouth shut, I still draw endless circles with my fingers, pushing her to the edge. She lets out a loud, "Ugh." So I shake my head and withdraw. My hand still gagging her, she whimpers with disappointment.

"Are you going to do as you are told?" I ask, trying hard not to laugh.

I like this game.

She nods vigorously behind my hand.

"Okay," I concede. "Quiet." I slide into her again. Her eyes close and she draws in a deep breath as I move, fingers still in place. She begins a rhythmic breathing. I watch her internalising all the sensation. I catch the odd flicker of her eyes and she's frowning in that cute way she does when she gets close. I can't take my eyes off her, she's the most incredible thing I've ever seen. She makes a tiny, clipped "mmh" and her eyes flicker open as she assesses my reaction to this slip up. I raise an eyebrow and stop moving. She shakes her head, pleading with her eyes for me not to stop.

I love this game!

I resume my pace and take it up a notch. Her eyes stay on mine until she can't take it anymore and she flickers them shut as she digs her fingers in the pillow and at the same time sinks her teeth into the palm of my hand to keep from making a sound. I feel rather than hear her intense orgasm and she whimpers slightly because I don't let up with my fingers while she rides it out, but I let her off. I'm so close to giving in, but watching her squirm is something wonderful. Her body tries to come down from the heights it has just visited, but my fingers won't let her, I wonder if she could go again?

I know from experience there is almost no limit to the number of times she can come, but I've never got her tripping one straight into the next like this, we always have a breather. But suddenly it becomes my mission in life to get her to come again, right now.

"You're going to come again," I whisper. Upping my efforts and allowing her to cry out.

"What?" she slurs, pushing my hand aside, still a little lost in the aftershocks and battling against my fingers, relentless on her oversensitive clit.

"You heard me. You're going to give me another one before I let you go." With that I pull out all the stops.

"I don't think I...I need a min...OH GOD!" She cries out and convulses beneath me, arching her back off the bed in the throes of a violent climax. Her grip on me from the inside almost takes me with her, almost. But I'm on a mission now and she groans and wriggles and then whimpers and pleads when she registers that I'm still not stopping.

"One more," I order. I'm loving this, she's normally so in control that pulling her apart is a dizzying power trip. I could get used to this, once she goes, she's putty. Mine to shape however I choose.

"Danny...please give me a...please...fuck!...it's too much...ah, sensitive...please..." She claws her way up the bed to get away from my relentless hand.

"Ssshh," I soothe, slowing my hand slightly. We have reached the huge upholstered headboard and I kneel, lifting her up so that she is sitting astride me and inch us closer to prop her up against it. She moans almost in despair when I push my fingers back against her, well this time it's just my thumb, but it still gets her full attention as it starts turning those circles that will bring her one more. One more that I'm having with her.

I grab her delicious butt with my other hand and hoist her up, raising up on my knees and pushing her into the cushiony wall behind us. Now I can really fuck her into another hotel wall, but it's soft enough that I don't have to feel bad. I give her everything I have, slamming into her again and again, still teasing those frayed nerves with my thumb.

"God, Liv...I love you," I growl, digging my fingers into her hip and burying my face in her neck. "Go on, one more."

I hear her gasp and then she lets go. She shudders against me, she would have doubled over if my body wasn't pressing her against the wall. "Danny," she whispers.

Hearing my name is all it takes. I tense and then lose myself in a free-fall. Fuck...amazing...perfect...Is this the best it has ever been?...I mean ever?...Can you ever really know that?...Do I need to be thinking about it now? Through all the thoughts crowding my brain, I can only get out one word. "Liv."

We flop back onto the bed, panting and exhausted. Liv lands on top of me and does not have the energy to peel herself off, so she just sighs heavily and gives in to it.

I run my fingers lightly up and down her spine. "Liv?"

"Yeah?"

"You okay?" I whisper.

She giggles slightly. "Okay?" She lifts her head to look at me, blowing a strand of her freshly fucked hair out of her eye. "You're asking me if I'm O.K…After THAT?"

"Uh-huh." I nod. "Are you?" I frown, she doesn't get it. I need to take care of her. She convinces me to not treat her any differently and then somehow we end up in that crazy frenzy and now I'm not supposed to show any concern.

"I'm fine, Danny." She shakes her head in exasperation. "More than fine actually, I'm floating. I probably won't be able to walk today, but that was beyond incredible." She laughs and drops her head back down on my chest.

"So it wasn't too much?" I ask, knowing it's going to piss her off, but I can't find a way not to ask.

She sighs. "If you do anything that is too much, I'll tell you then and there and if you won't stop killing my buzz then I'm afraid it's your turn to shut the fuck up." She lifts her jelly-like hand and carelessly mashes it onto my face.

"Liv?" My voice is muffled and distorted by her hand.

She lifts her head and narrows her eyes, daring me to bring her any further out of her post-orgasmic haze.

"Wanna go again?" I laugh.

"Fuck off!" she says laughing with me. I pull her up my chest and our mouths lock.

"Three times? Fuck off, you're so full of shit!" Scott shouts, waving my claim off. "Three times in one night, fine, but three times in ten minutes? Fuck off!"

I shrug. "I'm telling you, she digs it. I tell her what to do and she falls apart."

"Liv? We are talking about Liv here, right?" Charlie laughs from across the table. "Liv? About your height, tattoos, nice girl, control freak, beautiful, wouldn't fuck with her…Are you sure you don't mean you tell her what to do and she slaps you in the head so you don't do it again?"

The three of us belly laugh. "I know, I nearly shit myself the first time I did it. But I swear, it gets results."

"Wow. Max won't believe this," Charlie says shaking his head and reaching for his coffee.

"Oh hell no! This is bachelor party talk. He made his choice when he when to the spa with the girls, this stays between us."

Charlie holds up his hands in surrender. "Alright, alright. I won't say a word. But you know they'll be discussing it right now. Liv tells Max everything."

"This is one twisted little circle we have got ourselves here," Scott mutters.

"Yeah, I think we went past twisted around Tuesday. There's no word for the place we are now." I joke, looking at Scott, still waiting for some sign that he's not fine with the whole my-sperm-inside-his-wife-thing.

"I think it's one of those situations where we have to agree that the details stay between us, I mean it works, but I doubt anyone would understand."

"We're not, like, gang-banging here!" I reply.

Charlie laughs, "No, but come on, there's you and Liv, right. You both have these questionably close friendships with members of the opposite sex. Just about everyone already accepts that. But here we are in Vegas, getting you secretly married because the first one was a fake, you've knocked your bride up already. Then you, hopefully, get your best friend pregnant while on your honeymoon. Now there is talk of Liv helping us if we want kids. People are going to think there's some bed swapping going on. "

"I don't care what anyone thinks, it is what it is. I'm happy." I watch the pool for a moment, reflecting on how utterly inadequate the words 'I'm happy' actually are. I'm complete, alive, ecstatic, delirious, content, excited, relaxed, overwhelmed and most of all deeply in love. Is there a word for that? Happy is a piss poor excuse if that is all there is. I shrug, with all that in my life, people can think what they like. They can't touch us. "So, what do we have planned?"

"We finish breakfast," says Scott. "Then we hit a strip joint." He wiggles his eyebrows.

Charlie groans and throws his head back, although I get the sense that he would tolerate it for the sake of the group. But I screw up my nose.

"I'm kidding! I'm not telling you what we have planned. Drink up." He grins.

"Easy, it's bad enough you are making me eat breakfast without Liv, now I'm on the clock?" I knock back the rest of my coffee, wishing secretly I could have gone to the spa.

"This is your bachelor party, suck it up. Tonight you'll be married, this is your last stand," Scott moans.

"I've been married for two weeks," I remind him. God, if he keeps mentioning it, I'm going to kill him. I can't wait to get this paperwork straight to shut him up.

"Whatever, come on let's go."

When I get back to the room its 4pm. Liv is drying her hair wearing a hotel robe and doesn't hear me come in. I watch her from the doorway to the bathroom. She's just beautiful. I could watch her all day. She looks up and shuts off the dryer.

"Hi, I didn't hear you come in," she says smiling sweetly.

"Sorry, I didn't mean to startle you." I step over to her and wrap my arms around her. We both face the mirror and look in each other's eyes. I kiss behind her ear. "How was your day? You smell fantastic."

"My day was very relaxing thanks. How about yours?"

"I wouldn't say it was relaxing, but it was awesome! We went to the Speedway, took a tour and got to drive some fast cars. Then we stopped in at the Shelby HQ for a tour. Honestly, you should have seen some of the cars, Liv; it was a great day."

"I can see you enjoyed it." She grins and kisses me on the forehead. "You look like you did when your dad gave you that BMX when you were eight."

I laugh, I love that she knows that much of my life. "I feel like an eight year old." I agree. "I'd better shower and get ready." I turn on the shower and Liv finishes her hair. Then we help each other get dressed. She straightens my tie and I zip up her dress.

"You should leave the jacket," she says. "It's way too hot. But here…" She turns back the cuffs of my dress shirt in wide neat folds until they are just above my elbows and then she buttons my vest. Then she steps back to appraise me. I put my hands in my pockets, self-conscious with her eyes on me.

"Do I pass?"

"Pass? You look perfect. I might make us fashionably late." She purrs running her hands around to my back and pulling me tight.

"No you won't, not for this, I need to get this done, it's been driving me crazy." I admit.

"Okay." She laughs. "Come on then."

I grab my wallet and shades and take her hand, lacing her fingers between mine. I stop and look at her. "You are perfect, you know that? I love you."

"I love you, too."

I hold the door open for her and she walks through still holding my hand tight. We stay like that, firmly connected while we knock for Max and Charlie, and then Jen and Scott. We ride in the lift and I lead her proudly through the lobby, wanting everyone to see how beautiful she is and that I'm the lucky guy she's marrying. We don't let go while we climb into the waiting limo and we're still holding hands when the limo arrives at The Chapel of the Flowers.

We fill out the papers and choose Liv a small bouquet from the flower shop, then we walk around to the cute white Victorian Chapel. While we wait for a few minutes, we're quiet as a group. I watch our friends. Following our lead, they're all holding hands. Jen and Scott sit on a leather couch in the marble reception and Jen is speaking softly to Scott, while he strokes his thumb back and forth across the back of her hand. She giggles at his reply. It makes me happy to see them like this despite the stress they have gone through recently.

Charlie and Max are standing by the window. Max lifts their intertwined hands to his lips and kisses Charlie's fingers. Charlie smiles shyly and smoothes Max's collar. Max smiles. They're so different at home than they seem separately and in moments like this, amongst friends, they can be so tender. I'm grateful for my time living with them so that I could really get to know them. I hope Liv and I are as happy after six years together.

Liv squeezes my hand. "Nervous?" she asks.

"No." I shake my head. "Happy." I kiss her on the cheek as she just reapplied the gloss that makes me want to get messy.

"We're ready for you now," says a lady from the doorway. We walk in as a group and Liv and I don't let go of each other once until the minister asks us to place rings on each other's fingers. Then we go right back to holding hands. It's a simple ceremony, because I still want our wedding two weeks ago to be the real one in our memories. This is just a renewal to me.

We have some photos taken outside, it was part of the package, like the flowers. But aside from the included extras, we don't really want all the Vegas crap added on. I chose this place because it wasn't tacky. It's still Vegas, but it's nice.

"Thank you," Liv whispers while we pose with our friends for a shot with Jen's camera.

"Anytime." I smile. "Mrs Morgan."

The limo is waiting when we're all done and we hit the town. Dinner, Chinese at Liv's request, was amazing, thanks to Scott's insider knowledge. I parade Liv around in her dress, showing her off like I just won the grand prize. We get a few congratulations from strangers and each one lifts me slightly higher. We wander through the casino back at the Bellagio and decide to have celebratory game or two. Then it happens. I find out something about my wife that I never knew.

My. Girl. Plays. Poker.

"What are you doing to me?" I whisper in her ear.

"What?" She looks puzzled.

"Poker? You're killing me. Do you have any idea how hot that is? I'm in enough trouble around you already." I shake my head.

"We play at the bar sometimes, Connie taught me."

Can she get any more perfect? Not only that but she and Max are good. In the end, us lesser mortals give up trying and gather around them at a table. She's something to watch. Does she go around doing stuff like learning how to play poker, just to make herself more irresistible to me? She must. I'm literally hard. I already have enough trouble with the mental image of her behind the wheel of the Shelby, now I have to have her at a poker table at the Bellagio wearing her wedding dress rolling around in my head too. I won't get anything done!

Then she does something only a woman could do, she quits while she's ahead and walks away $600 up.

"I have to have you right now!" I tell her as I scoop her into my arms.

Laughing, she pouts. "But I want to dance."

I sigh. "Seriously, you're going to be the end of me. You think I can go rub myself up against you when I already feel like this?" I settle her down and pull her tight so she can feel the extent of my predicament.

She smirks and presses in. "You'll survive. Besides, anticipation is half the fun."

"Jesus," I mutter and follow her to cash in her chips.

We end up at The Bank, the club inside the Bellagio and Liv drags me straight out onto the dance floor. This is another experience I've yet to have with her. We danced at our wedding and a couple of times when there was live music in the bar. But we have never been to a club together. Our friends join us and it's clear that we both have the same setup with our friends. Scott doesn't dance and Jen loves it, so I was usually her dance partner. It seems like Max and Liv dance and Charlie doesn't so much. Well tonight everyone makes an effort. Before long Charlie and Scott head to the bar, leaving Liv to torture me and Max to more than adequately partner Jen.

Liv can move. I mean it was obvious. She is unbelievable at everything else and I've seen her move her body in countless other ways. How could she be bad? But I'm in serious trouble, like the elevator last night but with about a thousand more witnesses. She faces away from me, but that doesn't mean I'm safe. She backs all the way up against me and the rhythm she is keeping with her hips ensures I don't get a break.

When I see that Scott and Charlie have secured a small table near the dance floor, I suggest we go cool down. I signal to Jen and she grabs Max and follows. They've got beers and cocktails waiting.

"Those had better be virgins," Liv shouts to Scott.

"Well you sure as hell ain't sweetheart!" he jokes.

Liv laughs, but clocks him in the arm anyway. She grins as she takes a gulp of her virgin daiquiri and winks at me. Seriously? How long do I have to put up with this shit before I can take her upstairs? I have maybe thirty minutes left in me and that's it. After that I can't be held accountable for my actions. After a quick pit stop, the girls drag Max and I back out onto the floor.

Liv turns and wraps her arms around my neck, looking in my eyes as she moves. We can't talk, it's too loud, but she says everything she wants to in that look.

I love you too, baby, you're everything to me.

Epilogue.

Liv

"I was just imagining them…"

"Oh don't, I was fighting that mental image." He cringes.

"No, but just think of how exciting this is for them." I point out as Danny winces again.

"Please stop telling me to think of them. I'll never be able to get it out of my head." He laughs, but shifts me off him. "Can we put the TV on or something before I start freaking out." He shudders.

"Oh stop being a baby!" I laugh. Grabbing the remote and scooting under the covers. "What do you fancy?" I ask casually. "Knocked up? Nine months? Oooh, what about What to expect when you're expecting?" I tease.

He narrows his eyes and presses his lips together, suppressing the smirk. "You're evil," he says, getting in bed beside me.

"Come on, laugh. This is quite funny and the more positive we are about it, the easier it will get."

"It's just…" He shudders again. "THAT bit of me…it's IN…THAT bit of her." Another shudder. "I know I didn't put it there, but it's there. That's weird isn't it?" His face twists in disgust. "I'd imagined myself blissfully oblivious when it happened. Not sat here waiting for their Skype call." He pulls the sheet over his head and starts rocking, hugging his knees. I'm beside myself by this point, hysterical and no help whatsoever.

"Thanks for your support!" he says huffily from under the covers.

"Oh don't! I have to pee!" I leap up and run to our bathroom. The new house certainly has its advantages. Right now, my favourite thing is the number of bathrooms at my disposal, because this baby took up residence on my bladder about six weeks ago and seems to like it there.

When I come back into the bedroom, Danny is still rocking under the covers. I pull them back and he grimaces.

"I don't think I can talk to them, can you just tell them I had to run to the bar?"

"No! It's you they want to tell." I wrap my arms around him and nuzzle his neck.

"Hmmm, that's nice." He sighs.

I drop a kiss behind his ear where he likes it. He rolls his head to the side, a clear invitation, which I accept, scraping my teeth on his earlobe. He groans and has me on my back in two seconds flat.

He stares at me and touches the end of his nose to mine. His lips curl into a tender smile that melts my heart. Then he raises his eyebrow and smirks as he presses himself against me.

Just then his laptop trills from the end of the bed.

"Oh for the love of…" Danny strops and drops down beside me.

I pat his shoulder. "Get used to it babe, because in a few days this little one will be calling all the shots."

"Ugh!" He groans, adjusting himself.

I grab the laptop and settle it on my knees and Danny yanks the sheet over his head, beside me.

"Hello!" I say happily as Jen and Scott appear on my screen.

"Hey!" they both reply in unison.

"Where's Danny?" Jen asks.

"Being a big baby." I laugh, elbowing him.

He waves his hand outside the sheets and I pull them off him.

"Hi," he says reluctantly.

"Oh there he is," says Scott. "The man who just tried to knock-up my wife!" He shakes his head slowly. "People have been trying to tell me for years it would happen, but would I listen?"

Danny groans and tries to cover himself back over. I don't let him, while Jen tells Scott off for teasing.

"So how did it go?" I ask Jen, Trying to ignore the boys

"Great!" She grins. "It all went smoothly, so now we just wait."

"And you can find out in a couple of weeks?"

"Yeah, but we aren't getting our hopes up. We know the odds, so we're just trying to put it out of our minds."

"Oh Jen, it will work, I just know it, we will get there eventually."

"Eventually," she says. "It's a long road. But thank you." Then she speaks just to Danny. "Thank you for what you've done, I'll never forget it."

Danny smiles and nods. He kisses his fingers and touches the screen and Jen does the same. I love watching the two of them together and it breaks my heart that it has to be via Skype most of the time. They still talk almost every day, but at times like this, they need to see each other. But I'm so close to my due date Danny refused to go when I suggested it. Still, they will be here soon. They're coming to meet the little nugget.

Epilogue.

Danny

"Sssssshhhhh!" I softly whisper as I place her on my shoulder and rub her back to soothe her. "Let Mommy sleep."

I pull the bedroom door closed quietly behind me and take her downstairs so that Liv can get a little more rest. She was up half the night. I rock back and forth while I try and work the damned coffee machine one-handed. Fuck this, I'm getting us some instant later! I don't care what she says, you NEED coffee when you have a baby and this machine is not a one-hander!

"Let me help you with that," Jen whispers from behind me.

"Oh, hey," I reply a little louder, kissing her cheek. Liv and I are trying not to do the whole tip-toe thing and while she's sleeping on one of us you can be as loud as you want, she never stirs.

Jen makes the coffee and I sit at the counter having my snuggle. I love the mornings when she lies awake after her first feed. I can watch her for hours. But this morning she just wanted to be held and then she went right back to sleep. I'm only too happy to oblige.

"Couldn't sleep?"

Jen wrinkles her nose. I give her a tight smile. She can do a pregnancy test today. US time, so not until this evening here, but it's bothering her. Every month before now, they knew it wasn't likely, but this is the real deal, if it doesn't work, which it probably won't, it will start to make her wonder if it ever will.

"So did you decide yet? That poor kid needs a name, you can't keep calling her Nugget, she'll get a complex."

I laugh. "Um, yeah I did actually, it came to me in the night, we'll just have to see if Liv likes it when she gets up."

"If it isn't on the shortlist, I'm going to kill you, just pick one, don't make it harder!"

"It's not, but trust me, it's the one. You'll see."

She shakes her head in despair.

"See what?" Liv's voice surprises me.

"Hey, I wanted you to sleep in," I say as she strokes Nugget's hair and bends to kiss me.

"Well I woke up and you were all gone. I missed you."

I look at her expectantly and she grins. I left the baby name book open on her nightstand with a note saying 'Strong, graceful, flexible, can withstand anything.'

She looks at Nugget asleep on my shoulder and then nods. "It's perfect," she whispers and kisses the top of her head softly, lingering to smell her hair.

"Shall I start breakfast?" I ask, carefully passing Nugget to her.

"Yeah, I'll text Max."

Thirty minutes later, Jen and I are preparing to serve up breakfast and Max is cooing over Nugget…I must stop calling her that! Charlie and Scott are trying to figure out the sound system. Liv comes down after her shower looking spectacular in jeans and my Guns 'n' Roses T-shirt. Her hair is all piled up except a couple of strands that have already fallen. I watch her. She is flawless, perfect…

"Danny?"

"Huh?"

Jen grins. "I said, where do you keep table mats? You're in your own world."

"Sorry, down there." I point to the cabinet beside her. I finish piling the bacon onto a serving dish and carry it to the table.

We all sit down to eat and of course Nugget just wants to be held…and what can I say? I'm a sucker for my princess, so I wander around with her sleeping on my shoulder until she properly settles then keep her with me when I sit down. Liv serves my food and cuts up the bacon for me and I eat with just my fork. We have this down now!

"So come on then, the suspense is killing me!" Jen suddenly exclaims. "What are you calling her?"

Liv looks at me and I wait for her to say something.

"I'm happy," she says. "I love it."

"Really, you're sure? You don't want to go back to the list?" Everyone groans. "Okay, okay! Settle down." I absently stroke Nugget's back…Ah! No more Nugget! Okay, here goes then…

"It just came to me in the night. It's perfect, it's so us." I look over at Liv and she smiles. "We're calling her Willow."

"I love it!" says Max. "Of course! God, I'm annoyed I didn't think of that. It's perfect."

"It means strong, graceful and flexible, and hopefully she'll be like our tree and be able to survive all the storms," I explain.

"It's beautiful!" Jen sobs. I didn't realise she was emotional and frown.

"Jen, don't cry…"

Scott puts his arm around her and tells her she's so silly, but I can see there is more to her emotions than just Willow's name.

"Jen?" I say quietly.

She looks up at me and tries to smile. "It's nothing," she says. "Just hormones."

Everyone else is discussing the name and its meaning and I just stare at Jen in disbelief.

The corner of her mouth curls up in a smile and I know. I glance at Scott…for the love of God man…notice what she just said!

"Wait? Hormones?" he suddenly says.

Jen grins through the tears and 'doing a Liv', pulls a pregnancy test out of her pocket.

Scott's face is vacant for a second while he stares at the stick, then the lights come back on. "Baby, is this for real?" he asks with a slightly desperate edge to his voice.

"It's for real," she says

He pulls her up out of her chair and into his arms and kisses her as if they're completely alone.

"I love you," he whispers.

"I love you, too." She laughs, through tears.

She turns to us and the room goes crazy, everyone is up and congratulating them. Breakfast is forgotten.

I just sit and stare.

We did it!

WE DID IT!

With Nugget…fuck it!…with Willow still snuggled into my neck, I get up and go to them. Liv and Jen are both crying and hugging and I can hear Jen thanking Liv. Liv waves it off, but Jen insists that while I've given them this gift, it's because Liv supported me that it was possible, and she's right.

Scott turns to me. We lock eyes for a second. I can see the appreciation there, but I really don't want to discuss it, he's going to be a father at last, I have no place in his moment. So I hold out my hand and he shakes it and smiles.

"Congratulations man."

"Thank you," he replies and pulls me in for a guy hug. "Thank you," he says again before we break apart. I pat him on the shoulder.

Then Jen turns to face me and, through the happy tears, she laughs. She slips her hands around my waist and I fold her in my free arm. She lays her head on my chest beside Willow and I feel her relax.

I kiss the top of her head and she looks up at me and smiles.

"I don't know how I'll ever be able to thank you," she says quietly.

"No thanks necessary."

"But what you did…"

I shake my head. "It's me who needs to thank you. I owe you everything."

"You owe me nothing." She frowns.

"Really? If it wasn't for you, my stubborn ass would still be living in

LA pretending to be happy. Jen, you made me see sense over and over. You pushed me to do the right thing even though you knew it would mean you would lose out. You never once said stay because I'll miss you. You know that's all it would have taken too, but you gave me up to make sure I was happy. I wouldn't have any of this if it wasn't for you. So, thank you."

She sighs and smiles. "You are happy aren't you?"

"Happy doesn't even cover it." I laugh.

I pull her closer and hold her. She lets me have my moment because she knows what I feel for her and how hard being apart can be, but she smiles and I do too. She has her life and I have mine, she rescued me when I was drowning more times than I can count and I finally feel like I've paid her back. I wish we could always be around each other. I wish I could look in her eyes and see her smile and have her with me every day, but I can't. Instead I've left some of me with her…and that's forever.

It isn't perfect, they're too far away, but I have Liv and Willow, my world. And I'm unbelievably happy.

Acknowledgements

My thanks remain much the same for this book as they were for the last, because I wrote them back to back.

To Steve and my babies, I am eternally grateful for your patience and understanding over the past year. I know I haven't always been easy to live with, but I am trying. I love you and nothing makes me happier or more proud than you.

I know I have neglected everyone while I have been making this happen and I know how lucky I am to have such an understanding family. I love you.

To my ever-forgiving friends, I haven't forgotten about you. I know we are all busy, but I have been truly appalling! Thank you for not writing me off.

To my Scaries, for your unwavering support during the release of Just Human, I will be forever grateful. Your beta comments have once again made this book better than it was and just having had you in my life made me so happy.

Dana, your 'exuberance and passion' (read: crazy) is so infectious, you fire us all up. I can't wait to eat pie with you and waffles and skittles and cronuts and Mexican and ...notice how its all about food? Anyway, I can't wait!

Kelly, I want to sit on your deck and eat your pie! (God that sounds dirty!) That's all I ask really, I wait patiently for the day! I'll always be around to scoop up the mush you turn to when certain people talk to you on TL

Jen & Jodie we would be lethal if we lived on the same continent! My filthy, funny friends! I truly love you girls. You just don't know what you've all done for me.

To my round two betas, Rachel, Ellen, Zoe, Andrea, Simone, SJ, Bianca and a few others. Thank you for giving it the once over and making sure you got the HEA you were looking for.

To the fab bloggers I know and love. I'm afraid to start listing, because I'll miss some of you out and I don't want to upset anyone. You are all amazing. The reviews for JH were beyond my wildest dreams. There's so much support in this community and I am truly grateful every day. I am happy to count some of you as friends, I will always be in awe of some of you. I will never cease to be thrilled to bits anytime one of you takes time to talk about my work. Indies would be nothing without you. Thank you.

Thanks to the fabulous Steph at www.romanceaddictbookblog.com for being my tour host, twice. You crack the whip at just the right moments and always get the job done! I love having someone to say 'yes boss' to. x

To the magnificent Katy Evans. You probably don't know it because it has happened in the background, but you have been the perfect mentor to me. I truly value your encouragement and support and I am very grateful for your wise words. You absolutely rock and I can't wait to see what you have in store for us next!

Thank you to my other amazing friends who support me in so many ways you just wouldn't believe. I'm so lucky to call you my friends and have you in my RL as well as my TL.
@Prodigalson_1 I adore you, plain and simple. You support me so much, you make me laugh, you make me grrr and you give me evil ideas. You are an evil genius and I love it! Thanks for being there. x

A special thank you goes to Megan, who fell and injured herself at exactly the right time to save me a shedload of medical research! I'm glad you're back on your feet again, but thanks for being clumsy enough to give me an idea! x

Oh and I just have to credit Dana @Smuttastic for being the absolute genius who came up with the name Willow. I asked her to pick a baby name out of three regular baby names and she replied,
"IF they have a little girl I think it should be something AMAZING like Willow :) You know, Willow means something like strong/bendable but can't be broken :) What do you think? Do you hate the idea?"
...Do I hate the idea? Pfft! I just hate being the idiot who didn't even

think of it!! Thank you for being the genius who did. x

Thanks again to Kelly at Ultimate Proof for whipping Liv and Danny into shape. It was a pleasure to work with you again.

And to all the readers, who loved Liv and Danny as much as I did, thank you. I get a kick out of every tweet and every message. Keep talking to me, it never gets old.

Coming 2014...

Meet Spencer...

Wednesday 17th April
Jazz

MAGS @Magspie1
@OMGJazzyP How's #SPENCERSTALK going?

JAZZ @OMGJazzyP
@Magspie1 Do you even need to ask? pic.twitter.com/KdbaJDRnaX #SPENCER

MAGS @Magspie1
@OMGJazzyP WOW! That is some tattoo! Aren't you supposed to be working?

JAZZ @OMGJazzyP
@Magspie1 Work schmurk! #Spencerstalk is work. The tattoo! I know, here's another pic.twitter.com/hsLjiWaSDf

MAGS @Magspie1
@OMGJazzyP THAT IS A WORK OF ART! (Stop licking the screen!)

JAZZ @OMGJazzyP
@Magspie1 I'm telling you, I'd lick that tattoo right of his body! #Spencer

MAGS @Magspie1
@OMGJazzyP I know you would, but does he? @TheSpencerRyan #Spencerstalk

JAZZ @OMGJazzyP

@Magspie1 :-O WHAT DID YOU JUST DO??? @TheSpencerRyan

SPENCER @TheSpencerRyan
@OMGJazzyP @Magspie1 Evening ladies! This looks like fun!

JAZZ @OMGJazzyP
@Magspie1 @TheSpencerRyan Er, hi! :) Mags I'm going to kill you!

SPENCER @TheSpencerRyan
@OMGJazzyP @Magspie1 No fighting now, I'm glad we were introduced.

MAGS @Magspie1
@OMGJazzyP @TheSpencerRyan See Jazz, he's glad you were introduced.

JAZZ @OMGJazzyP
@Magspie1 @TheSpencerRyan Sorry about her, I can't control her!

SPENCER @TheSpencerRyan
@OMGJazzyP @Magspie1 So you are familiar with my work?

JAZZ @OMGJazzyP
@Magspie1 @TheSpencerRyan Not really.

SPENCER @TheSpencerRyan
@OMGJazzyP @Magspie1 Your pictures say you're lying!

You were followed by @TheSpencerRyan

MAGS @Magspie1
@OMGJazzyP @TheSpencerRyan BWAHAHAHAHAHAHA! This is brilliant!

JAZZ @OMGJazzyP
@Magspie1 I hate you! Not you @TheSpencerRyan

MAGS @Magspie1
@OMGJazzyP @TheSpencerRyan No, she REALLY doesn't hate you!

SPENCER @TheSpencerRyan
@OMGJazzyP @Magspie1 Do I need to lock my windows tonight?

MAGS @Magspie1
@OMGJazzyP @TheSpencerRyan It's ok, you are protected by the Atlanitc ocean

SPENCER @TheSpencerRyan
@OMGJazzyP @Magspie1 Thats a shame ;) Where are you?

MAGS @Magspie1
@OMGJazzyP @TheSpencerRyan NYC

JAZZ @OMGJazzyP
@Magspie1 @TheSpencerRyan Um, Hello!!!! I'm still here!

MAGS @Magspie1
@OMGJazzyP @TheSpencerRyan Ssshh! I'm chatting!

SPENCER @TheSpencerRyan
@OMGJazzyP @Magspie1 Well I have to run ladies, here's a new pic for your collection pic.twitter.com/hsoUgTHsAg happy #Spencerstalking

JAZZ @OMGJazzyP
@TheSpencerRyan @Magspie1 Thanks!

JAZZ @OMGJazzyP
@Magspie1 I seriously HATE YOU right now!

MAGS @Magspie1
@OMGJazzyP What for introducing you to your future husband? No you don't.

JAZZ @OMGJazzyP
@Magspie1 I'm out, I have work to do.

MAGS @Magspie1
@OMGJazzyP Ok, but you'll thank me one day. Pick up salad on ur way home.

JAZZ @OMGJazzyP
@Magspie1 Bite me!

MAGS @Magspie1
@OMGJazzyP <3

Kerry Heavens

Terrible wife, mediocre mother, appalling housewife,
Fashion graduate, wedding co-ordinator, Sex toy salesperson, shop manager, designer,
Font collector, romance addict
Fancier of nice men,
Ok, fancier of almost all men,
Awesome cupcake baker, Incessant singer
Film buff, friend
Writer

Website:
http://www.kerryheavens.com

Contact:
kerryheavens@kerryheavens.com

Facebook:
Kerry Heavens Author

Twitter:
@kerryheavens

Pinterest:
kerryheavens
Visit Pinterest to see my inspirations for the characters in my stories.

Thank you for reading! x

Made in the USA
Charleston, SC
25 June 2014